SACRATI

KATE SHERWOOD

RIPTIDE
PUBLISHING

Riptide Publishing
PO Box 6652
Hillsborough, NJ 08844
www.riptidepublishing.com

Sacrati

Cover art: Kanaxa, www.kanaxa.com
Editor: Carole-ann Galloway
Layout: L.C. Chase, lcchase.com/design.htm

ISBN: 978-1-62649-254-7

First edition
April, 2015

Also available in ebook:
ISBN: 978-1-62649-253-0

SACRATI

KATE SHERWOOD

RIPTIDE
PUBLISHING

TABLE OF CONTENTS

PART I

CHAPTER  1

Theos checked his map one more time, then looked at Andros, his second-in-command. It all seemed clear, but this was Theos's first time as iyatis and he needed to be careful. Fighting came naturally to him, but this situation called for caution—not his strong point.

"They're well over the border," Andros confirmed. Then he grinned, and Theos pulled his own lips back, half-smile, half-snarl. It was time for battle.

Which meant all room for doubt or questions was gone.

Both sides had already noticed the other's presence, and both sides had found cover in the dense forest on opposite banks of a small stream. Theos had seen about twenty of the enemy, and there were sixteen in Theos's patrol, so the odds were good. At two-to-one Theos might have begun to consider withdrawal, but even then it wouldn't have been likely, not when he was fighting with the Sacrati, the elite of the Torian army. No, twenty men was not nearly enough to make Theos hesitate.

But it was never good to be careless. He gave the orders for his team to spread out, four circling around to cut off any possible escape. And then, with a battle song singing from his heart to every fiber of his body, Theos led the charge.

The battle was short. The Elkati fought back, but not well. Theos bloodied his sword on one and elbowed another in the face for a satisfying crunch of bone, but there was no real challenge in a fight like this. It was disappointing, but not surprising.

Four of the Elkati died before Theos knocked away the weapon of the one he supposed was their leader, an older man with some sort of decorative plume on his helmet. Theos held his sword to the old man's throat and spoke one of the few Elkati words he'd bothered to learn. "Surrender."

But the old man surprised him, dodging Theos's sword and pulling a dagger. He lunged upward and Theos stepped to the side, then kicked him in the face. The man was flipped over and landed hard on the ground. Theos stomped down on his enemy's arm, then brought the tip of his sword to the man's throat again. He pressed in enough for a little blood to flow, and in a more exasperated tone, as if speaking to a child struggling with a simple lesson, he repeated, "Surrender."

The old man's only answer was a glare. But a younger, lighter voice rang out through the forest. Theos didn't understand the words, but he saw their effect as the Elkati disengaged and stood with heads bowed.

Theos's men knew the drill. The enemy soldiers were quickly disarmed and their hands tied tightly together. Their feet were bound with only a little slack in the rope; they could walk, but not lengthen their stride into a run. Then their weapons were inspected and their packs plundered while Theos sat back and supervised it all, ensuring that no one was careless.

He wasn't sure which of the Elkati had ordered the surrender, and he watched them now, trying to understand their structure. They certainly seemed concerned about the old man. Maybe *too* concerned; they were more protective than deferential. Was he their leader, or their mascot?

It didn't really matter. The men *had* no leader now, other than Theos. Whatever their structure had been, whatever their *lives* had been, it'd all been lost to them as soon as they'd had the bad luck to be discovered on their illicit trip into Torian lands.

No one in Theos's squad spoke sufficient Elkati to interrogate the prisoners, so there was no point in further delay. His men loaded the Elkati down with whatever had seemed worth scavenging from their packs and added a few of the heavier items from the Torian kits, then they started off. They'd been on the last leg of their moon-long patrol as it was, so they didn't have to divert from their original course in order to head for home.

Theos pushed a little harder than he might have without the prisoners, making sure they were sufficiently far away from the border to make rescue attempts unlikely, before giving the order to make camp for the night. He also set out an extra sentry, further back along their trail, to give advance warning if anyone was tracking them. They were in the mountains, with most of the land impassable, so there weren't many directions from which they could be attacked. Having done his job, he allowed himself to relax just a little.

After another quick inspection, Theos loosened the hands of two of the prisoners, giving them freedom to prepare food for the other Elkati. And then one of the prisoners still bound, a young man with barely enough beard to earn the name, stood and shuffled toward him. He held his own hands out, tugging on the ropes. Theos raised an eyebrow, and the Elkati pointed with his chin, gesturing toward two of his comrades who'd been injured in the battle.

"You want to patch them up?" Theos assessed the boy, then shrugged and loosened the rope around his wrists. After all, the prisoners would be more valuable if they were in good health. The boy started working with what seemed like competence. He looked at Theos for permission a few more times, first to take a pot to the spring and fill it with water, then to burrow through one of the Elkati packs for a bag of healing salves. The Elkati were renowned as scholars and doctors, so the Sacrati who'd sorted through their gear had known these potions might have value. But they probably hadn't intended them to be used on the prisoners themselves. Still, Theos couldn't bring himself to object. Not until the boy returned to Theos and pointed at his waist.

"You want . . . you want my knife?" Theos shook his head. These Elkati were all brain and no heart; they had no understanding of what was important. "No."

The boy held up his hands as if promising a truce, but Theos hadn't refused to lend his knife because he thought it would be used as a weapon. He would have been *more* likely to lend it if there was a chance it would shed blood. To allow his oath-blade, the sacred steel of his initiation into the Sacrati brotherhood, to be handed to the enemy for use in some menial task? Unthinkable. The question was a sign of the Elkati's ignorance.

"Here," Andros said. He picked up one of the kitchen knives and held it out to the boy, handle first. "Will this do?"

The boy frowned, made a gesture of sharpening, and waited until Andros found the whetstone and handed that over too. Then he nodded, just a quick jerk of his head that seemed merely an acknowledgment, not a thanks, and turned back to the other prisoners.

"Demanding," Theos commented.

Andros grinned. "I think he's pretty."

Theos snorted. "I put Xeno on sentry duty for one night and you're already prowling for company?"

"I expect Xeno will think he's pretty, too. We're always happy to share."

"Not until we're back to town," Theos said, letting just a touch of his authority slip into his voice. "You know how strange the Elkati are about sex. They're good little prisoners now, and I want to keep it that way; you will *not* set off some holy rebellion because you have an itch."

"I thought coming on patrol with you as iyatis would be fun," Andros said with a sigh. He leaned back and watched the young prisoner sharpen the knife. "I thought, 'Theos is young, and he likes adventure. I'll go with *him*.'"

"You were *assigned* to come with me. And you were assigned because I asked for you. And I *asked* for you because you have good sense. Don't ruin that now."

Andros sighed again in exaggerated disappointment. They sat together for a while, eating the dinner brought to them by the soldier on food duty, absentmindedly observing the prisoners as darkness fell on the camp.

"Which one are you going to keep?" Andros asked as he took Theos's empty plate.

Theos hadn't considered the question yet. As leader of the patrol that had captured the prisoners, he had the right to claim one of them. The rest would be divided up and sold, with most of the profit going to the army but a small bonus paid to each of the soldiers on the patrol. "I don't know. I'll ask the evaluators, I guess, and take the one worth the most."

"And then just sell him?"

"What else would I do with him?"

Andros shrugged. "Nothing, I guess. You're not likely to start a band of mercenaries, are you? And you're still young and pretty enough to find your own bedmates; it wouldn't make sense to have a captive bedwarmer."

Theos snorted. "No, it wouldn't."

"Not to mention how worn out you must be with so many calls to the city . . ." Andros grinned. He got a fair share of calls himself.

"Right," Theos said. "So I'll just take whoever's most valuable, sell him, and spend the money on new armor so I can fight better and take *more* prisoners."

"That's the spirit," Andros said. He raised his tankard of creek water in toast, and Theos returned the gesture. It *was* the spirit. What more could a man want than good armor, a good sword, and good men to fight by his side? And then to *lie* by his side at night, of course.

Theos had been abstaining since he was in command of the patrol; sex wasn't forbidden for an iyatis, but he hadn't wanted the distraction. Now, though, he looked over at the prisoners, at the "pretty" boy Andros had admired, and he let his mind wander a little. The boy's skin and hair were fair. Theos, like most Torians, was a mix of practically every culture the Empire had absorbed over the past several generations and had the usual brown skin and dark hair. What would it be like to be pressed against someone so pale?

What would any of it be like, with someone like that? Theos had always been precocious as a warrior *and* a lover, and he'd found his way into the barracks when he was much younger than the prisoner was now. For the first couple of years he'd been the less experienced, less aggressive partner to whomever could teach him. Later he'd found himself in bed with men who were his equals, and he'd enjoyed the comradeship, the boisterous challenges and easy laughter so much like the interactions on the drill grounds. Now he was often more dominant, but he didn't do much *teaching*. What would it be like with someone who needed guidance? The boy was Elkati, and everyone knew they were strange about sex. Was it possible the prisoner had never taken someone to bed? How would it feel to be his first? To teach him how to find and give pleasure, to touch him in ways no one had ever touched him before . . .

Theos shifted to give himself more room, and Andros glanced at his crotch and laughed. "You've been quiet this whole patrol," he said. "Keeping to yourself. That's not like you." He reached over and laid a friendly hand on the fabric covering Theos's growing erection. "You want a little attention? I'm a bit tired, myself, but my hand or my mouth . . ."

It wouldn't be the first time one of them had given the other relief. They were friends, after all. And the camp was quiet; a few of the soldiers had paired off and there were soft moans and murmurs coming from their blankets. The prisoners were huddled together, clearly working hard to pretend they were somewhere else, or that they didn't notice what the Sacrati were doing. And the rest of the soldiers were either on duty or getting ready for sleep. No one would care if Theos let his guard down for a few brief minutes.

He shifted away anyhow. "No, I'm okay. I should get some sleep."

But first he had to make sure everything in the camp was safe. So he stood, ignoring the roughness of his canvas trousers against the sensitive skin of his erection, and headed for the prisoners.

He found the boy and held out his hand. "Knife," he said quietly.

The boy handed over the whetstone.

"Knife," Theos repeated more firmly.

The boy rolled his eyes and produced the knife, handing it to Theos with exaggerated care. Theos squinted at him. The small show of rebellion, as if anyone would ask for a whetstone when he knew a prisoner had a knife.

"Hands," Theos ordered, gesturing to show what he wanted. The boy raised his hands and Theos took the slack out of the rope and then refastened it. He tugged, testing the strength, and found no give. But there was still something he didn't like. Something he didn't trust. He stood there, watching the boy feign confused indifference, and thought back. The kid had spent time with three prisoners. Two of them had pretty obvious injuries. The third? The kid had fussed over him, over his hands . . .

Theos took a couple of large steps, not too careful about any prisoners he might be landing on, and found the kid's third patient. A big man. His hand was bandaged, but there was no sign of blood. Theos yanked on the ropes holding the man's hands together, and felt them give. The kid had sawed almost through them, leaving just a few strands to make them look secure. Theos yanked again and the ropes split. The man sprang to his feet, and that was when Theos saw the rock in his fist.

The other prisoners were part of it now, roiling and struggling up, all still bound but trying to help their comrade. Theos lost his balance as they rolled into his knees, and the freed prisoner lunged forward, his feet clearly untied as well, the rock aimed right for Theos's head.

Theos got his feet under himself and ducked beneath the man's reach. Then he brought his hand up, the heel of his palm hard and flat, right into the man's nose. The enemy had been coming toward him and Theos had put his full strength behind the blow, so he wasn't surprised when the man toppled. The bone of his nose had been driven back into his brain, killing him instantly.

The camp was silent, the prisoners still and shocked, staring at their fallen friend. Theos turned to the boy who'd started it all and pointed at the dead man. "Your fault," he said quietly. He didn't know if the kid understood the words, but he was pretty sure he got the message. The man had been alive, and now he was dead, and there'd been no point to it. A stupid waste, just because the Elkati boy had thought he was clever.

Theos stepped carefully out of the crowd of prisoners. "Leave the body there," he told his men, who'd been drawn by the ruckus. "As a reminder. Check all of their bonds and make sure they're tight." He shook his head. "And keep that scrawny Elkati tied up—no more knives."

So that was that. It should have been over. They'd been a little careless, but Theos had caught the problem before it got serious.

Except he hadn't, because there was a dead body lying among the prisoners. A man who'd never see another sunrise. And it was partly the kid's fault, sure, but it was partly Theos's fault too. These prisoners were his responsibility, and now one of them was dead.

Theos spat his disgust out onto the dirt.

Andros approached cautiously. "Apologies."

Theos glanced at him, then turned back to watching the prisoners as they were reinspected. "I was right there, letting you give him the knife. If I'd thought it was a bad idea, I would have stopped it."

"Aye," Andros acknowledged. "But now you *really* need to let me suck you. You're all keyed up, and you'll never get to sleep otherwise. We've got another four days until we're home; you need your rest."

It was good advice, and Theos took it. He leaned against a tree and looked down as Andros knelt, and just that was enough to help him relax. Everything was fine. They were still alive, and the prisoner . . . Theos made himself stop thinking about the prisoner. Well, the dead one. Instead, he pictured the other one. The young one, who'd caused the trouble in the first place.

But instead of the earlier visions of teaching the boy about pleasure, Theos imagined showing the boy who was in charge. Making him beg, making him *need* release and withholding it because he hadn't done anything to deserve it. And then finally, when neither of them could stand it anymore, Theos would drive himself into the boy, would claim and tame and control him.

Andros grunted and shifted, trying to accommodate Theos's too-vigorous thrusting, and Theos managed to calm himself a little. He ran an appreciative hand through Andros's short, dark hair, and then glanced over to find the boy staring at them. The rest of the prisoners were huddled together, their heads turned away, but the boy's eyes were wide and gleaming in the firelight, his gaze fixed on Theos, and on Andros, and on the place where their bodies were joined. Theos pushed in, hard and deep, and felt Andros swallow desperately around him. And he saw the boy's eyes widen just a little bit more.

Theos looked away then, and made himself focus on the simple sensations, the warmth and the pressure and the wetness and Andros's busy, generous tongue. But when he felt the tension building, he took a few more thrusts and then pulled out, bringing his hand down to stroke himself as he spurted thick white strands onto Andros's face. And in the middle of it he turned back and saw the boy still staring, and another wave of pleasure crashed in, making him close his eyes and give in to it all.

When Theos was done, Andros wiped his face clean and laughed quietly. "Putting on a show?" he asked, climbing to his feet.

"I just wasn't sure you could handle it all. Didn't want to choke you." He nodded at Andros's crotch. "You want your turn?"

"You can owe me. Like I said, I'm tired."

Theos nodded. "Okay. Thanks." He refastened his pants, stretched his arms above his head, and refused to look over at the prisoners. "You were right, I wouldn't have slept without that."

"I'm very wise," Andros agreed. He headed off toward his own bedroll, and Theos undid his pack and spread his blankets close to the fire. After checking that the guard was in place and alert, he lay down and let himself relax. He tried to clear his mind, and almost managed it. But there, floating in the darkness, was a pair of wide blue eyes, staring at him. And Theos fell asleep still wondering just what the man behind the eyes had been thinking.

CHAPTER 2

They spent the next day walking, and the day after that too. It was still midfall in the valleys, but up in the mountains winter was fast approaching. Theos had heard of lands away to the west where the terrain was flat, where cities and farms could spread as far as their inhabitants wished, but he'd never lived in such a place, or even visited one. This was the only world he knew, with tall, hostile mountains covering almost all of the land, and human habitation limited to isolated valleys.

There were *many* valleys, it was true; at last count he'd heard the Torian Empire contained seventy-eight of them, each a semi-independent city-state united more by culture and principles than by government. Well, there was an empress, technically, but she was far away from Theos's valley and was more a receptor of tribute than an issuer of orders. The valleys sent soldiers back to fight along the eastern border of the Empire, where the enemies were larger and better organized. The west was left to its own devices, defending and expanding however it could, and no one seemed to be too interested in them, as long as they sent their taxes and recruits east each year.

Of course, there were valleys that hadn't been absorbed into the Empire yet, although they were fewer every year. The Elkati should be the next to be conquered, clearly; they were close to the western border, rich, and as a midsize city-state, with no more than ten thousand inhabitants, they would never be able to stand up to the Empire. But no one had bothered to convince them of that, yet.

So Theos and other soldiers from Windthorn patrolled the borders, as did soldiers from nearby valleys Cragview and Greenbrook, and they all waited for the order to invade, and start teaching the Elkati about civilization. And, occasionally, they found someone on the wrong side of the invisible line and took prisoners.

Theos looked over at the Elkati he'd captured. They were showing the strain, now. The two who'd been patched up by the boy seemed better, which was good; still they were all exhausted. The Elkati were fit enough, but the Sacrati were the elite of the elite, and had been hardened by conditions these Elkati would never know, and certainly never survive. And the Elkati were carrying heavier packs and hiking with their hands tied tight, and Theos had no intention of changing that just to make it easier for them to walk. He wanted to push the Elkati as much as he could without breaking them; it was wise to keep them tired, and it would be nice to get off the damn mountain before the snow came.

The Elkati boy had protested, after a fashion. He'd found ways to ask for special privileges: more food for one of the prisoners after he'd spilled his dinner on the ground; time to stop and bandage another prisoner's knees when a stumble had turned into a nasty fall; more blankets for them at night since they slept farther from the fire. Theos had refused every request without much consideration. He'd given the boy a chance once, and a man had died. The time for making deals was over. The prisoners would just have to make do. They had no choice.

Still, they were getting ragged. So Theos wasn't completely surprised, in the middle of the third afternoon, when he heard a voice cry out from somewhere near the front of the procession. But he was shocked to peer ahead and realize that it was Andros who was hurt, slumping to the side as the soldiers around him hacked at something on the ground.

Theos sprinted forward, then skidded to a stop when he saw the sliced remains of a rock viper at Andros's feet. He looked up and saw the glassiness already coming into the man's eyes. The viper's poison was potent enough to protect it against bears and mountain lions, and was almost always deadly to humans.

"Where?" Theos demanded. He fell to his knees and felt Andros's legs, up above the midcalf boots, and found a swollen bump that made Andros bite back a scream when it was touched.

One of the other soldiers had made a tourniquet, and Theos pushed Andros to the ground before slicing through his pant leg. The red lump was unmistakeable, with two spots already blackening in the middle where the venom had been injected and tissue was beginning to die.

Theos cut hard and deep, his dagger slicing into the flesh as Andros held himself rigidly still. The blood poured out in a cleansing rush, but the original wound was only part of the problem. Even if Theos had caught the putrescence and kept it from spreading, the poison was also in the bloodstream, traveling through Andros's body. The tourniquet would slow its progress and the venom might be diluted enough to not kill instantly, but that could just make death slower and more painful.

Then Xeno was there, called up from the back of the procession, and he eased in behind Andros and cradled him, kissing his hair and murmuring comforting words, ignoring the tears that were falling from his eyes onto Andros's too-pale face.

This shouldn't be happening. The damn viper should have been hibernating, not creeping around, attacking good men for no reason.

It was no way for a warrior to die. No way for *anyone* to die.

Theos stood up. The prisoners were standing, waiting, and Theos pushed through them until he found the boy who'd healed the other Elkati. "You! Fix him!" Theos knew volume wouldn't help when someone didn't know the words, but he let himself yell anyhow. Let the kid know how serious he was. He pointed to one of the Elkati packs, hopefully the one that held the medicine, and then pointed back to Andros. The boy just stared at him.

There was no way the little coward didn't understand. He just didn't care. He wasn't going to help because he didn't *care* if Andros lived or died. Theos took a deep breath. He pointed at Andros again, then rolled his own eyes back, mimicking death. Then he pointed at one of the other prisoners and drew a finger across his own throat. If Andros died, that prisoner died. But that wasn't enough, because Andros was a Sacrati, by the sword, and these useless Elkati were *nothing* compared to him. So Theos pointed to another prisoner, and then another, and made the same throat-slitting gesture. He waved his arm to indicate all the prisoners, drew his hand across his throat again, and then stared at the boy, making it clear that the threat was absolutely real. If Andros died, every prisoner on the mountain would follow him.

The boy swallowed, looked down at the ground, then up at Theos and started talking. His words made no sense, of course, just endless Elkati gibberish, and Theos raised his hand to strike him into silence. But before he could land the blow, the old man was there. He'd been quiet since the capture, sitting back and watching, following directions and acting like just another prisoner. Now, though, he caught the boy's shoulders in his hands and shook him, just once, but hard. He growled a phrase that sounded like an order, and when the boy began to protest, the old man said something else and pushed him toward the pack. Theos nodded his approval, then reached out and sliced through the ropes on the boy's hands with one tug of his knife. He bent and freed his feet as well. He didn't care what trouble the Elkati got into, not if he saved Andros first.

They were on a narrow pass, and the boy peered around as if trying to find something he needed. Apparently not finding it, he pushed past the soldiers and ran down the trail in front of them, waving an arm to indicate that they should follow.

"Bring the prisoners," Theos ordered his soldiers, and then he jogged to Xeno's side. "We'll carry Andros. The boy . . . he's our best chance. And Andros is tough."

Xeno nodded, swallowed hard, and then grabbed hold of Theos's wrists, the two of them making a chair to carry their friend. They lifted him carefully, then moved as quickly and smoothly as possible, following the boy.

The path wound around the side of the mountain, the curvature making it impossible to see ahead more than a few paces at a time, and Theos's gut began to tighten as they ran. The boy had gone. Theos had cut him free, and he'd escaped.

But then the ground leveled out and they rounded one more corner to find a small clearing, flat on one side, with a grassy slope on the other. The boy was there, breaking small branches off a fallen tree, clearly preparing to start a fire. Theos and Xeno settled Andros as gently as they could near the fire site, and then Theos was back in motion, finding tinder and flint and steel, yelling at one of his men to find a pot and the others to produce their waterskins in case whatever the boy was up to required water . . . What else? What else?

The boy was busy. He'd found his medicines and had them spread out in front of him, picking up jars and reading the labels with almost feverish intensity.

Finally he seized one of the jars and a wad of clean fabric and headed toward Andros.

Theos tore his eyes away from the boy. He was the leader of this patrol, and he had responsibilities to all of them, not just Andros. He scanned the area and decided that while the site wasn't perfect, it was good enough for a night, and set his men to finding water, building a cook fire, and securing the prisoners. This far from the border there was little need of a sentry, but Theos posted one anyway; he didn't want anything else to go wrong.

All through that night, Andros struggled and groaned, and the rest of the camp was subdued by his pain. In the morning, Theos evaluated their remaining supplies and then Andros himself—finally still, but pale and breathing only in weak, pained gasps.

The Sacrati could survive indefinitely in the mountains if they had to. If they stayed with Andros and the winter came, they could hunt and scavenge for food and build rough shelters using the materials the mountain provided. No, they wouldn't die, but their condition would be diminished. Theos would have left on his first patrol as iyatis with a band of healthy men and returned with a group of scrawny survivors. And fewer prisoners too, because how many of them were strong enough to last the winter?

In the end, his decision wasn't based on pride, but responsibility. He'd been entrusted with the care of his fellow Sacrati, and he should return them in the same or better condition than he had received them. But Andros was Sacrati too.

"We're splitting up," Theos announced to his soldiers. "Xeno and two volunteers will stay with Andros and the boy. They'll follow us when Andros is ready to be moved." He held the men's gazes for a moment, long enough to make it clear that Andros's recovery was the only acceptable outcome. "The rest of us will take the prisoners on ahead."

It was a good plan. It was the right thing to do. But that didn't make it easier for Theos to walk away from his friend, his *responsibility*. So his feet were heavy as he made himself start along the path, and they weighed just as much two days later when he led his patrol down off the forested slopes and into the pasture lands of Windthorn valley. A sentry greeted him from the raised observation post, and Theos said wearily, "Theos of the Sacrati, returning from patrol. Eleven Sacrati with me, four more to follow as they are able. Sixteen Elkati prisoners, one more to follow with the other Sacrati."

Another sentry peered over the edge of his platform. "Sixteen, huh? Not bad for a first patrol, especially when we aren't technically at war. Good to see, Theos."

It would have been easier to accept the praise if *all* of Theos's Sacrati had returned with him. As it was, he grunted an acknowledgment and nodded his band forward. As they passed the platform, each of his men pulled the tiny leather bag of soil from around his neck and hung it back on the long hooks with many other bags already on them. The men carried soil from the valley into the mountains with them so if they fell in the field, they would rest with at least a little touch of home nearby. The valley dirt would be enough to let their spirits leave their bodies behind, believing they were lying somewhere safe. A small ritual, but an important one.

The pastures gave way to cropland on the valley floor, the fields full of workers from the city weeding or harvesting or . . . whatever it was one did with crops. Young Theos had been enlisted to help in the fields, just as all children were, but he'd never paid much attention to what he was doing; he'd been too busy practicing his swordsmanship with a crooked stick, or wrestling the other boys in their endless fight for status and dominance. Agriculture, like everything else that wasn't directly related to the Torian war machine, was women's work. Theos appreciated the fruits of the women's labor, but he didn't presume to understand the details of it all, just as the women appreciated the efforts of the warriors but didn't bother with learning the finer points of warfare.

No, Theos's home wasn't in the city with the women and children. He belonged in the barracks, the low, rough buildings that circled the walled town as one more layer of protection against any hazards. As he approached the larger buildings that squatted on either side of the city's main gates, he let his shoulders relax a little. He might wish his homecoming was a purer triumph, but at least he'd gotten *most* of his men home.

He watched his men herd the prisoners into the roofed holding pen adjacent to the military headquarters. There were others already inside, captured on previous missions by other Torians. Theos stepped closer and squinted at the prisoners, reassuring himself they were secure and behaving themselves, then squared his shoulders and headed to the office to give his report. As Sacrati, he bypassed the tables set up in the main room and strode directly to one of the two private offices in the rear of the building; technically the warlord outranked the Sacrati captain, but the matched size of their offices was a more accurate reflection of their relative power.

Theos knocked on the open door and stepped into the office.

"Welcome back," Tamon said, standing and crossing the room to land a friendly clap on Theos's shoulder. "Report now, and we can catch up later."

So Theos told his tale, the captain listened, consulted the map to see exactly where the prisoners had been captured, and frowned. "What were they doing that far inside our territory?" he demanded.

"None of my men speak the language," Theos said. "We didn't question the prisoners."

The captain didn't seem surprised by that. Sacrati were warriors, not spies; they weren't expected to learn the language of every valley they conquered. "Well, they'll be questioned now." Tamon seemed personally insulted by the Elkati trespass. "So we won't be sending any of them to the evaluators for a few days. You'll have to wait for your share."

"Actually, sir, I was hoping to be sent back out, to help bring Andros back."

The captain gave Theos a long look before saying, "You left three Sacrati with him; do you doubt their ability to perform a fairly simple task?"

"No, sir. But I do doubt my ability to rest properly until *all* of the men I took out with me are safely returned."

Tamon sighed. "You're going to lose men, Theos. Hopefully not this time—although if your young Elkati has found a treatment for rock viper bites, I'm going to have more to question him about than just his reasons for crossing the border—but eventually. Every leader does."

"Yes, sir. But I'd like to put it off as long as possible. And I'd like to *know*. Sir."

Tamon nodded slowly. "Uncertainty makes everything more difficult," he agreed. "Stay in the barracks tonight. Have a meal and a good night's sleep. You can go back out tomorrow morning."

"Thank you, sir."

The captain dismissed him, and Theos headed for his quarters. He'd get cleaned up, as ordered, and later on, he'd get some rest. But in between the two? His men had worked hard and fought well, and he would make sure they had ale and wine enough to celebrate their return. That was his duty as a leader.

Then he'd go to bed, and the next morning he'd perform his *other* duty as a leader. He'd head back to the mountains, and he'd make sure all of his men were accounted for, one way or another.

CHAPTER 3

Theos pushed himself hard on the way back up the mountain. He wanted to get where he was going, but more importantly he wanted to be distracted. If all his concentration was needed to find secure footing and pull his tired body along step after step, there would be no energy left for him to imagine what he was heading toward.

Because, of course, he was going to find Andros dead. The young prisoner had known he couldn't cure a rock viper bite; that was why he'd protested when Theos told him to try. He'd only gone along with the stupid plan because Theos had threatened to kill the other prisoners, not because there'd been any chance of success.

That was what his mind told him. And if he'd *known* that it was true, he'd have slowed down. There was no need to run up a mountain in order to help bury a friend. Alternatively, if he'd known for sure that Andros was fine, there'd be no need to go up the mountain at all. He could just wait in the valley, make his visits to the city, and be content.

It was the tiny nugget of doubt that pushed him forward. He made himself stop for the night when it became too dark to move safely, but he just rolled himself in his blankets and chewed some jerky rather than starting a fire, and at first light the doubt roused him and sent him on his way.

Snow clouds appeared midmorning, still far to the west but coming closer, and the wind developed a damp, sharp bite. It wouldn't be the first snow of the season, not in the mountains, but any fresh snow was one more complication to consider. Theos hastened his already quick steps.

Then, in the dying light of that second day, he turned around a bend and saw the dancing glow of a fire not far distant.

He advanced with care, not because he expected hostility but because it was never wise to blunder into a camp of highly trained soldiers. He heard the sentry stir from the trees by the side of the path, just where he should be, and then, "Hold and identify yourself."

"It's Theos, Xeno."

"I thought it might be. Thanks for coming back. Go on in."

There was no emotion in the man's voice, nothing to help Theos guess what he was heading into. So he walked on cautiously, and when he saw the bundle of blankets over by the trees, he knew he'd been right. Andros had died, and they'd wrapped him and put him over there awaiting burial. Maybe they'd found no soil on the mountain deep enough for a grave and were going to carry him into the valley. But then the blankets stirred, just a little, and the boy rose from his spot by the fire and walked over to his patient. He spoke gentle words, none comprehensible, and then crouched down.

Theos strode toward the fire and was greeted by Achus and Elios, the two Sacrati who'd volunteered to stay behind, and the boy stared for a moment before returning his attention to his patient. Worrying whether his work was good enough, hopefully.

Theos dropped his pack by the fire and then approached. Andros was bundled up in blankets beyond what the weather required, his face pale and drawn, but he was alive, his breathing more natural than it had been when Theos left.

"Come to carry me home?" Andros said hoarsely, and Theos crouched beside him, edging the boy out since he didn't seem to be doing anything anyway.

"I shouldn't have to," Theos replied. "You're Sacrati—a little nip like this shouldn't be a problem. You've already had four days off, and now you want special treatment? You bring shame on yourself, Andros."

Andros's weak cough was probably meant to be a laugh. Theos wanted to touch his friend; it felt strange to avoid the casual contact that had always been how they'd communicated best. But Theos didn't know the rules for dealing with sick people.

He let himself run the fingertips of his hand down over Andros's cheek, then turned back to Achus and Elios. "He's hot. Fevered."

"He's been hot and cold for days," Achus said. "Finnvid says it's normal."

Theos frowned at the Sacrati by the fire, then at the prisoner now crouched by Andros's head. "Finnvid?"

"My nursemaid," Andros whispered. "He's more than just pretty."

There was something going on. "He 'says' it's normal?" he asked.

"Not 'says,'" Elios clarified. "Not in words. But he's noticed, and he's not worried about it."

Theos raised his eyebrows at the boy. "Finnvid?" he said, and the boy raised defiant eyes to meet his. "Can he move?" He made his fingers walk in the direction of the valley. "Tomorrow morning, can he move?"

The boy—Finnvid—grimaced. He pointed at Andros, mimicked the walking gesture, and shook his head emphatically.

"Snow's coming," Theos replied, though he didn't know why he was bothering to use words at all. He pointed to the sky, mimed that something was falling, and then rubbed his arms and shivered with mock cold.

Finnvid bit his lip, then rummaged through the debris on the forest floor. He found two twigs, held them parallel, and laid a leaf on top of them.

"A stretcher," Theos interpreted. "We could carry him." They'd have to take the longer paths for some of the way down, the ones followed by traders with their mules instead of sure-footed soldiers. And they'd have to rest more often, if being moved was hard on Andros.

Maybe it would be better to build a shelter, do some hunting, and wait out the season. But just because full-strength Sacrati could survive a winter in the mountains, it didn't mean that Andros could, not in his weakened state. He'd be better off recovering in the warmth of the valley, with tasty foods and a soft bed.

"Maybe I *did* come to carry you home," Theos murmured. He leaned over and kissed his friend's forehead. "Do you think you'd be able to make it on a stretcher?"

Andros took a deep breath, then choked a little as he released it. "Everything hurts," he admitted. "All of me. But . . . I could manage."

Theos nodded. He looked at the Elkati and said, "Tomorrow? We'll carry him down?" and went through the whole ridiculous series of pantomimes.

The boy nodded cautiously.

So the decision was made. Theos spent what light was left finding two strong sticks, and then went out to take Xeno's sentry post, leaving Xeno free to sleep in the camp with Andros. They all woke the next morning and shook the fallen snow from their blankets and ate a quick breakfast of dried fruit. Then they strung blankets between the long sticks, rolled Andros on board, and started moving.

Even with two teams of Sacrati to take turns carrying their injured comrade, travel was slow. By midmorning, Andros was breathing in ragged gasps, and Theos reluctantly ordered a break. He waved the prisoner over to tend his patient, and stood watching with a careful eye.

"I'm surprised the boy can think with you making that face at him," Xeno said as he gently lifted Andros's head to allow sips of water from his waterskin.

"Does he *need* to think? He's not doing much."

"Maybe he's trying to *think* about what to do." Xeno looked up at Theos and said, "He was good, Theos. When Andros was at his worst? Finnvid was good. He knew what he was doing. He saved Andros's life."

"Not yet he hasn't."

Xeno scowled at him but didn't reply, and Theos stamped away to the far side of the trail. He hated feeling useless, hated facing a challenge that couldn't be met with strength or courage or cunning. Everything in him cried for action, and everything outside him told him to be patient. He preferred to trust his insides.

So he built a fire, filled a cookpot with snow, and added dried meat and vegetables until he had a passable stew. There was enough for all of them, and he put a little in a bowl and carried it over to where Andros was lying.

"Can he eat?" he asked Finnvid, showing him the bowl.

The Elkati shook his head at the food, then at Theos, and pushed the bowl away impatiently.

Theos turned to Xeno. "Has he not eaten? In this whole time, he's not been eating?"

"He's had broth," Xeno said.

"No wonder he's so pale; he's starving to death!"

"Finnvid knows what he's doing."

"Starving someone to death?" Theos frowned at the prisoner. "Why?" He mimed feeding the stew to Andros and then made a questioning face. If Andros ate, what would happen?

Finnvid made a puking sound and lifted his hands to show imaginary food pouring out of his mouth.

Theos held his fingers close together. "We'd just give him a little bit, not a feast!"

Finnvid shook his head stubbornly, his expression almost scornful.

Theos huffed and rose to his feet. He had no idea whether to trust the boy's knowledge *or* his intentions, but he absolutely didn't like his attitude. "The prisoner eats what Andros eats," he declared. "No different, no more. If Andros can survive on sips of broth, then so will the Elkati."

Xeno seemed as if he wanted to argue, but then looked at Andros's drawn face and nodded.

"Tell me when you think he's ready to move, Xeno." Theos stepped away, then added, "When *you* think so. Not when the precious Elkati gives his permission."

Another grudging nod, and Theos turned back to the fire and added food to the bowl before sitting down to eat it. When he was finished, he checked his equipment and did some basic exercises, enough to maintain his flexibility and balance without draining strength he might need. And then he waited. Not entirely patiently.

By early afternoon, Xeno and Andros decided they could manage a little more traveling, so Theos grabbed an end of the stretcher, happy to be doing something. Again their progress was slow, and again they only made it a few hours before Andros was clearly in too much pain to continue, but at least they'd made some progress. They stopped at one of the most-used campsites on the route, a grassy clearing next to a cold, burbling stream, and Theos sent Achus fishing while Elios stood watch and Xeno helped settle Andros. By the time Theos had the fire set up and their blankets hung to air and be warmed by the flames, there were four fat trout waiting to be grilled. Four. Good. One for each of the people eating, and he'd boil up the skin and bones to make a broth for the two who weren't.

The fish smelled delicious as it cooked, and Theos found himself anticipating the Elkati's reaction when he was denied a taste. Petty, maybe, but there was something about the boy that just grated. His quiet self-confidence was frustrating.

And it was even more annoying when Theos doled out the cooked fish and the Elkati didn't even look in his direction. As if he'd known he wouldn't be getting any. As if he'd known . . .

"Xeno?" Theos said. "Andros is healing, right? The Elkati isn't really *doing* anything anymore? Just starving him and fussing over him? No real medicine?"

Xeno frowned. "Well . . . he's still using his potions . . ."

"But you've been watching? You know which ones to use?" Theos rose easily to his feet, his trout half-finished on the ground. He stalked toward Andros and the prisoner. "I've put up with enough from him. He's the enemy, he's already been part of an escape attempt, and I don't trust him when I close my eyes to sleep. I'm going to kill him now. My dagger right through his spine."

"There's no need of that!" Xeno protested, and Andros half-pushed himself off the stretcher.

Theos was behind the boy now, but Finnvid didn't move. He stayed crouched by Andros's head. Then Theos took half a step closer, and the boy leaped to his feet, whirling toward Theos with a bottle in his hand, ready to smash it into Theos's skull.

As the boy swung, Theos dodged inside the arc just as he had with the other prisoner days earlier, but this time he didn't punch the Elkati's nose. Instead, he caught the boy's wrist, twisting it behind his back until the bottle dropped, unharmed, into Theos's free hand. The attack had been doomed to failure, and had clearly been a desperate last attempt to survive. Theos wrapped his arm around the boy's throat and leaned forward until his mouth was right by the boy's ear. "You speak Torian," Theos said gently. It was the only way the boy could have anticipated his actions.

Finnvid's body stayed rigid for a moment, then slumped. "Elkati are educated," he hissed in Torian, his words practically accentless. "We bother to learn things about our attackers."

"Your 'conquerors,' you mean." Theos made sure he was angled well away from Andros before he shoved the boy into a graceless sprawl on the frost-whitened grass. "You wanted to be well-placed for a position in the new society once we take over. That makes sense. If I were a weaponless coward like you, maybe I'd have made the same decision."

"I was laughing at you," the boy retorted. "All the time with your silly gestures and your little shows, trying to make me understand what you meant, when all along I'd understood every word."

"Yes, yes, very humorous. You, my captive, off to live in slavery in my empire, completely under my control . . . you found a tiny, pathetic way to feel powerful. That's nice. If it helps, you can imagine me as an ant tonight as you sleep, and in your dreams you can stomp on me." Theos smiled, showing his teeth. "None of these games will change your reality, of course."

"You understand nothing! You're a brute, a thug!"

"I'm Sacrati," Theos corrected. He didn't need to make any more arguments, not with evidence like that behind him. "Now, let's go back to pretending you can't speak. I'll even do the entertaining hand signs, if you like." He pointed at the boy, then used both hands to cover his own mouth.

"Be nice," Andros croaked from his blankets.

Theos snorted at him. "Why? Because you think he's pretty?"

"Because he saved my life."

"Not yet," the Elkati said, his mouth twisted in a sneer as he echoed Theos's earlier words.

Theos moved fast, grabbing the boy by his hair and half lifting him off the ground. No flinch, a part of Theos's mind noted with approval, but most of him had no time for compliments. "The promise still stands," he growled. "If Andros dies, all the other prisoners die too." He ran his fingers along the boy's jaw, noting how soft the hair of his beard still was. "But not you. Not right away. If Andros dies, you live for a little bit longer than your friends. Long enough to see them die, and long enough to learn your lesson. You understand?"

The boy raised his lips in a wordless snarl, and Theos tossed him backward onto the grass. The Elkati had understood.

Theos stalked over to his abandoned fish and flopped down beside it.

"Nice to see you making friends," Xeno said lightly. He leaned in a little so no one else could hear. "And, iyatis or not, if I hear you talking about Andros dying again, anywhere Andros can hear? I'll cut out your tongue and shove it up your ass." He eased away then, but his eyes stayed locked on Theos's.

Theos had beaten Xeno in every sparring match they'd had since they were youngsters. But sometimes a threat didn't have to be frightening to convey a message, and Theos made himself nod. "Understood."

Xeno held his gaze for just a moment longer, then said at normal volume, "Good catch on Finnvid. I was getting pretty tired of acting everything out for him."

"You're saying it wrong," Finnvid said from his spot back by Andros's head. "It's Finnvid, not Feenveed."

"Careful," Theos warned. "If I decide your name is Dickless, that'll be your name. So, ask yourself: is Feenveed really all that bad?"

The boy didn't answer, which Theos took as a victory. He finished his fish and tossed the remains into the pot over the fire. Xeno did the same, with a thoughtful frown toward Andros. Maybe Xeno was finally remembering that Finnvid was the enemy, and shouldn't be completely trusted. Shouldn't be trusted at all, really.

But Xeno didn't *say* he'd changed his mind about Finnvid, didn't suggest that they try feeding Andros something solid, and Theos decided not to push it, not yet.

He took the first watch that night, standing guard on the edge of camp as Xeno retied Finnvid's hands and feet and then settled beside Andros. Achus and Elios had finished their fish and were staring at the flames, sitting close enough together that Theos knew what they'd be up to before they went to sleep.

The night was quiet, guard duty a formality rather than a necessity, and Theos found his attention being drawn to the Elkati.

By the time Xeno replaced him on watch, Theos had drawn some conclusions. When he saw Andros awake, staring at the flames of the fire Xeno had just rebuilt, Theos sank down next to him.

"He's the leader. He's the one who ordered the surrender that first day." It was strange to think of this boy in charge of a band of soldiers, but it fit what Theos had seen.

Andros didn't seem surprised by the idea. "He kept trying to look after them. Set up that escape, and did his healing."

"That healing might be his chance." Theos wasn't sure if the boy was asleep or just pretending to be, but Theos wasn't saying anything secret. Actually, it might be good to say a bit more, to be sure the boy understood his position. "If he can prove he's good for something, he can earn his freedom." If Finnvid had been a woman, he'd have had lots of choices. Women ran the city, controlled the trade, crafted the tools and weapons, and grew the crops. Even if the incoming prisoners had no skills, they could usually get pregnant and contribute through the production of new Torians. Any woman bearing a Torian child simply had to take an oath of fealty and she'd be made a free citizen. As her child grew up in the Torian Empire, her maternal love was expected to keep her loyal.

For men, though? There was only war.

Theos squinted at the boy. "He's probably not going to get much taller; hopefully he still has some filling out to do. But he hasn't been trained properly. Best chance is for him to be a medic."

Theos wouldn't admit it while the boy might be listening, but he knew the Torians never had much luck training their own healers. The women had their medicine, of course, and they'd help any soldier who could be brought back to the safety of the city. But they knew better than to venture out into the fields of battle.

"Either that or a bedwarmer," Theos mused.

"He's pretty enough," Andros mumbled.

Yes, he probably was. And when a bedwarmer *wasn't* busy serving his master however required, he could spend his time training, trying to find some way to earn a place for himself.

If that didn't work? The boy might be sent back east to one of the huge mines in the central valleys where he would labor underground, or he might be used for whatever skill-less jobs the army came up with. Theos had seen useless slaves sent to clear paths of traps before more valuable soldiers came through, and he'd heard of them being pushed onto the battlefield as arrow-fodder, distracting the enemy while the true soldiers approached under better cover. It was no way for a man to die.

"He needs to be smart," Theos said, still not really for Andros's benefit.

"He is," Andros replied.

"Well, he needs to *act* smart. Needs to remember who's in charge." A foolish suggestion, probably. It was pointless to speculate. Finding jobs for prisoners was the task of the evaluators, not the Sacrati.

So he left Andros to his blankets and took a brief tour around the camp, looking for dangers he knew he wouldn't find, stepping carefully to avoid Achus and Elios's tangle of writhing, half-naked Sacrati, trying to ignore the stir in his own groin. He thought briefly about approaching Xeno, but Andros had always been closer to Theos, and finding relief with Xeno while Andros lay there unable to join in didn't seem right. So Theos laid another log on the fire and settled back. The Elkati was sitting up, now, and working hard at not watching Achus and Elios. The boy wasn't going to have much fun as a bedwarmer if he got this flustered when someone *else* was having sex. But that wasn't Theos's problem.

CHAPTER 4

They made slow but steady progress the next day, and at dinnertime Finnvid allowed Andros to eat some finely minced vegetables and a tiny bit of the rabbit Xeno had caught and roasted. Finnvid clearly knew Theos was watching him around the food, and after feeding Andros he defiantly pushed away the vegetables and meat Xeno offered him. "I'm not really hungry," the Elkati said. "I think I'll just have a little more broth."

"Good," Theos grunted. He reached across and lifted the rejected plate off the ground by Finnvid's side. "I didn't get quite enough meat. Does anyone want more vegetables, or should I eat those too?"

He waited a moment for an answer he didn't get, then started eating. The rabbit was greasy and delicious, almost enough to make him forget that the vegetables had been dried and chopped into something closer to flour than to recognizable forms. Dried fruit, dried grain, dried vegetables, dried meat, reconstituted only if there was time to camp and start a fire—that was the diet of a soldier in the field. The rabbit made this meal a luxury, even if there was no replacement for the vegetable slush.

The next morning, the Elkati ate the same breakfast as everyone else, and Andros managed a half serving of oatmeal. They traveled faster that day, too. By the time the sun was setting, they'd reached the sentry at the top of the valley, and Theos helped Andros pull the leather bag from around his neck. They were home, and their spirits didn't need to be fooled anymore. Theos hung the bags up on the hook, then told Andros, "We can camp here, if you want, or else spend another few hours on the road and you can sleep in your own bed. It's your decision."

"I'm already *in* bed," Andros said, patting the sides of his stretcher with satisfaction. "I'm happy either way."

Theos looked at the other men. The Sacrati would be happy to get home, and walking through the flat valley in the dark wasn't dangerous. Five Sacrati who wanted their beds . . . Theos caught the Elkati's eye. Finnvid was trying to look unconcerned, but not really managing it. He had no idea what was waiting for him when they reached the city, and Theos didn't know much himself. The other prisoners had been heading for interrogation when he'd left the valley; what had they said? Why had they been on the wrong side of the border, and why had they been led by a healer instead of . . . well, instead of just about anyone else?

And even if the questions had been answered in the most innocent ways, what was waiting for Finnvid after the evaluators saw him?

"We'll camp," Theos decided. They'd left the cold behind on the mountain, and it would be pleasant to have a night under the stars without shivering. One last night before returning to the usual routine. Well, routine for five of them.

The sentry post was well stocked with food and miscellaneous cooking tools; Theos thought back to his own time on sentry duty and didn't remember the same level of luxury. It was probably a sign of moral decline that the sentries were living so well now, but he was too happy to see fresh bread to worry too much about it. He just commandeered what he wanted and left the sentries sputtering indignantly. Living on jerky until they were relieved of duty would be good for the soldiers' characters.

Theos, on the other hand? He and the others grilled slabs of ham, roasted freshly dug potatoes and carrots, and made a sort of apple-berry cobbler for dessert. A few jugs of ale might have completed the feast, but no one complained. They just ate, and sat around the fire. Even Andros, after having a taste of all of their foods, was more-or-less upright, leaning back against Xeno.

"Almost as good as the harvest feast," Achus said, patting his belly contentedly.

"I always wondered why they fed us so well on those nights," Elios mused. "After a big meal, I just want to sleep. Pleasing a woman seems like a lot of work."

"That would explain why you don't get many invitations to the city," Xeno said. "You'll be stuck with one or two kids a year if you can't make the women want you more often. Theos, though . . . Theos, how many have you got so far? Must be almost fifty?"

"Forty-six, I think. Two more on the way, though."

Elios shook his head. "Too much trouble. Why get cleaned up, walk all the way to the city, and go through all their nonsense, just to fuck a woman, when I could roll over right now and do whatever I wanted to Achus?"

"You have forty-six . . . Are you talking about— You've fathered forty-six *children*?" The Elkati was staring at Theos, his expression a mix of disbelief and something that looked like disgust. "I've heard about the Torian practices, but . . . *forty-six*? You aren't even— You're quite *young*! When did you start having children?"

"My oldest is coming to the barracks this winter. He's almost nine." Theos wasn't sure whether to be annoyed or amused by the Elkati's reaction.

"You've had forty-six children in nine years?"

Theos looked to Andros to see if he wanted to jump into the conversation, but Andros just said, "Carry on. You're seven kids ahead of me, and I started before you. Explain yourself to the foreigner."

Theos shrugged. "Three festivals a year. Babies don't always come from festival couplings, of course, but . . . one or two a year, from that. And then an invitation to the city most cycles, when I'm not on campaign, and they time it all carefully, so quite a few of those visits result in babies. So maybe five or six visits a year, for three or four more babies a year . . ." The math seemed simple.

"We don't all get the extra invitations," Achus told Finnvid patiently. "You wouldn't know it to look at him right now, but when Theos shaves and cleans up, he's a handsome devil. And the women look at his career too, and hear reports from officers and from other women. They like him because he's good stock so he'll probably give them good babies." Achus lowered his voice a little as he added, "And because he makes them *scream* with pleasure."

"While men like Elios are sleeping off a big meal," Theos said with a laugh. Then he turned his attention to Finnvid. Was it cruel to ask him about his old life, the one he'd never be able to go back to? Maybe, but it seemed awkward to ignore the topic altogether. So he tried to keep his question general. "I've heard rumors that Elkati mate for life, like beavers."

"Beavers?"

"One male beaver, one female beaver, in their lodge. Beavers."

Finnvid clearly didn't like the comparison. "We—we *marry*. We make vows to be faithful to each other."

"To have sex *only* with each other, forever?" Theos frowned. "What if you get tired of each other? What if your couplings don't produce babies? What if one of you dies?"

"If one of us *dies*, the other could remarry," Finnvid said, straightening his shoulders. "But otherwise . . . we remain faithful."

"Sex with *one* person. *Forever.*" Theos realized he'd expected to be laughed at when he'd brought up the rumors. How could anything so ridiculous actually be true? "So, have you married?" Theos was curious. "Will your woman marry again, now that you're gone?"

Finnvid looked as if he wanted to argue, maybe to insist that his captivity was only temporary. But instead he said, "I don't have a . . . you don't have a Torian word for it, then? A 'wife'? I don't have one."

"So . . . wait. If you only have sex with the one you're married to, and you've never married . . ."

The other men around the campfire had faded out of the conversation at some point, but now their attention was back, and they were staring at Finnvid with wide eyes.

"Have you never had sex?" Xeno asked, the disbelief clear in his tone.

"That's private," Finnvid replied. He sounded prim and disapproving, but Theos could hear the insecurity beneath it and decided to take pity on him with a less personal line of questioning.

"So, when Elkati are married," he said, "do you only *speak* to each other, as well? Only *look* at each other? If one of you is away on a campaign, the other one . . . just . . . doesn't have sex? At all?"

"Torian men spend most of the summer away from home," Finnvid countered. "So it's the same problem, isn't it? Your women can't have sex when *you're* not around."

Theos looked at him blankly, then turned toward his fellow Sacrati, hoping one of them could interpret the Elkati's words. Receiving no help, he said slowly, "They have sex with *each other*. They don't need *us* for sex, any more than we need them. That's . . ." He was still searching for some different meaning in the boy's words. Finnvid was supposed to be a healer, so surely he'd understand these things? "You need a man and a woman for *babies*," Theos explained. "That's all."

"But . . ." Even in the firelight the boy's blush was clear to see. Theos wondered if the skin would feel as hot as it appeared. "Yes, thank you," Finnvid managed to say. "I know about babies. But . . . it doesn't *have* to be just for babies. You can sleep with women for, you know, for pleasure. Companionship. All of that. As *well* as babies."

Theos was having to rethink his assessment of the Elkati. How could someone so clever about some things be so clueless about others?

"The women live *in the city*." He felt like he was speaking more slowly with every sentence. "We *could* sleep with them for pleasure, but they're far away. And it'd be a nuisance to have to get approval from the temple every time."

It was ridiculous that *Finnvid* could be confused by this conversation, but that was the only interpretation of the expression on the boy's face. "The temple? Why is the temple involved?"

"To make sure it's an approved mating. Not too closely related, not too many kids with the same blood being produced—"

"You've fathered *forty-six* children in nine years and you're worried about too many children with the same blood?"

"*I'm* not worried. The temple is. That's why they won't approve me for more than five or six extra partners a year, outside of the festivals."

"Otherwise every baby in the city would be his," Andros said with a grin.

"You're just as popular," Theos retorted. "We'd have made a lot of women unhappy if we'd left you up on the mountain with the snakes."

It would have been easier to let the conversation drift back in that familiar direction. But Finnvid clearly didn't want to move on. "But if you're sleeping with all these women . . . there must be an imbalance. There must be some men who *can't* sleep with a woman, because you've taken them all. That's not fair."

"Fair? Women aren't kegs of ale; they aren't to be divided up equally for the enjoyment of all the drinkers. If Andros and I have more children, that's because the women *want* to have our babies. It's their choice. Nothing to do with being fair to men."

"That's easy for you to say, when you're the one with all the women! What about the men who are alone?"

"Alone? Being invited to the city . . . that's . . . well, counting the festivals, it's maybe ten nights a year, at the most. Being with women isn't going to keep anyone from being *alone*." Theos nodded at Andros and Xeno, reclining together with their legs entwined. "Your *friends* keep you from being alone. Not women."

"But it *could* be women. You don't *have* to . . . you know. You don't have to do unnatural things. You could just be with women."

"The women are in the city—" Theos started again, but Finnvid interrupted him.

"The women could *leave* the city! Or the men could go there! You've built this whole artificial *culture* around a simple peculiarity of population distribution—"

"The women stay in the city because they're *safe* there. We need them, as many as possible, and we need them to be healthy. One man can have many children in a year; we don't need as many men. So men go to war and keep the valleys safe, and women stay in the cities where they're protected. They take care of business, and they build things and raise children." Theos raised an eyebrow. "What's so *unnatural* about that?"

"Your women are happy with this system? They don't want to settle down with one man and have a family?"

"If they aren't happy, they can speak up."

"And the men will listen? Who will make sure the women have voices? How can they know they're safe to speak, with no mate to protect them?"

"Why would they need a mate to protect them when they have a whole army?"

"What if it's the army they need to be protected against?"

"Well, one man isn't going to do much good against a whole army. But, really, why would the army want to attack a woman?"

"Because she challenged your crazy social structure?"

"Women can challenge things. They can go to the city council and say what they want."

"Without being shouted down by the men?"

Theos was getting impatient. "It's the *city* council. There *are* no men." He looked up at the stars for a moment, then said, "Remember back when the world was fresh and new? Back when you were pretending you didn't speak Torian? Those were good times, weren't they?"

Finnvid's snort was suspiciously like a laugh. "They were certainly simpler times," he admitted. He was quiet for a while, then tilted his face toward the same stars Theos had been gazing at. "Do Torians have stories about them?"

"About what?"

"The stars. Do you make pictures from them, and tell stories about them?"

"I don't understand. Make pictures from the stars?"

Finnvid nodded, and pointed upward. "Like those stars there. You see the brightest one? And then down from it, and over, how it makes a box? And the little stars in the middle are almost lined up. That's Greanna's loom."

"Who's Greanna?"

"The mother of all." Finnvid sounded like a man telling a tale to children. "She creates our lives, and then she and her daughters weave us together on the loom and determine how everything will go."

"Her daughters?"

"Three pairs of twins: Love and Hate, Birth and Death, Laughter and Tears."

"What kind of a mother would name her daughter Death? Or even Tears?"

"You don't object to Hate?"

"Well, I guess Hate isn't too nice either. I wouldn't mind spending a night with Laughter, though. She sounds like fun."

"You'd prefer Laughter to Love?"

"Love would be too complicated." Theos lifted his hand to point at the stars. "That one? And then . . . that one . . . yes, I see the box. That's their loom. What else do they do?"

"Well, that's about the only story for that constellation. It's just the easiest one to see. But . . . up from there, and off to the right. Do you see those two stars close together, and then the other one beyond them? That's Varin's sword. The hilt, and then the tip. And his shield is over there, those five stars in a sort of circle?"

"Aye, I see it . . . but who's Varin?"

"He's the greatest hero the world has ever known," Finnvid said confidently. He leaned back on his elbows and stared at the stars and began to tell Theos stories of the hero. And Theos listened, although he spent as much time looking at Finnvid as he did at the stars.

The next morning they woke early, had breakfast, and walked the rest of the way into town. Andros insisted on climbing off the stretcher once they reached the drilling yards and everyone slowed down to wait for his careful, tight steps. When they arrived at the barracks, Elios and Achus accepted Andros's thanks and then drifted off toward their quarters, and Xeno said he would take Andros to the medics to be checked out. Before they left, they both hugged Finnvid and thanked him, and Andros gave Theos a look that probably contained a message, but not one he could understand.

He walked Finnvid over to the holding pens and peered inside. The other Elkati prisoners were still there, a few of them with fresh bruises and cuts. Theos sighed. "Seems like some more work for you." Maybe Finnvid would feel better about stepping into the cage if he felt he had a purpose.

But as it happened, Theos couldn't see how Finnvid was reacting to the prospect. The Elkati's expression was as closed and unreadable as it had been in the early days, back when he was planning escapes and pretending not to speak Torian.

Which was as it should be, Theos reminded himself. Finnvid was Elkati. He was the enemy. He'd been captured well over the border, and now he'd face the consequences. None of it was Theos's problem, and none of it was within his power to change. "Good luck," he said, feeling like a fool as soon as the words were past his lips.

But Finnvid didn't mock him. He didn't say a thing as Theos unlocked the cage and Finnvid stepped into it. He kept his shoulders straight and his head high, and strode toward his men without so much as a glance in Theos's direction.

Theos shut the door behind him, made sure it was locked, then went to give his report to the captain.

CHAPTER 5

"They're saying it was a *dare*?" Andros said with disgust. He'd been lying on his bed when Theos arrived to check on him, but now he was propped up on his elbows and seemed about to swing his legs over the side of the bed and march off to right a wrong. "Does Finnvid really seem like the sort of person to cross a border on a dare? Like a raw recruit trying to earn his sword?"

"According to them, Finnvid wasn't the leader," Theos grumbled. He'd already gone through disbelief and was settling down into resignation, heavily tinged with confusion. "They said it was the old guy. He'd just been passed over for a promotion and wanted to prove he still had balls, so he led his men into our territory."

"There's no way the old guy was in charge. Finnvid was. It's obvious. You need to go tell them the prisoners lied."

"I already told them. And you know, the Elkati were a bit bruised when I dropped Finnvid off, but they weren't *really* messed up. Not like they'd been beaten hard." Theos frowned. There was more to this situation than incompetent interrogation, but he wasn't quite sure what it was. "The interrogators didn't listen. For some reason it was the warlord's crew who were in charge, and . . ." He realized what the problem had been. "They acted like being Sacrati meant nothing. Like I was just another soldier with a stupid opinion they didn't need to listen to."

"There are always rust stains who are like that," Andros said slowly. "Usually it's the ones who thought they should have been chosen, but weren't."

"No. I'm used to that. This was . . . It was something different. And when I asked to see the captain, he was busy."

"On the yards, doing training."

"No. He was in his office. I saw him."

"He was in his office, and he was too busy to talk to a Sacrati iyatis?"

"I know. It's— It didn't make sense. But that's what they said."

"What's going on, Theos?" Andros's voice was quiet and serious, and somehow reassuring. Theos wasn't being paranoid. "There's something not right."

Theos pushed himself to his feet. "Keep quiet about it, okay? For now, at least. Tell Xeno to lay low, and I'll talk to the other two. We shouldn't say anything different than what the interrogators found. Just until I can talk to the captain and figure out what's going on."

Andros nodded. "If you need support, tell me. There's no way that old guy was in charge. No way. So we still don't know what they were doing on our side of the line. But if they had a cover story figured out, and they were all strong enough to stick to it during interrogation . . ."

"I know." Theos stood up and clapped a hand onto Andros's shoulder. "But I'll take care of it; you focus on recovery. The rest of the world will still be around when you're better, and I want you at full strength."

Andros lifted a hand and laced his fingers through Theos's. He lay down again, keeping Theos's hand where it was so Theos had to lean over him. Then Andros raised his other hand and wrapped it around the back of Theos's neck, tugging gently.

Theos obliged, lowering his head to Andros's and kissing him. Just lightly at first, but when Andros didn't release his grip, Theos deepened the kiss.

It wasn't the start of anything; Andros was mending, but still not fit enough for sex. It was just to show solidarity. Whatever was happening at the higher levels of the military, Andros and Theos would present a united front.

There was a quiet thud behind them, and Theos turned his head to see Xeno standing in the doorway, smiling at them both.

"Feeling better, then?" he asked. He took the two steps across the room and crouched down next to them. A quick kiss for Theos, and then Xeno's attention was all on Andros. "I got the poppy juice, but they said to use as little as possible. Let me know if the pain gets to be too much, but otherwise we'll just give you a few drops before you sleep. And I can get a mat for the floor, so you'll have more room . . ."

"There's room here," Andros said. He'd taken his hand away from Theos and was gripping Xeno's wrist now. "Lots of room. I want you in bed with me."

Theos stood up and headed for the door. He and Andros were friends, but Andros and Xeno had been a pair for years. Finnvid seemed quite clever, sometimes, so how could he have missed their devotion? How could he think that they must be lonely because there were no *women* in their beds most nights? It made no sense.

Just one more thing that was hard to understand, Theos reminded himself as he jogged down the stairs toward his quarters. And not one of the more urgent puzzles to be solved. He needed to put the Elkati boy out of his mind, and figure out what was going on in his own barracks yard.

He picked up clean clothes and headed for the communal baths, one of the few luxuries in the barracks.

On this late-fall day, the shutters of the bathhouse were thrown open, light shining in as steam poured out. Most of the soldiers had duties during the daytime, so Theos had the place to himself. It was nice to be warm enough to strip right down, to look at the Torian tattoo on the rounded ball of his shoulder, the Sacrati brand on his hip. He'd gotten the tattoo as a young man, and it had stretched and faded a little as he'd grown, so he checked on it now and then to be sure it wasn't gone entirely. The brand had been hard-won; he liked to look at that too, sometimes, to run his fingers over the roughened skin and remember what he'd achieved.

And it was always good to pull the leather bracers from his wrists. Every Torian warrior used them, not just to protect their arms but to keep the bracelets underneath them safe. Now that he was in the barracks, though, he could shed the bracers and let the bracelets be seen. He ran his hands over them all, then stepped into one of the large communal tubs.

Theos soaked for a while, then scrubbed himself clean, rinsed off in the fresh water, and headed to the mirrors to shave. He was almost done before he noticed that he had company.

Theos knew the soldier's face, but not his name. There were well over two thousand men on active duty in the valley's military, with a couple hundred new recruits each year to replace the men who were killed or who went east to fight on the other border. This was just another soldier in a long line of them.

"Shouldn't you be on duty?" Theos asked, wiping the last of the shaving oil from his face.

"I'm the night guard this month," the soldier said. "It's not a bad job, but there's no one to spend time with when I'm not at work."

"But there is today." Theos moved closer, and the soldier smiled.

"There is today," the man echoed, and he pulled his tunic up over his head.

Their coupling was friendly, casual. The soldier just shed his remaining clothes and dropped to his knees, using his mouth to bring Theos to hardness, and then smeared some of the shaving oil on his cock. Theos buried himself in the other man's body, and the soldier braced himself against the wall and arched his back.

It was nothing special, yet it was just what Theos needed. A return to the ordinary, a reminder of the simple things in life: tight, slick heat; a body strong enough to take whatever Theos gave; grunts of enjoyment and encouragement; and a climax that took them both away, at least temporarily, from their worries.

They rinsed off together under the flow of water, and then Theos clapped the soldier's shoulder and wished him luck staying awake on sentry duty, and that was it. Theos dressed in clean clothes and set his laundry to soak in the tanks next to the bathhouse.

Fresh and clean, he went down to the kitchen in search of food. Technically the soldiers were all supposed to eat at meal times, but Theos was Sacrati, he was just back from the field, and he was hungry. The recruits scurried around to put food together for him, and he grinned. Life in the barracks was a nice change from the mountains.

Theos took his meal outdoors, intending to eat it while he watched the drills under the warm sun. But before he got to the drill yards he was stopped short by a procession in front of the holding pens.

Prisoners were being taken out of the pen and lined up in the road. Not the Elkati Theos had brought in; these men must have come from someone else's patrol. They already had heavy iron slave collars around their necks, and as they joined their fellows, the blacksmith was hammering red-hot iron into chain links, her hands quick and sure as she worked. She was fastening the prisoners together into a web that would hold until their heads came off or someone with a forge and the proper tools released them.

This was the preparation for a mass slave transport. Not that uncommon, but they usually happened after significant battles, and Theos would have heard from the captain if there'd been one of those lately. He strode forward and spoke to a one-armed man who was watching the work with an overseer's critical eye. "Where are you taking them?"

"Who are you to ask?" The man's accent was subtly different; he wasn't from Windthorn valley.

"I'm Sacrati." But why was Theos wasting words on this man? He moved a little closer and made his expression dull and threatening. "Where are you taking them?"

The man sighed as if he were tired of stupid questions. "Back east, to the central valleys."

"Why?" Slaves were usually kept in the valley that captured them until they'd been trained for their new lives. If they proved useless as soldiers, they might be sent to the mines, or if they had special skills, they might be transported to where they were needed, but it wasn't routine.

"I was told to," the slaver grunted.

"It's going to be winter before you get anywhere. You'll be lucky to make it to the next valley before you're snowed in."

"Extra risk means extra rewards," the man said with an oily smile. Then he turned away.

Theos stepped back and tried to find sense in the situation. The chosen prisoners were young. They were all male, but that made sense; females were captured when the Torians took over a valley, not when they captured trespassers, and there'd been no new valleys claimed recently. But still, there was something about the prisoners . . .

The boys were all pretty, and didn't seem to have anything else in common. "You're taking them to be bedwarmers?"

The trader wagged his eyebrows. "They'll fetch a good price back east."

It didn't feel right. This many young, healthy men had failed to meet the army standards? It was unheard of. "Who authorized this?"

"I did." The voice was chilly, and Theos turned to see the warlord striding toward him. Tall and lean with a hawklike face and eyes that seemed to see everything, the man was imposing. But Theos was Sacrati.

"Why are you sending them? They haven't been here long, have they?" The pens had been almost empty when Theos had left on patrol. "They haven't been given a chance."

"Remember yourself, soldier. Remember your place." The words were wielded like a whip, but they didn't sting when they landed.

"Sacrati," Theos corrected calmly.

"Sacrati are still soldiers, and it's time you all remembered that. Now, get back to your duties." The man's eyes raked over the food in Theos's hands. "Or your *picnic*. Whatever you were doing, start doing it again. This is none of your business."

The next prisoner was pulled out of the pen. Finnvid. His face was tight with anger or fear or a combination of both, and his eyes skimmed past Theos without any sign of recognition. Theos was just another Torian, another slaver. And Finnvid was a leader being dragged away from his men, and being sent on a dangerous journey to an unknowable fate.

"Sir," Theos said. "I have some concerns about this prisoner. Information I received while on the mountain suggests—"

"No, you have *no* concerns about this prisoner. He's none of your business." The warlord didn't even glance toward Theos this time. "Leave the area, soldier."

Sacrati, Theos wanted to insist again. He took half a step backward, casting around the courtyard hoping to find a solution he couldn't quite imagine on his own. He saw Andros standing on the steps of one of the barracks' buildings. He was leaning on Xeno, pale and weak, but he was standing. He was alive. "Sir," Theos said, stepping forward. "As patrol leader, I have the right to first pick of the prisoners we captured. I haven't made my choice yet."

The warlord curled his lips into an ugly sneer. "And the business of the valley should cease while you ponder?"

Theos knew what he was doing. That was the frustrating part. Displeasing a leader of the camp, getting involved in something he didn't understand—he knew it was stupid. And he did it anyway. "I chose that prisoner, sir. Finnvid of the Elkati. I claim him." He pointed to the boy.

The warlord glared at him for a moment, then jerked his chin toward the office building. "So go tell them inside, and they'll give you the coin."

A final chance to escape, but Theos didn't take it. "No, sir, I don't want the value. I want the prisoner."

The warlord's expression became even more hawklike. "What? You want to . . ." The veins in his neck were standing out, but then he gave a smile, tight and almost more intimidating than his scowl. "You're a young man, Theos. You're . . . I know, I said Sacrati were just soldiers, but we both know you get extra attention as one of the chosen. You have no need of a bedwarmer. And they're expensive, you know. If they're not contributing to the empire, *you* have to pay for their food, and for any clothing or medicine they need."

"But if they have any income, I get to keep that, right?"

"You're thinking of making him a whore?" The warlord shrugged a little, visibly trying to relax. His voice was lighter as he continued, "Fine, maybe that's not a bad idea. But . . . just between you and me. As comrades. Choose one of the others, one of the more tractable ones, and I'll mark it down as if he came from your patrol's capture. You'll get a better slave out of the deal."

And the warlord would be doing it because he and Theos were comrades. Theos managed to hide his disbelief and tried to think of a way to make his interest seem less peculiar. "Thank you, sir, but I've already spent time with this prisoner. I like his—his way. His skills. I know he's a nuisance, but I'll keep him under control."

The game was over now; the warlord wasn't trying to control his anger anymore. He stepped closer to Theos and hissed, "Take another prisoner."

"I'd prefer to follow the rules," Theos said quietly. "I'll take Finnvid of the Elkati, sir. Thank you."

For a moment it truly seemed that the warlord would refuse. Possibly with a bonus assault. Then he exhaled some of his aggression in an angry huff. "Fine," he growled. He turned to the woman who had just finished positioning Finnvid in the apparatus used for attaching the collars. The boy was on his hands and knees, his head stuffed between an anvil and a block of wood, strapped in place with a thick band of leather. It wasn't a scene that should have made Theos's cock stir.

"Let him up," the warlord snarled, and the blacksmith undid the straps. Finnvid staggered to his feet, rubbing his neck as if the collar had actually been attached.

Theos stood quietly as the slave trader wrapped a leather rope around Finnvid's neck. "Enjoy your new toy," the trader said with a lascivious smile, and handed the end of the rope to Theos.

Theos forced his fingers to accept the strip, and he turned and strode away with what dignity he could find, forcing Finnvid to jog to keep up.

"What's going on?" the Elkati demanded when they were safely beyond earshot of the rest.

"I have no idea," Theos growled. He whirled and stared at the boy. "But I'm going to find out. And by the sword, Elkati—you'll help me. You belong to me, now, and that means that whatever's going on in your busy little brain is my property. You'd better spread it out for inspection."

CHAPTER 6

N ot surprisingly, Finnvid didn't react too well to threats. He began by denying all knowledge of a mission, then stopped speaking altogether, and then, when Theos said he could speak or do without food, he'd started talking again: in Elkati. There was a constant song of gibberish coming out of the boy's mouth by the time Theos finally dragged him up the stairs to Andros's room.

He pushed the door open, shoved Finnvid inside so hard the boy tripped and landed on his hands and knees, and turned to Andros, who'd made his way up from downstairs and was lying on the bed.

"I saved his life, and he's repaying me with stubbornness and idiocy."

"Well, that must be very annoying," Andros said calmly. "Finnvid, can I offer you something to eat or drink?"

"He'll have neither," Theos interrupted. "Not until he starts talking."

Andros nodded as if he'd expected nothing else. "Ah, yes. Stubborn idiocy."

Theos stared at his friend. Had that insult been aimed at Finnvid, or . . . "He was across the border for a *reason*," Theos insisted. Andros had known all this only hours ago. "He and his men *lied* about what that reason was, so we still don't know why they were in our territory." Theos lowered his voice so he wouldn't be heard in the corridor. "I couldn't speak to the captain about it, and it's too late in the season for a caravan to be heading off. Full of young men who should have been able to earn their chance in the army. At least *some* of them. And when I claimed Finnvid, the warlord argued with me. He wanted me to take any other slave in the whole train." Theos shook his head in

Finnvid's direction. "I *could* have taken one who would cooperate and answer simple questions."

"Simple questions about his valley's defenses? About his mission? Just general questions that would help us understand the Elkati strategy, and make it easier for us to conquer them?" Andros's voice was annoyingly patient. "The same questions you would be totally cooperative about, if *you* were ever captured."

Theos squinted at his friend, then turned to Finnvid. "When I leave here, I'm going to talk to the captain. He'll understand what I'm saying, and you and your men will be reinterrogated. This time by Sacrati interrogators. They won't let you get away with your nonsense. Do you understand that?"

Finnvid didn't reply, but the bleak expression on his face made it clear that he understood all too well.

"So you can save yourself a lot of pain—you can save your *men* a lot of pain—if you just speak up now." Theos stared at the wall behind the boy's head and waited. When Finnvid said nothing, Theos made himself continue. "If you don't respond to the pain, they'll go further. They'll kill one of you. That's the advantage of there being so many. They have lots of spares, so they won't have to worry about wasting a few. So, aye, kill one of you, and probably hack his head off and hang it in your pen. Maybe the whole body, so you can smell it rot; I don't know. They'll castrate another two or three, if it goes that far. Chop off an ear or a nose. If they can't get the truth out of you, they'll stop worrying about your worth as slaves, and they'll take your hands and feet. All those men you led into danger, and they're going to be mutilated and tortured, just because you're slow in giving answers that you *know* we'll get out of you eventually."

Theos crouched down next to the boy. "What do you think they'll take from you?" He reached out, a strange mix of horror and fascination as he thought about an axe hacking through the delicate bones of the boy's wrist. When Theos touched the narrowest part with one gentle finger, Finnvid jerked his arm away. He was trembling, now, but he still wasn't saying anything.

Theos shook off the strange mood and tried to sound calm and reasonable. "I don't want any of that to happen, Finnvid. I want you to be a healer, or whatever else you're good for, and I want you to earn your citizenship. When we take over your valley, you can come with us and help us rebuild. You can help your people *that* way. And I want your men to be soldiers. I want them to die as men, if they must die, not as animals. The old man, the one with the plumed helmet, I want him to be a trainer for the new recruits. He may not have enough years left to earn his citizenship, but he could earn a home for himself, and be safe and warm and useful."

There was still no response. Theos stood slowly. "Andros is your friend, right? You trust Andros?" Even though Theos had just saved the boy's life, and Andros had done nothing but get bitten by a snake, Theos bet Andros would be favored. "I'm going to leave you here with him. You can talk to him. And you can ask whether anything I said is a lie, or even an exaggeration. You can ask him for advice. And then when I come back, by the sword, you *will* tell me what you were doing in our territory, and why it was so important to the warlord that you be shipped out as soon as possible."

Theos looked at Andros but couldn't read his expression. Well, Andros was Sacrati; he'd do what needed to be done. Two steps to the door, and then Theos turned back to Finnvid. "You'll stay with Andros until I return. If he gets sick of you, you'll sit in the hallway just outside his door and wait for me. If you aren't in one of those places, I'll consider you a runaway slave. You'll be punished when you're caught. And your men will be punished as well."

Finnvid finally lifted his head, yet his expression was anything but cooperative as he sneered, "Thank you, *master*. Your instructions are a gift, *master*."

"My *patience* is a gift," Theos corrected. "But it's not one that I'll keep giving indefinitely." He frowned at Andros. "Make him see sense," he ordered, and then he whirled and left, slamming the door behind him.

He decided it would be foolhardy rather than brave to go to the headquarters searching for the Sacrati captain; the warlord spent most of his time in that building. And Theos had been heading toward the drill yards earlier in the day before running into the slavers. He'd been planning to eat, his stomach reminded him, and he tried to remember what he'd done with the food he'd been carrying. But he didn't have time for another trip to the kitchen.

Instead, he headed for the yards. He was greeted by the familiar sounds of men shouting commands, curses, and war cries; the smells of sweat and leather and well-oiled steel; and the sight of sweaty, fit bodies being used as they were born to be: in toil and fierce battle. Theos loved every part of it, and he took a moment just to enjoy the sensations and be glad he was back home. Then he scanned the crowd, looking for the Sacrati.

Other than the ceremonial daggers they all wore at their waists, there was nothing that immediately set the Sacrati apart. They tended to be a bit larger than the other soldiers, but the difference wasn't dramatic. They wore the same armor and used the same weapons, although the Sacrati saw more action and victories, so they had coin enough to make sure their armor was perfectly fitted and their weapons were customized as needed. Theos's own sword was two inches longer than the Torian standard and had a special pattern etched into the grip that kept it from getting slippery with sweat and blood. But that sort of thing couldn't be spotted at a distance in a crowded training yard.

He just searched for the intensity. Where was the group that was pushing a little harder? The group with a few more scars? Where were the grunts of pain followed immediately by laughter and shouts of encouragement? All Torian soldiers fought with strength and skill; Theos searched for the ones who fought with passion, as well.

And he found them, down by the pond, trampling around in the mud and working on finding their footing in the slippery terrain. As he approached he was hailed, and his clean clothes were immediately covered in filth from hugs and sloppy, playful projectiles.

"Welcome back," Galen said with one hand gripping Theos's forearm as the other clapped him on the shoulder. Galen was the most senior iyatis in the Sacrati, second-in-command to the captain.

Theos leaned into the gesture, rubbing their cheeks together roughly and taking the chance to whisper, "I need to talk to you. And the captain."

Galen leaned away. The smile on his lips was for their audience; the warning in his eyes was for Theos alone. "We need to share some drinks! You can tell me about your adventures."

And Galen could explain whatever was happening in the valley. Theos nodded enthusiastically. "Tonight?"

"I thought you'd be busy tonight," a mischievous voice added from somewhere in the mud. Whoever it was raised his volume enough for all to hear him say, "Did you know Theos has claimed a bedwarmer for himself? Everyone's talking about it up at the barracks! Iyatis for one month and already he's too good to find pleasure with the rest of us!"

Galen's face was frozen halfway between a frown and a smile, and Theos just shrugged. "It's a long story," he muttered. Then he lifted his own voice and told the crowd, "I wanted a tight ass, and with only you sloppy old men to choose from—"

"An ass that's tight around your tiny dick?" someone responded. "Are you sure you're not fucking his nostril?"

Ah, yes. Theos was home, and his brothers were welcoming him.

He grabbed a wooden practice sword and joined the drills, sparring and wrestling and sliding around with the rest of them. For an inexperienced warrior, rough terrain could be a great equalizer, adding an element of chance that made it possible for a weak opponent to beat a stronger one. But Sacrati tried to overcome this by training to take advantage of any opportunity; for them, terrain was just one more weapon to be used in battle.

Theos found a rock outcrop, no larger than his fist but firmly anchored in the mud, and used it as a base for one of his feet, giving him a tiny edge of stability that'd allow him to defend against all comers, at least for a while. When the others realized what he was up to, they fought him for possession of the lone rock, trying to push him off in a strange version of king of the hill.

Finally, three of them attacked at once and sent him slipping away to land in the mud at the bottom of the slope, laughing at his comrades as they fought.

His oldest son would be coming to the barracks soon: a well-grown boy, healthy and clever and ready to start training. Theos smiled to think of the boy finding his own brothers, forging the bonds truer than blood that came from working and fighting and living together year after year. One day, Damios would stand on this hill, maybe as a Sacrati himself, and he would struggle and win, and struggle and win, and eventually struggle and fail, as everyone did.

Theos hoped he'd be around long enough to see some of the boy's victories.

But in the meantime, he had his own battles to fight. He pushed himself to his feet, waited for an opportunity, and then launched himself back into the fray, tackling a man off the little outcrop with sheer weight and aggression, tumbling halfway down the hill before clawing his way up to take his rightful spot again. He would hold it as long as he could. That was all a warrior could do.

CHAPTER 7

Theos went back to the barracks and found Finnvid slumped in the hallway outside Andros's room. He felt guilty for having left the boy for so long, then remembered that he was the master, Finnvid the slave. Making him sit in a hallway was *not* cruel.

So Theos ignored the boy and shoved open the door to Andros's room. He and Xeno were in bed, wrapped around each other, dozing with such contentment on their faces that Theos knew what he would have seen if he'd come through the door just a little earlier. It was good to know Andros was feeling better.

"Wake up, lazies," Theos said, jarring the bed with his foot.

Xeno opened his eyes with a growl, then sighed and nudged Andros awake. "Your master is here," he whispered, and grinned wickedly at Theos. "I mean, *Finnvid's* master. I knew you couldn't resist that boy! It might have been Andros *calling* him pretty, but—"

"I kept him because he's needed," Theos snapped. He might not have been thinking in those terms at the time he'd made the decision, but he'd been acting on instinct. Clearly his instinct had been a little ahead of his brain. "Andros, did you get anything out of him?"

"I learned quite a few Elkati curse words," Andros mumbled. "Some of them are pretty good."

"Did you learn anything more useful? Like what he was doing in our territory?"

"No." Andros sat up. "I repeated everything you said. I made it clear that everyone breaks if they're tortured long enough. *Everyone.*" He shrugged. "I think he believed me. He seemed . . . you know. Worried. Upset. Still, he wouldn't talk."

Theos shook his head in disgust. "I didn't find the captain," he said. "Got sidelined by some training. But I talked to Galen. He made it clear there's a problem of *some* sort." He turned his attention to Xeno. "What have you been up to? You weren't at training."

"Doing my own investigations. I know a boy who works in the warlord's office, so I talked to him."

"And?"

"Nothing too specific. He confirmed that there's something going on. Between the captain and the warlord, at least, but he seemed to think maybe there was more? He couldn't say what, though. He just said everything's tense."

Theos thought back wistfully to the battle on the mud hill. Problems were so much simpler when they could be solved with strength and cunning instead of investigation and planning. "I'll talk to Galen. Try to get hold of the captain. I can't think of anything else to do."

"And Finnvid?" Andros asked.

"I don't know. I'll have to turn him over for questioning, I suppose, if I can get anyone to agree that it needs to be done." Theos hated the idea. He wanted the boy to just *talk*, without having to go through all the things he'd threatened. "In the meantime . . . I don't know."

"Treat him like a bedwarmer," Andros said firmly. "You told the warlord you wanted him for that, so you'd better follow through."

"How's a bedwarmer supposed to be treated? What am I supposed to do with him?"

Xeno snorted. "You really need lessons?"

Andros was grinning, too, but he was a little more useful. "Get him cleaned up. Get him something to wear. Not a warrior's tunic, something softer. And then look after him in public. Men with bedwarmers are protective of them. They don't want other men poaching, not once they've paid for exclusive access. So leave him in your room when you don't need him, and if you take him out, stay close."

Theos couldn't see why anyone would ever bother with it all, not when other options were so much less trouble. But Finnvid had saved Andros's life. Andros wanted him taken care of, and Theos was still grateful enough to have his friend alive to feel soft. "Fine. I'm going to go bathe, and I'll take him with me." He pointed sternly at the bed. "You, Andros, continue healing. And Xeno—I'd better see you at training tomorrow. There's a patch of mud waiting for your attention."

"I wouldn't have thought there'd be any mud left, after you've tracked so much of it over my floor," Andros shot back.

Theos had the door open by then and he said, "If you like, I'll send my slave to clean for you later. He's not good for too much else." He scowled down at Finnvid, daring him to disagree, but Finnvid just stared at him defiantly.

Theos shut the door. "Get up. We're going to the baths."

Finnvid stood, and Theos started walking before the boy could ask too many questions. He stopped by his room for another set of clean clothes, then looked at the boy. After days of hiking, the rags Finnvid was wearing would probably dissolve as soon as they were removed. Theos might be able to find something of the sort Andros had described—something *soft*—at the next market. But the Elkati couldn't walk around naked until then, so Theos pulled out another one of his own tunics and an extra pair of trousers. He didn't have an extensive wardrobe, and if he was going to be getting this muddy *and* sharing his clothes with someone else, there would be a problem.

But maybe there was also a solution. "I'll show you where the laundry is when we're down there," he said, heading out the door. "New recruits are in charge of doing the work, usually, but they're slow. It can take several days for clothes to be returned. You can do it faster."

"So I'm to do your laundry?" Finnvid sounded insulted.

Theos stopped walking. He turned to face the boy. "Are you living in a different world? Do you not understand what's happening in this one? You're a prisoner. A slave. *My* slave. You'll do whatever I tell you to do." Theos eased in, close enough that he could feel Finnvid having to fight to keep himself from backing away. "Everyone *thinks* I've bought you as a bedwarmer. Do you know what that is?"

"I can imagine," the boy said stiffly.

"So, if I want to, I'll fuck you. I'll make you suck me. I'll do whatever the hell I choose with this body that I have earned and that I *own*."

"And *will* you do that? Those things? To me?" There was still insolence in his voice, but there was also a tightness that betrayed his fear.

Theos stepped back, just a little. "I have no interest in fucking a resisting virgin when there's no shortage of *enthusiastic* partners waiting for me. But I make no promises. I own you, and I'll do what I want with you." And then, back to the main point. "So if I ask . . . no, wait. If I *tell* you to do some laundry? I suggest you just *do it*, without acting as if it's an affront to your precious dignity. Understood?"

He made himself wait, and was eventually rewarded with a tiny, reluctant nod. It wasn't much, but it was something.

They walked to the baths in silence. When they reached the large room, they found a very different scene than the one that had greeted Theos earlier. The baths were now crowded and raucous, full of soldiers unwinding after a long day's training.

"Stay close," Theos warned, and he found a spot on the long bench around the outside of the room where he could leave their clean clothes. "Do you have baths in Elkat?"

"Not—not like this," the boy said, his eyes wide.

Theos tried to see the scene from Finnvid's perspective. Huge tubs of water, a lot of steam . . . and a lot of naked men. It was probably the last of those three that had the boy cowed for a change. Damn, if all it took was nudity to shut him up, Theos would be willing to never wear clothes again.

"Strip down," he ordered, pulling his filthy tunic off. "We'll start in that one, the biggest tub. That's for basic cleaning: the water flows through fast, so it's where you want to lose the worst of the grime. Then if you're just having a quick wash, you can go right from it to rinsing under the stream of water, over there. Or if you want to sit and soak for a while, you can move to one of the smaller tubs. The water in them circulates, but not as fast, so you don't want to get into them until you're pretty clean." Theos frowned at the immobile boy. "Strip down," he repeated as he tugged off his own trousers.

"I can just— I don't need to bathe—"

Theos snorted. "Yes, you do. You stink like a month in the forest, and you'll be sleeping in my room tonight. You'll get cleaned up, and you should shave; wearing beards is fine in the field, but we don't do it when we're in the barracks."

"I don't—"

"You'll strip yourself or I'll strip you," Theos said firmly. He didn't have time for this Elkati squeamishness.

The words got Finnvid moving, at least, although he glared as he did. After the fuss, Theos half expected to see some shameful deformity hidden beneath the boy's rags, but his body was . . .

It was healthy, Theos told himself. Anything beyond that was none of his concern. He shouldn't give in to his fascination with the flawless, pale skin, like the marble of the statues in the temple. He wouldn't stare at the patch of fair hair between the Elkati's legs, certainly wouldn't try to get a better view of what else lay in that area.

No, Theos wouldn't do that. But everyone else in the baths was getting a good eyeful. It probably wasn't the first time they'd seen a naked Elkati, yet there was something beautiful about the boy, something they all seemed to notice. Knowing the Elkati was a Sacrati's bedwarmer probably added to the mystique. What qualities must he possess to entrance a man like Theos?

Theos resisted the urge to toss a towel over the boy and instead just threw angry glares at anyone who got too close, anyone who might want to do more than look.

Finnvid kept his gaze locked on the floor, hopefully not aware of the attention.

"Come soak," Theos said, and he led the way to the big tub. It was crowded, and there were several invitations for Finnvid to sit on various laps, which turned into a competition, which turned into wrestling and splashing. Finnvid might not have seen the staring, but he'd have to be blind and deaf not to notice all this.

Theos sighed. He'd made a ridiculous decision to keep the boy, and now he needed to tolerate the fuss until the excitement subsided and the men found something else to be stupid about. "You," he said, reaching down and hauling on the arm of one of the younger combatants. "You and your friends—out of the tub. You're clean enough."

The youngster narrowed his eyes, and Theos anticipated spit in his food or maybe grime on his laundry, but the child clearly wasn't ready for open rebellion yet. Which was almost too bad, because Theos would have liked to vent some tension by knocking an insolent recruit around a little. Instead, he glared until the boy and his friends climbed out, then nudged Finnvid's shoulder. The Elkati jerked away as if the touch burned, and Theos sighed again. "Get in. There's a bench about halfway down inside the tub. You see where everyone's sitting? Step on that."

The boy reluctantly did as he was told, and Theos then stepped into the tub himself.

One of the men in the tub was older, not Sacrati but a veteran of many campaigns. Theos had fought with him in three different valleys, and they'd always gotten along, so he nodded a greeting. The man said, "I heard you were planning to rent him out. Put my name on the list."

Theos shouldn't have wanted to punch his comrade in the face. "I'm keeping him to myself for a while," he replied as evenly as he could. "But when I get tired of him, I'll let you know."

Other offers started coming in then, some joking, some serious, and Theos realized that he was not going to have a long, relaxing soak in the tubs that evening. "Scrub clean," he told Finnvid. "There's soap here, and use those brushes."

The boy sat still, maybe trying to figure out a way to drown himself in the steaming water. Theos grabbed one of the brushes and whacked Finnvid on the head with it. "Hey. Let's go." He tossed a chunk of soap at the boy. "The faster you do it, the faster you can get your clothes on and get out of here."

That was a good incentive, apparently, since the boy got to work. Theos had only needed a rinse to get the caked mud off him, so he had some time to waste while he waited for Finnvid to finish. He tried to keep his eyes to himself, but it was somewhat difficult when everyone else in the room was staring in one direction. So, okay, maybe he snuck a few peeks.

The boy needed more muscle. He was thin from insufficient food, which Theos tried not to feel guilty over, and also from growing too fast *up* and not enough *out*. But more food and lots of exercise would have him in good condition; he probably would have been able to make it as a soldier, if he'd been given the chance. Well, he would have if his attitude hadn't gotten in the way, which seemed pretty unlikely, really.

Now that the boy had begun his task, he was meticulous, scrubbing his entire body as if preparing for his initiation ritual. His hair became several shades lighter after he lathered it up and rinsed it out, and Theos's hand twitched with eagerness to touch it. Instead, he flicked Finnvid's shoulder. "Ready to rinse? Then you can shave, and we can get out of here."

Finnvid didn't reply immediately. He stared at the far wall, the ceiling, anywhere but at Theos or the other men.

"You're going to have to get out of the tub eventually," Theos said. "If you're waiting for a time when no one else is around, you're going to dissolve into the water and be washed down the drain."

"That sounds fine," Finnvid finally muttered.

Theos snorted. "Not fine with me. I have things to do tonight, so I'm leaving. You can come with me or you can take your chances here on your own."

Another successful threat; Finnvid turned and reached for a towel. But in his attempt to keep as much of himself underwater as possible, he ended up crouching on the submerged bench, stretching forward, his ass bobbing out from the water at just the right height for . . .

Theos gripped the edges of the tub with one hand and used the other to yank Finnvid back. "No towels yet," he said when he'd regained control of his voice. "You're not clean until you're rinsed."

"I have to walk over there naked?"

"You making a fuss is what's getting everyone interested." It wasn't the whole truth, but it was probably a factor. By the sword, if Theos hadn't known Finnvid was an uninterested virgin, he'd have shifted over behind him while he was reaching for the towel, slid inside, fucked him senseless, and then this obsession would be finished with. The boy would have gone back to being an annoying military problem.

But Theos wasn't that lucky. So he pulled himself out of the water, ignoring the demands of his body, and stared pointedly down at Finnvid. "Let's go."

The boy seemed as if he was going to refuse, but finally stood, his hands cupped protectively around . . .

Theos laughed, a welcome release. "You *like* the attention, do you?" If Finnvid had been Torian, Theos would have given him a half hug, maybe slapped playfully at the boy's erection, and they both would have laughed at the uncontrollable urges their bodies sometimes inflicted on them. In this case, though, he just shook his head. "Don't be stupid. At your age you're probably getting hard if a butterfly flaps its wings near your cock. The flowing of the water feels good, that's all." Theos gestured to his own half-hard cock and decided not to mention that it hadn't been an issue until Finnvid reached for his towel.

"Come rinse, and then you can wrap up. Not that it's going to hide *that*." Theos wished he could take a moment to appreciate the boy's beauty, but instead he headed for the rinse water. "I guess you can use my razor to shave. I don't really know how all this works; am I supposed to buy you *everything* for yourself? I know I have to pay for your food." He tried to keep up the inane blather, trying to help Finnvid relax . . . trying to keep his own mind away from Finnvid's cock, and wondering if it would feel different under Theos's tongue than a Torian cock.

He tossed a towel to the Elkati and led the way to the mirrors. Shaving oil, razor. Theos tried not to think about anything else, and wished he hadn't shaved that afternoon so he could have something to do as he waited. He couldn't have shaved anyway, though, not with Finnvid holding the only razor in his strong, long-fingered hand. Those fingers that would feel just right . . .

Theos turned away. Tagan, a young Sacrati, was beside him, fresh from rinsing off the same mud Theos had just lost, his curious gaze on Finnvid's oiled face.

"Not him," Theos grunted as he stepped toward the man. "But me."

There was no argument. They kissed as they moved, hot bites and shared gasps, and they only made it a few steps away from the shaving mirrors before they dropped their towels and reached down together to grasp each other's cocks.

"Not saving yourself for your bedwarmer?" Tagan murmured as he tightened his grip.

"I've got enough to go around." Theos dropped to his knees and took the man in his mouth. It should always be this simple, this easy.

"Elkati!" Tagan called. "You, bedwarmer!" Theos turned his eyes to see Finnvid staring at them. "Toss me the oil."

After a stunned moment, Finnvid complied, and the Sacrati caught it and passed it down to Theos. "Oil me while you suck. Then fuck me."

Aye, this was how it should be. Theos didn't argue with the instructions, and he didn't waste much time prepping his partner, either. After covering the basics, he rose to his feet, lined up, and couldn't keep himself from looking at Finnvid as he buried himself in the Sacrati's ass.

And he kept looking as he fucked. Finnvid's face was rosy with heat and his beautiful blush, and he'd stopped shaving with half his skin still covered in beard. He stared at Theos, and Theos stared back, then slowly, carefully, reached around to find Tagan's cock with his hand. He nodded, just the hint of a suggestion, and watched as Finnvid's hand tentatively lowered. Theos almost froze; he was captivated by what might be about to happen. But then Tagan grunted something and rocked back into Theos.

That broke the spell, and Finnvid's hand jerked away from his cock. Stupid Elkati.

Theos closed his eyes. He let the vision replay behind his lids, the way Finnvid's blush had spread all down his chest, the way his hand had trembled. The way he'd stared before finally turning away. Theos imagined himself driving into Finnvid's pale, eager ass, imagined the way the muscles would tighten around him, and his orgasm came fast, sweeping over him like a spring avalanche. He was dimly aware of Tagan arching and swearing as he found his own release, but it wasn't important to him.

By the time Theos had recovered, Finnvid was trying to shave again. His hand was trembling dangerously and his chest rose in quick, shallow breaths, but he seemed to be back in his own world. And Theos didn't think it was a happy world, at least not right then. Damn it, what was wrong with these Elkatis? Why did they have to make something so simple into something so complicated?

Tagan straightened up and turned with a sly smile to say, "Everyone said you were crazy, taking on the trouble of a bedwarmer when you could have any ass in the barracks. But maybe you had your reasons."

Theos snorted agreement, then made his way over to the running water for another rinse. He kept a subtle eye on Finnvid, noting that he didn't move the whole time Theos was away. The boy just stood there, so tense he was almost shaking. It wasn't Theos's fault Elkatis were strange about sex. Why was he feeling guilty about this?

He strolled back to Finnvid. "Finish shaving," he said gently. "And stop thinking so much. You followed the Elkati rules when you were in Elkat, but now you're Torian. Things are different here. You should relax and let yourself enjoy it."

"I doubt they'd agree with that in Elkat," the boy said softly.

Theos bit his tongue. Probably not the best time to remind the boy that he wouldn't be *going* back to Elkat, not until it was part of the Empire and learning new rules. "They're there; you're here. Two different worlds. Keep them separate." He waited while Finnvid appeared to think about that idea, then added, "And finish shaving. You don't want to walk around with half a beard."

Finnvid didn't obey immediately, but when he did pick up the razor, his hand was steady and he finished his job without incident.

Theos took it as a victory. "You can rinse off if you want," he offered. "Then put those clothes on. We'll get dinner, and I'll explain to the kitchen that they'll have to bill me for your expenses."

"I thought I didn't get to eat or drink until I answered your questions."

Theos had forgotten about that. He shrugged. "I'm losing interest in your little secrets, to be honest." An orgasm had helped calm his mind, as it always did. "I'm tired of worrying over your nonsense. The Elkati military is weak and poorly trained. The Torian Empire will take your valley whenever we choose to. There's nothing you can do to stop it, so I don't need to get involved."

Now he was speaking to himself more than to Finnvid. "I jumped in where I shouldn't have, and now I'm stuck paying for and protecting a sneaking, lying, pain-in-the-ass 'bedwarmer' who acts like it's the end of the world when he *almost* jerks himself off. When the captain finds time to talk to me, I'll tell him what I think and he may or may not want you and your men tortured until you spill the truth. If that doesn't happen, you've got roughly five months to make yourself useful at my expense. If you haven't found a way to earn your keep by the time the snow goes, I'll send you out on the first slave train, and you can go east and see how much *they* care about your Elkati ideas of 'unnatural.'"

By the sword, he'd talked himself out of his postcoital ease and into a bad mood. "So, aye, go ahead. Eat all you want to. Get yourself nice and fat, if you like, so you'll be warm for the winter. I don't care."

He stepped away and scowled at the still Elkati in front of him. "And already I take back some of those words. I *do* care what you do, because I'm hungry and I want to eat. You can get your clothes on and come with me to the dining hall, or you can stay here by yourself. If you're coming with me, hurry up."

Finnvid hurried. And Theos stared at the door, wishing he could go through it on his own, without dragging Finnvid's turmoil along with him.

CHAPTER † 8

Galen wasn't at dinner, and he wasn't in the Sacrati hall afterward, either. Well, that was fine. Good, even. It would be easier to withdraw from whatever was happening if Theos never learned any more details.

Xeno and Andros came down for a quick drink, and as the Sacrati all inspected the healing wound on Andros's leg, Theos let himself relax.

Yes, that was the real reason he'd pulled the Elkati out of the slave chain. Finnvid had saved Andros's life, so Theos had repaid him with five or six months' reprieve from his fate. That was fair. And while Finnvid was around anyway . . .

"The healer responsible for Andros's recovery is right here," Theos announced in a voice loud enough to carry through the room. "How many of you have little injuries that won't heal right? Bring them to Finnvid and let him see what he can do. If he doesn't succeed, you'll only pay to cover his medicines, but if he *does* succeed? Well, how much would you pay to get rid of the one annoying thing that's keeping you from being your absolute best as a warrior?"

Some of the men looked thoughtful, and Theos nodded in satisfaction. "Tell your friends," he advised. "Common soldiers, Sacrati . . . he's open for business, of that sort at least. We all know the Elkati like their books and their potions. Here's our chance to take advantage of that!" He pushed Finnvid into the crowd. "See what they've got," he ordered, and Finnvid slowly complied.

Andros raised an eyebrow as Theos came closer. "You're planning to profit from my near-death?"

63

"Absolutely," Theos agreed. "I need to pull *something* useful from this mess."

"It might not be bad for Finnvid," Andros mused. "Gives him a chance to establish himself and be useful."

"Well, I'm glad you're looking out for *Finnvid*," Theos said with asperity. "I'm glad *Finnvid* will be okay through all this."

"What are you complaining about? He saved my life; I like him; I'd like him to do well."

"He's the enemy, and probably a spy," Theos countered. "He only saved you because I threatened to kill them all if he didn't. He's shown no loyalty or affection for any of us, and yet we're breaking our backs to make sure he's happy. Does that make sense to you?"

"Well," Andros said slowly, "he *is* very pretty. I like him shaved. Makes him look a bit older. I'd have thought the reverse would be true."

Theos stepped away. He wasn't interested in the boy's attractiveness. He wasn't interested in anything to do with Finnvid or Elkatis in general. "Why don't you take him tonight?" he suggested. "You're such good friends, after all. Why don't you have him sleep in your room? Actually, he can sleep in your room forever. That could be fun, right? And you'd have a medic there if you needed him—"

"No," Andros said firmly. "I don't want him lying in my room and acting as if it's a crime every time Xeno and I touch each other. I like him, but he's a pain in the ass about sex."

He certainly was. And Theos was going to have a pain in a different part of his anatomy if he had to lie down that night with Finnvid's tempting body within easy reach but totally out of bounds. "Elkati," he barked. If he was going to have a restless night, he might as well start early. "Let's go."

"I was just about to show him this terrible swelling I've got," one of the Sacrati called, grabbing his crotch.

"I could lance it for you, if someone brought me a sharp knife," Finnvid replied, and there were howls of laughter.

Theos tried not to smile. He didn't want to encourage any more impertinence from the boy. "There are no guarantees made for the quality of any treatments," he said, and he waited for Finnvid to join him.

Unfortunately, it seemed the boy would rather stay in this crowd of ruffians than go to a quiet place with Theos. That was the kind of gratitude the Elkati was showing.

And then Theos caught himself: Finnvid was the enemy. A spy, or something like it. Gratitude from him would be a sign that Theos was doing his job wrong.

So he tried not to resent it when Finnvid trailed along behind him, dragging his feet like he was being led to his execution. They visited the toilet at the end of the hall, and Theos showed the boy how to turn the water on and off, and where the brushes for their teeth were kept. He cleaned his own teeth and handed the brush to the boy. "Maybe we'll be able to go to the city tomorrow, and I can buy you some things of your own," he said.

Finnvid made a face and set the brush down where Theos had found it. "I can wait until then," he said.

Theos was out of patience. "Fine." He led the way to his room, which was barely lit by the moonlight coming through the narrow window, and looked at the bed. It had been big enough for himself and another man many times. This time, though, he pulled a blanket out of the closet and tossed it in Finnvid's direction; he'd want it back before it got really cold, but that was a worry for later.

Finnvid caught the blanket awkwardly and stood there as Theos climbed into bed and dragged the covers over himself. He had his eyes closed by the time Finnvid said, "I'm allowed to sleep on the floor?"

"You're *required* to sleep on the floor. And to shut up."

There was a long pause before Finnvid said, "I'm sorry if I've angered you."

"You're angering me right now by not shutting up."

"I'm sorry I can't tell you what you want to know."

"If you can't settle and be quiet here, I suppose I could just return you to the prisoner pens. I'd probably still have to pay a little extra for your food, and you wouldn't have the chance to earn your citizenship, but I don't find myself all that interested in helping you become a citizen. And that way I wouldn't have to pay for clothes or toiletries or any of the extras. And, more importantly, that way I could sleep in peace."

Finnvid was quiet for just long enough that Theos began to hope he'd gotten the message. But then Finnvid said, "Perhaps you'd allow me to *visit* the prisoners?"

"Come up here and suck me," Theos said.

A stunned silence before Finnvid said, "What?"

"Come up here and suck me. You do that for me, and I'll think about doing favors for you."

"I don't— I can't—"

"Then *shut up.*"

Finally, Finnvid did. They lay there together in the dark, and listened to the sounds of the barracks shutting down for the night. At some point, Theos drifted off to sleep, but he woke up the next morning just as frustrated.

"What am I supposed to do with him during the day?" he asked Andros as they ate breakfast. Finnvid was at the far end of the long table, where Theos had ordered him to sit. With the crowd of other men between them, there was no way Finnvid could hear this conversation. Not that Theos was trying to spare the Elkati's feelings. "I *think* he'll stick around, knowing that his men will be punished in his stead if he leaves. And of course there's nowhere for him to go." There were only two paths out of the valley, and they were both well-guarded. "If I give him free time, is he going to . . . I don't know. Be a spy? Sabotage something? It's hard to predict what he'll do when I have no idea what he's already *done.* But he's not likely to do anything *good*, right?"

"Might save some lives," Andros said looking down at himself.

"Only if threatened," Theos reminded him.

Andros shrugged. Then his attention seemed to shift to something over Theos's shoulder. "Don't turn around."

Theos froze for a moment before forcing his body to relax. They were in the dining hall; how serious could the threat be?

"Shit," Andros said, casting his eyes toward his meal and clearly trying to sound casual. "Warlord's coming over, and he looks less than happy."

"Get Finnvid and keep him with you." Theos made sure he didn't glance in the boy's direction, didn't give the warlord any reason to send his attention that way. "They can't do anything to me. Keep an eye on *him*."

Andros nodded, then looked up in a convincing presentation of surprise. "Sir! Good morning."

Theos turned toward the man who was ignoring Andros's greeting. "Sir."

"We need to talk. Come with me."

Theos did as he was told. Technically the Sacrati were separate from the usual military command structure and were supposed to answer only to other Sacrati, but the Sacrati captain answered to the warlord, so Theos knew what he had to do. He left his breakfast behind and followed the burly man through the crowd of curious soldiers and into the courtyard, where the frost was still white on the ground.

The warlord walked briskly through the cool air, apparently intent on doing laps around the small space. He frowned over at Theos, then said bluntly, "I want your bedwarmer."

That caught Theos off guard, and he snorted before managing a reply. "Sir? You— For yourself, you mean?"

The man curled his lip but then snarled, "Yes. For myself."

If the warlord truly wanted Finnvid, he wouldn't have been so eager to ship him out into the snowy mountains the prior day. Theos wondered what would happen if he gave the boy up now. Would he end up falling down the stairs and breaking his neck, or being stabbed after "attacking" a senior officer? Slave owners weren't actually allowed to kill their property, but Theos couldn't imagine anyone would ask many questions of the warlord.

"I'm sorry, sir, but he's not for sale. I'm still enjoying him."

"Really? I'd heard you two weren't getting along too well. I was told you took another soldier right in front of the boy in the baths yesterday."

"All part of the game, sir." Theos had never been particularly interested in games, at least of this sort, but he didn't think the warlord would know that.

The man drew closer, and wrapped an arm around Theos's shoulders. "I would consider it a personal favor, soldier."

"*Sacrati*," Theos said with quiet intensity, stepping out of the man's half-embrace. "And I'm sorry, sir, but I'm not willing to give him up yet. I'd be pleased to help you in another way, if I could be of service."

"I'm not making myself clear, *soldier*." The warlord had given up the pretense of comradeship. "*I want the Elkati. Now.*"

"Under what authority would you take him from me, sir?"

"Under *my* authority, by the sword!"

"Sir, I don't believe you have the authority to confiscate personal property. Do you?"

"Is this what Sacrati have become? Rule-quoters? Little boys hiding behind *laws*?"

"I'd be more than pleased to face you as a Sacrati, sir. Armed combat or hand-to-hand, whichever you chose. Sacrati are now, as they have always been, warriors. And we fight for the Empire, and the rules and traditions of the Torian people." Theos's voice was tight with controlled anger.

"You don't understand what's going on here, soldier."

"You're right, sir. I have no idea what's going on. If you want to explain it to me, maybe I can try to be more helpful. But as it is . . ."

"Do you really want to make me into your enemy?"

"No, sir. I don't want that at all."

"But you're not going to sell me the Elkati."

"No, sir. He's not for sale."

The warlord glared at him a moment longer, then turned and stalked away.

Theos exhaled roughly. He just wanted to be a warrior. He wanted to fight the enemies of the Torian Empire and find victory for his people. Instead . . . this.

Soldiers were streaming out of the dining hall now, and Theos spotted Andros and jerked his chin toward one of the courtyard gates. Finnvid followed Andros, cringing like a puppy who expected to be scolded.

"Why does the warlord want you?" Theos demanded as soon as they were close enough to speak.

Finnvid's eyes widened but he didn't say anything. Theos waited. "I don't know," Finnvid finally replied.

"You're lying." Theos said it conversationally. The sky was blue, winter was coming, and Finnvid the Elkati was telling lies. Nothing to be surprised about. "I told him no. Made him angry, which was *not* part of my career plan. And that was my decision, so I'm not holding you responsible for it. But it would be nice to know *why* I just threw away the respect of one of the leaders of the valley. I refused his reasonable request, made him angry . . . for *what*, Elkati?"

Finnvid just shook his head, his mouth closed in a thin, stubborn line.

Theos turned to Andros. "Can you babysit him today? We'll have to figure something else out when you're well enough to train again, but for today?"

Andros nodded. He looked almost as upset as Theos, though it all seemed to be making him more sad than angry. "You ready?" he asked Finnvid, who nodded and followed along, obedient for once.

Theos took himself to the drilling yards and worked with a group of new recruits before joining the Sacrati for unarmed combat drills. It felt good to be doing something physical, something with a clear goal and an obvious way to reach it. He ate lunch with the rest of the soldiers, and by midafternoon he'd tired himself out enough to think calmly again.

Of course, calmness didn't do him much good when he didn't have sufficient facts to work with. So instead of taking a break with the rest of the soldiers, he jogged up the hill to the command building and knocked on the captain's open door. Galen was inside, standing behind the seated captain as they worked on papers at the desk. They both looked up at the knock and then at each other, a silent communication with a message Theos couldn't begin to guess.

"I was hoping to speak to you about the Elkati prisoners, sir."

Tamon nodded. "You have some concerns," he said quietly. "You think the interrogation was inadequate and the true story is not what we were told."

"I'm not sure the interrogation happened at all. The true story is definitely not what you were told. And I think the warlord—"

Tamon held up a hand. "Careful, Sacrati. Careful what you say, for it cannot be unsaid."

"I don't need to unsay it, as long as it's the truth."

"How charmingly naive you are."

Theos didn't try to deflect the words. "I don't understand what's going on, that's certain. But I know *something* is."

The captain nodded again and stood up from behind his desk, coming to stand next to Theos with a tired smile. "We know it, too," he said. "And we're doing what we can. But Sacrati . . . We're in a delicate situation. The balance of power between the warlord and us has grown very, very fragile. We're being careful not to push too hard, and so far, so's the warlord. But we can't be sure how long he'll keep the peace. Everyone's stuck in this valley for the next five months or more. Until the spring comes, we can expect no outside help, and have no real way to escape. Can you see why that makes it important that we all get along?"

"It's that bad?" Theos wasn't sure he believed any of it.

"We're still figuring things out," Galen said. "But, yes. Potentially, it's that bad."

"So I . . . ignore it? I don't know about the big picture. I'm not good at ideas, or big strategies. If we're trying not to anger the warlord, should I just give him the Elkati spy?" Theos tried to ignore his gut's reaction to that idea.

"The damage has been done, there; the warlord is angry, but he hasn't exploded. So we should maintain the current situation, which means the Elkati should stay with you until we figure out why he's important. Keep an eye on him, and keep him safe."

Theos shook his head. "I should have just walked away," he said, mostly to himself.

"Too late now," Galen responded. "You own him; you need to take care of him."

"Don't suppose either of you is looking for a bedwarmer?"

Tamon snorted. "I've got enough troubles of my own; I'm not taking on yours." He gripped Theos's shoulder. "Keep an eye on him, Sacrati. That's an order."

Theos couldn't think of any way out of it. So he nodded his understanding, if not his approval, and left the office. He was halfway down the square on the way to the practice yards when he heard an unfamiliar sound, or perhaps his warrior's instinct kicked in . . . *something* made him turn around and look at the headquarters building. Even from a distance, there was no mistaking the blond hair and pale skin of the figure striding away from the building and back toward the barracks. Finnvid was supposed to be with Andros, but here he was, marching out of the headquarters building, prancing about as if he owned the whole valley.

What in the name of a rust-stained sword was the Elkati up to? Who had he been meeting with, and what had been said?

Theos wanted to run after the boy and grab hold of him, beat him until he spoke the truth, and find out what was really going on. But Galen and Tamon had made it clear that Theos was stuck with the Elkati, and they'd given him no instructions about interrogation. They hadn't expressly forbidden it, of course . . .

He tried to imagine striking the boy. In anger, maybe. But as part of a cold, purposeful interrogation? He could do it if necessary, he supposed. He didn't want to, though, not at all.

So he swallowed his frustration and made himself continue down to the drill yards. His mind might be confused and useless, but his body? His body would fight. It was all it knew to do.

CHAPTER  9

"He was here," Andros said. "I mean, I slept a bit in the afternoon. But he was here when I went to sleep, and here when I woke up."

"Well, he was sneaking around sometime in the middle." Theos frowned. Even injured, Andros was Sacrati, and he should have been more alert and aware of his surroundings. "Did he give you anything? To make you sleep?"

"Some medicine," Andros admitted slowly. "He said it was just a tonic, to make sure I kept healing. But I did fall asleep pretty soon afterward."

Theos nodded. Drugging the man he was supposed to be healing; one more crime to add to the Elkati's long list. "Don't take any more medicine from him."

Andros frowned for a moment, but then sighed and nodded. "Aye. Okay."

"I'll take him with me from now on. He can . . . Well, I guess he can do some training. He isn't infirm, after all."

"He's not—"

"Not the enemy? Not a liar and a spy? Not a *poisoner*?"

Andros shrugged. "Aye, but he's really *very* pretty."

"You're hopeless." Theos stood and headed for the hallway, jerking the door open to see if Finnvid had been eavesdropping. But the Elkati was too clever to be caught like that. He was sitting against the wall on the far side of the corridor, face as sullen as always, and he barely looked up when Theos stepped out of Andros's room.

"Heel, Elkati," Theos ordered. He took three steps, then scowled back at the boy, who hadn't moved. "You don't want to test my temper today."

Finnvid seemed to be thinking about it, but instead he rolled to his feet and ambled in Theos's direction.

"Laundry," Theos said when they reached the bathhouse. He practically dragged Finnvid to the service room, then waved a hand to summon the recruit in charge. "This slave needs to clean my clothes. But he can't be trusted, so you're in charge of keeping watch over him. If he misbehaves, come get me from the bath. Understood?"

The recruit nodded, eyes wide. This was probably a bit more interesting than the usual laundry duty. Then Theos turned toward Finnvid. "You clean my clothes while I clean my body. You can't get into too much trouble in the laundry room, I hope. If you want a bath, you can splash yourself with laundry water."

Finnvid didn't respond, but he did gather the clothes Theos indicated.

Finally, after all the trouble Finnvid caused, Theos had found one small way in which it was beneficial to have a slave. Unless, of course the Elkati found a technique to destroy his clothes or embed them with an itch-causing herb, or in some other fashion made Theos wish his patrol had never found the Elkati at all.

Theos ignored the boy through dinner and then through drinks and gaming in the common room, and he didn't step in when a young Sacrati named Nero approached Finnvid and tried to make conversation.

Nero was clearly nervous, glancing over toward Theos as if expecting a—possibly violent—intervention. And after a few moments, Finnvid himself looked over as though to see if Theos would get involved. He thought Theos was going to *protect* him. As if it was Theos's job to protect the comforts of an enemy spy.

Theos took a long swallow of ale and deliberately turned away, giving his full regard to the Sacrati entertaining his table with a tale of incompetent recruits struggling with the simplest of drills. That was what Theos wanted to care about, not anything more complicated.

Unfortunately, it wasn't long before the attention of his table was drawn over toward Finnvid, and Theos reluctantly swiveled to see what was happening. Nero was still there, but he was frowning at Finnvid now.

"Unnatural?" Nero said, his voice loud in the growing hush of the room.

"Disgusting," Finnvid replied, just as loud and somehow even clearer. "Immoral. Sinful. An affront to the gods."

"The gods?" Nero seemed a bit confused by that one; Torians weren't much for religion. But he did a good job of pulling himself back to the main point. "We're disgusting?"

"You're using your bodies as they were not meant to be used." Finnvid wasn't backing down. Indeed, he was the first to rise, a clear challenge in his body language.

"That's true," Nero said, standing to stare at Finnvid eye-to-eye. "Torians are warriors. Our bodies are *meant* to be used for war. For *fighting*." And with that, he threw a punch.

Finnvid was quick, Theos would give him that. He didn't manage to dodge completely, but he moved fast enough to take the blow at half-strength, which allowed him to keep his feet. Still, he staggered and didn't have his balance before the Sacrati was on him again.

Another blow, this one light and almost taunting, but still sufficient to snap Finnvid's head back and bloody his nose. Then a few jabs to his gut, and when Finnvid stumbled Nero grabbed him by the collar of his tunic and sent him flying into a nearby table.

Theos just watched. Fights weren't a big deal; Sacrati were disciplined, even in their recreation time, and they knew better than to let a petty squabble get out of control. Already Nero had tempered his blows, clearly realizing he was fighting an unworthy opponent, and now he glanced over at Theos as if unsure whether to continue.

"Use your judgment," Theos said, just as he would have if Finnvid had been a Torian recruit who was being taught a little respect.

The young Sacrati nodded, and looked down at Finnvid, who was struggling to raise himself off the floor. "Enough, then," Nero said. He stepped back and half turned, holding out his knuckles to display their bloodiness to a friend. But Theos approved of the way he kept himself angled, a good position to keep an eye on Finnvid.

Who apparently hadn't given up yet. He pulled himself to his feet, took a deep breath, and charged.

Nero laughed, stepping to the side at just the right moment to catch Finnvid and flip him over. The Elkati landed flat on his back and lay there for a long moment, his eyes wide, struggling to breathe.

Theos stepped in at last and crouched beside the boy. "Your wind's knocked out of you," he said, and he laid a calming hand flat on Finnvid's chest. "Relax. You'll be okay. Try to take a few deep breaths."

Finnvid stared at him, eyes still wide, chest not moving.

"Breathe," Theos ordered, and Finnvid took a shallow, trembling breath. "Let it out slowly. Good. Now breathe again, deeper this time."

Finnvid managed that.

Theos stood up and nodded respectfully to Nero. He'd behaved honorably in the face of an unready opponent; a good character, if not a good fight. "I wish I could promise an apology, but I doubt he'd mean it even if I made him say it." Theos didn't bother to add that he'd not generally had any luck making the Elkati say a damn thing he didn't want to. That wasn't the point. "Still, I think he'll remember your objections."

The young Sacrati nodded, then came to stand near Finnvid's feet. "You don't seem to know too much about how to use your body for anything useful; maybe you should keep your mouth shut about ways to use it for anything fun."

Theos smiled, and wondered if there was a way to assign Finnvid to this young Sacrati for regular tutoring.

He nudged Finnvid with his toe. "You breathing? When you've got yourself under control, go wash your face. Try not to annoy anyone too much while you're doing it. Be back here by the time I finish my drink."

Finnvid stared at him for a moment. He'd gotten his breath back and apparently his rebelliousness had come with it. But after a brief, all-too-visible battle with his self-control, he composed himself and jerked his head in acknowledgment.

Theos returned to his ale and paid only a little attention to Finnvid as he rolled to his feet and staggered toward the doorway.

"Don't Elkati fight at *all*?" Andros asked as they watched Finnvid leave. "The rest of the men we captured were no match for us, but they seemed to at least have basic training. Why not Finnvid?"

Theos thought about it. "He should have done better," he agreed. "He fought like a raw recruit. Maybe he's a full-time medic, at home." He thought a little longer. "But then why the hell would he have been in charge of a patrol that snuck across the border?"

Andros shook his head. "As usual, more questions than answers."

Theos was getting pretty tired of that state of affairs. He called for another mug of ale, hoping to find wisdom in its depths, but when it was empty he had just as many questions as he'd had before.

He gathered Finnvid, who had returned to the room and found a quiet spot along the wall to sit and stare at the floor, and they headed back to the barracks.

"That was a disgrace," Theos said calmly as they walked through the torchlit halls. "If my nine-year-old son can't fight better than that when he arrives in the barracks as a fresh recruit, I'll contact the temple and ask them to double-check whether he's really mine."

Finnvid didn't answer.

Theos shrugged. "Starting tomorrow, you'll train. No more sitting around. I'll take you to the yards with me and show you some exercises. And you can watch others train, and learn from them. If we can get you to *any* level of competence, we can try to find a group for you to join, but for now it'll be private instruction, I think."

"I'd like that," Finnvid said. "Thank you."

"It's certainly my top priority to make sure you like the terms of your servitude," Theos replied calmly. "But you might want to wait until after tomorrow before you thank me. You have a *lot* of ground to make up, and you're not going to do it by being coddled."

"I understand."

"No, you don't." And he wouldn't, not until the next day.

Still, Theos fell asleep with a little more peace in his heart than he'd felt the night before. He had a plan. There was still a lying, spying, virgin Elkati sleeping on his floor, and the blow to the nose seemed to have added "snoring" to the list of Finnvid's negative qualities, but at least Theos had a goal. He would add "fighting capably" to the list of the Elkati's qualities. It was enough to let him fade into a peaceful sleep.

The sense of serenity lasted through the next morning. After breakfast, he took Finnvid to the training yards and they joined in the mass run, thousands of soldiers coursing around the outside of the yards in a continuous, seething mass. It was one of Theos's favorite exercises; it reminded him that he was part of something larger, something mobile and powerful. This was what it meant to be Torian.

Finnvid kept up. As bodies started dropping out of the mass, heading off to whatever other training they had scheduled for the day, Finnvid looked wistful as they left, but he didn't stop running.

"This could be your skill," Theos told him as they ran. "You're starting too late to ever be a great soldier, and I'm not sure you're going to fill out enough to even be a good one. But you could be a runner, carrying messages." It was better than nothing. He glanced over at the Elkati. "How old are you, anyway? You've got your full height, I expect?"

"I've been confirmed," Finnvid said between gasps.

Too bad he wasted his breath on something so meaningless. "*Confirmed*? As what?"

"As a man." Finnvid was keeping his eyes on the track in front of them. "Surely you have initiation rituals?"

"We do." Not that Finnvid would have passed any of them. Well, he could have gotten into the barracks as a recruit. All *that* required was basic health and fitness. But any further? "We have different initiations. To become a soldier, recruits must run the tests at one of the festivals. There's another ritual after the first enemy is killed. To become a Sacrati, warriors must excel in all areas of training and warfare, spend a winter in the mountains alone, and be voted in by the other Sacrati." He looked curiously at Finnvid. "What were the requirements for being *confirmed*?"

"I had my twentieth birthday," Finnvid replied without meeting Theos's gaze.

"Oh." So, not an achievement exactly. "How long ago was that?"

"Last spring."

"So you'll probably still put on some muscle," Theos decided. "But you'll always be light. So running should be good for you. Or archery, possibly." Generally, only women trained as archers, since it was considered a defensive skill and they could stay behind the city walls and send death down on anyone foolish enough to threaten the city while the men were away fighting. But Theos had heard talk of archers used as an offensive force, and maybe that would be something Finnvid could try. "Do you hunt? Can you use a bow?"

"I've hunted. But not with a bow."

"Snares? Spears?"

Finnvid hesitated, then said, "Falcons."

Theos tried to figure that out. "You hunt falcons? For food? How do you kill them without using bows or snares?"

"No, we hunt *with* falcons. For rabbits, or small birds . . . that sort of thing."

Finnvid's Torian was almost perfect, and sometimes Theos forgot that it wasn't his first language. "A falcon is a wild bird," he explained. "I'm trying to think of what word you mean, but there's nothing really close—"

Finnvid stopped running, stepping off the track so those behind them could get by. Theos stepped aside well, and stared as Finnvid explained, "We train the birds. We breed them and raise them and train them, and they hunt for us." He was still gasping for air, but the words were clear enough, even if hard to accept.

"Falcons?"

Finnvid managed a grin, and lifted his arms a little to flap in demonstration. "Falcons."

"They fly away, find game, and come back to you?" Finnvid nodded, and Theos said, "I'd like to see that someday." Finally, the Elkati civilization had produced something interesting. "When we take over the valley, I'll have to make sure the— Where do the falcons live? Are there people who work with them full-time? How many of them are there?"

"They live in a mews—it's a small building, like a henhouse. There are full-time falconers. Not many, because it's not the most efficient way to get meat, so hunting with them is a bit of a luxury. But there are a few. And I think there are about twenty falcons in the mews, last time I checked." He raised his eyes. "Any more questions?"

"Well, having found ones that you'll answer, I suppose I'm a bit overexcited." Theos thought for a moment, then nodded decisively. "Yes, when we take over the valley, I'll have someone show me the mews, and I'll make sure they're protected. I'd like to see the falcons at work."

"And that's within your power?" Finnvid asked. "To protect something your compatriots have just conquered?"

Theos shrugged. "Not if it were strategically important, or something really valuable. But if I decided to guard a little building and some birds? Nobody in authority would object to that. And I can look after myself if it's just other soldiers causing trouble."

"I'm sure you can," Finnvid said. He didn't sound sarcastic, but who could ever know, for sure?

Anyway, it was time to get back to business. "So you can't use a bow. You're obviously not much good at hand-to-hand. Do you have *any* sword training?"

"The basics." Finnvid frowned, then shrugged. "Even in the Elkat valley, I'm not known as a great swordsman. Here . . . I suppose here I'll be even lower in the rankings."

"I expect so," Theos said mildly. "I can teach you a little, but, really, you'll probably *always* be low in the rankings, here. You've wasted too much of your life."

"Wasted my life? Learning languages and rhetoric and philosophy? Improving my brain?"

"Aye." For someone with an improved brain, Finnvid asked a lot of stupid questions. "You've wasted your life."

"Was the time I spent learning about *healing* wasted? Would Andros say that it was?"

"No," Theos conceded. "*That* might actually be a bit useful. It's all the *rest* that was a waste."

Finnvid shook his head. "It's impossible for me to even explain all that you're missing, because one of the things you're missing is the ability to understand my explanations."

"That must be very frustrating for you." Theos turned and strode off toward the small pond at one end of the field, speaking over his shoulder as Finnvid tried to keep up. "I think we'll start with basic footwork. Balance and mobility are the keys to almost everything else you're going to be working on."

"Balance and mobility," Finnvid said, apparently leaving his haughtiness behind at the promise of learning something. "Okay. What do I do?"

Theos took the Elkati over to the floating logs in the pond. "The bigger the log, the easier. Start with the biggest. When you can make it from one end to the other without falling in the water, shift over to the next smallest log."

Finnvid squinted at the water. "This is how you train soldiers? With logs?"

"We train soldiers with everything. This is somewhere to start."

After a moment, Finnvid stripped off his tunic and bent to tug at his boots. "Okay," he said, his voice full of determination. "Start at the biggest log, move to the smaller ones." He jogged purposefully toward the water.

Theos waited for the first splash, which came when Finnvid was only a few steps on to the bobbing, spinning log. "Keep at it," he ordered when Finnvid's head bobbed to the surface. "I'll come back in a while and check on you."

Finnvid looked as if he was fighting the temptation to rebel, but finally he dragged himself out of the muddy water and started back toward the logs.

Theos headed for his own training. He heard the next splash but pretended he hadn't. The boy was trying, and Theos wouldn't laugh at him, no matter how tempting it was.

So he went down to train with the wooden swords, and if he was a little less focused than usual, it didn't mean anything. Maybe he was still tired from his time in the field, or maybe the distractions of trying to deal with the political situation had gotten to him. Maybe he shouldn't have had the third mug of ale the night before.

Any of those reasons were better than admitting that maybe his mind was somewhere else. That maybe he was thinking about a stubborn Elkati, and what it would have felt like if Theos had extended a hand to pull the boy from the pond. Maybe they would have stumbled a little, and fallen into each other, and Theos could have discovered whether Finnvid's smooth skin was still warm from exercise or whether the water had made it cool and slippery.

No. He wasn't thinking about any of that.

When he finished his drill and went to check on the boy, he walked quickly because he wanted to get things done that day, not because—not because anything! He wasn't hurrying because he wanted to see Finnvid. He didn't want anything to do with him.

And when he saw Finnvid on the second-largest log, scrambling from one end to the other like a drunken otter, the warmth he felt was just . . .

Damn it. He had an itch for the Elkati. The sullen, spying, lying Elkati virgin bedwarmer. Theos wanted the boy, and the boy didn't want him back. Finnvid thought Theos's urges were unnatural and shameful.

And they were meant to share a bedroom through the long, cold winter.

All because Theos couldn't keep his mouth shut and had gone diving into something that should never have been his business.

"Don't look down!" he ordered, and his voice broke Finnvid's concentration. The boy slipped, spun, and fell into the water with a splash and a curse. "And don't get distracted," he added when the boy's head surfaced.

Good advice for himself as well, of course. He sighed, trying not to notice the way Finnvid's wet trousers clung to his legs as he sloshed out of the pond. It was going to be a long winter.

CHAPTER † 10

They fell into a pattern after that. Long days of training, baths before dinner, and then drinking and gaming in the common room. Theos tried to treat Finnvid like a raw recruit, but he found himself struggling with that attitude.

Parts of his reluctance were quite practical: Finnvid didn't sleep with the recruits because he was supposed to be Theos's bedwarmer. So Finnvid was spared the loud, crude, rough dormitory life. Finnvid bathed more often than the recruits because Theos didn't want a smelly creature sleeping on his floor. And recruits weren't allowed in the Sacrati hall, but Theos wanted to be there, and he needed to keep an eye on Finnvid, so Finnvid came along.

Giving him ale, and letting him learn the dice games? Well, that was harder to justify. But Theos was tired of being angry, tired of being a guard when he just wanted to be a soldier. So he let go of a little tension.

And so, it seemed, did Finnvid. He stopped flinching and walking around with his eyes on his feet in the baths, and he started relaxing into the heat and steam. He even spent some time talking to Nero, the young Sacrati who'd beaten him in the common room, and while Theos didn't hear the words, he was pretty sure Finnvid apologized for starting the fight. A few Sacrati approached Finnvid with medical issues, and Finnvid seemed pleased to offer suggestions. And when they went back to Theos's room at night, Finnvid began telling his stories before they fell asleep, tales of the heroes and gods in the stars.

Despite all this, Theos was fucking his way through half the soldiers in the barracks. He was trying, unsuccessfully, to find someone who'd make him forget his fascination with Finnvid's smooth skin and lean body. When Finnvid was breathless after their morning run, Theos wanted to think about the boy's lack of fitness, not about other ways Theos could make him gasp. When Finnvid grunted in exertion during calisthenics, Theos didn't want to get hard, didn't want to imagine himself driving the breath out of the boy's body with long, deep thrusts...

"You're acting like a randy recruit," Andros said one morning while they were taking a break from sparring. "Do you actually have a plan, or are you just operating on instinct?"

"A plan? Not a plan, exactly, but, aye, I have some idea of what's going to happen."

Andros raised an eyebrow.

"I'm going to keep going like this until one night I roll over and catch a glimpse of a bit of his skin slipped out from under his blanket, and then my dick will explode and I'll bleed to death and this whole stupid thing will finally be done with."

Andros nodded slowly. "Messy, but you're right. At least it'll be an end."

"This is all your fault. You're Sacrati, by the sword! You should know enough to watch where you walk. If you hadn't stepped on that snake—"

"I wonder what *would* have happened," Andros said thoughtfully, "if we'd brought him in with the others, stuffed him in the pen, and forgotten about him. You'd have chosen a different prisoner as your prize, taken the money, and everything would have gone on as normal. But for Finnvid?"

"He'd have been able to do his spying and lying and sneaking around with less of an audience."

"Or he would have been shipped out to freeze to death in the mountains."

"Sounds perfect," Theos said, but they both knew he didn't mean it. As annoying as the Elkati sometimes was, Theos didn't want him dead. Not really.

The days passed. By the time of the midwinter soldiers' council, it had all become... not quite routine, just familiar. Theos had forgotten what it felt like to sleep alone in his room, without a crabby virgin on the floor beside his bed. But he didn't miss his solitude.

He sat near the front of the room for the council, as an iyatis should, yet didn't pay much attention to the proceedings. The warlord and Sacrati captain both served five-year terms, with their start dates staggered to ensure continuity of leadership, but neither post was up for a vote that year. So this council was mostly dealing with bureaucratic nonsense, and Theos wished he was sitting at the back with Andros and Finnvid. Still, he kept his posture straight and tried to look interested.

He'd almost dozed off by the time the warlord stood and announced that there would be a new iyatis for the coming season. So it took him longer than it should have to absorb the next words. He heard the warlord say that Ekakios would take Theos's place as iyatis and just sat still for a moment, wondering what had gone wrong with this poor Theos's leadership. Then the message sank in.

Theos jerked his gaze toward the Sacrati captain. Tamon was looking straight back at Theos, his expression intense, and Theos knew he was supposed to stay quiet and pretend none of it mattered. So he did, not because of the captain's unspoken order but because he was too shocked by the demotion to know how to respond.

He'd never been particularly ambitious and hadn't campaigned to become iyatis like some Sacrati did, but he'd been proud to be selected. Now? He took deep breaths, forced his face to stay calm, and tried to ignore the sick churning in his gut. He'd been demoted. No warning, no explanation. Just humiliation.

The warlord was watching him, greedy for a reaction, and Theos made himself remain impassive. This was his punishment for interfering with Finnvid? That was fine. It didn't bother him.

When the meeting broke up, he stayed in the room for the chitchat that always followed these events. He saw Tamon coming and was conscious of every muscle his face used to create the illusion of a smile.

"I'm sorry, Theos," the captain said. "There was . . . It's a delicate time. I'm trying to keep the peace. You're young. You'll have other chances."

Theos couldn't listen to this. He'd been publicly embarrassed because the warlord carried a grudge, and because the man who should have spoken up for him hadn't bothered to do so. And now he was supposed to listen to excuses. "Of course," he said, and he didn't worry too much about making his smile seem genuine anymore. He just nodded briskly, said, "Excuse me," and headed for the exit.

He was almost there, almost free, when he saw Finnvid working through the crowd toward him. It would be easier to dodge the Elkati and lick his wounds in private. Easier, but maybe not better, so he slowed and let Finnvid catch up. Theos glanced over at the warlord, and saw him watching again.

So Theos smiled at Finnvid. "More time for fucking," he said.

And Finnvid didn't object. More than that. He stepped closer and wrapped one hand in the front of Theos's tunic. "Good," he proclaimed.

It was stupid. Theos had done enough to save a little face, and he shouldn't press for more. His head knew that, but his hand moved on its own, finding a spot on the back of Finnvid's neck as if it had no other resting place. Finnvid blinked hard, but didn't pull away, and when Theos tugged, Finnvid shuffled toward him. Theos tilted his head down, and Finnvid tilted his up, and their kiss was warm and easy, like an established couple.

It was just for the audience. Theos knew that, and he knew he'd owe Finnvid a month without laundry duty in gratitude, but still his tongue savored the taste of Finnvid's mouth, still his body drew closer and tried to find warmth.

And when Finnvid pulled away, his eyes wide, Theos's cock swelled in appreciation and anticipation, no matter what signals his brain was sending out.

"Should we go?" Finnvid asked breathlessly, lacing his fingers through Theos's.

"Aye," Theos breathed. Finnvid had rescued him, making it look like he was driven off by lust, not humiliation. Probably Finnvid should never do laundry again. And if Finnvid actually followed through on the promise Theos's cock hoped he'd made . . .

But as soon as they were away from the meeting room, Finnvid let go of Theos's hand. No dramatics, just . . . the end of the contact. Finnvid had helped him, but now he was done.

They silently made their way back to Theos's room, then pulled off their outer clothes and lay down in their usual places. Theos was beginning to believe the night was over and he could forget it all when Finnvid whispered, "Andros said that was because of me. He said you lost your rank because you defied the warlord and kept me out of the slave trade."

"Andros is kind. Maybe I just wasn't good at the job."

Finnvid was silent for a while, then said, "I've told you about Varin. The greatest warrior in history?"

"Aye," Theos said cautiously.

"I've told you some of his trials. You know the gods frowned on him and sent him deep beneath the earth, and another time the avalanche caught him, and later he had to rescue his son from the rock trolls."

"Aye," Theos said. He rolled over onto his side so he could look into the darkness where Finnvid was lying.

"But I haven't told you about King Lordan, have I?"

"I don't think so."

"Lordan was Varin's king, and Varin was a loyal subject. He fought for Lordan, and led his armies to many victories."

"Lordan didn't lead his own armies?"

"No. He stayed at home, safe and warm, and sent his soldiers out to do battle."

Theos knew how Torians would deal with a leader who didn't at least take part in the big fights, but Elkati were different. "Did Varin like that?"

"He accepted it. He was loyal, and Lordan was his king. But one day, while Varin was off on some adventure, Lordan came by his home and saw Varin's wife. And she was beautiful, of course."

They'd already covered that: how Varin's mate had been a swan until the gods made her human, and how she'd kept her grace and beauty through the transformation. Theos hoped she'd softened a bit in the beak area, but hadn't pushed for answers about that. When Theos asked too many questions, Finnvid tended to stop telling his stories, and Theos liked the stories. So he stayed quiet, and Finnvid kept talking.

"As soon as Lordan saw Varin's wife, he was overcome with lust for her. But he knew she was a virtuous woman who wouldn't be unfaithful to her mate. So he decided he needed to make her . . . What's the word in Torian? For a woman after her mate dies?"

"You have a word for that? And, wait, do you mean *Varin* is going to die?"

"We have a word in Elkati, yes. And, yes, the king decided he should kill Varin so his wife would be free."

"He's going to kill Varin just so he can sleep with Varin's wife? Does she even have a name? Does she *want* to sleep with Lordan? Does Varin have to *die* just so two other people can have sex?" Theos took a deep breath. Probably the story wasn't worth getting quite this upset over. Still . . . "Do you begin to understand how ridiculous your Elkati system is?"

"Do you want to hear the rest of the story or not?"

"I don't know. Does Varin die?"

"You'll have to be quiet if you want to find out."

Theos huffed, but then he lay still. He needed to hear the ending now that he'd heard the start.

When Finnvid seemed satisfied by the silence, he continued. "But King Lordan couldn't just have Varin killed. The people loved their hero too much, and might revolt if he was murdered by their king. And Lordan wasn't strong enough to kill Varin in a fair fight. No one was." Of course not. Theos had come to think of Varin as the original Sacrati, which made the stories much easier to appreciate. "So Lordan set traps for Varin. He sent him on impossible missions . . . I've already told you some of those stories, and we know how Varin managed to win against all obstacles. And then he'd return to the arms of his beautiful wife—and, no, I don't think she has a name—and the king would see them together and come up with an even more impossible mission."

"When Varin came back from fighting the star god, Lordan must have wanted to punch him in the face."

"Probably," Finnvid agreed. "The king had stopped caring about Varin's beautiful wife quite so much because he was too busy hating Varin. Being jealous of him. Especially since Varin was the only one strong enough to lift the star god's sword, so now Varin had an even *better* weapon to fight with."

Theos tucked his arm behind his head and looked up into the darkness of the room. This was a good story.

"But after that fight," Finnvid continued, "Varin was tired. He needed to recover from his many injuries, and he wanted to spend some time with his beautiful wife. So when the king summoned him to a royal audience, he went, and he was respectful and polite. But the king said he had another mission for Varin to go on; Varin refused. Politely. He said he was injured, and tired. He said he needed a little more time."

"How'd the king like that?"

"Well, secretly he was very pleased because it gave him the excuse he needed. He said Varin was no true hero if he wouldn't follow the orders of his king. And right there in the grand hall, with all the nobles watching, he declared another man the hero of the realm."

Theos was quiet for a moment. "Is this a real story?"

"It *is*. But you're right, it's not a coincidence that I'm telling it to you now."

"No." The story was beginning to taste more like medicine than a treat. "So . . . what happened then?" Best to get it over with.

"Varin thanked the king. He said the other man was a good fighter and would be a good hero, and Varin was looking forward to spending more time with his wife. And right there in front of everyone, he pulled his wife to him and gave her a big kiss."

"Wait. You were being my wife in the hall?"

"The story isn't over yet. Do you want to hear the rest?"

"Probably not. Why don't you just tell me more about your wifely duties and responsibilities. Should you be sleeping on the floor, now that we're married?"

"So Varin went back to his home with his wife, and they were very happy."

"Did she sleep on the floor? Did he like that?"

"You're about to miss the ending of the story. I'll just roll right over and go to sleep, and you'll be lying up there trying to guess what happens, but you won't be able to because your imagination isn't all that good."

"My imagination is excellent. I just use it for more interesting thoughts than stories about silly Elkati kings and marriages."

"Fine. You lie up there imagining whatever you like. And I'll just go to sleep."

Theos lasted for three breaths, then said, "Slave, I order you to tell me the rest of the story."

"Ask nicely."

"I *ordered*. You *are* a slave, you know."

"I don't agree."

It was true, Theos realized. Finnvid still acted as though he was just spending time with slightly surly friends before returning to his old life in Elkat. And Theos had been letting him believe it. So he might as well continue with the charade, at least long enough to find out what happened to Varin. "Please tell me how the story ends."

The room was too dark to see Finnvid's smug smile, but Theos could hear it in his voice as he said, "Everything was fine until the dragon came."

"Wait? There's a dragon?" Theos had almost missed the best part of the story.

"Aye, a fierce old beast. Claws as long as a man's arm, and eight of them on each foot."

"Eight? That seems like a lot."

"It *is* a lot! It was a terrible dragon."

"But not Varin's problem."

"Well, not right away. First, the king sent the other hero. And that hero was a good man. Next to Varin, he was the best warrior in the kingdom."

"But he got eaten all the same."

"Have you already heard this story?"

"I've heard your other stories. I've noticed a pattern."

"Well, I don't know about that, but as it happens, yes, in this one case, the other hero *did* get eaten by the dragon. And all the villagers screamed and wailed, and they begged the king to summon Varin. But the king was too proud. So he called together his ten best knights, and sent *them* after the dragon."

"Why doesn't he just send everyone at once? What's he going to do when the ten knights get eaten, send the next twenty?"

"So you *have* heard this story before."

Theos was smiling. Lying there in the dark, listening to his crazy virgin Elkati floorwarmer, and smiling to himself. It was strange, but it felt good. "I haven't heard the story. Keep going."

"Well, let's skip over the multiple failures from increasingly large groups of knights and warriors. But we should be clear that all this time the dragon isn't just eating the people who come to fight it, it's eating innocent villagers too. So finally the villagers approach the king, and they're angry. Everyone knows who can kill the dragon."

"But Varin's balls-deep in his beautiful wife and doesn't even know there *is* a dragon."

"He's not— He's *with* his beautiful wife. In their home. Just— *with* her."

"Fucking."

"That's between Varin and his beautiful wife."

"I'm going to lose most of my respect for Varin *and* his beautiful wife if they're not spending a *lot* of time fucking."

"Varin and his wife don't care what you think."

"That's because they're too busy fucking."

"If there is one more interruption, story time will be over."

Theos made himself be silent, and finally Finnvid said, "Even though he knew Varin was the last chance for the land, the king refused to call him. But the villagers couldn't just sit around waiting to be eaten, so they sent a delegation of their oldest, wisest men to ask Varin to help them. And as soon as he heard of their plight, he buckled on his armor and grabbed the star god's sword and headed off. As he walked through the village, the people fell in behind him, cheering him on. The king heard the noise, came out on the palace balcony to see what was happening, and he seethed with rage. But there was nothing he could do. Varin found the dragon, and the battle was fierce. The dragon's long claws were only one of the problems; he also had horrible teeth, and there were spikes on his tail sharp enough to impale a man right through the strongest of armor. Varin had to use all his strength and cunning and speed, but finally he managed to dart in underneath the monster's jaws and slice the creature open from belly to chin."

Of course he did. Finnvid wasn't much good at giving details of the battles in these stories, but Theos could fill many of them in for himself. He could practically feel the tough dragon hide surrendering to his sharp sword, the heat of the blood that would pour down on his head from the wound . . .

"So naturally Varin won," Finnvid said. "But you know what the best part was?"

"The victory fucking?"

"No. Is that really–is there *victory fucking*? Do you do that?"

"I'm sorry, I think you're getting distracted from your story. You should stay focused, or I'll stop listening and go to sleep."

Finnvid paused before he said, "You know what the best part was? It was when Varin walked back through the village, with all the cheering villagers behind him. The king was out on his balcony watching them, and Varin didn't even glance in his direction. He'd realized the king didn't matter. He was a hero because of who he was, not because of a title some old man gave him or took away from him. He didn't need the king's approval to be who he was meant to be."

Theos let the message sink in. It was a good story. Still, "I think that Varin ignoring the king was probably the *second* best part. It was good, but really, the best part was almost certainly the victory fucking."

Finnvid made a disgusted sound, and Theos heard the blankets rustle as he rolled over. They lay in silence for a while, and then Theos said, "Thank you for the story, Finnvid. And for the kiss. They both helped."

"You're welcome," Finnvid said quietly, and then they both lay still until they fell asleep.

CHAPTER 11

The kiss might have helped Theos deal with his surprising demotion, but it did nothing to cool the desire for his uninterested slave. Frustration with his career *and* with his sex life led him to train more intensely than ever, trying to tire himself out enough to keep his emotions under control.

"Festival tomorrow," Andros remarked. Theos had just knocked him to the frozen mud of the training grounds, but Andros didn't seem concerned. He let Theos help him up, then clapped him on the shoulder. "Maybe that's what you need. You can't forget about Finnvid when you're fucking other *men*, because they're too similar. If you're fucking a woman, though, it'll be totally different. You should try for a really soft one . . . big tits and a round ass, nothing like your little pile-of-bones bedwarmer. That'll make you forget all about him."

Theos had his doubts, but he put them aside as they started sparring again. And the next day, walking through the gates into the city, he was excited, almost happy. He glanced over at Finnvid, who was looking around at the buildings and finely dressed citizens, and smiled. "Not like the barracks, is it?"

Finnvid shook his head. "It isn't. This is the city that was here before the Torians took over? The buildings seem more—more refined, I suppose. The graceful lines, the carvings . . . Torians wouldn't approve of that sort of ornamentation, would they?"

Theos had never paid much attention to the city's architecture. "It's the old city. We almost always keep the old buildings. We build up the walls, maybe, and tear down things that clearly aren't needed, but it's a lot more efficient to adapt than to rebuild from scratch."

"But the homes. They'd all be designed for families, and you don't really have those, do you?"

"Not the same way you do. Not one man and one woman and all the offspring they produce. Usually two or three women will share a house, and they'll have their youngest kids with them. That's a family, for us."

"That's how you were raised? Do you still see your mother?"

"Sometimes. I get along better with her housemates, though, so I'm more likely to visit them." It was strange, talking like this. Explaining everything to Finnvid made Theos think about details he'd never spent much time on. He wasn't sure he liked it.

But Finnvid nodded as if he understood. "I have an aunt like that. My mother's sister. She's much—much easier to get along with." He paused, frowned, and then in a more careful voice added, "Not that my mother isn't a wonderful woman."

"Mine too," Theos agreed seriously, and then he grinned.

And Finnvid grinned back. Just like that. Like they were friends. In that moment, Theos wanted to wrap his arm around Finnvid's shoulders, not to draw him in for anything more, anything lustful . . . simply to touch him.

But he didn't dare. Finnvid didn't want to be touched.

So it was a bit surprising to feel the boy's hand on his shoulder, gripping tight for a flash of easy affection before they stepped farther apart and kept walking along the street as if nothing had happened.

Theos tried to control his racing heart. Why was he so excited? Because his *slave* had touched him kindly? Had he lost all sense? Just because he'd chosen not to force himself on the boy didn't mean they weren't still master and property!

Would Theos have been this excited if a *dog* he owned had shown him some affection?

Well, that thought calmed him down a little, because he was pretty sure he *would* be excited about a dog, if the dog had been wild, or an enemy war dog. Theos was *taming* Finnvid. That was why he was excited. He wouldn't push, but if he kept being slow and steady and kind, maybe eventually Finnvid would be tame all the time. Maybe he'd share his secrets, and Theos would finally figure out what was going on. And maybe Finnvid would get over his stupid Elkati ideas about sex and realize that there was nothing unnatural about two people giving each other pleasure.

And maybe then he'd flap his wings and start to fly. But it was festival day, a good day for crazy dreams, so Theos let himself believe this one, just a little.

They reached the market square, and Theos steered Finnvid toward the stall of a healer they'd been planning to talk to. Finnvid needed potions of some sort—Theos had stopped listening to the explanation pretty soon after it had started—and the city healers seemed like the most likely source. So he made the introductions and then stood back, watching the women in the square. And the men who approached them.

"What's that lineup for?" Finnvid asked from close to Theos's elbow.

"You done already?"

"She's gone to get some things from her shop. The lineup?"

"Couples who've already decided on their partners for the night. They need to register to be sure it's an approved match."

"What? Who makes the approvals?"

"The people in the temple. That's the building they're in front of."

"Why do they get to decide? I heard that festivals were the only time of the year when men got to choose their partners. Are you saying that isn't really true? They *still* have to get approval from the temple?"

"Well, it's harder to get approval from the *woman*, really. We get to choose, but they can refuse the choice. Sometimes there's ten men who all want the same woman, and she picks one. She might make note of a couple others and request them during the rest of the year, but on a festival night she only takes one. Then they have to get it approved by the temple to make sure they're not too closely related."

Finnvid made a face. "They wouldn't just *know*?"

Theos snorted. "My father had one hundred and seventeen children, and he died in midlife. There are older men who have even more. The temple puts a lid on them after a while, or else transfers the man or some of the grown children off to another valley; in the meantime, though, people don't just *know*. They can ask, obviously, and figure out if they share a direct parent, but there are complications. I don't know who my father's siblings are, or my mother's, and I don't know all of my siblings, or the children they may have had. Most people don't. So the temple keeps track and makes sure everything's good."

"Wouldn't it be simpler to just—" Finnvid stopped. Then he nodded, as if confirming something with himself. "Okay. That's interesting. So you'll be approaching a woman today? Do you have one in mind?"

Theos shook his head. "I usually just see what happens. I stand back and watch, and maybe I'll see someone . . . I don't know. The last festival there was a woman who was messing with the spit for the roast pork—the thing was supposed to turn automatically, I think, but it wasn't working and she was trying to fix it—and I got kind of fascinated with the way her arms moved. They were so much smaller than mine, yet she still seemed strong . . ." Again, he was saying more than he usually would. But he'd started, so he'd better finish. "I just liked watching her. So when she was done I went over and we talked for a while, and we got along, so . . ."

"So you went to the temple and got permission?"

"No. The temple's just for early on. Later, they have tables set up at the festival grounds, and there are kids wandering around taking names; you give your names to the kid and they run over to the tables and get you checked out. It's more trouble for the temple, I guess, but less for us."

"And the people running the tables? They don't get to take part in the . . . festivities?"

"Older women, or those who don't want another child yet. Sometimes women who are already pregnant."

Finnvid nodded slowly. "It's all worked out."

Theos shrugged. "It's not perfect. There are fights every year—two men after the same woman, usually. If she's got any sense, she'll leave them to it and choose a third to go off with, but some women seem to like the fighting. Like animals, I guess, the males competing for the females' attention."

"But not you." Finnvid raised an eyebrow mockingly. "You're above all that. You wouldn't fight for a woman; you just wait for them to come to you."

Theos raised his own eyebrow in return. "I'm not interested in fighting for partners, or in being with someone who doesn't want to be with me. You of all people should remember that."

They didn't talk much for a while, but their silence was friendly. They wandered through the market and looked at the wares on display, and when Finnvid admired a warm winter coat, Theos bought it for him. It wasn't fancy, but it wasn't inexpensive, either, and Theos began to wonder just how much coin he'd have left by the time spring arrived and he was able to go out and earn more. He'd better start looking for contests and bets around the barracks: ways to earn a little extra. And while he'd been generous for a while, it was probably time to start charging for Finnvid's medical advice.

There was no formal lunch during festivals, just lots of snacking at various stalls all through the day, with a lull starting in midafternoon. "We should go get cleaned up," Theos said as he saw the crowd begin to disperse.

Finnvid was still agreeable and relaxed as they bathed, then returned to Theos's room. "Slave women are allowed to partner, at the festivals, but not the men," Theos said, feeling slightly apologetic as he pulled on his best tunic. "But it's a good meal, and there's music and dancing afterward."

Finnvid hesitated for the first time that day. "Actually, I was thinking . . . hoping— It's not that I disapprove! I understand that you do things differently. Not worse, not better, just different. But I'm really not comfortable with it. Not yet. I was hoping maybe I could stay here."

Theos frowned. He was supposed to keep an eye on the boy. "No, you should come with me. It's not like the bathhouse, you know. The partners go off to private places. There's a bit of kissing, maybe, on the festival grounds, but that's all. There are lots of children present." He grinned. "You could probably make friends with them."

Finnvid was quiet for a moment, then looked away quickly. "It's not the generalities," he said. His voice was tight and all the easiness was gone from his face. "It's . . . I don't want to see *you* going off with some woman. I mean, with the men . . . I can stand it. Barely, but . . . I know you don't feel that way, but for me it's not real, with them. With a woman it would be . . . for me . . . and . . . I don't want to see that."

Theos stared at him. "What are you talking about?"

Finnvid kept his gaze locked on the floor somewhere behind Theos's feet. "You know," he mumbled.

"No. I don't know. Are you saying . . . are you saying you'd be *jealous*?"

Finnvid snorted, then darted a glance at Theos. "Maybe," he said finally. "I don't know. I'm trying to understand it. I know . . . I know I've never felt like this before. Not about a man, certainly, but . . . not about anyone, I don't think. And it's strange, and new, and I don't know what to think, and I just need some time! I need a few damn hours where I can't hear you and smell you and when I don't feel tempted to reach over and touch you. Just a few hours of peace to get things straightened out."

"I don't know if I *want* you to get it straightened out. Not if having it crooked means you want me." Theos took a cautious step forward. Finnvid's body tensed, but he didn't move away. "Look at me," Theos said quietly.

Slowly, reluctantly, Finnvid raised his eyes. There were too many emotions on his face for Theos to decipher them all, but his confusion and desperation were obvious. Theos raised his hand and brushed the backs of his fingers against Finnvid's freshly shaved cheek.

Finnvid breathed out, a tense, shuddering sound, and then gasped as Theos ran his thumb over the boy's lips. Could this be real? If Theos continued to be patient, could he make this work?

"A few hours," he said gently, and he stretched his fingers to cradle Finnvid's jawline, then leaned in. Slowly, careful not to scare the boy . . . but Theos needed something.

His stomach was tight, waiting for the disgust, the refusal. It didn't come. His mouth found Finnvid's, just a quick brush of skin against skin, and he felt the desire churn through his whole body. The boy was *his*, and Theos ached to grab him, tear off his clothes, and throw him on the bed. He knew exactly how it would feel, his own strength and Finnvid's lithe grace, and he *needed* it, needed to break through the boy's stupid ideas and show him how they could be together. By the sword, had he not been tested enough? Did he not deserve his prize?

For a moment they were frozen there, their lips a breath apart, Theos fighting with himself, Finnvid . . . maybe Finnvid fighting with himself too, but on a different battlefield. When Theos finally trusted himself to move, he began to pull away, only to find strong fingers wrapped around his neck, holding him still. Theos opened his eyes as Finnvid leaned back and whispered, "Thank you." Then the boy brought their mouths together again.

This time, there was more. Finnvid's lips were softer, and Theos let himself lick, just a taste. Finnvid drew in a shuddering breath, then sighed into Theos's mouth as his whole body relaxed and he leaned toward the kiss.

It didn't last long. Theos was still savoring the first wash of sensations when Finnvid pushed away, his hands flat on Theos's chest, cheeks flaming, eyes wild and staring anywhere but at Theos.

"You okay?" Theos asked softly.

Finnvid's smile was too quick, too wide. "Yes! I'm . . . sorry, I—" He took a deep breath, then said, "I definitely do need that time alone. I just need to catch up to some things, I think."

"We don't have to go fast," Theos promised, and made himself add, "or at all. Not if—if you decide this isn't what you want. We don't have to do anything."

The smile he got in return was still automatic. "I appreciate your patience. Your forbearance. We don't have the same customs in Elkat . . . We don't give our prisoners jobs, we just keep them in cells."

"Easier to treat them that way when you rarely *take* prisoners," Theos observed.

Finnvid shrugged. "My point was, it *is* the custom of your people. One of many ways we differ. Nobody here would have blamed you or even been surprised if you'd . . . done whatever you wanted with me. Right?"

"Well, there's people who'd be surprised, I think. People who know me well enough to think I'd be kind."

Finnvid nodded. "Well, now I'm one of those people. And I appreciate your kindness. Thank you."

Theos couldn't resist. He smiled as winningly as he could manage and said, "I could be kind in a whole lot of ways you haven't experienced yet, if you'd care to open your mind a little and let me in."

"I believe you. I just . . . It's customary for the men to stay in the city overnight, isn't it? I'll see you tomorrow morning when you return, and I'll be much calmer. I just need some time to get my head sorted out."

Theos frowned. "You said a few hours. When this started, you said a few hours."

"I guess I was thinking in terms of the time we'd be awake for. I mean, you *do* normally sleep in the city, don't you? I don't want you to insult your partner by leaving early."

Nodding slowly, Theos agreed, "Aye. Tomorrow, then." He tugged his tunic back into place and smoothed his hands over his trousers. "I look presentable?"

"You do."

Theos left. He headed down the stairs with a crowd of rowdy young men, but stepped aside so he wouldn't have to walk into the city with them. He needed his own time alone to think.

CHAPTER 12

Theos stayed by the doorway of the barracks until the sun began to set. He could hear the distant sounds of music and revelry in the city, and every now and then he caught a whiff of the roast pork, carried to him on the cool autumn wind. But when he finally moved, he didn't head in the direction of the city gates.

Instead, he found his way down along the backs of the buildings, through a narrow alley, and then into an alcove. A different smell, here, the odor of men kept too close together, without the benefits of the baths. Theos hoped he was in the wrong place, but he didn't think he was.

And sure enough, shortly after the moon rose, Finnvid appeared. He moved carefully, but didn't sneak. If there was anyone else left in the barracks to see him, they'd think he was on official business. By the sword, the boy was a natural.

Finnvid headed straight for the door of the prisoner pen. Theos had a good view of the pens, and was interested in discovering how the spy planned to get past the heavy iron lock.

He frowned and leaned forward in disbelief when he realized what he was seeing. The boy—the Elkati *spy*—he had a *key*.

There was no time to think about it right then. Theos sprinted across the yard, saw Finnvid's startled face, saw the little coward trying to change his expression into a smile, or an apology, or whatever else it would take to fool big, stupid Theos again.

This time, Theos didn't give him the chance. He slammed his fist into Finnvid's gut and as he doubled over Theos dropped his elbow into the back of the boy's lying, spying Elkati skull.

He wished he'd had more time to teach the boy to fight, because it was over too soon. Finnvid managed to keep himself vertical for a moment by grabbing hold of the bars of the pen, but his dizziness proved too much for him and he slid down into the mud. Theos grabbed him by the back of his collar. He was wearing his new coat, the one he'd tricked Theos into buying for him that afternoon. It would be good for traveling in the winter. But had he really expected his men to survive without being better equipped? Or did he only need them to fight past the sentries, and didn't care if they made it the rest of the way?

Or had the same person who'd given him the key also left a cache of winter equipment somewhere? Had the person left *weapons* they could use to escape the valley? To *kill* the sentries?

Too many questions, and Theos was done with not having answers. He dragged Finnvid, groggy and disoriented, through the abandoned barracks until he found some leather armor straps, and he used them to tie the spy's hands and feet together. Then it was time for more dragging.

He was halfway through the city gates before he calmed down sufficiently to remember the occasion. Pulling a sputtering Elkati, bound hand and foot, into the central square probably wouldn't contribute to the mood of the evening. So he changed course, turning left down a narrow street, cutting through an alley, and coming out behind the main administrative building. Theos had spent the first decade of his life running through these streets, and he still knew them well. The back door was unlocked, as most city doors tended to be, and he pulled the Elkati up the steps, down a hall, and into the outer office. His luck abandoned him there, as he tried the next door and found it locked. Sensitive materials inside, maybe.

He glared down at the spy. There was blood from his nose smeared all over him, and some extra bumps and scratches from his rough trip, but otherwise he looked healthy enough. Still, he'd been dizzy earlier, so obviously his brain had been affected at least a little.

"I don't want to gag you in case you puke. There's no point in having kept you alive this long just to have you choke to death now, so I'm going to leave your mouth free, but I don't want you disrupting the festival. If you make any noise, I'll beat you bloody. Do you understand what I'm saying? You haven't had a beating yet, and I don't really like giving them. But in this case? For you? I'd make an exception. I'd make you *suffer*. You understand?"

The Elkati nodded reluctantly. Theos took the end of the leather strap he'd brought from the barracks and threw it over a post halfway up the nearby staircase, then pulled it down to the spy's hands and tied it so he was almost, but not quite, suspended. Tight enough that he had no room to squirm or cause trouble. And hopefully tight enough to cause the lying little coward some pain.

Theos left him then. He strode out the front door and through the city streets, trying to hang on to his anger because it was easier to feel that way than to give in to the hurt and confusion. The humiliation of having been a fool, of having believed, even for a moment, that the Elkati was being genuine. No, Theos would much rather be angry.

He found the reeve in the main square, watching the dancing with her typical small frown. The earlier exchange with the Elkati over difficult mothers flashed through his mind, and then he made himself step forward into her line of sight.

Photina raised an eyebrow. "Where have you been? You've been missed."

Her tone made it clear that *she* hadn't missed him. She just didn't like her women being slighted by a man who neglected to show them proper admiration.

"My apologies. I was kept away by something important. Something I need to speak to you about."

She let him guide her a few steps away from the crowd before she said, "You're referring to your Elkati, I assume?" She snorted at his reaction. "Don't look so surprised. Do you think tales of your exotic bedwarmer didn't climb over the city walls? Do you imagine I wouldn't ask some questions, once I heard?"

"I suppose I didn't think you were interested in that sort of thing."

"About you taking a slave? I *wouldn't* care, normally. Well, I'd think it peculiar, and maybe a little pathetic, but I wouldn't consider it my business."

"And you think this is different somehow?"

"Don't be slow, Theos. I know why you took him, and I know you've been told to stop pushing and to keep things calm. So the only thing I *don't* know is why you're here, apparently about to make a fuss when you've been clearly told *not* to."

Theos stepped closer. "Things have changed. He tried to escape tonight."

"Really? It was my understanding that part of your job with him was to prevent that sort of incident from occurring."

"He had help." This was the thing Theos couldn't grasp. "Someone gave him a key to the prisoner pens. I expect he was going to try to fight his way past the sentries into the mountains." He waited for her to react, and when she didn't, he peered around to make sure no one could overhear, then hissed, "A *Torian* gave him a key so he could get loose and attack our guards! So he could *kill* Torians. We're supposed to be pretending there's nothing wrong while we're all winter-stuck, but we've got people plotting murders. Is that really something we can ignore?"

She frowned at him as if he was the one who'd made all this happen, then sighed. "Where's the Elkati now?"

"In your office."

"Really. What an inappropriate place for him."

"Where would be *more* appropriate? Should I have dragged him into the festival? Or left him down in the barracks to be freed again?"

"Enough theatrics, Theos. You're Sacrati—aren't you supposed to be stoic?"

"You're the reeve—aren't you supposed to care about the safety of your people?"

Her eyes flared. "You think I should show how much I care by igniting a civil conflict in an enclosed space? Really?"

"The conflict's *been* ignited. Or at least, there are sparks flying all around, and I seem to be the only person trying to put them out, so sooner or later one of them's going to find tinder and blaze up."

"How poetic." She half turned. "Your absence was noticed, and now your agitation has surely been seen as well. The other side will be hoping you're upset about a successful slave escape, but you would have gone to the captain about that, not to me. Right? So they'll suspect something different. They'll suspect you've thwarted the escape and are demanding answers." She shook her head. "I hate it when the other side knows the truth. But what will they *do*, now they know it?"

She whirled back toward him. "Were you discreet? When you left the Elkati in my office, did anyone see you?"

"I don't think so."

"But you don't know for sure. Someone may have followed you as you charged up from the barracks, intent on vengeance." She was energized. "Return to the Elkati and make sure he stays safe; if they've been unable to get him out of the valley safely, they may choose a more permanent method of silencing him. I'll go find the captain and consult."

She turned and strode away without waiting for his agreement. It was frustrating, but he didn't have a better plan himself; he did as he was told. A few Sacrati caught at his arms as he walked past their festive tables, but he shook them off and kept moving. If Photina was right and people *were* watching him, he didn't mind if they saw him being angry. He *wanted* them to see his anger, and understand that it was directed at them. He wanted them to be afraid.

But when he got back to the administrative building, *he* became the apprehensive one. He couldn't say why the hair stood up on the back of his neck, didn't know what his body had noticed, but he'd learned to pay attention to it at times like this. He slowed his pace and let his senses absorb clues from the surroundings, and when his heart rate picked up a little, he stepped out of the moonlight and into the shadows by the front of the building.

He eased the door open, moving slow and quiet, and wished he had at least a knife with him. But no one brought weapons to a festival. He could only hope that anyone else in the building had been dressed for the same occasion he had been.

And there *was* someone else in the building. Someone hiding in the shadows, waiting for him. He might not understand the rest of it, but fighting? This was in his blood, and he trusted his feelings even when he couldn't trust his thoughts. It was a relief to be back to something familiar.

Still, he was too disciplined to charge forward. Did they know he was in the building? Any warrior worth the name would have noticed the front door opening, even as quiet as Theos had been. He'd let in a bit of a breeze, cold evening air washing in, and probably the shadows had changed a little as the solid door had opened and admitted the moonlight. Even without Theos's sixth sense, any Torian—

And that was where he caught himself. Any *Torian*. The people inside the building now, the people he was so eager to fight and kill ... they were Torians. His fellows. His brothers in arms. There was no one else in the valley, besides the prisoners, and they were all locked up. Whoever was hiding in the darkness ahead was a Torian.

Whoever was *waiting for him* was Torian. What were their plans? Did they want to kill him? Did they have the same hesitations he did? Did they *know* him?

He stopped in the middle of the corridor. "I'm coming in," he announced, his voice ringing down the almost-empty halls. "If you'd like to discuss this peacefully, speak up now. If you stay hidden, I'll assume you're hostile."

There was motion behind him. Smooth but fast. An attack.

Theos's body took over and moved as it had been bred and trained to do. There was no room for doubts; one of his hands found the enemy's wrist and twisted, the other grabbed the knife from the man's weakened fingers. Everything happened quickly, instinctively, and before Theos's drew his next breath, the attacker had taken his last, the blade in his throat ending him forever. It was too dark to see his face, and Theos didn't drag the body into the light.

Instead, he pulled the blade free and stepped away. He was trained to kill, but he wished he'd taken this man captive. Still, there was no time for second thoughts. "One down," he called, "and now I'm armed. If you have a full patrol in there, stand and fight, and we'll see who wins. But if there's less of you than that ..."

Theos could almost smell his opponent's fear, and when he heard movement, he knew the intruder was heading out the back door, trying to escape.

Theos didn't want to kill anyone else, but he'd be damned if he'd let the man go free. So he sprinted, arriving at the back door just as it was opening, and wrapped his arm around the man's neck—quick and tight, at just the right angle. The enemy struggled, of course, bringing his arm up to stab ineffectively over his shoulder. Theos lowered his head, felt the knife puncture his scalp and bounce off his skull, and then the struggling body collapsed, so suddenly heavy it almost dragged Theos to the floor.

He held the choke hold for an extra couple of seconds to ensure the man was out, then released him. Moonlight shone through the open door on to the man's unconscious face.

Familiar, but not intimate. Torian, but not Sacrati. Theos had probably seen the man around, maybe even trained with him, but they'd never gotten drunk together. Never fucked, he was pretty sure. So that was something.

He heaved the man onto his back and carried him to the room where he'd left the Elkati. His stomach sank when he saw the empty space, but before it had even hit bottom he noticed a darker shadow in a gap between the large desk and the wall. The boy must have gotten partly loose somehow and worked his way into a hiding spot. He was still in the building though, and still alive: Theos knew what death smelled like, and there was none of its stench in the room.

"Elkati," he barked. "Worm your way out of there. I have someone to share your bonds."

The boy didn't move.

"If I have to drag you, I'm going to drive my knife into your thigh and use it as a handle."

After a moment's hesitation, the dark shape began squirming from its cave. An obedient Elkati and a live Torian prisoner. Theos's luck was improving.

CHAPTER 13

Of course, everything went wrong when his mother and the captain arrived.

"There's a body in my foyer," Photina growled at Theos. "That's a problem."

Theos shrugged. "It's not mine."

"Not your *body*, or not your *problem*?"

"Neither." He watched Photina light the wall lamps, then he walked over and put the dead man's knife on the desk in front of Tamon. "He was carrying this. It's well-balanced, but there's nothing special about it that I could see. Typical Torian blade."

The captain spoke slowly. "You killed a Torian."

Aye, that was the part Theos had been trying not to think about. "He attacked me; I had no choice." That had to be true. "The other one tried to get away, so he's still alive." Theos gestured toward the two men tied back-to-back on the floor at the far end of the room. "He returned to himself a while ago, though he's pretending to still be knocked out. He's Torian too, but I don't know his name. He's not Sacrati." And that was all he had to report. At least about the *recent* events. "Photina told you about the spy?"

"She did." He frowned at the two bound men. "I wonder if it's time to include our Elkati visitor in the conversation."

"Not if you want to hear anything useful or truthful," Theos said with a bitter laugh. "If you want to be lied to, though? Absolutely. He's your man."

"I was thinking that I'd be the one doing the talking," the captain said. He looked at Theos, then shook his head. "No. You first, and then I'll move on to him. Secure the door so no one can get in while we're busy, and we'll go into the inner office." He paused and glanced in Photina's direction. "With your leave."

She nodded, and Theos shoved the large desk over in front of the door. A strong man might be able to get the door open with the desk there, but not without making enough noise to alert the whole city.

Tamon nodded his satisfaction and stood aside for Photina to lead the way into her office. Theos followed. Now that he had the chance to learn the truth, he wondered if ignorance might not be better.

But it was too late for that, so he shut the door behind himself and leaned against it, waiting. Photina scowled at him, then at Tamon. "Don't you train your men to stand up straight?"

"I train my men to conserve energy whenever they're not using it productively."

That had sounded almost like he was defending Theos. Was he more sympathetic than he'd seemed?

Tamon smiled regretfully at him. "This is frustrating for all of us," he said. "But you've had it a little worse, maybe, because we haven't given you the full story. I think it's time we changed that."

It was well *past* time, but it probably wouldn't do him any good to point it out right then. So he kept quiet.

Tamon squinted at him. "You've never been back east, have you? Never seen the capital, or the cities in the central valleys? Never seen the way people live there?"

"No," Theos said cautiously. He was a warrior, and the best place for a warrior was at the battlefront. He might have passed through the central valleys on the way to the far borders, if he'd chosen that adventure, but he'd always found enough to keep him busy in the west.

"Things are different there," the captain explained. "More . . . your Elkati would probably call it more civilized. I'd be inclined to call it more decadent. People don't live communally, as they do here. At least, the wealthy don't. They don't focus on the function of things; they look for luxury. Pointless, ostentatious collections of wealth in the hands of a few, while the poor there . . . well, there *are* poor there. There are people starving."

That was hard for Theos to imagine. Everyone in Windthorn was expected to work, of course, but there was food for everyone, and places to sleep. Luxuries like Theos's private room had to be earned through seniority and achievement, and little extras came to successful squads, but those were *extras*. "Starving?" he asked with a frown. "In the central valleys? Where does all their produce go, then? And our tribute?"

"Into the hands of the wealthy. Men and women who never lift their hand in labor, but who know the right people or have made the right alliances."

Theos frowned. It didn't sound anything like the Torian values he'd been raised to respect. But still . . . "What does that have to do with an Elkati spy?"

Tamon sighed. "Nothing directly. But it may have rather a lot to do with the man who's *helping* the spy."

"There's a faction within Windthorn that feels we are too austere," Photina said. Her tone made it clear what she thought of such whining. "A group that would like us to adopt many practices of the central valleys." She glanced at Tamon, then looked back at Theos. "You may think we've been sitting around, but in reality we've been working hard, trying to determine how strong each side's support is here. Figuring out who is allied with whom. If it comes to a battle, even if we won, it would still be costly to the valley, with many dead or injured. And it would be even worse if we *lost*."

Theos didn't want to think about that for too long. "They'd actually fight for this? For the right to . . . be lazier? To have more belongings than someone else?"

"That's not how they'd present it," Tamon said. "They'd say they're fighting for freedom, I expect. The freedom to succeed. They'd say they work hard, and it's unfair to take their wealth, or the wealth of their parents, and give it to people who are too stupid or lazy to earn their own."

Freedom. Yes, people might fight for that. "Are we sure they're wrong?" Theos ventured.

Tamon raised an eyebrow. "You're strong and smart. You'd do better in that sort of system. Is that what you're thinking?"

"Me? No. I'm just a soldier. But if someone *was* smarter than others, or did work harder, wouldn't they deserve a reward?"

"Maybe," Tamon said with a shrug. "But there's a Torian way to do that. We talk about ideas, and vote on them. We don't sneak around and weaken the empire from within."

"So why aren't they doing things the right way?"

"Because they know they'd lose if they did," Photina said. "If they had the support of the majority, they'd come out in the open. They're sneaking around because they know most of us *don't* want the changes. Hoarding property for themselves and treating women *like* property, to be possessed by a man? No. The majority don't want that. So the only way the warlord can hope to succeed is by stealth."

Theos felt the truth of those words. "And you're sure the warlord is involved in the sneaking part?"

Photina nodded decisively. "Yes. We're quite sure of that, now."

"Why was he trying to ship the spy back east? And was he the one who tried to help him escape tonight?"

"We think the first attempt—shipping him east—was meant to be another escape," Tamon said. "The warlord was probably going to have his men attack the traders as soon as they were away from the valley and set the Elkati free. So both were attempts to help him escape."

Photina added, "Both attempts were very risky, though. The battle at the start, and then the long travel in the winter mountains? The warlord wanted the Elkati out of our control, absolutely. We assume he was worried the boy would talk, or give in under torture. So if he couldn't get him safely away, he'd have been happy to just have him die in the attempt."

"He tried to take him from me. Tried to buy him."

"That worried us." The captain frowned. "I thought about ordering you to give him up. Or giving him to the warlord for more questioning."

"You *wanted* the warlord to have him?" This entire situation was making Theos's head spin.

"No. But we were worried that desperation might be enough to push the warlord out into the open. If he'd taken the boy from you, and you'd pushed back—which I assume you would have—it all could have exploded. We're still hoping to solve this by negotiation, and, luckily, it seems the warlord is hoping for that too."

"Unless he's just biding his time," the reeve said darkly. "He may not be ready to strike *yet*, but that doesn't mean he isn't marshaling his strength and getting ready to move. Unfortunately, we're still not sure what direction he'll move *in*."

"So the men who came tonight. The warlord sent them. And they came to kill the Elkati, you think?" Theos might be happy to kill Finnvid himself, but he didn't want anyone else doing it.

"I can't imagine they thought they could get him out of the valley, not once we'd been warned." Tamon nodded. "So, yes, I expect they came to kill him. He'd be a useful asset alive, but he's too dangerous to leave in our hands indefinitely."

"*Why*?" Theos demanded. "What's so special about him?"

Tamon and Photina exchanged a look, then Photina said, "I imagine the warlord wasn't pleased that the boy seemed to be growing close with a Sacrati. Tell me, did you get him into your bed, yet? My understanding is that bets were being taken on how long he'd hold out."

She wasn't really answering his question, but she was distracting him pretty effectively. Theos thought of the kisses. The first one had been public, for a reason he couldn't now discern. But the second had clearly been designed to mislead him. "He's a very good liar. If people thought he was warming toward me, it's because he *wanted* them to see it. I have no idea why he'd want that."

"Neither do I," Photina said. "But, whatever the reason, I can imagine the warlord seeing your apparently growing friendship and becoming concerned."

"About *what*, though?" This was the most confusing part. "What does some stupid Elkati have to do with anything? Who cares about Elkat?"

The captain's smile was bitter, but when he spoke he sounded like an old man telling a tale around a campfire. "It's usually easy for us to take over valleys. Because we're strong, yes, but also because they *make* it easy. They know we're coming, they know they have no chance of defeating us, and still they fight alone. They depend on their gods, or on some desperate chance, rather than trusting their neighbors and uniting to at least put up a good fight. We say it's because they lack leadership. It's because there's no one in any of these little valleys who's strong enough to pull them all together. And then we laugh, and we wonder whether they'll ever figure it out."

"You're saying they did?"

Tamon nodded. "They found a leader."

Theos stared. "Not that spying rat! He's . . . in ten years, maybe. But now? He's a boy!"

"No, not him. The young king of Elkat, a man named Alrik. But apparently there's a younger brother. We're told he's a handsome fellow, a bit of a scholar, who was trained in healing before he was recruited to help his brother form alliances against the Torian threat. Sound familiar?"

"He was well within our territory when we found him. Who would he have been 'forming alliances' with back here?"

Theos had thought the question was intelligent enough, but Photina looked at him almost pityingly and didn't speak.

Theos worked it through. "With the warlord?" he demanded. "That's—that's treason!"

"Not yet," Tamon said. "Not until we formally declare war on the Elkati. If that happens, and the warlord refuses to invade, or helps them in any way? *Then* it would be treason."

"Why *haven't* we declared war? If we knew this alliance was a threat, why didn't we strike quickly and end it?"

The captain grimaced. "Because the Elkati have been buying time. Emptying their coffers, and possibly those of their neighbors, sending bribes to the Torian warlords in the nearby valleys. Sending bribes back east, too, we believe."

"What's the point of taking bribes? Why not just attack and take their treasures once we've conquered them?"

"Because the proceeds of an invasion are divided up," Photina said as if it were obvious. "As a soldier, you'd get some. Your commanders would get some. A fair part of the rest would be shipped to the central valleys, some of it would go into the general coffers of our valley. But bribes? Bribes go to individuals, those who are powerful enough to postpone the invasion even if they *don't* have good reasons for it."

"But what about the central valleys? If someone misbehaves here . . . I mean, if the warlord . . . You make it sound like there could be civil war! Like he might have his men attack other Torians!" Theos waited for them to object, but they didn't. "Surely the central valleys wouldn't tolerate it. The warlord can't be planning for that, can he? There's no point in him seizing control of Windthorn for the winter if he's executed for treason in the spring!"

"The Empire doesn't much care who's in charge of the western valleys, not as long as we keep sending slaves and soldiers and tribute in their direction," the captain said with a rueful shake of his head. "And an alliance with Elkat would give the warlord the resources he'd need to send his own bribes east, enough money to take care of anyone who *does* bother to question what's happening out here."

Theos's head was spinning. "So . . ." He left the door and sank into one of the deep leather chairs by the reeve's desk. "For some time, there's been corruption in the Empire. People have been living in luxury while fellow Torians starve. The warlord here and maybe warlords in neighboring valleys wanted a taste of this. They were approached by Finnvid, or some other Elkati, and were offered bribes to hold off on invading Elkat. Then, while we hesitated, the Elkati have been building alliances in order to better defend themselves. The warlord wants to take control of Windthorn, and east isn't likely to interfere with his plan. He wants Finnvid gone or dead in order to keep us from finding out about all this." He looked up at them. "Is that it?"

Tamon nodded. "That's the big part, yes. The warlord kept us from questioning the Elkati prisoners, so we don't have as many details as we'd like. But based on what we do know? I assume the warlord would prefer to have Finnvid escape alive; it would be much harder for him to cement an alliance with the Elkati if they know their young prince died on his watch." He hesitated, then said, "I imagine that if the prince *does* die, the warlord will have someone in mind to blame. Maybe the same man who's been treating the prince like a slave . . ."

Theos nodded. He wasn't too worried about a bunch of Elkati wanting his blood. "So what's next? Is it finally time to *do* something, or will you be sitting around and waiting for a bit longer?"

"I've organized a search of the barracks, looking for a possible equipment or weapons cache to aid the escape."

"And if you find it?"

"We can try to identify the source. Examine the materials and see if there's anything distinctive about any of it."

"What about the key? There aren't many of those, are there? Couldn't you figure out whose is missing?"

"There are quite a few in circulation. And it wouldn't be hard for a locksmith to make a new one, if requested."

"So couldn't we ask the locksmiths if anyone had asked for a key to be made?"

"All this will be done," Tamon said. "We'll investigate."

"Wait," Theos said. "Who's 'we'? Who's involved in all this?"

"That's not anything you need to know," Photina said firmly. "Until things are finalized, we intend to maintain confidentiality."

Theos sighed. He was being shut out again; then he remembered that he *wanted* out of this mess. "Fine. Is that it? I'm done?"

Tamon didn't say anything, so Theos headed toward the door. "I'm sure you can handle it without me," he offered. "Maybe it's not too late for me to find a festival partner." Or at least something to drink.

"I need your help with the prisoner," Tamon said.

"Just one? There are two prisoners, aren't there?"

Photina shook her head and strode toward the exit. "No. There's one prisoner, and one honored guest of the reeve of Windthorn." She opened the door and stepped into the outer office, carrying their lantern with her. Theos could imagine the formal smile on her face as he heard her say, "Prince Finnvid, is it? I apologize for this misunderstanding. We've only recently become aware of your true identity. But now that we know you're here, we're eager to discuss a possible relationship between our valleys. I hope you haven't been too uncomfortable."

Theos whirled toward Tamon, who winced. "Divide and conquer," he muttered. "If the other valleys are allied with the Elkati and their neighbors, we can't stand against them. But if the Elkati confederacy can be persuaded to support *us* . . ."

"We're playing their games, now? Secret allies, favored friends? Will *our* allies be supported with Elkati bribes as well?" Theos frowned. "Wait. Not 'we.' Not 'our.' I'm not part of this. I stumbled into it, but now I'm out. I'm done." He turned his back on Tamon and started for the door.

He was in the outer office, ignoring Photina where she was crouched beside the Elkati, sawing at his bonds, when he heard the captain bark, "Sacrati!"

Theos froze. He was Sacrati, and this was his sworn commander. "Sir," he forced himself to say.

"You'll assist me with the prisoner," the captain said firmly as he walked into the room. "I don't expect a direct attack, but I can't be sure. I've got Galen and Andros on guard out front; call them in, and we'll get going."

"Galen and *Andros*?" Theos stared at the captain. His peripheral vision told him Photina had straightened and was watching them with interest. He tried to ignore the audience. "Andros is working with you?"

"He is."

"You've told *Andros* all this? He knew all along? About the—the alliances, and the Elkati, and . . . all of it?"

"There hasn't been an 'all along,'" the captain retorted. "We've been working it out as we go."

"But . . . 'we.' Andros is part of this."

"He is."

Theos tried to make sense of it. Andros. His friend. The one he'd complained to, joked with. The one he'd trusted. Andros was Sacrati. He was Theos's brother-in-arms. Theos had been talking things through with him, trying to figure out what was going on, while Andros had known *exactly* what was going on. But Andros hadn't trusted him with the truth, and neither had anyone else. "You trust Andros, but not me."

"Andros is easier to read," Photina said. Her voice was just as neutral as Theos's, and he wondered whether she was hiding the same turmoil. Probably not. Probably she really didn't care. She went on, "You're a loyal soldier. You do as you're told without giving much thought to why the orders were given. You need to understand, Theos: if you had known what we were up to and it had gone wrong, you could have been in direct violation of orders from the warlord. We could all end up disobeying the Empress. How would you react if you were given an order you didn't agree with? You're so well trained. So . . . dedicated. If you received an order, would you question it?"

"Would I question an order from authority?" Theos asked quietly. He glanced at the captain. "Authority like yours. I mean, the only reason I follow your orders is because of your place in the command structure. If the command structure is contaminated, corrupted, then does it still *have* authority?" Theos's brain was twisting and turning, roiling like a pit of snakes. "You think I'm too brainwashed to resist. You think I'm a trained dog who can only follow orders, not think for himself." He nodded slowly. This made sense. They'd been happy to use him, forcing him to spend time with their pet Elkati, but that didn't mean they trusted him. "Maybe I've got no mind of my own," he said. He looked at his mother, saw her impassive face, and shrugged. "Or maybe I do." The first step toward the door felt right, so he took another.

Then he half turned, just enough to catch the captain's gaze. "You can escort your own prisoner," he said. "I'm done."

And he spun sharply and strode out of the building, taking the back door because he didn't want to look at Andros's lying face.

The remains of the festival were between him and the city gates, but he didn't even glance over. He wasn't fit for any sort of company, so he headed for the drill grounds and groped around in the dark equipment shed until he found the weighted iron swords. One in each hand, he jogged to the heavy wooden beam and began his drills. Hacking, slashing, using his whole body so the metal hit the wood with maximum power. The jolts traveled up his arm and through his core, and he welcomed the numbness that soon followed. It was stupid to push too hard at a drill like this, knew he was inviting an injury, but he didn't care, and pressed on.

It took longer than it should have, but eventually he found his discipline again. He had no doubts, and no weakness. He was what he was meant to be: he was Sacrati.

But there was no ignoring the truth hidden beneath the title. He was still Sacrati; but he no longer knew what that meant.

PART II

CHAPTER 14

Finnvid lay in bed that night feeling safe for the first time in far too long. He was clean, well fed, and had some blessed privacy, without any leering or scowling Torians in his immediate personal space. He was in a soft bed, wearing a nightshirt that, while perhaps not up to Elkati standards, was at least made of something other than leather or wool. And he'd retired for the evening at *his* initiative, not because his so-called owner had decided it was time to sleep. He was free again, and fairly certain he'd be able to negotiate freedom for his men.

Everything was much brighter, so there was absolutely no reason for the restlessness that pushed him out of bed.

No reason except for the memory of Theos's face. The way the man had looked as he'd stalked away from the Sacrati captain, or worse, when he'd found Finnvid with the key at the prisoners' pen. Or even further back, the surprisingly sweet smile when he'd pulled back from Finnvid's kiss.

And, of course, his recollection of the kiss itself. Finnvid felt his body start to respond at just the hint of the memory, and quickly forced his mind from the thought. He'd been brainwashed. That was all. His time as a prisoner might not have been physically traumatic, but that didn't mean he hadn't suffered emotional strain. A few nights in civilized accommodation, some time to think and gather his resources, and everything would be back to normal.

It took him longer than it should have to fall asleep, but the next morning he slept until he roused himself, not until a brutish Torian decided it was time for him to wake. He sat up and stretched, his muscles complaining as they had every day since he'd begun exercising with Theos. That was over too, he supposed. He'd no longer have sore muscles because there was no one pushing him to work so hard.

He pulled on the clothes that had been left for him the night before and wondered where they'd come from. There was no way any self-respecting Torian male would wear something so light and soft. The shirt felt as if it would rip if Finnvid ran his fingernails over it, let alone the edge of a practice blade. He had a wardrobe full of such garments in Elkat. Would he ever wear them again without feeling effeminate?

There was a gentle tapping at his chamber door, just loud enough to catch his attention. He opened the door to find a tall young woman, her beautiful features serene and confident. This was not the cowering servant he'd expected.

"Prince Finnvid? I'm Roxa. Photina asked me to show you to the dining hall and the baths, and to wherever else you might like to go."

He nodded, and tried to remember how to make his smile gracious without seeming deferential. "Thank you. I'd appreciate your guidance."

"Are you ready to eat?"

"I could be, yes. Let me find my boots." They hadn't replaced those, he noted, and felt glad of it. These were the boots he'd worn when he left Elkat, and it was nice to have at least one thing that hadn't changed in the last month or so. He gestured toward the small room at the end of the hall. "I'll just stop off for a moment before we go too far," he added. For all their primitive culture, the Torians certainly had a way with water; the sinks and toilets in Windthorn would be the envy of the Elkati palace, and he wasn't sure he'd ever be able to explain the miracle of the bathhouse.

He shut the door behind him and leaned over the sink, splashing water on his face as he tried to stop thinking about the baths, about Theos's strong brown body soaking, or indulging in other pleasures. No, Finnvid admired the Torian engineering, not the decadent uses they had found for their inventions.

He and Roxa went outside and made their way through the bustling streets. Hardly any horses here or even oxen, but many pedestrians. All women, he realized with a start. "Are there *any* men in the city, other than me?"

Roxa said, "Right now, yes. Anyone who needs a tradesperson or who has other business is welcome to visit during the day. And if there was a threat in the valley, we'd give shelter to any men who were ill or injured. But normally, at night, it's only women. And the male children, of course."

So Finnvid was lumped in with the children and the infirm. Compared to the strength he'd seen on display at the training yards, he supposed it made sense. But he couldn't help musing about what the men were doing. Breakfast probably was over, so maybe they were running, the huge mass of them surging around like a river in spring flood. He'd been part of that, however briefly, and now . . . now he was set apart again.

Roxa continued, "And, with you here, everything's a bit different. We had two regular soldiers *and* a Sacrati guarding you last night." She shook her head, clearly amazed that any Torian would care that much about someone who wasn't strong enough to defend himself. Then she glanced over her shoulder. "They're still following us."

Finnvid whirled around. Sure enough, there were two unfamiliar men about ten paces behind him, and off to the side was Andros.

Finnvid wanted to go talk to him. Andros wasn't only a familiar face, he was a *friendly* face. He might not be pleased with Finnvid right then, but he'd always been kind to him before, and he really didn't seem like the sort to hold a grudge. Finnvid wanted to be Andros's friend, wanted to hug him in greeting and walk beside him.

But Finnvid was an ambassador now, caught between two factions of a society that was accustomed to using war to solve differences of opinion. So he made himself smile at all three men as he walked back toward them, ignoring the privacy they'd been giving him. "I was guarded overnight?" Each side protecting him from the attacks of the other, he supposed. "Thank you. I knew I felt safe, but I didn't realize all the effort that went into that."

And those were enough joint pleasantries. He wanted to find a way to speak to Andros alone, but it would be too much of a risk. "I'm hoping to meet with each of your leaders shortly," he said instead. "I'm on my way to breakfast, so after that?"

"The warlord is at your disposal," one of the soldiers replied with an attempt at a gracious bow.

Andros raised an eyebrow. "The captain is busy with various important duties. But he was planning to come up here midmorning to check in." There was no bow.

Finnvid wasn't sure which style he preferred, but it didn't matter. "Is there any point to us all meeting together? I've already spoken to both men alone, after all." Though more times with the warlord, from their initial negotiations in the wilderness to the meeting outside the laundry room a few days earlier where Finnvid had received the key and instructions for his escape.

The soldiers seemed uncertain, and Andros's shrug didn't speak of confidence either. But at least he had an answer. "I suppose it depends what your goals are. And of course you've kept your own council on that, so I couldn't begin to offer advice."

So there it was. Theos's anger might be more acute, but Andros was obviously harboring resentment as well. Finnvid didn't like it. Not just strategically, in terms of finding allies, but also personally. He wanted a friend, and that *should* be his first priority, as long as he remembered that his friends should be Elkati, not Torian.

"I want to have my men released. If we're treating my capture as a misunderstanding, then surely my men should be freed too."

Andros nodded as if he'd been expecting the request. "So you should meet with both leaders," he said. "Let them sort it all out."

Andros clearly wanted to wash his hands of it all, as Theos had tried to do so many times. But he'd been just as unable to escape Finnvid as Finnvid had been unable to escape him.

That was a thought for another time. "How do I send a request to the captain?" They'd spoken briefly the night before, and neither of them had committed to anything beyond an agreement to speak more in the future. Finnvid wasn't certain just how far he was authorized to go on his own; he'd been sent to the Windthorn valley to meet with the warlord and cement their alliance, not to start a whole new political relationship.

"I can arrange a meeting," Roxa said, inserting herself smoothly into the conversation. "And perhaps I could send an invitation to the reeve, as well? She isn't directly involved with the prisoners, but talk may move to other matters, and I'm sure she'd have a great deal to contribute."

The right path would be clearer if he knew more about the internal politics of Windthorn: how was power distributed, and what was the etiquette for these sorts of meetings? He was in over his head.

"I assume we'll be meeting in the city." Andros spoke directly to Finnvid. "So I'm sure we'd all understand if you wanted to include your host in the meeting."

It wasn't clear whether Andros was taking pity on him or if he was just arranging for his side's ally to be present, but either way, Finnvid was grateful for the suggestion. "Of course," he agreed, nodding to Roxa. "I'd appreciate it if you could set up a meeting. At everyone's earliest convenience?"

So while he ate his breakfast, alone, she went off and made the arrangements and Andros and the soldiers went back to their respectful distance. Finnvid wished he had something more to do with his time while he waited, and ended up finding his way onto the city walls, peering down through the crenellations at the barracks below. The masses of men in the drilling yards were training and working as if it were just another day.

"Looking for someone?" Andros asked from nearby. His face was impassive, but his eyes were locked on Finnvid's face.

Finnvid shook his head quickly. "No. Just . . . watching."

"Your men will have a better eye for judging our defenses," Andros said. "And they've been training with us as well. I doubt you'll see any weaknesses they haven't already uncovered."

"So there *are* weaknesses? The mighty Torians aren't invulnerable?"

Andros shrugged. "No one's successfully attacked a Torian valley in the history of the empire. I sincerely doubt that's going to change anytime soon. Your people are on the defensive, here; you won't be attacking Windthorn."

No, Finnvid thought. They wouldn't be. He didn't need to be a military strategist to realize there'd be no chance of success. "We want peace," he said firmly.

Andros snorted. "The weak always do."

"You sound like Theos."

"There are worse things."

Finnvid frowned. "When you're with him, you disagree with practically every word he says. But now that you're *not* with him, he's a source of wisdom?"

"When *you're* with him, you frown and sulk and try to escape. But now that you're not with him, you're staring over the battlements, clearly looking for someone."

"No. I'm not looking for anyone."

"Oh, there he is," Andros said, pointing to a spot quite near the wall on which they stood.

Finnvid spun to see, squinted . . . and turned more slowly back to Andros, who was smirking in satisfaction.

"Childish games," Finnvid scolded. "These are serious times. Do you really have nothing else with which to occupy yourself?"

"I'm babysitting a spy," Andros said. "It doesn't take a great deal of my attention." He stepped in a little closer. "Theos spent the night at the drilling yards, and now he's gone to ground somewhere. Sacrati train on their own initiative and schedules, so no one's going to worry about him too much. I expect he'll be avoiding us both. But if he does come near you? Be . . ." Andros frowned. "Be gentle," he finally said. "He tried to do the right thing. And if you'd been who you claimed to be, you would have been grateful for his kindness."

That was true enough. Theos had been more generous than Finnvid could have ever expected. And he'd repaid him with lies and betrayal. "I think I can do him the greatest kindness by staying away from him."

Andros nodded. "That's probably true."

They climbed down off the walls shortly after and were escorted to the reeve's office. The soldiers all stayed in the antechamber, leaving Finnvid alone with the warlord, the Sacrati captain, and the reeve. He felt young and untried in their company, but reminded himself that he was a prince, and deserved their respect. "My first priority is the freedom of my men," he said as soon as greetings were complete.

The warlord smiled. "I don't see a problem with that. Things are still up in the air, of course . . . as I told you at our earlier meeting, there are some discipline issues in our military and I can't guarantee your safety; that's why I encouraged you to keep your identity secret until you could leave the city." He glanced over at the captain and continued, "But now that your presence is being announced from the rooftops, I see no reason to maintain the illusion. I'll order your men released at once."

"And where will they stay?" the captain asked dryly.

With an expansive if somewhat unfocused wave, the warlord said, "We have room for them."

"Do we? The barracks are full . . . it's been too long since we had a war. Behind the walls, then?" The captain frowned at the reeve. "It wouldn't be my decision, of course. However, we all know the Elkati are . . . different . . . in their treatment of women. I don't think we could expect them to behave with proper respect and decorum."

Finnvid wanted to argue with that, but he wasn't sure he could. He didn't absolutely understand the Torian system himself, and he could only imagine what a common Elkati soldier would do if he discovered the city of Windthorn was full of unprotected and unmarried women. "They could camp out," Finnvid offered.

The captain shrugged. "If you think your men would be more comfortable camping in the snow than sleeping in the prisoner pens, I suppose that's your choice."

The warlord said, "If they're camping anyway, perhaps they'd like to try returning to Elkat. They're good men. Strong. And we could equip them properly."

"And I could accompany them," Finnvid said. That had been the idea behind his latest escape attempt, after all. Things were less desperate now, but spending the winter trapped behind the Windthorn walls would make him as much of a prisoner as he'd been before. "If we were careful and well provisioned, we could make it, surely."

The captain shook his head at Finnvid. "I realize you're new to Windthorn, but surely you're not new to the *world*? Do Elkati cross the mountains in winter for anything but the direst emergencies?"

"Isn't spending an entire winter in the mountains, *alone*, one of the initiation rites for Sacrati?" Finnvid demanded. "That's not a dire emergency, is it?"

"For *Sacrati*," the captain replied. "And when we do it, we're staying still. We make a camp, collect food and fuel when the weather allows, and when the weather is bad we hide in our camp and fight to survive. *Sacrati* have to work that hard." His expression made it clear that if a task was difficult for a Sacrati, it would be impossible for Finnvid.

"It hasn't been a bad winter," Finnvid argued. "If we took our time—"

"It hasn't been a bad winter *here*," the captain objected. "We have no idea what conditions are like in the peaks."

But Finnvid wouldn't be scaling the peaks. He'd suspected it when he'd traveled with the Torians before, but now he was certain. The Torians didn't know about the lower route between their valleys. Which made sense, he supposed. The Torians were new to the area; they'd conquered Windthorn only decades ago. Obviously they hadn't yet discovered all the secrets of their mountainous home, and if the natives had known, they must have kept it to themselves. The Torians hadn't found the twisting, tortuous route that had nothing to recommend it to summer travelers. But the trail stayed low, running from one narrow valley to another, and while it wasn't an *easy* trip in the winter, it would certainly be easier than taking the straighter route through the mountain passes. This was a valuable secret for the Elkati to keep, and just as valuable to know that it *was* still secret.

"If we're truly free, then we're free to make our own decisions," Finnvid said firmly. "I'll consult with my men. We'll either camp out or leave; either way, I'm afraid I'll have to impose on you for some basic equipment and supplies, but I'm sure I can arrange to have the value of whatever you can spare sent to you in the spring."

"While I'm concerned for your safety, I certainly support your right to follow your wishes," the warlord said. "I'll have your men released and you can meet them . . . Well, do you feel safe traveling to the barracks? I can arrange a guard for you, of course."

"Haven't you already?"

"A larger contingent."

Finnvid decided to push, just a little. It was because of this man's machinations that Finnvid had been kept as a slave. If Theos had decided to actually use Finnvid as a bedwarmer, the warlord wouldn't have stopped him. "I must say I'm somewhat concerned about this lack of safety. My understanding was that we were dealing with the man in charge of the Windthorn military. Since arriving here I've found that there is, in fact, a significant body of the Windthorn army *not* under your direct command, *and* I've learned you have so little control of the men that it was necessary to resort to subterfuge to secure my freedom. When we first met out in the wilderness, you suggested it was the Sacrati captain who might be hostile to me, but he's on our side and still I need guards? Who is the enemy now, Warlord?"

The captain seemed just as interested in the answer as Finnvid was, but the warlord's smile was tight and angry. "I'm afraid you've misunderstood a few things. First, the Sacrati *are* under my command. I have delegated some of my authority to the captain and he handles them day-to-day; still, I command the Windthorn army. The *entire* army." He stared at the captain as if daring him to disagree. The man stayed silent so the warlord continued. "Further . . . these are delicate times. You are safe from organized attacks because I control the organization. But someone apart from that?" Again, he glared at the captain. "Someone operating outside of the chain of command? It could be termed sedition, and anyone guilty of it would be caught and executed. Of course, that wouldn't do *you* much good, young prince, not if you already had a sword in your gut."

"And who do you suspect of this sedition?" the captain asked, his voice full of overstated concern. "Do you have evidence to suggest such a problem? How can we support you if you don't share your worries with us?"

"Enough." Finnvid was probably speaking out of turn, but he was tired of being the scrap of meat these lions fought over. "I will consult with my men and let you know whether we require supplies for camping or for traveling."

Neither man seemed pleased with the dismissal, but it was the reeve who spoke up. "Perhaps you and I could speak together, Prince Finnvid? The men are so busy with war they sometimes forget there are other aspects of life that must be considered." She smiled sweetly. "Sometimes they charge straight ahead, no matter the obstacles and danger, and fail to notice other paths."

He kept himself from staring at her. Maybe the words had been a coincidence. Maybe. But he couldn't take that chance. "Of course," he said with a smile of his own. "I'd be pleased to discuss anything that concerns you."

So the two of them waited impatiently for the warlord and captain to depart. After a moment, the men shuffled off, and the reeve crossed to the door and watched them leave the outer office before turning to him. "My shepherds spend a lot of time in the mountains in the summer," she said simply. "They sometimes find interesting things, and report back to me."

He nodded, and she smiled again, though without a trace of friendship or joy. "I'd like to see you and your men safely out of Windthorn before you can stir up any more trouble," she said. "But I'm not inclined to let you leave if you're going to go back with news of an alliance that doesn't suit my purpose." She crossed the room and sat in one of the large leather chairs by the desk, and then patted the seat next to her. "Come," she invited. "We'll talk. We'll decide what's best for everyone involved. And when we're done, we'll make the captain and the warlord think it was all their idea." Another smile, this time more genuine, before she added, "That's the Torian way."

CHAPTER 15

"**S**o, what do *you* think is best for everyone?" Finnvid asked cautiously. There was something about this woman that put him on guard. He had a sudden, reckless urge to introduce her to his mother; he suspected they would either be good friends or instantly set about trying to have the other assassinated.

"Well, as in all cases, I start by deciding what's best for the women. They are the people I serve. The men?" She waved a dismissive hand. "They'll do as they're told."

"The captain and the warlord will do as they're told?"

She shrugged. "Eventually. I can be patient." She frowned at him. "But you, apparently, cannot. I don't care what route you take, it's still dangerous to travel in the wintertime. And as far as I'm concerned, you'd be going home with a job unfinished. You were sent here to establish an alliance with the leader of Windthorn, were you not? You thought that person would be the warlord." She leaned back in her chair and her eyes glinted. "You were wrong."

Finnvid had seen enough interactions between the reeve and the others to know she had a point. "But he's the *military* leader. Correct? At this point, our primary concern is preventing an invasion, which would be a military issue. We'd certainly be interested in establishing trade later on; I saw some lovely crafts at the market the other day that I'm sure could find a home in Elkat. However—"

"You think that's what I'm in charge of? *Crafts?*" She caught herself. "Of course, I'm very proud of my sisters' work in that area. But I'm in charge of *everything* that doesn't directly involve men marching around and killing each other. The food they eat whether they're in the barracks or off fighting? My farmers and hunters provide it. The weapons they carry? My miners find and refine the ore and then my blacksmiths forge the weapons and armor. And just as important? The young soldiers, the boys who will replace those who die in the campaigns? My women provide *those*, as well."

Finnvid nodded. Phrased that way, she did have more power than he'd been giving her credit for. But still . . . "They could *take* all those things, if they decided to. Right? I mean, the Torian army? Nobody stands up to the Torian army."

She snorted. "Nobody stands up to a Torian mother, either." She seemed amused by his surprise. "There have been, to my knowledge, three attempts by Torian warlords to seize control of the cities they were sworn to protect. In all three situations, there was an immediate mutiny as soon as the orders were given. No planning, no negotiations or power brokering. The men simply refused to raise their swords to the women who'd given them life. The women who *still* gave them life, through food and clothing and medicine." She shook her head. "The men will never attack the city. That is a guarantee."

Finnvid thought of Theos, surely one of the more aggressive Torian males, and tried to remember any word of his that had been less than respectful toward the women of the valley. Any suggestion that he might resent them or feel they were too powerful. There had been none, Finnvid was quite sure. As inexplicable as it all was to his Elkati mind, he had to believe what the woman was saying. And that meant he needed to take a different approach. "So . . . yes. I *did* misjudge the power structure. My job *is* unfinished. Tell me, please, Reeve: what are your interests in the matter? What will be best for your women?"

She smiled. "We like it the way it is," she said firmly. "I've traveled. I've seen how women are treated elsewhere—*including* in the Elkat valley. Treated *only* as mothers? Tied to one man, often one chosen by a parent rather than the woman herself? Isolated in their homes, given no voice or power of their own? No. My women don't want that. There's no amount of luxury that would make up for a lack of freedom."

"Is that—is that something you think might happen?"

"No, because I won't *allow* it to happen. Not here. Which means I need to be on my guard. I've traveled to the east too, and seen the way things are starting to go back there. I might wish our Windthorn men were less obsessed with war, but I have to admit it keeps them busy. In the central valleys, those with no battles to distract them, the men have turned to domestic affairs, and are trying to take over women's concerns. Now that they've seen the potential for accumulating wealth, they're spending all their time worrying about *that*. I've heard some of them are already agitating for one man per woman, just so they can keep better track of whose children are theirs. They want to train the next wave of *businessmen*, and they want to be sure the fortunes they've hoarded stay together, in the hands of one of their own children."

Finnvid wasn't sure he agreed with all the conclusions she'd drawn, but he couldn't argue with what she'd seen. "So you want your men to go to war with Elkat to distract them from what you're doing?"

She frowned. "I'm not quite that hard-hearted. And I don't care about them going to war, with Elkat or anyone else." She leaned forward as if telling him a secret. "One of the reasons the men give for protecting the women as they do is that we are needed for reproduction. They say that the Torian war machine needs fuel, in the shape of young recruits."

He nodded cautiously. Theos had explained things the same way.

She leaned back with a satisfied smirk. "We actually have *fewer* babies per woman than most nations, because the women control reproduction. I have five children, and that's actually a bit higher than average. Our women are strong and healthy and not exhausted from constant pregnancies, so we have a good survival rate for our young, but in terms of actual numbers, we don't have that many. And we could have even fewer, if our men stopped getting themselves killed in wars."

"I know a Torian who has forty-six children, with two more on the way. And he's still quite young."

She nodded. "Theos is very popular. However, there are other men who have no children, or only one. We track fertility through the women, not the men."

"But you knew which man I was referring to, just because I mentioned the number of children?"

"Those children are my grandchildren," she said quietly. "Theos is my only son, so it's not too hard for me to keep track."

Theos's mother. The Sacrati had *said* his relationship with his mother was difficult, but surely this went beyond "difficult." "You have a son who could die in a war between our valleys, but you're not concerned whether one starts or not?"

"I have one son. I have *four* daughters. And Theos?" She sighed. "Theos has been looking for a heroic death since he was old enough to crawl toward danger. War or peace, he'll find a way to die young. There's nothing I can do about that."

Finnvid stared at her. He wasn't sure if he was more horrified by the idea of strong, vibrant Theos dying, or by the reeve's apparent indifference to his fate. "Maybe he just needs something to *live* for! Maybe his energy could be redirected, if he found the right reason."

She raised an eyebrow at him. "Well, I'd certainly like to thank you for all you've done in that regard. Losing his rank and his faith in his leader and friends? I'm sure that's gone a long way toward giving him a reason to live. Not to mention whatever went on between the two of you personally."

She held his eyes for a moment, then smiled, clearly serene in the knowledge that her point had been made. "So. Neither one of us has been able to do much for Theos. But I want my women content and free, and that will be most probable if we can hold off any attempts to 'reform' or 'modernize' the Torian system that has served us so well. I'm confident that the Sacrati captain shares my goals in that area, and I therefore support him. I am much less confident about the warlord. It's very troubling that he hid your presence from the rest of us for as long as he did, and I certainly don't like hearing that he was meeting with you behind our backs. So, Elkati prince . . . I will support your nation's quest for peace, if you will support my goal of maintaining the traditional Torian way of life."

She watched him closely as she added, "What's more, I have been in communication with the reeves of Cragview and Greenbrook, and they agree with me in principle. They do not support any changes to the Torian system. If they feel that Elkat is their ally in this, they will be inclined toward peace with your valley."

The room was quiet for a moment, both of them waiting for what came next. "And of course," the reeve said, "if any of us see Elkat as a problem . . . if we find that Elkat has made alliances with factions from our valleys that threaten to upset the lives we currently enjoy . . . then we will urge our men to respond to the threat. And as I'm sure you know, our men respond to threats in only one way."

She relaxed back into her chair and gave him another peaceful smile. "You made a mistake, dealing with the warlord instead of with me. But now you have a chance to rectify that mistake. I suggest you take advantage of the opportunity."

She was clearly done with him, which was just as well because he had no idea how to reply. So he stood up and bowed formally; the reeve inclined her head in return. "Go see your men," she said, as if sending a boy to look at a litter of puppies. "But don't take them anywhere. Not until you've come to say good-bye."

It wasn't quite an order, but it was close. "I certainly wouldn't want to leave without thanking you for your hospitality," he agreed mildly.

When he left the outer office, he found Andros and the other two soldiers waiting for him in the hallway. "I'd like to go see my men," Finnvid told them. He realized he was talking mostly to Andros, hoping for some renewal of their familiarity. "Do I really need a larger contingent of guards?"

Andros shrugged. "Who's after you?"

"I have no idea. No one, I hope."

"If no one's after you, you don't need guards at all." He looked over at the other soldiers. "I'd say we're here to keep an eye on you, not to guard you."

"Theos isn't babysitting me anymore, so you are?"

Andros ignored the question. "Which means we're probably enough, but if you want more, I can arrange it."

"No, I don't want more." He wanted less. Strange as it was, he wanted to go back in time, just a little. The day of the festival had been good, walking through the city with Theos, sampling foods, talking . . . and all the while, Finnvid's duplicitous mind had been split between enjoying the present and planning for the future. Planning for his escape that night.

No. If he was going to go back in time, he'd go back to the day before they were captured, so he could change their route and avoid all the confusion and doubt that had come from spending time with his enemies. But there was something in this idea that didn't feel right. *Would* he want to erase the time he'd spent with the Torians? With Theos?

The questions were a stupid distraction. He couldn't go back in time; he could only go forward. He could get out of Windthorn and back to his old life and he could make himself forget the strange feelings. But the reeve had been right: he needed to finish his job here first.

By the time he and his escort arrived at the training yards, his men were gathered. Finnvid gestured for the Torians to stay behind, and he approached his men alone. He'd caught glimpses of them training with the regular soldiers as he'd worked under Theos's direction, but he'd rarely gotten close. And they'd been returned to the pens every night, locked up after their efforts while he bathed and ate hot meals.

As they saw him approach, they clearly realized something was going on, and when he drew close enough for them to notice his new clothes, he saw several nods of approval. Torians might like their leaders down in the dirt with them, but Elkati preferred that distinctions be maintained.

At least, some of them did. A few of the others looked a little less happy to see him in his changed state. He ignored their reactions for the moment, and strode forward to grasp Gunnald's forearm in greeting.

The old man beamed at him. "About time," he said gruffly. "What'd you have to do to free us?"

Nothing. Finnvid had done nothing. The one time Finnvid had tried to stage an escape, he'd gotten one of his men killed.

Killed by Theos, he reminded himself. He needed to remember that sort of thing. And he needed to pay attention to the current conversation. "I didn't have to do much," he admitted, but he made it sound like he was joking. "I think they were just glad to be rid of you."

"Tired of us showing them up at their training," Gunnald said.

"That must be it." Finnvid moved then, circulating among the men in greeting, and checking on their health.

"They took good care of us," Hrodi said. "And the training?" He looked at his fellows and shook his head in amazement. "We need to take their system back with us. There's so much more we could be doing."

"You think anyone at home would put up with all that?" Nasi demanded. "We were *forced* to do it, and their recruits are brainwashed into it. But no sane, free man would train as hard as these Torians do."

"I guess that's why they're the best," replied Hrodi. "While we're . . . What are we? Just soldiers, and not even for a *good* army."

"Enough," Gunnald barked, as if he was used to breaking up this sort of debate. Apparently Finnvid wasn't the only one whose perspective had been changed by his time with the Torians. Gunnald continued, "Your prince is here, and he doesn't want to hear that sort of disloyalty." He turned back and said, "Is there a plan, sir? Have you heard from your brother?"

"No message," Finnvid said. "But, yes, the beginning of a plan." He raised his voice enough to address all the men. "I need your opinions, though. We've been offered hospitality here for the winter . . . to an extent. Apparently they're low on space. I offered to have us camp out, though I expect they'll come up with something a bit better than that, if they're given a little time. The other option is to head for home. It's a horrible time of year, but . . ." He lowered his voice. "We Elkati have our secrets."

"We could be home by the late-winter holidays," one man said, amazement in his voice.

"Or frozen in a snowbank until spring thaw," another countered.

"I may not be able to give you the choice," Finnvid said with sufficient volume to regain their attention. "I'm still working through things with the Torians. But think about it, and if you have a preference, be ready to share it if I ask you."

The men nodded, and Finnvid gestured with his chin, drawing Gunnald away from the others.

"May not have been wise to give them the choice, sir," Gunnald said when they were safely out of hearing range. "Once you let them think for themselves, they don't like to stop doing it. Generally better to *tell* them rather than ask them. Sir."

Finnvid knew that was the Elkati way. The way he'd been raised, and more importantly, the way the *men* had been raised. But surely they'd all seen Theos interacting with his men. There had been some orders, certainly, yet there had also been comradeship and consultation. Finnvid squinted at Gunnald and thought about bringing all that up. Instead he nodded. "I thought I'd give it a try," he said. "But . . . I hope they want to go. The political situation here is unstable. I think we should lay a foundation of partnership with all parties and then get out before we're forced to choose sides or get too deeply involved. We can come back in the spring and see who's in charge."

"And they'll let us leave?" Gunnald asked skeptically.

"Most of them seem thrilled by the possibility. I don't find them a terribly political people, at least not compared to our intrigues. While I'm here they're forced to think about things they'd rather ignore; much easier to send me home with messages of tentative friendship."

Gunnald still didn't look convinced. "They're *Torians*. All they know is war. 'Tentative friendship' is not part of their mindset."

"I don't think they're as warlike as we've been led to believe," Finnvid said. "And it seems like they've got quite a few serious internal issues they're trying to sort out; when they've got that resolved we might be in trouble again, but at least we'll have bought ourselves some time. We can start the training the men were discussing, build our defenses—from the sound of things, the Torian Empire still expands on its borders, but there isn't much support from the center anymore. Some soldiers are sent from the western front to the east, apparently, but the main government is more or less out of the conquering business; it's mostly individual valleys doing the work now. So there isn't really one single Torian mindset, not in the way we've always thought."

"This is what they told you? And you believe them?" Gunnald scoffed.

Finnvid bit back harsh words. Gunnald was a valuable family advisor, sent along to support Finnvid on his first mission. He'd known Finnvid since he was a baby, and maybe he still thought of him that way. Annoying, but not worth getting angry about. "Can you think of a reason for them to lie?"

"So we distract ourselves trying to promote peace while they arrange a surprise attack."

"Torians aren't known for their subtlety. They generally give *lots* of warning of their attacks; did you realize that more than a third of the time valleys surrender without a fight?"

"*We* won't surrender without a fight, and they know that."

"They also know we post sentries all through the mountains on our side of the border in marching season. They could sneak a few men by, probably, but a full attack-force? No, not with only a few possible paths for them to take." This felt right. "I appreciate your caution, Gunnald, but I don't think they're planning a surprise attack. And if they were, surely they'd be more likely to kill us all than to send us home to join the defense forces."

Gunnald didn't seem to have a counter argument. Finnvid was just about to turn the conversation toward the practicalities of a winter trip home when he noticed a familiar shape looming from the crowd of Torians jogging past. Even among the physically masterful Sacrati, there was something about Theos that made him stand out. He was tall, but not the tallest; his shoulders were wide, but not the widest. Yet somehow he seemed to be *more* than all the others. More intense, more vital, more . . . something Finnvid couldn't put in words. But he couldn't deny its impact on him either. He hadn't even realized he'd stepped forward until he felt Gunnald's fingers wrap around his biceps and pull him back.

Still, the Sacrati had seen him. Several of them gave him smiles, others looked at him and then over at Theos, as if waiting for a reaction.

But Theos gave them nothing. He gave *Finnvid* nothing. His eyes stayed locked on the path ahead and his body didn't slow. He ran right by, as if Finnvid didn't even exist.

Finnvid stared after them, and then Gunnald tossed an arm over his shoulders. "You'll get past it," he said comfortingly. "The best thing to do is forget about the whole thing. Whatever that animal did, it's nothing to do with *you*."

"He did nothing," Finnvid protested.

Gunnald nodded. "Good. Yes. He did nothing."

Finnvid didn't argue anymore. "What would we need to travel safely?" he asked instead. Better to focus on practical matters. There was nothing to be done about Theos.

CHAPTER 16

His men wanted to go home, and Finnvid wasn't inclined to argue with them. He went to see each of the Torian leaders individually, assuring them that Elkat wished for peace with all, carefully committing to nothing. He told them he'd speak to his brother, and they'd send emissaries early in the spring. He told the warlord that of course the Elkati were interested in supporting their friends in Windthorn, and he told the Sacrati captain and the reeve that Elkat valued tradition but hoped there might be room for a few minor changes in order to make everyone happy.

He knew they all resented him for pushing his nose into their business, and he had to agree that none of it was his concern. But they'd approached him as factions, not as a united front, and they clearly wanted him to choose a side. He'd come to realize that the main benefit of an Elkat alliance was the supply of bribes; if the warlord could give gifts to his supporters, funded by Elkat coffers, he could buy loyalty. He wanted that, and the other two wanted to make sure it didn't happen. So the captain and the reeve weren't so much interested in an alliance for themselves as they were in making sure there was no alliance for the warlord.

It was exhausting. After each meeting, Gunnald stayed behind a little longer, tidying up whatever messes Finnvid had created, and Finnvid would find himself pacing around, running over the mental exercises Theos had taught him, the tools to focus his mind. He needed as much focus as he could find.

On the last night, he slept in his warm city room while his men camped on the hard floor of the barracks dining hall, complaining that they'd had better accommodations in the prisoner pens. Bright and early the next morning, Finnvid ate, dressed in layers of warm clothes, and said good-bye to the city of Windthorn.

But when he made his way to the barracks, he found more men waiting for him than he'd expected; all of them were dressed for a long winter expedition, all carrying packs of supplies. He saw Theos, off to one side, and Andros off on the other; it was the Sacrati who'd been made iyatis in Theos's place who stepped forward to greet Finnvid. "Sir," Ekakios said with an efficient salute. "Your escort is ready."

"My escort?" He looked at his own men, then back at Ekakios. "I believe I *have* an escort."

Another man joined the conversation, this one unfamiliar to Finnvid. "The warlord wishes to ensure your safety. After all, the last time you traveled unescorted on Torian lands, things did not go smoothly." He nodded a more official greeting and said, "I am Zenain, leader of the Torian troops on this mission."

Ekakios's smile was tight. "And you know me, sir. I am the iyatis for this band of Sacrati."

Jockeying for position already. The rivalry in the Torian valley was coming with them into the mountains. And more importantly, the *men* from the Torian valley were coming with them, meaning that Finnvid could not take the warmer, safer route without exposing a valuable secret. "That really isn't necessary," Finnvid said. Then, a little more strongly, he added, "I would prefer to travel alone."

"Unadvisable, sir." It was Gunnald joining in, and Finnvid wanted to strike him. This was the downside of looking for feedback from his men, he supposed; they would sometimes give it at inappropriate times. Gunnald continued, "We should accept the escort. They can carry more supplies, and they're trained in winter survival."

"Yes," Finnvid said tightly. Then he scowled fiercely, trying to remind Gunnald of the secret route.

But he didn't get the chance because that was when Theos stepped into their circle. He spoke only to Ekakios, as if the others were beneath his notice, and even to the iyatis his voice was bored and close to insolent. "The princeling doesn't want us to discover one of his many secrets."

Finnvid jerked in surprise, wondering how he'd given himself away, but Theos still wasn't looking in his direction. Instead, the

Sacrati gestured toward one of the other well-bundled men, and it was only when Finnvid turned his full attention toward the figure that he realized it wasn't a man at all. "I was summoned to the city late last night, for less pleasant reasons than usual," Theos drawled. "The reeve told me there's a valley route to Elkat. This is Apala, who knows the way. The Elkati were trying to keep the path secret so they could use it for their spying."

"This information should have come through the warlord," Zenain blustered.

Theos barely shrugged. "Take it up with the reeve."

"And is that why *you* were chosen for this mission?" Zenain sneered. "To report back to your darling mother?"

"You'll have to talk to Ekakios about why I'm along," Theos said, picking casually at a seam on his heavy coat. "I certainly tried my best to get out of the job."

Finnvid tried to regroup. "We had no intention of using the route for spying." He wasn't sure if anyone believed him or not. "But, yes, we *did* prefer that it remain unknown. As it's too late for that, though, yes, we know the route. We don't require a guide, or an escort. And I don't think it's a good idea for a young lady to travel with ... well, with a group of soldiers. I can't guarantee that she won't be—"

"*I* can," Theos growled. He turned to the Elkati men and raised his voice loud enough for them all to hear. "Apala is a Torian woman, under Torian protection. Anyone who lays a hand on her without her permission will lose his hand. Anyone who touches her with any other body part, without her permission, will lose that body part. She's not here for your disgusting, immoral, unnatural ways." He still didn't look at Finnvid, even after echoing his words so accurately. He kept his gaze on the Elkati soldiers, fierce and proud and unyielding. "By the Sacrati sword," he vowed, thumping a fist over his heart for emphasis.

And the Sacrati in the group, even Ekakios, thumped their own chests and declared, "By the sword."

There was silence for a moment. Finnvid honestly couldn't guess at the other men's reactions, but he knew what he was feeling. Envy. To be part of a group like that. To live by a code of honor, even one enforced by threats and violence. To make an oath and know that there were men standing behind you, swearing their own oaths in your support. Theos was strong on his own, but with these men on his side, surely he was invincible. Finnvid tried to imagine standing in the Great Hall of the Elkat castle and making such a spectacle of himself, especially over the safety of a common-born woman. He'd be laughed out of the room.

But he was with Torians, and they did things differently. He cleared his throat and spoke into the silence. "So she's safe." He turned to Apala. "At least from the men. All the same, this will be a dangerous road, even through the southern valleys. It would be better for you to stay at home. It's an unnecessary risk for you to accompany us."

She didn't look to Theos or anyone else for guidance, just gave her own laconic shrug. "I'd be more than happy to stay by the fire. But I've been shepherding in these mountains since I was old enough to walk out at lambing season. I know them as well as any and much better than most. You and your men may know the Elkat side of things, but I know the Torian side. I'm here to help you with that."

"And the plan is to accompany us to the border?" Finnvid asked, turning his attention back to Zenain. He couldn't really think of a way to absolutely refuse an escort while they were on Torian lands.

Zenain nodded. "As I said, the warlord wants to avoid any further incidents."

"Well, then," Finnvid said, trying to sound jovial, "let's get started!"

They spread out along the wide, snow-packed road and started moving. Theos walked beside Apala; maybe he wasn't sure his threat was quite enough to keep her safe, or maybe he was still angry at Andros. Theos and the woman didn't seem to be talking much, but sometimes company could be good even without conversation.

And, Finnvid was reminded as he tried to listen to the inane pleasantries Zenain and Gunnald were exchanging, sometimes conversation could ruin company. He wished they would shut up. Theos had just bent down and said something to Apala, something that made her smile at him, and Finnvid hadn't been able to hear what it was.

Not that he should care. Not that he *did* care. Damn it, he was acting like . . . well, he wasn't sure what he was acting like. Certainly not like a prince, not like a man entrusted with conducting important foreign relations for his endangered valley.

So Finnvid ran the political situation over in his head a few more times. He didn't come to any new conclusions, but he decided he was doing the right thing, getting back to Elkat to report on the new developments.

When they reached the sentry post, they stopped long enough for Zenain and Ekakios to speak to the men on duty, and for the Torians to collect their little leather bags, then carried on.

It should have felt momentous, but it didn't. There was no great sense of relief at their escape, and Finnvid didn't feel anything from his men, either. The truth was, being a Torian prisoner really hadn't been that bad.

It could have been. If the warlord hadn't protected the men from interrogation, or if Theos had been a different sort of man. Everything could have been much worse for all of them. But as it was, they were leaving relative safety behind, heading into danger that couldn't be controlled by strategy or human decency.

It was a sobering thought. Sixteen Elkati, twelve Torian regulars, and twelve Sacrati, plus an innocent Torian shepherdess, facing weeks in the harsh, icy wilderness just because Finnvid had said so. He hoped they wouldn't regret following him.

The dusting of snow on the valley floor turned into knee-high drifts as they started climbing the slope of the mountain, and soon the Torians broke out the oversized, sinew-latticed "snow flats" that they strapped to the bottom of their boots for easier walking in deep snow. They'd insisted on supplying a pair for all the Elkati travelers, and there was a bit of a break as Finnvid and his soldiers discovered how to walk with their feet wider apart and without catching their toes with every step. After this, the Torians took turns blazing the trail, moving in a slow shuffling jog which seemed effortless to them but left Finnvid struggling to keep up.

There was more jockeying for position around midday when Zenain decided it was time to stop for lunch and gave the order without consulting Gunnald or Ekakios. The Torian regulars unslung their packs and started to find food while Finnvid's men looked torn and the Sacrati watched in amusement. They'd been snacking as they marched, Finnvid had noticed; he'd seen Theos sharing food with the shepherdess. And they were probably too fit to need a break from simple walking.

"You're on Torian land," Zenain said to Gunnald. "You're our guests, yes, but guests eat when the meals are served, not when it suits them."

"This isn't an ideal place to stop," Ekakios observed. "Prime avalanche territory . . . see how there's no trees?"

"This isn't avalanche weather!" Zenain snapped at him.

Finnvid thought he was right, but Ekakios just shrugged. "The Sacrati will scout ahead." He gestured across the open slope where they were perched, to where the trees started growing again. "We'll see what the trail looks like. And if the snow comes down, maybe we'll be able to dig you out."

"Fine," Zenain sneered. "Suit yourselves."

Finnvid wished there was a way he could go with the Sacrati. He wasn't worried about an avalanche, but he was pretty sure he'd prefer their company.

Not that they wanted his. At least, Theos certainly didn't, and even though he was no longer the formal leader of the group, the others were apparently following his example. After their initial greeting, they'd kept away from him, keeping to themselves and treating him like an outsider. Still, they'd once been friendly, if not quite friends.

He turned back to his own men and saw one of them watching the shepherdess as she bent to pull something out of her pack. The man noticed Finnvid scowling at him and quickly averted his eyes.

Finnvid felt almost guilty as he swiveled his head toward Theos and saw the man watching the exchange. Theos's frown seemed to be directed at Finnvid as much as at the errant Elkati soldier, and Finnvid returned the expression. He wouldn't take responsibility for a man happening to glance at an attractive woman, and if Theos didn't like it, that was Theos's problem.

His indignation allowed him to turn his back on the departing Sacrati and hunt through his pack for his own food. The Torians made a sort of biscuit, mostly just corn flour held together with fruit and animal fat, that they swore by for winter travel. But as much as Finnvid trusted the Torian expertise on all things practical, he couldn't bring himself to eat the "cakes." He'd tried it twice, back in the city when the supplies were being put together, and had gagged as soon as his teeth sank into the gritty lard. He'd seen the other Elkati react the same way. The cakes might have everything their bodies needed to stay healthy in winter conditions, but they wouldn't do much good if the Elkati couldn't get the food into their stomachs. So he'd filled his pack with dried food and hoped for the best.

After their short break they set out again, the Torians seemingly inexhaustible, the Elkati starting to drag. By the time they reached a clearing in the forest and paused to regroup, Finnvid decided it was time for him to look after his men, and himself. "This seems like a good camping site," he observed, careful to speak to the air somewhere between Zenain and Ekakios. "And the sun's getting low. Should we stop here and set up camp?"

Both men grudgingly agreed, and the Sacrati almost immediately disappeared into the woods, spread out in various directions, apparently on some secret mission. They were away longer than the firewood they returned with justified, but Finnvid was too happy to see the start of a fire to think about them too much.

He helped Gunnald set up the tent they'd agreed to share. It had been scavenged from the equipment the Elkati had been carrying when they'd been captured, so at least he knew what he was doing with it. He sensed some of the Torians watching him and the other Elkati with curiosity, and it soothed his pride. The Torians might be physically superior, but they weren't innovators. They were probably still sleeping in tents that were little more than a canvas thrown over a tree-tied rope. The Elkati tents were carefully designed, vastly superior—

Then he noticed that the Torians weren't setting up tents at all. They'd made a long, narrow fire down the centre of the clearing, nestled some snow-filled cookpots into the flames, and now they were just sitting around. Well, no. A couple of them were busy, working away with shovels and the snow.

Andros approached him carefully, almost reluctantly. "The tents are fine," he said, "as long as it doesn't get too cold or windy. But if we hit a storm, you'll all have to den up. Do you know what that means?"

Finnvid stared at the digging men. They were making man-sized tunnels in the snow . . . "You're going to *sleep* in those?"

"Snow's a good insulator. It's nice to have a tent or two so there's somewhere with space to move that's out of the wind. But for sleeping, we den up."

"You stay warm by burying yourselves in snow?"

"Aye. When we stay in one place for a while—like for our Sacrati initiation—we build a whole house out of snow, and it's warm enough to strip down and bathe in, and to sleep in with just a couple blankets. Quite comfortable, really." Andros kicked at the white stuff on the ground. "Horrible for traveling through, but very useful for living in. 'A winter without snow is a cold winter indeed.'"

"We have the same expression," Finnvid said. "But I think we mean it differently."

Andros shrugged. "So, den up," he concluded. "We can show you how. Also . . ." He lowered his voice a little. "Good job earlier. Suggesting the campsite." He made a face in the direction of the Torian leaders. "I think those two are going to be a bit of a problem. Playing games, competing . . . there's no energy to spare for that nonsense. If your men or you need a break, *you* need to call for it. If anything else needs to be decided, you decide it. Don't get sucked into their games. Aye?"

"Aye," Finnvid agreed. "But . . . well, I know when my men are tired. But I don't know enough about winter travel to be in charge of any real decisions."

"We'll try to give you suggestions," Andros said. "Quietly, though."

"*We?*" Finnvid asked. He tried not to sound pathetically hopeful. And it *was* pathetic, this desperate need he had for Theos's approval, or for any sort of contact with the man. Even the frown from earlier had been *something*, because Theos had at least acknowledged Finnvid's existence.

Andros just raised an eyebrow. "The Sacrati. All of us." He glanced toward his group, then turned back to Finnvid. "But leave Theos alone. He's wound too tight right now. No room for extra aggravation."

"He appears happy enough," Finnvid said as Theos laughed at whatever the shepherdess was saying.

"It's an act." Andros's eyes were downcast. "When Theos really laughs, it's practically silent. Just a little huff of breath and a smile. This . . . this is for show."

Finnvid stared at the man next to him. There'd been something about the way he spoke . . . "You love him." The words should seem absurd when talking about one man's feelings for another, but somehow they weren't.

Andros looked away quickly. "Of course. He's my brother."

"No, not like that. Not because you're both Sacrati. He's special to you—" Suddenly, Andros's expression made Finnvid realize it might be cruel to continue. "Listen to me, pretending to know about these things!" He made his smile bright. "So, the tents are suitable for tonight. And as they're already constructed we'll leave them, I think. But tomorrow the men and I will learn to den up."

Andros nodded, clearly relieved to be back to business. "Good. And you'll keep the idiots from killing each other, or from getting any of us killed because they're too busy arguing to do their jobs." He stopped for a second, then grinned a little as he added, "And you'll keep your men away from Apala, and you'll keep yourself away from Theos. You'll learn to sleep while buried in a snowbank, and by the sword, we'll have you eating cakes before this trip is over. You'll keep up with the trained soldiers on a winter march, and you'll let your second do his job without letting him take over yours. And while you're at it, maybe you could compose a nice song for us to sing as we walk, and make some crafts out of fallen pine cones and bits of bear dung. I'll teach you sword fighting in the morning breaks, and help you with hand-to-hand combat after dinner." He glanced at the fire, then quickly back at Finnvid. "Did I mention that you should prepare the dinner, then serve it and clean up as well?"

It felt good. That little bit of acknowledgment, just knowing that someone *saw* the challenges Finnvid was facing. "I'll see what I can do," Finnvid said lightly.

Andros clapped him on the shoulder. "I'm sure you'll do well." Then he left, going back to the easy comradeship of the Sacrati fire while Finnvid stared at his tent, and realized that the walls he'd thought would protect him were worth nothing at all.

CHAPTER 17

Despite his frustrations, Finnvid slept well that night, and woke the next day ready for walking. Which was a good thing, because that was all they did. Even taking the lower route there were hills to climb and descend and a lot of snow to fight through, and though he hiked in the middle of the pack with the Torians breaking the trail ahead of him, his thighs were trembling by the time they stopped for a midday rest. The day before had been the warm-up, but now the Torians were in marching mode, and they were tireless.

Finnvid knew Andros was watching him and the other Elkati, and felt a flash of hope when he saw the Sacrati speak quietly to his patrol leader. He was too proud to admit his weakness, but not too proud to have someone else point it out.

He tried not to look pathetic when Andros came over to him after the conversation. "Stretch," the Sacrati said gently. "Any time we stop for a break, make sure you keep moving at least a little. And stretch your muscles out. Otherwise they'll freeze up and you'll have trouble starting again."

That wasn't quite the news Finnvid had been wishing for, and as soon as he realized it, he felt ashamed. This whole trip had been his idea. No one had forced him to walk home in the wintertime, and no one had told him it would be easy. It was his second day on the trail and he was already wishing they could take more breaks? Spend more time in the wilderness, where a blizzard could strike at any moment?

"Thank you," he said to Andros. "And . . . do you have any ideas for eating the cakes? I just . . . the texture . . ."

"Start small," Andros said easily. "And eat them with something else. You've got dried fruit, right? A nibble of cake with a chunk of apple to begin with, and then gradually start eating more cake, less apple." He grinned. "I've been eating them since I was a kid, so I've never had a problem. But when we get new recruits from outside the Empire, that's what they do."

"Thank you," Finnvid said again. He wondered how many kindnesses this man had already shown him, and how many more were to come. "Andros," he said slowly. It might be a mistake, but he needed to be honest. "The snakebite . . . when I . . . you know . . ."

"When you saved my life?"

"Well . . . about that." He was too far in to quit. "I just— I didn't have a treatment for the snakebite. Theos threatened to kill my men if I didn't cure you, but . . . I didn't know what I was doing. I just . . . I mean, I treated the symptoms. I wasn't just feeding you bitter water. But, you know, in terms of an actual *cure* . . ."

There wasn't even a tense moment. Andros had started smiling partway through Finnvid's stammered explanation, and by the end he had thrown his head back and was laughing. "You didn't save my life! I'm too tough to die!"

"I may have *helped*. Maybe."

Andros looked over toward Theos and his expression darkened a little. "I wish I could tell him. But the mood he's in, it'd be one more example of Elkati trickery." He sighed. "And probably a sign of my deceptiveness, too, daring to recover just to give you a better story."

"I'm sorry," Finnvid said. Not only for pretending to be a better healer than he was, but for everything going on between Andros and Theos, for the tension between the Sacrati and the other Torian soldiers . . . for all of it. For the disruption of his presence in their lives. Then he thought about the disruption to Elkati lives if something hadn't been done to keep the Torians away, and he stopped feeling guilty in favor of being confused. Nothing was as simple as it had seemed months earlier when his brother had sent him on a mission to meet with the warlord of the barbarian invaders.

"I may need more breaks," he said, surprising himself with the confession. "I'll work as hard as I can, I promise. But . . . I'm not as fit as you are. Not even as fit as the other Elkati."

"I'm going to take most of your pack," Andros said as if it had already been decided. "We can leave the tents behind, with your permission. And I'll distribute the rest of the weight among the Torians. We'll take some of your men's gear too. I can tell the Torians it's training. Or maybe turn it into a contest between the Sacrati and the others, to see who can carry more."

"I don't want to be a burden."

"It would break our Torian hearts if you were able to keep up. You'll be doing us a service if you allow us to continue feeling superior."

Finnvid let himself agree, and as the day dragged on, he was glad of it. The Torians grumbled but didn't actually seem too put out, and the Elkati were sufficiently tired to swallow their pride and accept the help. Even with his lighter pack, by the time the sun was low enough for Finnvid to feel justified in suggesting they stop for the night, he could barely feel his legs. He carefully stretched his muscles, but knew he'd be sore the next day.

The Sacrati dropped their packs and then disappeared into the forest again. He'd asked about it the night before and been told they were setting snares; that morning, the Sacrati had gone out to retrieve their prizes, then gutted and skinned the captured animals. Now, as the Sacrati returned from the forest, they pulled half-frozen meat from the outside of their packs and set it to cooking on the fires.

Finnvid watched cautiously as the shepherdess approached the Elkati fire, a skinned rabbit in her hands. "We have extra," she said, "if you'd like a share."

"Will you sit with us as we eat it?" one of the men said, a lascivious grin on his face.

Finnvid winced, but the woman didn't seem affected. "No, I prefer to eat with better company. Shall I leave the rabbit?"

"Thank you," Finnvid said quickly. "We appreciate it."

She nodded in his direction and tossed the rabbit into the snow by his feet.

Andros came over later and showed the Elkati how to den up, and that was about all the interaction between the two groups for the first several days.

By the evening of the fifth day, Finnvid's soreness was wearing off, and being replaced by a deeper, more troubling exhaustion. It wasn't just the endless work, but the constant cold. Even denned up like the Torians he was never really comfortable, and every morning the daylight called him out of his burrow to face the biting wind. They weren't even at the border yet, and he was barely able to keep going. It was too late to turn around, though, so he knew he had to keep moving or lie down and die.

That night at the campfire, it was Theos who approached with a couple snared squirrels. The Sacrati had been good about sharing their food, giving some to the Elkati and some to the other Torians. Divided among the men there was barely more than a mouthful of meat for each; not enough to give them the energy they needed, but an appreciated bit of flavor nonetheless. This night, though, with Theos standing there staring down at them, it was clear that something more was in the works.

"You're starting to drag," he said. It wasn't quite an accusation, but it certainly wasn't a compliment.

"We're doing our best," Nasi protested.

"You need to do better." Theos pulled two of the fat cakes out of his pack and tossed them into the cookpot, where the lard began to sizzle immediately. "Fry the meat. Then make a paste with the vegetable flour and make it into balls, and fry that. Fry dried-up *leaves*, if you have to. Don't stop frying things until all that fat is in your bellies." He took a step away, then turned back and said, "Tomorrow you'll have three cakes to eat. The day after that will be four. I'll keep adding to the number until you can keep up on the trail."

"We'll be at the border soon enough, and we'll be rid of you," Nasi growled.

"The rate you're going you'll still be in Torian territory come springtime. Of course, you'll be frozen in a snowbank by then, waiting for the vultures to find when they come back from the south." And with that, Theos stalked off.

Finnvid should have left it, but he was on his feet before his mind knew what he was doing. He stumbled after Theos, and when the man stopped and whirled to stare at him, he blurted, "Thank you."

Theos's scowl didn't disappear, but after a moment, he grudgingly said, "My oldest boy didn't like cakes. That's how his mother got him to eat them."

"And now he likes them?"

"Now he *eats* them. I don't think anybody really *likes* them."

It was almost a conversation. Not friendly, exactly, but at least an exchange of words. "Well, we'll hope for that, then. And I didn't just mean to thank you for the advice about the cakes. I meant for everything. For trying to help me. For not—not being cruel to me. Before. Thank you."

Now the man's scowl deepened. "I didn't help you."

Finnvid wasn't sure how to respond. "You meant to, though."

"I'm foolish that way." Theos turned away, clearly ready to stop talking. "I'm trying to get smarter."

"I hope it doesn't work," Finnvid said. He meant it. He liked Theos just the way he was. "And, Theos . . . Andros didn't know much. Not for long. And I know he was ordered not to tell. It wasn't his choice. I don't think he'd ever choose to keep secrets from you."

"Thank you for your wisdom, princeling. I'll be sure to consult you in the future, if I need anything else explained to me."

And that was the end of it. Theos returned to his own campfire, and Finnvid turned back to his. It should have been enough. Finnvid had thanked Theos, Theos had been typically ungracious, and now their association was over. But later that night, as Finnvid watched the Torians head for their dens, some alone but others in pairs, he couldn't keep his mind from wandering. What would it be like to crawl into a den with Theos? To share space, warmth, breath . . . to press against the man's broad torso and long, strong legs, and to not be ashamed, because they had the excuse of needing heat.

Or not to be ashamed, regardless. To not look for an excuse, as the Torians didn't. What would it be like to stretch his body out next to Theos's just because they wanted to touch each other?

Two men together was unnatural. Men and women were built to fit, men and men were . . . wrong.

Finnvid crawled into his den, trying to ignore the cold, claustrophobic walls and trying not to wonder how much more pleasant it would be with some company.

He should be fantasizing about the shepherdess. She was an attractive young woman. Theos had warned the men to keep their hands off her, but he hadn't mentioned their minds. Finnvid should be thinking about her.

He didn't even remember her name, he realized with a start. The only woman for many days' walk in either direction, and he'd noticed her so little he didn't even know what she was called.

He wasn't thinking about men—about Theos—because there were no women around. No, there was more to his fascination. Lying there in his dark tunnel, he let himself admit it; there'd *always* been something fascinating about men, even before he'd come to Windthorn. Back in Elkat there had just been confusing, quickly repressed urges. He'd known he would marry a woman, and had looked forward to the event with a mix of optimism and dread. He'd hoped that once he had the right body in front of him he'd stop thinking about the wrong bodies. But if he didn't . . . if marriage didn't cure him . . .

He squirmed, trying to find a more comfortable position. And he cursed his time in Windthorn. If he'd never traveled, he'd never have realized just how bleak his future would be if marriage didn't cure him. Never have realized what he was missing. Never have known how simple and perfect it could all be. How *natural* it was.

And now he was fighting to get back to Elkat. He'd really thought he'd be able to forget what he'd seen if he just got away from it quickly enough? He was a fool, alone in a cold, snowy grave.

He considered crawling out and going to find Theos. The man had wanted Finnvid; of course, Theos seemed to want practically anyone who wandered into sight. Still, that could be good. Finnvid had apologized with words, and maybe he could also apologize with his body . . .

No, it wouldn't be an apology. It would be a plea. For forgiveness first, and then for so much more.

Finnvid knew he wouldn't move. But he let himself imagine it. A different Finnvid, braver and less confused, sliding out of his tunnel, reborn as a man who followed his own instincts, not the rules of his valley. He'd find Theos, surprise him, and Theos's body would tighten at first, ready, as it always was, to fight. And there would be a moment when it wasn't clear what Theos would do, but then he'd relax, his frown gentling from anger to amusement, and he'd pull Finnvid in next to him, and their bodies would align, their lips would meet . . .

Finnvid fumbled with his clothes, fighting to get through the layers to the pulsing heat at his core. He'd refused to give in to the urges when he was sleeping in Theos's room. It would have been too real, too intense, to find release while the object of his fantasies was lying within arm's reach. And Theos was a light sleeper. If he'd woken up and realized what Finnvid was doing—it had been too terrifying, too tantalizing, to take the chance.

He'd barely wrapped his hand around himself before he was gasping, and then the images began flashing into his mind, too many, too quickly for him to focus on just one. Theos in the baths, muscles everywhere and warm brown skin glowing with health and vitality; the Torian tattoo on his shoulder, the Sacrati brand on his upper thigh; Theos driving into someone, thrusting and groaning and shaking; Theos kissing someone else, rough bites and punishing strength; and then, the kisses with Finnvid, somehow gentler and sweeter than with the others. Then Finnvid wasn't seeing anything but brightness and beauty. His body spasmed over and over, releasing his need and his desire into the cold snow wall.

He lay there, drained and exhausted, and for a few moments he thought he'd found peace. Perhaps giving in to the fantasies had been enough to dispel them. Then, unbidden, his imagination sent him the idea of having Theos there beside him. He'd wrap a warm, heavy arm around Finnvid's body, pull him in tight and safe, and they'd sleep entwined together.

And with that thought, the yearning was back. But it was changed, now. He didn't crave the heat and passion, at least at the moment; he wanted the warmth and affection. He wanted to wake up with Theos, or even better, to wake up and find Theos already at the campfire so they could exchange sleepy, easy smiles like Andros and Xeno did. So everyone could see them, and know that there was something between them, something special and pure and real.

That was where the fantasy fell apart, though, because there would be Elkati around the fire.

Some of the Elkati soldiers seemed to have accepted the Torian ways; Finnvid wasn't completely sure that a few of them hadn't indulged a little themselves. Despite that, the dominant mood was still disapproval and disgust. If the Elkati felt that their *prince* had given in? Finnvid couldn't imagine their reactions. His skin tightened and itched just at the thought of it. The Elkati soldiers would be bad enough, but if they went home and told his brother? His *mother*?

All the lovely tranquility was gone, replaced with a mix of anxiety and despair. He could play whatever games he wanted to, in his mind. But he could never act on his fantasies, not in the real world. Not when he was surrounded by Elkati.

He'd lost his chance. When he'd been a slave, there'd been freedom. He and Theos could have done whatever they'd wanted without worrying about who saw them. But Finnvid had been too wrapped up in his own pride and fear and anger to take advantage of the opportunity.

And now it was gone. He was on his way home. In a few days, they'd reach the border and Finnvid would say good-bye to Theos forever.

It took him a long time to fall asleep that night, and when he finally did drop off, it felt like surrender.

He woke the next morning, slid out of his den and saw Theos sitting by the fire, stirring a cookpot. The Sacrati glanced up at him, and everything fell away until it was just the two of them. Theos didn't smile, but he didn't frown, either. He just looked, and Finnvid looked back. Then somebody nearby moved, breaking the spell, and Theos jerked his gaze free. Finnvid froze, hoping against hope that Theos might turn to him again. And he knew that, if Theos smiled, Finnvid would go to him, and sit with him and touch him in any way the Sacrati allowed, regardless of the Elkati audience. Finnvid would abandon everything he'd known for a chance at something new.

But Theos didn't glance back, and eventually Finnvid stumbled to the edge of the camp to pee, and the day went on as the days before it had. Finnvid was still trapped. But now he knew it, and that made it so much harder to bear.

CHAPTER 18

It was three and a half more days before they made it to the border. There wasn't really anything to see, no landmark to make it clear, but the shepherdess and Gunnald seemed to agree that they'd found the right spot.

Halfway, Finnvid told himself. More than half, really, because the Elkati territory wasn't as large as Windthorn's, so walking to its center wasn't such a trek.

It was still a long way, though, and even with the addition of the fat cakes, Finnvid was tired. Then he caught a few snippets of the conversation among Zenain, Ekakios, and Gunnald and realized he had more important things to worry about.

"My orders have been clear from the start," Zenain said firmly. "We are to escort the Elkati prince all the way home."

"You want us to go uninvited into Elkati territory?" Ekakios grinned in true Sacrati fashion. "That might make this trip a little more interesting than it's been so far."

"We do *not* require an escort," Gunnald said icily. "We appreciate your efforts, but do not need you anymore."

"You're ready to carry all your own gear?" Zenain asked. "Because you've barely been keeping up with us as it is."

"We won't need to *keep up* with you once you're walking in the opposite direction."

"You'll still want to move as quickly as you can, though. We've been lucky with the weather so far, but you can't count on that to continue. For maximum safety, you need to get your prince and yourselves back down in your valley, in out of the cold, as soon as possible. Right?"

Gunnald scowled. Finnvid eased into the conversation, and made his voice as mild and inoffensive as he could. "It would be problematic for foreign troops to trespass on Elkati soil without permission."

"I agree, Prince Finnvid. It is not our intention to trespass. We were expecting to be invited. I'm sure you can understand how interested we are in seeing you home safely. Not only for your own sake, but for the sake of the peace between our two valleys. It is our fault that you did not make it home before the snow fell, so it is our responsibility to see the situation rectified now."

It was a nice speech, one that felt carefully practiced. Finnvid tried to think it through. Bringing the Torian soldiers onto Elkat soil—was that dangerous? There weren't enough of them, even with Sacrati among their number, to pose a threat to the full Elkati army. The visit *would* give the Torians an opportunity to spy a little, just as Finnvid had done in Windthorn, but that might not be a bad thing. Let them notice the progress Elkat had made in arming itself, and hear about the many allied troops prepared to join them. Elkat was not a ripe berry to be plucked effortlessly from a thornless bush. Not anymore. And the Torians should have the chance to see that firsthand.

"I would appreciate your continued assistance," Finnvid said at last. He hoped he was doing the right thing. "We can offer you hospitality when we arrive, a chance to restock your supplies as needed."

Zenain's evident triumph made Finnvid question his decision immediately, but it was too late to change his mind without seeming weak. So he smiled apologetically at Gunnald; it was all he could do.

The Torians took a few moments to reorganize; Finnvid heard groans and discontent from the regular soldiers, but nothing from the Sacrati. Apparently they were too stoic to be upset by an extended mission.

He watched as the men set off toward the Elkati side of the border, then frowned as he saw the young shepherdess heading in the opposite direction. He stepped forward without thinking, and it was mostly coincidence that the nearest Torian was Theos. "She's going home? *Alone?*"

Theos didn't seem alarmed. "She spends most of her summer in these mountains alone. It's no different in the winter, is it? Less chance of human trouble, at least."

"But it's not safe!"

"The biggest risk is the weather, and being in a larger group doesn't help much with that. Safer for her to go back now, alone, than for her to travel farther with us and then have to turn around and travel back, too."

Finnvid hadn't really thought about the extra danger he was imposing on the Torians by having them accompany him all the way home. They seemed invincible, but he needed to remind himself that they weren't.

"She could come with us and stay until spring," he tried, but he knew before the words were out of his mouth that the idea would be rejected.

"She wouldn't want to live among Elkati," Theos said simply. "Especially without other Torians. And I assume you aren't mad enough to consider inviting all of us to stay for the winter."

"You could camp out. Just as we were going to do if we'd stayed in Windthorn."

"But you decided it was better to travel through the winter mountains rather than spend extra time in the enemy camp. Do you think Torians would feel differently? Especially when traveling is less difficult for us than for you?"

"Do you still think of us as enemies?" Finnvid was pleased that his voice sounded casual, with no hint of the turmoil that had churned inside him at Theos's choice of words. They weren't still *enemies*, surely.

Theos turned to him, his gaze cold. "I find it best not to think of you at all," he said, and then he started walking and left Finnvid behind.

Finnvid rejoined his men as they stepped over the border and back into Elkat. It shouldn't have felt like walking into a prison, and Finnvid tried to ignore the tightness in his shoulders, as if they were bracing to carry a weight heavier than any pack the Torians were carrying.

He trudged on through the day, lost in his thoughts, barely noticing the cold wind that had picked up shortly after they crossed the border and started climbing the slope on the Elkati side. Eating the fat cakes had helped give him energy, but he was still pushing himself hard every day just to keep moving. He'd learned to let himself fall into a sort of trance, focusing only on the path ahead of him. There *was* no destination, no end to the toil; there was only snow, and cold, and brutal trudging.

And when he finally heard the call to stop moving and set up camp, there was no real sense of relief. He helped to gather wood for the fires, his fingers numb even inside his heavy mittens, and waited for his turn with a shovel so he could dig his frozen grave for the coming night.

But something was different this time. Finnvid had to squint through blowing snow to see Zenain and Gunnald and Ekakios arguing again. He approached reluctantly, wishing they could just work it all out without him. "What's wrong?" he asked Gunnald.

"The mighty Torians are afraid of the snow," Gunnald sneered. "They want to build a *big* camp, and stay here for several days."

"We'll only stay if the storm comes," Ekakios said. "It's stupid to try to walk through a blizzard. Better to stay safe and warm in good shelters than to get lost in the storm." He frowned at Gunnald. "Elkati must know that. Even if you don't travel as much as Torians do, you still live through winter every year. You know what's sensible."

But Gunnald was resentful of the Torians' continued presence, Finnvid realized. He didn't want to spend any more time with them than he had to, and he certainly didn't want to admit that they were right about anything.

"Is there any harm in building the shelters?" Finnvid asked, trying to sound conciliatory. He really didn't want to override Gunnald's opinion for the second time that day, not if he could help it. "Then if we don't need them, we can just leave them behind and walk on tomorrow."

"We could walk on *today*," Gunnald insisted, "if these Torians weren't set on stopping early so they can build their little forts."

"Maybe the Elkati should walk on," a new voice said, and Finnvid turned to see Theos standing just behind him. He stepped further into their circle, keeping his gaze on Ekakios. "They'll tire soon, carrying their own gear without their pack mules, but it would certainly make things easier for us. We can wait out the storm here, then turn around and go home. The Elkati bodies will be found in the spring, and surely we can't be blamed for them freezing to death in a blizzard well inside Elkat territory."

"That's not the best outcome," Ekakios said mildly. "Although, yes, it would be easier for us." Then he raised an eyebrow, clearly asking why Theos had interrupted the meeting.

Theos ignored the reprimand and said, "There's plenty of men working on the shelters. I'm going to go see if I can find any game bigger than squirrels and rabbits."

Ekakios nodded distractedly. "If they don't need your help on the shelters, then hunting would be good. Don't get lost in the storm, though."

"That's an excellent suggestion. Thank you." There was nothing but courtesy in Theos's voice, but the sarcasm, however well veiled, was there.

Finnvid watched as Theos stalked away and Ekakios frowned after him. The balance between the two Sacrati was clearly still delicate; Finnvid wondered what would have happened if Ekakios had challenged Theos and told him to do something else, and the thought brought shivers unrelated to the cold wind. The winter was harsh enough without a Sacrati brawl.

Then he shivered a little more as he remembered the callous way Theos had contemplated the possibility of Elkati deaths. It made sense: Theos tried not to think of the Elkati at all. The Elkati were the enemy. And Finnvid was, of course, Elkati. Theos didn't care if he lived or died.

"I could use a break," Finnvid said, bringing his mind back to the current discussion. "And so could the men. If we have good shelters, a few extra hours in camp wouldn't be a bad thing." Here was the Elkati version of the power struggle, and Finnvid was uncomfortably aware that he was playing Ekakios's role in it. He was the leader because of a title, not because he was the best man for the job. "It would give us a chance to rest a little so we can really push hard once we're ready to go."

Gunnald didn't look convinced, but he made a quick bow and said, "As you wish," before spinning and heading over to the Elkati men. Some of them were following Torian directions in heaping snow onto the huge mounds, others were working on fires or organizing packs. Everyone had a job, except Finnvid.

"Is there something I should be doing?" he asked. He wasn't sure who the question was directed to, but both Torians answered almost at once.

"You should just rest," Zenain said.

"We could use more firewood," Ekakios suggested.

"Firewood," Finnvid said decisively. They'd managed to stay below the tree line for almost the whole trip, so it wasn't a challenge to find trees, but living wood didn't burn well, so it was better to drag in fallen branches that hadn't rotted yet. Not easy to find such treasures under all the snow. The next option was to find dead trees that hadn't fallen, and either push them over or chop them down. "Right."

"He shouldn't leave camp," Zenain objected. "If the wind comes up harder, he won't be able to see, and he could get lost."

"Don't go far," Ekakios said dryly to Finnvid. "Keep track of landmarks. Don't get lost."

Finnvid grinned as he echoed Theos's earlier words. "Excellent suggestion. Thank you."

It *was* a bit frightening to head into the woods alone, and Finnvid soon realized that the Torians weren't being alarmist about the storm. The trees provided some shelter from the wind, but not nearly enough, and the snow was falling fast and blowing sideways in front of his eyes. So Finnvid stayed close to camp, dragging in what he could find nearby. It was hard work, and he found himself sweating, which wasn't good; wet clothes would freeze him once he stopped moving. But he needed to contribute to the camp's efforts, so he kept going.

He noted the progress on the snow mounds as he came to and from camp. There were six of them, taking up practically the whole clearing, and the men were alternately shoveling more snow onto them and then stomping all over to pack it down. For a while after they stopped adding snow, the mounds were ignored as the men built a long snow wall around one side of the clearing. A windbreak, Finnvid realized.

Eventually, he came back and saw men digging into the mounds, pushing snow out for their colleagues to add to the windbreak. It was a lot of work, hard work, enough to make Finnvid happy he was only fetching firewood.

By the time the men had finished with the mounds, Finnvid was exhausted. His usual state by this point of the day, but generally it was mostly his legs that ached rather than his whole body. Still, he'd built a good pile of wood, and it was gratifying to see the men pulling logs and sticks from it to feed their fires. The smells of cooking soon filled the camp, and Finnvid found a spot out of the wind and close to a fire, trying to ignore the chill that was spreading over his body as his heat leached away through his wet clothes.

Of course, as soon as his mind had a moment of peace it began looking for trouble, and as usual, that trouble was Theos-shaped. Finnvid couldn't find the Sacrati's familiar form, and that was enough to make him start wondering. Maybe he was taking shelter in one of the snow mounds? But that didn't seem like him. Finnvid stood, his body creaking and his skin complaining as it brushed against parts of his clothing that had frozen solid.

Andros looked up as Finnvid approached the Sacrati fire. "He's not back yet," he said, as if there was no other reason Finnvid might have wandered over. "I'd be happier if he were, but he's smart and tough. If the conditions are worse where he is, he may den up out there and come find us when the storm breaks. Or he could be back any second." Andros watched Finnvid digest that, then said, "It's better to not worry about things you can't control. And you definitely can't control Theos."

"I don't seem to be able to control my worries, either," Finnvid confessed.

Andros smiled. "That's always the problem, isn't it?" Then he frowned up at the darkening sky and inhaled deeply. "There's a lot of snow ready to come down. We're going to be here for a while. Work on getting comfortable—pick a mound and crawl inside, spread your gear around so it has a chance to air out and get dry. Mend your boots, tend your blisters, rub fat on your wind-burned skin. Sleep, and dream of summer." He raised his eyebrows and said, "Ideally, find someone to snuggle up with and share body heat. You can sleep naked in a snow mound if there are enough other bodies to keep you warm."

Finnvid felt the blush heating his face, but Andros's laugh was kind, not mocking. He sounded more serious as he added, "Keep an eye on your men. There've been a few comments lately about who

Torians chose to den up with, but everyone's tired so we've just been ignoring it. In the mounds, it's all going to be more obvious, and everyone's going to have more free time for saying stupid things *and* for beating the crap out of people who say stupid things. If your men don't like Torian ways, they can go set up a damn tent in the blizzard."

"I'll speak to them," Finnvid said. "And if you see something building, something I'm not around for, try to let me know. I'll fix it if I can."

Andros nodded. Then he peered at Finnvid a little longer and said, "You're doing well, you know. You're the only one of us who's not used to this kind of work, and you're keeping up. You're making good decisions. Everyone's still alive, so . . . well done."

Finnvid wished it were that simple, but he couldn't find the words to express his doubts, so he just shrugged and backed away. The Elkati men were deep-frying vegetable cakes and chewing on jerky, and Finnvid joined them, trying to think of the best words to prevent hostility and violence. Finally he said, "The Torians are different from us. They have different knowledge. These snow mounds . . . if they're as warm as the Torians say, they'll be valuable, just as learning to den up was."

The reactions were about what he'd expected. The Elkati who'd been impressed with the Torians in Windthorn continued to be impressed with them. The Elkati who'd resented the Torians continued to resent them, even as they made plans to crawl inside one of the mounds and take it for themselves.

"I think that's a good idea," Finnvid said firmly. He could tell by the men's looks that they'd expected him to protest. "You should take over a mound and stay in it. If you don't like the Torians, and don't like their ways, you should stay away from them. Be in the one mound—take one of the ones at the end, I think—or be outside. Don't mix if you can't adapt."

"We're on Elkati soil, now," Nasi said. "*They* should be adapting, not us."

"They're our guests. And they're not insisting that any of us join in their ways. Leave them alone, and they'll leave us alone."

"Is that how it worked for you?" Nasi asked. "When you were that Torian's whore? He *left you alone*, did he?"

Gunnald half rose in protest; Finnvid waved him down and fixed his gaze on Nasi. "Yes, he did."

The man clearly didn't believe him, but turned away with a grunted, "If you say so."

Nasi would have been punished if they were at home. Serious punishment for such disrespect. Here, though, in the mountains . . . No. It wasn't just the location, it was Finnvid. He'd changed. He didn't expect the same sort of deference that he was used to, not after being humbled so many times on this trip. This man . . . well, this man was an ass, but surely that was his right?

Finnvid pushed himself to his feet and walked away from the fire. He hadn't realized how much the wind had picked up until he left the shelter of the snow wall and his chest tightened with the cold, making it hard to breathe.

And Theos was out in this. Maybe he'd denned up, as Andros had suggested, but what if he'd fallen and hurt himself? Sacrati were strong, but not completely invulnerable.

Finnvid peered anxiously into the forest, but could barely see the trees a few paces ahead of him. He stumbled forward, wading through hip-high drifts in places that had been almost free of snow when they'd made camp.

Theos. Finnvid tried to focus on the man's name, tried to picture him in his mind and send the thought out like a beacon, guiding the man safely back through the storm. Then he stepped further into the woods.

The trees cut the wind a little. The branches caught some of the snow, but much of it still landed on the ground. "Theos!" Finnvid yelled. The wind would carry his voice away from camp, into the forest. "We're here! Theos!"

It felt pointless. It *was* pointless. The forest was vast, the storm fierce, and neither Finnvid's mental beacon nor his feeble voice was enough to shine any light into the darkness.

Except . . . except there was movement ahead of him. A dark shape against the white snow, moving slowly, but steadily, wading through the drifts. From the shape, it could have been an angry bear startled out of hibernation by Finnvid's racket, but he knew the way

Theos moved, even when burdened. "Theos!" he yelled, and the shape changed course and came toward him.

The Sacrati had a deer slung across his shoulders. Of course his hunt had been successful. Of course he'd returned safely to camp. Finnvid felt foolish for doubting it.

Suddenly Theos stumbled and fell, catching himself on one hand and staying there as if frozen. Too exhausted to pull himself to his feet.

Finnvid lurched forward to meet him. He dragged the deer off the man's shoulders and then fell to his own knees, bringing their faces to the same level. "It's only a few more steps," he promised. "The camp is close. You can smell the smoke. Right?"

Theos's eyes were dark and fixed on Finnvid's, and his mitten-covered hands grasped Finnvid's arms. "I can smell *you*."

Something changed. Finnvid stopped caring about survival; it seemed like a petty concern compared to the heat in his gut. He nodded, eyes wide.

Theos shifted, somehow, falling forward, too heavy for Finnvid to catch and hold, and they tumbled into the snow together, Finnvid's legs bent painfully, Theos flat on top of him. Had the man passed out?

But then Theos moved. His leg found its way between Finnvid's, and his cheek, ice-cold and covered with frozen stubble, brushed against Finnvid's almost-as-chilled face. Finnvid squirmed, wriggling just enough to straighten, and Theos responded by pushing his weight down, holding Finnvid in place. He'd thought Finnvid was trying to escape, and he'd stopped it.

Theos's power, even when diminished by exhaustion, was too much for Finnvid. Whatever the Sacrati wanted? It was going to happen. Finnvid was at his mercy.

CHAPTER 19

Finnvid lay in the snow, staring up at the shadowy face of the man holding him down. A brutish, angry Torian had attacked him. Out here in the forest, away from any help, where it would be easy to hide his body. Finnvid was pinned, and even if he'd been able to get free, he couldn't outrun his attacker, and certainly couldn't outfight him.

And yet, he was not afraid. Nervous, maybe, but not afraid. This was *Theos*, and that meant Finnvid was safe. He wasn't even cold anymore, not with the snow puffed up beside them to block the wind and with Theos's body on top of him. He brought his hands up, wishing he could take off the bulky mittens, and grabbed the back of Theos's head.

He saw the flash of shock in the Sacrati's eyes, and then things happened too quickly to truly understand. Theos's lips, hard and chapped against Finnvid's, and then his tongue, the first taste of warmth Finnvid had felt in far too long. A desperate, hungry sound, half-growl and half-moan, ripped from Theos's throat and was lost in the wind before Finnvid had time to fully cherish it. Theos's hands held Finnvid's unresisting shoulders, and Theos's body pushed and drove and rutted against Finnvid's, the tension and hardness and need clear even through all the layers of clothing.

Finnvid arched up to meet the sensations, then fought one leg free so he could wrap it around Theos's thighs and pull him in tighter. There were no thoughts, no plans, no attempts to shed clothing. There were only their bodies, their mouths, and more than anything, their eyes. They stared at each other and Finnvid saw it all. Theos's anger, his frustration, his desire. His need and his want. Finnvid saw Theos's excitement building, and it spread easily to his own body. There shouldn't have been enough contact, enough friction, but this was *Theos*.

Finnvid moaned into Theos's mouth, clawed at his back with ineffective hands, and he begged, almost chanted, "Please. Theos, please. Theos, Theos. Please."

Theos didn't reply in words, but his grunts and gasps were an answer for Finnvid. They came together, both of them throwing back their heads and finally letting their eyes shut in ecstasy.

Even after he calmed, Finnvid didn't want to move. He wanted to stay there in the snow forever, with Theos a comforting, essential weight on top of him. It didn't matter if they both froze to death; their bodies could be found in the springtime, still wrapped around each other, and hopefully they'd be buried together so this embrace never had to end.

Fortunately for both of them, Theos was more practical. He eased backward, careful of his weight, and pulled himself up until he was kneeling, gazing down at Finnvid. And from that angle, Finnvid had a clear view as Theos's expression changed. In a matter of seconds it went from open and relaxed and affectionate to confused and almost alarmed. Then it settled on sardonic.

"What were you trying to distract me from this time?" he asked quietly. "Have your men stolen the deer while we were busy? Is there murder and mayhem back at camp, and you didn't want me to interrupt?"

Finnvid supposed he deserved that. He *knew* he deserved it. But Theos was hardly an innocent victim. "I'm sorry. I guess the habits of slavery die hard. After months of being treated like property and expected to care about your every whim, I guess I was still inclined to *serve* you."

"I don't remember you caring about my *every* whim," Theos replied. He staggered to his feet, clearly not past his exhaustion, but just as clearly ready to get away from Finnvid and back to camp. He looked down at Finnvid and rubbed his own crotch in distaste. "I need to do some laundry while we're stopped. I hope the storm lasts long enough for things to dry, but even if it doesn't, I'd rather wear something damp than something that reminds me of my stupidity with every step."

The hard words hurt, but Finnvid refused to show the sting. "How unexpectedly poetic you are. A treatise on washing seed out of clothing. Of course, I suppose you'd be the expert on that sort of thing."

"Most of my seed finds more receptive homes." Theos turned and nudged the deer with his foot, then sneered at Finnvid. "Carry that in, why don't you? There may as well be *something* productive to come from your little trip into the woods." He took a step toward camp, then stopped and squinted. "What *were* you doing out here? What kind of spying happens in the middle of a blizzard?"

Finnvid wanted to lie, but he wanted to tell the truth more. "I was looking for you. I was *worried* about you." He struggled to his feet. "So you're not the only one feeling foolish." He took his own step toward camp and then spun to say, "You can carry your own stupid deer."

Petty, maybe, but he didn't care. He made his way back to camp, the dampness of his underclothes quickly cooling into an uncomfortable mess, and tried to understand what had happened.

It had been nothing. Clearly that was true for Theos, and so it should be true for Finnvid as well.

But he remembered how Theos had moved, how he'd sounded and smelled and felt. He remembered the fierce concentration on the other man's face, as if he was memorizing Finnvid, claiming him and owning him. Finnvid felt his cock stirring again and tried to ignore it. He needed to think about something else. He needed to stop shaking.

The Elkati were sitting around one of the campfires, but he couldn't join them. They'd know. They'd realize he'd just— What had he done? He'd never touched a woman like that, never even kissed in a more than friendly way, and now he'd . . . done *that* . . . with another man. A Torian. A *Sacrati*. Rutting like animals in the forest, soiling their clothes, risking their lives in the cold . . . Theos was right. It had been stupid. Worse than stupid. Dirty, unnatural, immoral. It had been wrong.

As Theos staggered into camp, the deer over his shoulders again, Finnvid crawled into the nearest snow mound. The tunnel ran down a bit and then up, and as he emerged into the soft glow cast by several small flames, he realized that it *was* warm in the shelter. Not hot, but above freezing, certainly. There was a bucket of water heating by one of the flames, probably a sign that someone else was planning to bathe.

But Finnvid didn't care about the etiquette of stealing someone's water. He pulled his clothing off as if it were on fire, dropping it in a heap on the snowy floor. Layer after layer, days' worth of grime, and then the final evidence of his depravity on his underthings. He stripped it all off, dipped his hands into the bucket of warm water and splashed it up and over himself. It would be better if he had a brush or even a rough cloth, but he made do with his hands. He scrubbed and scrubbed, and as the water in the bucket was consumed he scooped snow off the floor of the structure and dumped it into the bucket, barely letting it thaw before he used it on his body.

He heard a sound from the side of the cavern and whirled, seeing only then that all the mounds were joined through little tunnels. It was Andros's familiar head that appeared at the low tunnel entrance, and he was dragging Finnvid's pack along with him.

"Do you have clean clothes?" he asked, as if he assisted Elkati princes with frenzied bathing as a matter of course. "Something dry? We can probably get the rest of your things washed and dried before we leave. At least the inner layers. But you'll need something to wear in the meantime."

Finnvid stared at him. It was all so prosaic. And Andros was, as always, so kind. Did he know what Finnvid had done? But even if he did, Andros wouldn't care. He did those things himself. He did them in public, with people all around him. It wasn't— For Andros, it wasn't shameful. It wasn't unnatural.

Could it ever be that way for Finnvid?

It *had* been, he realized with a start. Of all the emotions that had washed over him in the forest with Theos, shame had been absent. Even after Theos had pulled away, Finnvid hadn't felt ashamed. Angry and embarrassed and hurt, certainly. But he hadn't felt shame until he returned to camp. Until he was back among his Elkati peers.

"You done washing?" Andros asked gently. He might not understand the exact reason for Finnvid's agitation, and apparently he didn't need to. Just as Finnvid had with Andros's snakebite, Andros was treating Finnvid's symptoms, if not the underlying injury. "You should get dressed. Stay warm."

Finnvid nodded, which prompted the rest of his body into action. He rummaged through his pack and found clothes that were somewhat cleaner than the ones he'd been wearing and pulled them on. "There's a way to wash the other stuff?"

"Lots of ways. If we were staying here longer, we could set up a line outside and hang the clothes on it, let the snow and the wind wash off the dirt. But that takes a couple days, and then you need drying time on top of that, so let's just use water."

Simple and matter-of-fact. Andros found a few more buckets, filled them with snow, and set them next to the small lamp to thaw.

"I didn't know you carried lamps with you," Finnvid said absently. "And fuel, too."

Andros just grinned and then reached into the metal bowl and ran his finger around in the fuel. Then he popped his finger in his mouth and licked it clean. "Mmmm," he hummed. "Fat cakes!"

Finnvid squinted at the lamp. "Fat cakes? Really?"

"They're good for everything."

"Everything except eating."

"You'll get used to them. Well, you *would* get used to them, if you ate them more. But I guess you won't, once you're back in Elkat." He frowned. "Strange to think of that. You not being around anymore."

"It's a little strange for me too."

Andros went back to his demonstration of the washing process, and showed how Finnvid would have to wring the clothes almost dry before hanging them because the cold air wouldn't absorb much of their moisture, and Finnvid saw that this was one more skill he'd never have the chance to use again. Not that he really *wanted* to be a launderer, but he'd learned some tricks from scrubbing Theos's clothes at Windthorn, and now he was learning new ways, and soon none of it would matter.

"Are we allowed to be in here?" he asked suddenly. "No one else has come in. Are they all still out in the cold?"

"It's not that bad, behind the windbreak and by the fires. And they're all waiting for their shares of venison. We've got some time."

Things were so calm and easy with Andros. Finnvid wondered what it would have been like if Andros had been the one to buy him. There'd have been less anger, certainly. Less frustration. Everything would have been easier.

He frowned at Andros and tried to imagine doing what he'd done in the forest with him. Despite all he'd seen of Andros and Xeno, and even Andros and Theos, he just couldn't picture Andros and himself. Theos's frustration was strong enough to match his own, his passion powerful enough to override Finnvid's hesitations. And Theos was . . . he was *Theos*. All the things that made him so difficult made time with him that much sweeter when he finally relaxed and let himself be easy.

"Thank you for helping," Finnvid said quietly.

"You're too much like him," Andros said as if he had a pretty good idea what had triggered Finnvid's feverish cleaning. "You both take things too seriously."

"He hates me." Finnvid felt like a child as he said it, and even more ridiculous when he realized how much he wanted Andros to contradict him.

Andros just smiled. "He doesn't. But he's definitely angry with you. Very angry."

"He kept me as a slave. I was a prisoner, and treated as the enemy. I was duty-bound to try to escape."

"Aye."

"So did I do anything wrong?"

Andros shrugged. "Wrong? I don't know. It's not about being right or wrong, I don't think. It's just . . . things got muddled. What you did was fine if you're the enemy, but him hating you is fine if you're the enemy, too. So neither one of you did anything *wrong*. Of course, if you're *not* the enemy, when did that happen? Did you both know it was happening? Did it happen for both of you at the same time?" He shook his head, then grinned. "I'm glad those are questions for you and not for me, because my brain would hurt if I tried to answer them." With a slap on Finnvid's shoulder he added, "You look tired. I think the Elkati are sleeping at the far end of the mounds, the last two in the line, so you can either crawl all the way through the tunnels or you can walk through the snow. But you should go and get some sleep, I'd say."

"What if I didn't sleep with them?" Finnvid hadn't known he was going to ask the question. He saw Andros's expression, and tried, "I could sleep here, couldn't I? Or with—you know—if he wasn't still angry..."

Andros raised an eyebrow. "And how would your men feel about that? Who would they tell when you get home? What would happen if people at home knew?"

Finnvid felt his gut clench and churn, his body freeze at that inconceivable outcome. People at home couldn't know. Not ever. "Of course," he whispered. "I was being stupid."

"You were dreaming," Andros said. "It's not the same as being stupid, as long as you remember not to act on it."

Finnvid nodded slowly, then crammed his gear into his pack and crouched to crawl through the tunnel to the Elkati snow mounds.

When Andros spoke, it was so quiet that Finnvid had to strain to hear. "I do love him. Not just as a brother, but the way you mean." Andros sounded... not sad, but resigned. "But it'd be impossible. He's too... too much. Too intense about everything. I love Xeno just as well, and we make a lot more sense together."

Finnvid wasn't sure what to say.

Andros shrugged and busied himself with emptying the buckets. "Just thought you might like to know. You're not the only one." He looked speculatively out in the general direction of the campfire, and his usual grin returned. "And we're probably not the only two."

"Maybe not," Finnvid replied, and then started crawling again. He wasn't sure how he felt about Andros's confession. Yes, it was nice to know he wasn't alone, but at the same time he liked to think he and Theos had something... well, something unique, if not special. Maybe that was completely one-sided. The very first night Finnvid had been with the Torians, Andros had given Theos the same relief Finnvid had just given, and that had seemed to be ... not nothing, yet close to it.

The next snow mound was empty, and Finnvid didn't bother standing up; he just kept crawling, dragging his pack behind him, suddenly realizing just how exhausted he was. The snow mound after that housed two Torians, both naked, both engaged in something much more interesting than a crawling Elkati, and Finnvid kept his gaze on the snow and continued. The next snow mound had more fat lanterns, clearly there for light as much as for heat, because there were quite a few men scattered around, stripped down to their underclothes, playing a Torian dice game; Torians and Elkati together, Finnvid noticed, and hoped that the gambling led to comradeship rather than hostility. At least there was no alcohol to fan the flames of any rivalries. He wondered if he should stay in case mediation was necessary, but he was too tired, so he crawled on.

Theos was in the next mound. He was alone, still wearing his old clothes, although he'd taken off his outer jacket and was sitting on one of the snow benches with the jacket between him and the snow wall. Theos was just . . . sitting there. Waiting? For Finnvid?

Too damn bad. Finnvid kept crawling.

"You didn't get any venison," Theos said quietly.

Finnvid didn't respond. He was all the way across the floor of the mound, ready to enter the next tunnel, when Theos said, "Stop."

And Finnvid did, damn it.

But he didn't back out, keeping his head inside the tunnel so Theos couldn't see his face. Then he realized the position he was in and dropped his ass as low as it would go, trying not to look like he was issuing any sort of invitation. He heard Theos huff out a breath, maybe in amusement.

Then a strong hand landed on Finnvid's ankle, and tugged. Not hard enough to force him out, not dragging him. But still somehow irresistible.

So Finnvid shuffled backward, slowly, and Theos kept his hand where it was, with a looser grip. When Finnvid was free of the tunnel, he jerked his ankle loose and spun around to stare at Theos, both of them on their knees so their faces were at the same level.

"What?" he spat.

Theos was examining his face as if trying to read a book written in a language he'd never learned.

"You're angry," Theos finally said. He paused and stared a little more. "Really angry, or just acting like it?"

"Why would I *act* angry if I wasn't?"

"Why do you do any of the things you do?"

Finnvid snorted in disgust and turned, heading for the tunnel. Theos's hand caught him on the shoulder. Again, there was no real force, yet Finnvid was unable to make himself pull away.

But this time at least he didn't look at Theos. "What do you *want*?" he demanded, staring into the cool darkness of the tunnel.

"What do *you* want?" The question was soft but intense.

There were too many words inside him, and Finnvid didn't trust any of them. So he kept them to himself. "I want sleep," he said firmly, even though he no longer felt all that tired.

Theos slowly released his grip, and Finnvid resisted the urge to catch his hand, to return it to his shoulder or find it an even better home elsewhere on his body. This was for the best. When the storm was over they'd be heading back to Elkat and Finnvid would have to start forgetting about Theos; the fewer memories he had, the easier it would be.

As soon as he emerged into the last snow mound, cold and empty, Finnvid wanted to go back. There was only one lamp burning, and despite the space, the mound felt more like a grave than the dens Finnvid had slept in so far. And he knew why.

He slumped against the frozen wall and yanked his mitts off, throwing them in frustration. He was killing a part of himself. Not Theos, nothing to *do* with Theos, really. It was *Finnvid* who was returning to a life where he had to pretend to be someone he wasn't, even to himself. For all Theos's savagery and anger, he was free, and Finnvid, for all his rank, was still a slave.

But his choice was made. He spread his blankets on the bench carved out of the snow and lay down, closed his eyes, and willed sleep to come. It did, to some extent, and he dozed as other Elkati came in and found their own spots in the mound, and woke occasionally to hear the grunts and farts and snoring of the men all around him, and to hear or imagine the different, more intriguing noises coming from the Torian mounds.

Finnvid was in the wrong place, with the wrong people. And there was nothing he could do to change it.

CHAPTER 20

The blizzard raged for three days. The men stayed inside the mounds most of the time, only venturing outside for hurried calls of nature and to ensure that the ventilation holes on the hills were clear of snow. Otherwise, the travelers might as well have been hibernating.

Finnvid kept to the Elkati mounds as much as possible. He fried the remains of the deer meat, rubbed fat on his wind-burned skin, and stared at the white walls. Sometimes he crawled to the opening of the mound and looked out at even more white. There seemed to be a fog over the whole world, a swirling, confusing mass.

Then he tried to dismiss such frivolous notions and find something constructive to do with his time.

Andros came to visit once, dragging most of the deer remains with him, and showed Finnvid how to render fat and boil the bones to make a rich broth. It was frustrating work with the limited amount of heat Andros would allow inside the snow mound, but it gave Finnvid a little more knowledge—albeit knowledge he would never use once he returned to his real life—and he was glad of the distraction, and suspected that Andros knew it.

Late in the afternoon of the third day, Gunnald came to find Finnvid and told him the wind was dying down; if it stayed calm, they'd set out again the next morning. Finnvid wasn't sure how to take the news. He wanted to leave the camp, of course, wanted to get home safely. But while they were stuck in the snow, he could still dream that there was some escape for him. Once they started moving again, he'd feel like he was marching to his doom.

He'd thought about running away, or refusing to go back. But he couldn't do it. His valley was facing a crisis, and he'd been entrusted with helping to find a solution. His first real responsibility, the first time he wasn't being treated as a child or an afterthought. He needed to go home, and make his report, and consult with his brother about the best way to face the Torian threat and capitalize on the divisions within the empire. Finnvid needed to be an adult and ignore the divisions within himself.

So when the next morning dawned cold and clear, he joined the other men in pulling on their outer layers and packing up the camp. It was strangely sad to leave the cramped quarters behind; the mounds hadn't been fancy, but had been home, at least for a little while.

As usual, Theos walked with the Sacrati at the front of the procession. Finnvid let himself watch, let himself dream. If the world were different, Finnvid could jog ahead and walk with Theos—and be scolded for distracting the man from his job. But that would be its own victory because the scolding would come with a smile and a reluctant kiss, and Finnvid would know that he was interesting enough to *be* a distraction. As it was, in this world, Finnvid may as well have been a snow-covered tree for all the attention Theos paid him. Which should have been what he wanted, of course.

Even with all the new snow they kept up a quicker pace than before the storm; clearly the rest had done them good. The Sacrati took turns breaking the trail, then the Torian soldiers packed the snow down, and finally the Elkati soldiers strengthened the packing. By the time Finnvid strolled along the trail, he might as well have been walking down a paved road. Almost.

That night, unfortunately, he denned up near a couple who weren't tired at all. He couldn't identify them, not by their voices alone, but he had no trouble identifying their activity. The soft voices, the deep chuckles, then the gasps and moans and grunted half words. It was nothing new; since coming to live with the Torians, he'd grown used to their lack of modesty. But somehow, this time it all seemed more poignant.

Those sounds, unnatural? Unsophisticated, maybe. Hell, he'd even say uncivilized, and not expect much argument from anybody.

Something this natural could only *be* uncivilized. Unvarnished, undisguised, honest, real.

Finnvid burrowed through his layers of clothes and tugged and squirmed and fought his cock free; he moved his hand in time with the other men and imagined that Theos was there with him. The strength, the aggression, the tenderness and humor. And, yes, the arms, the chest, the ass, and the cock. All of it. All natural. He gasped as he came, pictured Theos gazing down on him with affection and warmth, then drifted off into a contented sleep.

The next morning when he wriggled out of his den, he wasn't completely shocked to see that one of the men crawling from the tunnel next to his was Hrodi. When the Elkati realized Finnvid had seen him, he went pale and then flushed. He turned and scurried away without a backward look at his partner, and the Torian shook his head and grimaced in Finnvid's direction.

"Do you all *enjoy* being so stupid about it? Is there something exciting in pretending it's forbidden?"

The Torian stalked off before Finnvid had time to answer, which was just as well. Anything he said would only have ended up getting him in trouble.

They marched on. The grind wore away at Finnvid, but for the first time he was aware of how it wore at the rest of them too. They all trudged; they all kept their heads down and their thoughts to themselves. Instead of being lost in his own fog, he found himself joined with the others in a huge migration of exhausted beasts. It was no less tiring, but at least he didn't feel so alone.

They slogged through that day, and the next one. And there was one after that, and then another, but at that point everything was blurring together. He was keeping up on the hike and functioning in camp; that was all.

One afternoon the snow became wetter and not as deep and the trees faded away, leaving open spaces. He was in a valley. *His* valley.

He noticed a Sacrati, Andros from the look of it, break away from the pack and head into the forest. Calls of nature were usually answered a few strides off the path, not deep in the woods. What was Andros doing?

Finnvid was still puzzling over that when he saw the small hut the Sacrati had stopped by, and the sentries from the building jogging toward them, swords drawn, searching for an Elkati in charge. Finnvid was suddenly dizzy and had to fight to stay on his feet. Now that he was home, back in the Elkat valley, it was as if all his hard-won strength had deserted him, and he was ready to collapse and be taken care of.

But his spine stayed straight, held erect by determination he hadn't known he possessed. He stepped forward, ahead of Gunnald, and said, "I am Finnvid. These are the men who left with me in the summer. We have returned."

The sentries squinted at him in disbelief, and he remembered he was wearing ragged clothes with wind-burned, chapped skin showing about an almost-full beard. Of course they didn't know him.

How ironic it would be to travel all that distance and be turned away at the gates of his home. But then Gunnald was recognized, and Zenain presented papers to the sentries with an order that they be sent by runner to the castle. Now they knew who Finnvid was, there was talk of waiting at the sentry hut for a sleigh to come out and convey him home, and various people had various opinions on the topic, so Finnvid started walking.

He was dimly aware of men falling in behind him: the Sacrati. Maybe they were expressing solidarity, or maybe they were just tired of standing around. But they were there.

The others must have joined the procession, although he never turned around to check. For a while, his eyes were busy absorbing the familiar sights of home: the snow-covered pastures, the croplands, the orchards, and the villages. Unlike Windthorn, the Elkat valley was designed for prosperity, not defense. The castle was fortified, yet everything else—every*one* else—was spread out in the places where the work was done. Instead of a single walled city, there were several smaller villages, protected by nothing but a guard post. With his newly trained eyes, he could see how exposed the valley was.

There were certainly advantages to the Elkat system. If he'd been tired enough or shameless enough, he could have ducked inside one of the larger houses in the first village and waited for that sleigh to come pick him up. If he made it a little farther, to the next village, there'd be a rough inn, one used by traders who couldn't drive their caravans all the way to the castle market in time for nightfall.

But he hadn't walked all that way to quit right on his doorstep. So he kept moving, and as the sun was setting, they reached the castle itself. Rough stone, few windows, a moat and a drawbridge; finally, the Elkat valley was showing its defenses. Of course Finnvid knew, and was sure the Torians could tell, that the castle wasn't large enough to have much food or water stored. It could protect its inhabitants from quick raids, yet it would never stand up to a patient siege. And Torian invaders were known for their patience.

"You're home, Prince Finnvid," Ekakios said. Finnvid turned to see the Sacrati step off the path. "We'll leave you here, safe."

"You need to resupply," Finnvid protested. "Rest, too, even if you only stay one night."

"It's not necessary," Ekakios said.

Then Zenain strode forward, and leaned in so only Ekakios and Finnvid could hear him. "We should stay the night," he said firmly. "My men need the break, and the supplies. If they know the Sacrati are out here, it will create resentment, and we don't need that right now. Bring your men in, and let them have a few drinks with their comrades before we head for home."

Ekakios frowned. "Our hosts may not appreciate having a band of drunken Torians under their roof."

"So tell your Sacrati to control themselves. Surely their famed discipline can extend that far?"

"The Sacrati are not my chief concern," Ekakios said pointedly.

"They should be." Zenain's voice was close to a growl. "They should be your *only* concern. Do not overstep yourself."

"I'm sure it won't be a problem," Finnvid interjected. "We have a Great Hall, where traders and travelers of all sorts feast and then sleep in the summer. And the messengers will have told my brother we were approaching; he'll have food prepared for us." He grinned as he saw Ekakios's wistful expression. "Roasts, and vegetables and fresh bread, and wine and ale, and cake and fruit. A *feast*. He'll be most put out if he has no one to share it with."

Ekakios looked at the castle, then at his men, and finally shrugged acquiescence. "I wouldn't want him to be put out."

Finnvid knew the wave of relief that washed over him was a sign of a larger problem, but he chose to ignore it, focusing instead on keeping his gaze away from Theos. He waved an arm somewhat grandiosely toward the castle and told the men, "Please, come inside. Welcome to Elkat Castle."

The men trailed in behind him, and he glanced around to see the Torians staring at the building: the mosaics on the wall, the light wells and the gas-powered lamps, the mirrors and carpets, and the soaring staircase in the main entry. It was much fancier than they were used to, maybe fancier than anything they'd ever seen.

But, he realized, that wasn't why they were staring. At least, not why the Sacrati were. They were assessing the defenses, scanning for hazards, memorizing the terrain and searching for advantages. And maybe that was why they were the first to become alarmed.

Finnvid saw the Sacrati step to the sides of the grand entry hall, looking for shelter, and followed their gazes to the archers in the upper gallery. "No, it's fine," he said with a laugh. "It's not unheard of for them to be there; just security, nothing to worry about."

He peered ahead and saw his brother step into the entry hall, his deep-purple, fur-lined coat swinging as he moved. "Alrik," Finnvid said in greeting, and he strode forward as his brother raised his arms for an embrace. The embrace was stronger than usual, almost fierce, more like wrestling than hugging, and Finnvid had to stagger to maintain his balance.

And then he was yanked forward—his brother was dragging him out of the entry hall! Finnvid struggled, but he was too shocked and confused to be effective. He heard screams from behind him, roars of anger, pounding feet, metal clashing against metal.

The archers. The archers were firing on the Sacrati. And Finnvid couldn't stop them.

CHAPTER 21

There were bodies everywhere.

It made no sense. None of it made sense.

It had taken only a minute for Finnvid to free himself from his brother's hold, but by the time he ran back to the door of the entry hall, it all seemed to be over.

The Elkati soldiers who'd been traveling with him had retreated into the antechamber, staring at the carnage. And the Torian soldiers, the non-Sacrati . . . they were still upright, over by the main doors. Zenain was standing in front of them, his arms wide as if shepherding them away from the massacre.

Finnvid tried to understand the scene in front of him. It was the Sacrati who'd been attacked. *Just* the Sacrati. They'd clearly counterattacked, somehow; there were Elkati bodies mixed in among the dead. But— The Sacrati— Finnvid stumbled forward, his brother's arm catching him again, holding him away from the bodies. From Theos.

Finnvid drove his elbow into his brother's ribs, twisted free, and launched himself toward the chaos. There was so much blood, and so many bodies. Some of the archers had fallen down from the gallery and they'd landed on top of other men. There were moans and cries from the survivors, and maybe one of them was Theos . . .

More hands caught at him now. Strong, trained hands, yanking at him, pinning him against the wall. If he'd had a knife, he would have plunged it unthinkingly into those restraining him. But he wasn't armed; he was helpless.

Still he struggled. And then she was there. Lifting her skirts as she stepped daintily through the carnage, her gaze never leaving his face to acknowledge the disaster surrounding her. "My son," she said. "You've returned safely. We must celebrate."

He stared at her, then twisted so he could see his brother. "What have you *done*?" he screamed. "Why?"

"We'll talk," his mother said calmly. "But you're exhausted. You need to rest now, and clean up." She turned to the guards holding him. "Take him to his rooms. There are servants waiting for him there."

He fought. He screamed and swore and kicked. But the men holding him were well armored, and strong, and there were too many of them. They dragged him to the rooms that had been his home since he left the nursery, and pushed him through the doorway. Servants *were* there, waiting for him, but he swore at them too, and struggled with the guards as they tried to pull him toward the bathing room. It couldn't be real. It couldn't have happened. He needed to go back downstairs and— He didn't know *what* he needed. He needed to make it not be true.

"Release him," his mother said.

Finnvid hadn't seen her follow them up the stairs, but the guards didn't seem surprised by her sudden presence, and let go of Finnvid so quickly that he stumbled to his knees.

He didn't bother to stand, just stared up at her and whispered, "Why? They came as *allies*."

She turned to the servants. "Leave us. Guards, wait outside, please."

As they all began to move, she stepped forward and then crouched to take Finnvid's hand. "Come," she said, and she guided him to his feet. But as she tried to lead him to the low padded bench by the window, he jerked his hand away.

"They may still be alive." He headed for the door. "I need to go to them! We can help them—"

"Listen to yourself," she said firmly. "You're talking about the Torians. Worrying about *them*. Did you notice how many of our own men those animals killed? Do you even *care* about the Elkati lives that were lost today?"

"I care." At some level, he was sure he did. "But they *attacked* the Sacrati! The Torians came in peace."

"*Torians* came in peace?" She sounded scornful, but her tone gentled as she added, "We know what they did to you. How they treated you. It's quite common for prisoners to get confused, and form bonds with their captors. Quite common for slaves to *die* in defense of the ones who took away their freedom. It will pass, Finnvid."

"My captors? They escorted me home! What kind of captors would deliver their prisoner to his family?"

"So you *willingly* traveled to Windthorn and stayed with the Torians all through the fall?"

"No, of course not. Initially, I was a prisoner. But the Sacrati thought I was trespassing on their land! *They* didn't know I'd been invited to a meeting with the Torian warlord. And he didn't tell them! *He* was the one who left me imprisoned." Finnvid's shocked brain finally began to understand what had happened. "And *he's* the one who sent the message to you. When we arrived in the valley, and the couriers were sent with messages . . . he sent his version of the story to you, and you read it and you believed it."

Finnvid shook his head vigorously and started for the door. "They may not be dead. Maybe not all of them." Arrows were lethal, especially at close range, but Sacrati were tough. Theos was invincible, surely, and the others almost as strong. The Sacrati, everyone who'd stood by him and befriended him, they couldn't all be dead. He wouldn't let that be true.

"We received the message, and we acted accordingly," his mother said. "What's done is done. You must understand: the Sacrati attacked us and we responded in self-defense. It's tragic, but it's over. We can't afford to have Sacrati returning to Windthorn and saying anything different."

"That's the story the other Torians will tell?" He spun toward her. "No. Maybe at first, but they'll tell the truth eventually."

"They didn't see what happened. They were still in the vestibule. They didn't *see* one of the Sacrati lunge at a guard, yet they'll believe it happened. Everyone knows Sacrati are aggressive, and our guards had no reason to attack other than self-defense."

Her tone was so level, so confident, that for a moment Finnvid doubted himself. Then he wondered how many other lies she'd told him in the same tone, lies he hadn't caught. "*I* won't believe it." He wouldn't sacrifice the only power he had left. "By the sword," he said, the Torian oath sounding strange in the Elkati, "*I* will know what happened."

This was right. He could feel it deep in his gut. "*I* will know. Maybe I can believe that it was a mistake, as long as you do the right thing *now*. The Sacrati need to be tended to. If any of them are still alive, they need healing. I will do it myself." He turned and started for the door again. What if someone *had* survived the attack, but had been killed as the bodies were sorted through, while Finnvid wasted time talking to his mother?

"No, Finnvid," she snapped. "We'll take care of them. You need to stay here. You need to get clean, and dress yourself as befits a prince." He could hear her following him. "If they twisted your mind, and made you someone you aren't, then they deserve to die. So if you want any survivors to live, you need to show me that you're the same loyal, obedient son you've always been."

Finnvid stood frozen.

"As soon as you agree to let the servants come in and bathe you, I will go downstairs and see what's to be done for any surviving Sacrati. If any *have* survived, they'll be cared for." Her voice was deceptively gentle. "But I'm a mother, and when my ability to protect is thwarted, I resort to my ability to take revenge. If I find that I wasn't able to protect you from their manipulations . . . I *will* take revenge on anyone within my reach."

It was chilling.

How would Theos respond to such a situation? But Finnvid couldn't smash something and then fuck whoever was handy. What about Andros? He'd smile and laugh and assume the other person was joking, because surely no one could ever be so cold-blooded. Yet Finnvid knew better than imaginary Andros. So he answered as himself—the older, wiser him that he'd become over the past months. "I understand," he said. "And I hope there *are* Sacrati alive, for your sake as well as theirs. Because if they survive and are cared for, you'll have a useful tool for controlling me. Without them? I'm honestly not sure how you'll make me do what you want."

They stared at each other for a moment until Finnvid said, "Call the servants, please. I'd like to bathe."

She gave him another look, then turned and headed for the door. He was gratified to see her moving briskly, but it wasn't enough to take away the shock and the fear. The servants came in and led him into the bathing room and added a few buckets of steaming water to the tub before encouraging him to undress and climb in. One part of him was aware of their clucking and fussing over every scratch from his adventures, but mostly he was elsewhere. In the warm bathhouse of Windthorn, on Theos's hard floor with the Sacrati sleeping almost beside him. At the training grounds, on the cold trail, in the stormy forest with Theos above him, in that moment of tenderness before it all went to hell.

And then in the hall below. Finnvid had laughed—*laughed*—when he'd seen the Sacrati's alarm. He'd given them foolish words of comfort. Had they listened to him? Had they believed him? Had Theos's last thought been that Finnvid had betrayed him again, lied to him *again*?

He pushed himself out of the tub, drawing a cry from the man who'd been trying to shave him. "I'll do it myself," Finnvid growled. He couldn't sit there any longer, being pampered while people he cared about were—what? Dead?

Yes, at least some of the Sacrati were dead. He'd seen too much of the carnage to believe otherwise. It seemed impossible that Theos could be among them; he was too vibrant, too alive. But which of the Sacrati *should* be vulnerable to something as puny as an arrow? What had happened in the hallway hadn't been in accordance with any rules Finnvid understood.

He needed to know. And he needed to avoid making things worse. "Give me the razor," he ordered. He'd shave, and he'd dress, and he'd play whatever games his mother wanted. But he wouldn't stay in his rooms, ignoring the larger world. He couldn't hide. Not from this.

CHAPTER 22

As soon as he was clean, Finnvid returned to the entry hall where the Sacrati had been attacked. At least, he tried to, but he found himself frozen on the threshold. He thought of Theos, and Andros, and for the first time remembered that Andros had broken away from the other Sacrati as they'd entered the valley. Andros was still alive. And Finnvid would find him, one day, and Andros would want answers. Finnvid needed to have them.

So he swallowed hard, once and then again, and forced himself into the room. There were servants cleaning up, but the bodies were all gone. So were the soldiers, Elkati and Torian alike, who'd witnessed the massacre. Were the Torians already headed back to Windthorn? What message would they bear? How would Theos's mother react to the news? Would she be resigned to her son finally finding the violent death she believed he'd been seeking? But, no, she hadn't said "violent"; she'd said "heroic." And there was nothing heroic about what had happened in that hall.

"Where's my brother?" Finnvid demanded of the nearest servant. The woman blinked up at him, her hands stained red from the blood she was scrubbing at, and he recoiled as if she'd been a viper. "The king," he managed. "Or the queen mother. Or— Were there any men taken from this room? Any *living* men?"

She stared at him wordlessly, and for a moment he wondered if she was strange in her head. Or maybe she was just as stunned by it all, just as horrified and torn apart and bewildered as he was. Then he remembered that he was in Elkat. Servants here might not be slaves, technically, but they were treated as barely human. This woman, confronted with an angry prince, was almost certainly expecting a blow. She wasn't ready to give him any helpful information.

He crouched down, trying to ignore the blood on the floor, trying not to think if it belonged to someone he knew. "Did they take anyone away for medicine?" he asked in a gentler voice.

This time the woman nodded.

"Where did they go?"

She pointed her eyes in the direction of the Great Hall, and he stood quickly. "Thank you," he said, then caught himself. Elkati princes did not thank servants.

That was what he was worried about, the propriety of it all? He'd been back in Elkat for such a short time, and already was falling into old patterns of thought. He nodded at her, then headed toward the Great Hall.

As he approached the ornately carved double doors, a scream rang from inside the room, and he stumbled to a halt. He reassured himself that the voice hadn't been familiar, as far as he could tell by a scream. But shouldn't he be *hoping* to recognize a voice? Even agony was preferably to death.

Finnvid made himself enter the room, and his nightmare changed from a frightening abstraction to something far too concrete and real. There were bodies everywhere, most of them close together and being ignored, but a few spaced out far enough that people could crouch by their sides and tend to them. The many dead, and the few living.

This was too close to home, with the bodies laid out in the room he usually saw decorated for dances and feasts. And Finnvid wasn't a soldier; he'd seen death, but not often. His mind was torn between the need to know and abject terror: it was all too much, and he sagged back against the doorjamb, trying to control himself before he ran from the room.

"Finn." His brother's voice wasn't gentle, exactly, but it wasn't cruel either. "Mother spoke to me."

And Finnvid's rage gave him strength. "You made a horrible mistake." He spun and glared at his brother. "The Sacrati are not the enemy. And Theos—one of the Sacrati—his mother is the reeve of Windthorn: the civilian leader. She was working with the reeves of Cragview and Greenbrook to ensure their support for peace. If you've killed her only son . . ."

Alrik shook his head. "We knew about her. It was in the letter the warlord sent. He said the reeves exaggerate their own importance, while the warlords are the ones who run the armies. Finnvid, we aren't worried about the Torian *women*."

"You should be," Finnvid snarled. But this wasn't what he needed to talk about. "Where are the Sacrati?" He made his voice calmer. "Did any survive?"

"Mother was right. She said you were more concerned about the enemy than about your own citizens."

"My own citizens aren't the ones I led into a trap," Finnvid said through gritted teeth. "And I know you'll take good care of them. So I'm worried about the Sacrati, yes."

Alrik looked around, then leaned in a little closer and lowered his voice. "The warlord told us what they did to you. The Sacrati. He said the Sacrati who—the one who—who thought he *owned* you—the one who abused you—the warlord arranged for him to be sent on this trip. Is that right?"

Finnvid stared. "No one— Do you mean *rape*? When you say 'abused,' is that what you mean? No one did that!"

"Of course," Alrik said hurriedly. "Of course not. But the one who *tried*. Is he here?"

"If a Sacrati had tried to rape me, I'd have been raped. But none of them tried."

"Finnvid, we know you were enslaved. Not just from the warlord; we've started questioning the men who were with you, and they're confirming the story. I understand why you'd want to deny it, and once we're done with this you need never speak of it again. But we *know*. And we will take revenge if we haven't already."

Finnvid wanted to scream. "I wasn't raped. Ask the men what they actually *saw*. I was claimed from a chain of others, and those others . . ." Finnvid didn't really want to think about the fate of the others. "They *were* intended for slavery, I assume of that sort. But Theos only claimed me as a way to *rescue* me. He never told me to do more than wash his clothes and train."

"Train?"

"As a warrior. That's how Sacrati measure manhood, so he was trying to help me become worth something. If he'd been planning to hurt me, he wouldn't have spent his time training me to defend myself!" And with that, Finnvid was out of patience. He pulled himself up straighter and said, "Did any Sacrati survive the attack?"

Alrik looked undecided, but finally nodded. "Yes. One."

Finnvid's entire body was tight, but he managed to make his voice sound almost normal. "Where is he?"

"You don't need to see him."

"Alrik. Where is the Sacrati?"

Another indecisive moment before Alrik jerked his chin in the direction of the back hallway, the one that led to the kitchen and storage rooms. Finnvid didn't listen to whatever words of warning Alrik tried to give him; he couldn't hear past the blood rushing through his veins.

Finnvid strode forward and didn't stop or even slow down, not while his stomach clenched, not while this strange mix of cold and heat washed over him. He reached the half-open door of a storage room and possibly he staggered a little from the sudden dizziness when he heard a mumbled, guttural curse in a voice that sounded like— No, he wouldn't hide behind a dream. He had to *know*.

But then he heard his mother's light voice and made himself freeze. He needed to ensure that he didn't make things worse. He wasn't a child, he was a man, so he needed to be strong, and responsible. And until he convinced his family of his mental fitness, he needed to be very, very careful. So he calmed himself and pretended he had no particular interest in the man lying in the storage room. Whoever he was, he was just a fellow traveler.

Gunnald's voice was low and close, as if he'd come over toward the doorway. "It's a miracle he survived."

"Not exactly." His mother spoke a little louder than Gunnald, as if she didn't care who heard her. "He's the one who made it up the gallery stairs. At close range, the archers didn't have the advantage. The bastard killed half a flight of our best men before enough guards got in to stop him. It's good you're back, Gunnald, because clearly our forces need your strong hand in training; this was supposed to be a precision attack, and instead the savages almost survived! They were close to winning the battle, and then what would have happened, with a band of enraged Sacrati loose in our castle?"

"They're great warriors." Gunnald didn't seem grudging in his praise. But he was more reluctant when he added, "And there are a couple hundred more of them in Windthorn. The conditions in that valley . . . I wish you'd waited to consult, your grace. I don't agree that the Torians will just believe the story you send back, and I'm not sure it would matter regardless. If we've killed Sacrati, we've proved ourselves dangerous. And Torians are not the sort to let a dangerous neighbor sit peacefully and get stronger."

"You forget your place," the queen mother said sharply. "You've been away for too long. You need to trust your king, and his advisors. We know things about the Torian situation that you do not, and we have made our decisions based on our superior knowledge and understanding."

Finnvid knew he should listen more and work out a plan, but he couldn't wait any longer to know. So he pushed away from the wall he'd been leaning on and eased the door open. His eyes glanced over his mother, then he addressed himself to Gunnald. "A Sacrati survivor?" He was proud of how level his voice sounded.

"Yes, sir."

"Who?" Finnvid asked, trying to act as though the world didn't depend on Gunnald's answer.

And Gunnald, bless him, turned a little, giving Finnvid an excuse to move with him so his face wasn't visible to his mother when Gunnald said, "It's Theos, sir. He's in rough shape, but still alive. At least for now."

Theos. Of course it was Theos: the most aggressive, the strongest. Finnvid kept his body upright and made himself nod as if this was just another interesting bit of news. He wouldn't let himself even glance in the direction of the man on the floor, not with his mother watching him. He bit the inside of his cheek, drove his nails into his palms, and fought to remain in control. When he had his expression schooled into something approaching calm, he turned to his mother. "I'd like to speak to you and Alrik, as soon as possible."

"We have rather a lot to deal with currently."

He shouldn't be surprised by her dismissal. He'd always been the lesser son, the baby, and for most of his life he'd been glad of the freedom he gained from their lack of interest. His mother and brother were a team, running the valley after the old king's death; Finnvid had been left to his studies. He'd known he didn't have their respect.

It would be so easy to quit. To retreat to his rooms, banish the servants, and sob his gratitude and shock and sorrow to the skies. But Theos wasn't safe yet. Theos needed him to be strong. "I appreciate that you're busy. However, Alrik sent me to Windthorn because he wanted me to become more involved in affairs of state, and I worked hard during my time with the Torians to gather intelligence. I have important information to share."

There was a little sound, just a rustle of fabric, and his eyes instinctively tracked it to its source. He tried not to gasp at Theos's bloodied face, or the way his eye was swollen shut, and made himself meet the furious stare from the Sacrati's one good eye. Theos didn't speak Elkati. He wouldn't have known exactly what Finnvid had said. But he'd have heard the tone, and seen Finnvid standing there unharmed and wearing fine clothes. Theos angrily jerked his arm, and it was only then Finnvid realized the man was chained to the wall.

Finnvid did what he had to. He sneered down at Theos and said in Torian, "Yes, I know, I'm a dirty Elkati spy. You hate me. I *know*, Torian. I just don't *care*." He turned away from the rage on Theos's face and shrugged at his mother, shifting back to Elkati to say, "They're great warriors, but not a sophisticated people. It wasn't hard to learn about their politics, and the tensions in their society. I think there are ways for us to take advantage of these weaknesses." And then the important part. "Alive, this man is a possible tool for our use. If he dies, we lose that potential."

His mother examined him, and he kept his gaze level. He'd been lying for his whole life, deceiving his family and everyone around him, and he was good at it. His skill might have hurt Theos in Windthorn, but in Elkat it might save him, as long as Finnvid could keep his cool.

"He could be useful," his mother admitted. "Possibly."

"Easy enough to kill him later. Very difficult to bring him back to life."

She narrowed her eyes at that, and Finnvid realized he'd gone too far. Usually his flippancy would be no surprise, but it had been less than an hour since she'd seen him raving and screaming as he was dragged to his quarters; the change had been too drastic.

So he made his smile a bit more tremulous. "I really should explain what I learned. But maybe you're right; maybe it could wait. I'm exhausted." He tried to look ashamed and apologetic. "This wasn't the homecoming I wanted, but I'm glad to be here anyway. Maybe I should sleep, and we can talk in the morning? I just wanted to be sure the Torian wasn't wasted. I think we need to keep him alive for now, and then we can decide what to do with him later."

She nodded slowly, still cautious, but believing him. He hoped.

"Yes, go and rest. You're right, this isn't the celebration we should have had. Soon, we will feast."

So Finnvid turned to go and saw Gunnald watching him closely. He had a feeling the older man had seen through his charade; it was lucky that Gunnald had recently been rebuked for speaking his mind, so he likely wouldn't share his suspicions.

Finnvid left the room without even looking at Theos. If they'd been alone, he'd have thrown himself on the cold flagstones, torn at his clothes to make bandages for Theos's wounds; he would have licked the man clean if there'd been no water to wash him. And he'd almost certainly have cried, and begged forgiveness, and if Theos granted it, Finnvid would have stayed with him for as long as he could. He'd have stayed with him forever.

But they weren't alone. So he walked calmly out of the room, then down through the kitchen and up the back stairs so he could avoid seeing his brother. He wondered where the other Torians were. They'd been his companions on the journey as well, and he'd invited them into the castle to eat and rest. But the only room large enough for all of them was the Great Hall, and it was being used as a field hospital. He was tired, but he forced himself to turn around to find someone who would know more.

He was startled to see that Gunnald had been following him. "I wanted to be sure you were safe," the older man said quickly. Then he stepped closer. "And I wanted to know what I should do."

Finnvid frowned. For their entire adventure together, Gunnald had been happy to take charge whenever Finnvid didn't insist on having a voice, and now he was feeling deferential? Yes, of course he was. Now that they were back in Elkat, independent action could get him in trouble, but actions taken on the direction of a member of the royal family might win him favor.

Of course, Finnvid wasn't the only member of the royal family Gunnald had recently been in contact with. He could very well have been sent by the queen mother to spy on her youngest son. "Are the other Torians cared for?" Finnvid asked. "I promised them food and beds."

"We sent them to the traders' inn. They'll be fine there."

Finnvid nodded. "And your men? They're well?"

"Your brother's men asked them a few questions and then sent them to the barracks. We'll grant them leave to go visit their families once we're sure they're not needed here."

"Then I think we've done everything we can." Finnvid knew it was an unnecessary risk, but he couldn't keep himself from adding, "You heard what I said about the Sacrati. About keeping him alive so he can be useful. Do you agree?"

Gunnald frowned. "It's a bad situation. Is it better to kill him and keep things tidy? We've already—" He stopped himself. "It's complicated," he said finally. "I'm not sure how Windthorn will react. I'm not sure the other Torians will tell the story we want them to. To be completely, coldly rational, it might be safer to kill them all, really. But if *no one* comes back from this trip alive? I can't imagine the Torians reacting well to that."

"You didn't know what the warlord's letter said? You didn't know this was going to happen?"

"I'm a soldier! Maybe not as skilled as the Torians, but I'm a man of honor. To live with them, train with them, travel with them, and then betray them?" Gunnald's outrage seemed genuine. "No, Prince Finnvid. I did not know what the letter said."

Finnvid believed him, and it was a relief. "But Zenain knew. He was ready for it when the Sacrati were attacked. He held his men back, kept them from joining the battle. If they'd fought, the Sacrati might have won. But he didn't let it happen."

"It would seem so."

"And insisting that we be accompanied all the way home . . . that was his idea, too. Ekakios was ready to go home at the border, but he didn't trust Zenain on his own. He worried that Zenain might hurt me, so he put his men in danger to protect me. *Me*. And I brought them to *this*." Ekakios was dead, the other Sacrati were dead . . . Finnvid thought of Andros again, stepping off the path as if to answer a call of nature. He was out there somewhere, and he didn't know that his comrades were dead, and Theos imprisoned. He didn't know how horribly wrong it had all gone.

Gunnald's hand was warm and strong on his shoulder. "You were betrayed too, my prince. You didn't know."

"It's a leader's *job* to know. I've been prancing around, acting important because my father was king, but what have I ever done to earn anyone's allegiance? Why should anyone trust *me*?"

Gunnald smiled grimly. "I had similar questions this summer when you were put in charge of the mission." He watched Finnvid for a moment, then shrugged. "I'm starting to change my mind."

Maybe that should have made Finnvid feel good, but instead it was just another weight on his already exhausted shoulders. He forced a smile and tried to think like an Elkati prince. "I appreciate that." And though they were alone in the hallway, he leaned in a little to say, "Can you keep an eye on things for me? You know, with the injured Sacrati, and the other Torians. Your men too, if there's any trouble there. I think my family expects me to give up on all my responsibilities now that I'm home, and I can see why they'd expect that; it's certainly consistent with how I've behaved in the past. But this was *my* mission, and I don't feel like it's over yet." That was good. No mention of his feelings for Theos, no overpowering guilt or anger. Just a sense of responsibility. If Gunnald reported this conversation to the queen mother, there should be no repercussions, and if he didn't, Finnvid might get some information from it.

Gunnald nodded, apparently pleased to have a mission. "I will. And if there's a problem . . . I can come to you for help?"

"Come to me," Finnvid agreed. He wasn't sure what help it would be in his power to give, but he supposed that was *his* job; he needed to spend his time doing what was needed to ensure that he *did* have power, and could be useful.

And the first step in that was acting as his family expected him to. "I'm retiring for the night. Get some sleep yourself, Gunnald."

The older man smiled, and Finnvid very much wanted to trust him. But he couldn't be sure, and guessing wrong would be disastrous.

So they parted without further conversation, and Finnvid went to his rooms and felt guilty about the soft, clean sheets he crawled between, while so many others were fighting for their lives. But there was nothing he could do about that, not right then, so he lay still and tried to clear his mind. It took longer than he'd have liked, yet eventually his exhaustion claimed him, and he faded off to sleep.

CHAPTER 23

"It's no use planning a strategy for where we were yesterday." Alrik was imposing, standing up and leaning over his desk to glare at Finnvid more effectively. They were in Alrik's study, morning light streaming in through the long, narrow windows. "Maybe we made a mistake. We were operating on the best intelligence we had, and I'm still not convinced it was wrong, but *maybe* it was a mistake. If so, it's been made. It's too late to change it based on anything you learned in Windthorn."

"No, it's *not* too late." Finnvid would never have dreamed of arguing with Alrik before the trip to Windthorn, but anyone who could defy an angry Sacrati could absolutely contradict his own brother. "It *was* a mistake yesterday. A horrible mistake. And it *did* change things, yet not so much that we're doomed, I don't think. We just need to adjust our strategy."

Alrik stared at him but didn't say anything, so Finnvid continued. "If we do nothing, then the warlord has gotten what he wanted. He's ensured that we're in his pocket, because every other Torian faction hates us. That must have been his motivation for ordering the attack, right? To get rid of a few strong Sacrati, and to ensure that we couldn't go behind his back and deal with the Sacrati *or* the reeve, since we'd just killed the Sacrati men *and* the reeve's son." It was easier to stay calm when he thought of Theos as a pawn rather than as a forceful, vibrant man.

Still he had to push a little. "But we *haven't* killed the reeve's son. Have we? He remains alive?"

"Alive," Alrik agreed. "He's hanging on. There were a couple arrows that did him no good, and a few slash wounds from when the guards reached him." He shrugged. "And the head injury, and maybe some extra bruises from afterward. The men were pretty pleased to have a Sacrati in their power."

"That needs to *stop*!" Finnvid caught himself and didn't speak again until he was sure he could control his voice. He let a little anger bleed in to cover for the horror that had been in his last words. "It's *stupid*, Alrik. Our only chance now is to claim that we made a mistake. We were tricked by the warlord. We followed *his* orders, but as soon as we realized they were wrong, we did everything we could to rectify the situation. We gave the Sacrati survivor the best treatment and we are willing to support our Windthorn allies as they work to deal with the problems in their valley that brought death and destruction to *our* castle."

"If there's internal conflict with the Torians, we need to back the winner," Alrik said with a frown. "Sacrati are legendary—and their performance yesterday shows that the legend is deserved—but there aren't many of them. And Torian regulars may not be quite so elite, yet they're still great warriors. I've spoken to some of the men who traveled with you about the Torian training they did, and they all admitted it was tougher than anything we'd even consider in Elkat. They weren't training with Sacrati, just regular Torian soldiers. You really think a small band of Sacrati could take on the Torian war machine?"

"You're leaving two factors out," Finnvid said. He tried to sound completely confident in his ideas. "You have to consider the resolve of the soldiers. The Sacrati would be fighting for their lives, and to revenge a savage attack on their own. They're a *tight* group, Alrik. They would be completely committed to their battle. The Torian regulars? The warlord is a skilled manipulator, I'll give him that. Yet I traveled with the Sacrati and the regulars on the way here, and they got along well. That's what I saw in training at Windthorn, too. The Sacrati were more intense, but they often exercised right alongside the others." Finnvid decided not to mention that the Sacrati and the Torian regulars had all probably had sex with each other. "I'm not sure the Torian regulars would follow the warlord into battle against their own."

Alrik didn't seem exactly pleased at being lectured by his previously worthless younger brother, but he was listening. He raised an eyebrow as he said, "And the second factor I'm leaving out?"

"The *women*," Finnvid said firmly. "It's not like we thought it was, before I left. The women aren't drudges, exhausted from being treated as broodmares and doing all the menial labor. The women run the valley. The economy, the crafts, the agriculture—they're absolutely in charge of everything but the military. Even reproduction. *They* call the men to the city when they want them. The children do a lot of the menial tasks—laundry or whatnot—and there really isn't as much of that sort of work there as there is here. No great dinners with white linens and fancy foods. They live more simply, but more equally, too. The women are a force to be reckoned with. And I've been told—and it makes sense, based on what I saw—that the men would never attack the city. Their mothers and sisters and children live in there, and they wouldn't endanger them."

Alrik pursed his lips and glanced over toward the rolled parchment on his desk. "You haven't read the warlord's letter," he said thoughtfully. "But you've guessed at a lot of it. Which makes me think you understand the situation over there fairly well."

"But there's something I'm missing?"

"Possibly." Alrik made a face, one Finnvid remembered from their childhood. Alrik was trying to decide how much information to share. Unfortunately, in their childhood capers Finnvid had usually let his brother down; he'd reported the theft of the sweet plums, or wandered off when he was supposed to be standing guard. But maybe Alrik had forgotten, because he finally waved an arm toward the desk. "Read it," he said. Apparently making it sound like an order was easier than admitting he'd like Finnvid's opinion.

And Finnvid didn't need to be ordered twice. He grabbed the letter and scanned it quickly. It was addressed to Alrik, written in Torian, and signed by the warlord. He returned to the top and went through it more carefully. He looked over at his brother, who was watching with more patience than usual, and then nodded slowly. "It's mostly lies," Finnvid said. "I can see why you thought you were protecting me. Or getting revenge, I suppose. But I've told you the truth. The Sacrati didn't abuse me. I was a terrible slave, really, disrespectful and sullen, and no one ever raised a hand to me. It was the *warlord* who knew who I was, and he left me enslaved because—" Finnvid stopped, frowned, then said, "*because he wasn't powerful enough to get me free.*" It was true, and it was important. "He tried to sneak me out in the slave train; I assume I'd have been rescued somewhere in the forest and sent home. Then he tried to bully Theos into giving me to him. But Theos didn't give in, and the warlord couldn't do a thing about it. If he had the sort of power over Windthorn that he claims, he'd just have ordered them to free me and it wouldn't have been an issue."

"It may have been a question of timing," Alrik said, but he didn't sound sure. "He may still have been consolidating his power. And we don't know what's happened over there since you left."

Finnvid couldn't argue with that. He looked down at the letter again. It was mostly what he'd expected. The first part was a cleverly worded manipulation: there was no actual *order* to attack the Sacrati, but there was a clear expression of understanding if such an attack were to occur, given the horrible treatment the Elkati prince had suffered at Sacrati hands. And then there were promises of alliances and mutual benefit, nothing that was new to Finnvid after the initial meeting with the warlord. But the third part was a puzzle. Until . . . "He wants *us* to attack the city," he gasped. "That's why he wants the exchange of troops. He'll send his most independent troops away from the city, to us or elsewhere, and we'll send him *our* men, for 'training,' and he'll use them to attack the city. The women aren't heavily armed, and they wouldn't be expecting it. It wouldn't take too many soldiers to take the place over."

Alrik nodded. "I think that may be it."

"It wouldn't work. Not long-term. Our men might be able to *take* the city, but they'd never hold it. Not once the women organized resistance, and certainly not once the Torian troops returned."

"I wonder how many Torian troops would be *left*," Alrik said. "If he can get the Sacrati fighting the regulars, there'd be huge casualties, surely. Is he that . . . merciless? Cruel? Could he be sinister enough to sacrifice his own men like that?"

"I don't know." Finnvid hoped not. "Maybe he's just planning to send for help from the central valleys. Even a *small* conflict between Sacrati and regular troops would be unheard of in the Torian Empire. I don't know how they'd handle it, but maybe they'd split the men up, and send new troops to serve under the warlord? Men who wouldn't be as loyal to the women in the city, and maybe men from the central valleys, who want Torian society to change in the same ways the warlord does."

Alrik shook his head in disgust. "We don't know. We just don't know enough to make good decisions."

"We know enough to make *some* good decisions," Finnvid objected. "We know the warlord's letter is full of lies, and he wanted us to do his dirty work for him." He left out any recriminating comments about just how easily Alrik had fallen into that trap, and tried not to think about the tragic results of his brother's mistake. "So surely we can decide not to work with him anymore, can't we? We can decide that his enemies are our friends?"

"We know not to trust him," Alrik agreed. "But, Finn… remember our ultimate goal here. We're not trying to solve the problems of the Torian Empire. We just want to look after Elkat."

The idea brought Finnvid up short. Alrik was right, of course. Alrik was thinking like a king, a *good* king, putting the interests of his people first. "But what does that *mean*? How do we do that?"

"We back the winner." Alrik sounded a little sad, but only a little, and his voice was more energetic as he added, "We aren't looking to make friends with the Torians. We aren't even looking at them as allies. We just want to be left alone."

"Will the winner do that? Or will he finish up in Windthorn and then look around for his next challenge? If we're not friends or allies, how do we ensure that we'll be left alone long-term?"

"We make our allies on the other side. The other valleys, the ones not yet under Torian control. We've started the process. We have treaties in place, but no one has built their armies enough, not to face a threat like this. If the Torians attacked, even just one valley of Torians, we'd have trouble defending ourselves. But every day we hold them off matters. We only started working on this a couple years ago, and we've already got several valleys willing to stand with us. If we can last another few years, especially if the Torians are weakening themselves with infighting, we'll have more allies, more troops, and a much better chance."

It made sense, but it also made Finnvid's skin crawl. The Torians weren't an abstraction to him, not any longer. They were living, breathing, kissing, fucking *people*. They weren't the horde. Were they?

"What if we could do something more?" he asked. "What if we could find some sort of common ground with the Torians? Their science is weak—they only learn from within the empire, without really talking to anyone outside. When they conquer new territory, the learning stays in that valley instead of spreading as it should. Their music, their art—it's very limited. But I think they'd enjoy those things if they had the chance. And maybe we could learn from them, too." Probably not a great time to discuss economic equality, but surely there were other contributions the Torians could make. "On the trip here, they built simple structures of snow to sleep in. Nothing too impressive, in terms of engineering, but none of us knew how to do it. We would have frozen to death if they hadn't shared their knowledge."

"You *did* get close to them." It didn't feel like an accusation, not like it did when their mother said it.

"I lived with them for months. And they treated us *well*. It was all based on their assumption that every living human would want to become a part of the Torian Empire, but once you get past that, they were kind. And honestly…" This part was probably a mistake. Probably not something Finnvid should be saying right then, or maybe ever. But this was his brother, and he wanted to be as honest as he could. "Have you ever heard of a valley revolting after it's been taken over by the Torians? I never have. And do you know why? It's because they get rid of the few people who will never agree to their ways—the royals, the nobles. They kill us or send us back east, I think. But for everyone else? The peasants, struggling to find food to eat and somewhere warm for the winter? They feed them, and give them clothes and beds. They expect work in exchange, of course, but we expect that too, and give less in return. For most people—" No, Finnvid wasn't stupid enough to complete that sentence, not even with Alrik. This wasn't the time to point out that for most people, things were *better* under Torian rule than under independence.

So he shrugged to show it wasn't a matter he would pursue. "They gave us chances, and they were patient." He remembered Theos's frequent bouts of frustration and smiled despite himself. "Well, not *always* patient. But always kind." Was that true? "Never cruel." He could stand behind that statement, at least.

"So you aren't their enemy." Alrik sounded *too* casual. "You'd like to be their friend." He smiled gently, as if inviting a confidence. "All of them, or one of them in particular?"

The hair on the back of Finnvid's neck stood on end. This was a trap. He had no idea what would happen to him if he fell into it, but he had a pretty good idea what would happen to Theos. "I spent more time with some than with others," he admitted. "One of them—" He stopped, wondering what Andros was up to and whether it would be wise to mention his presence to Alrik. "There was one who didn't come all the way with us. But his name is Andros, and he's . . . We think of Torians as being ill-humored, but he's not, at all. Andros was a good friend."

"Andros." Alrik looked surprised. "What about the one we've captured? The one who thought he owned you?"

"Theos?" Finnvid forced a shrug. "I think he has good intentions. Not quite as smart as Andros, maybe; less aware of the larger world. He was almost completely unable to admit that Torians aren't the best at every single thing. But he wasn't a problem."

"Mother said—" Alrik frowned before continuing. "She was worried. She thought you'd . . . She said you might have 'formed an unnatural attachment' to him."

Finnvid couldn't help himself. He schooled his face to innocence and said, "'Unnatural'? What do you mean?"

"She didn't say," Alrik said stiffly.

"Oh. Well . . ." Finnvid reflected for a moment and realized he could say it honestly. "No. Nothing unnatural, I don't think."

"But you still want him alive?"

"Well, yes. He was good to me. And more importantly, I think he could be useful."

They left it at that. Finnvid thought about asking to see Theos; he could visit the Elkat soldiers injured in the battle as well, and offer his healing skills, such as they were, to everyone.

Unfortunately, the queen mother remained a factor. Finnvid had ensured that she was busy elsewhere when he'd asked for his brother's time, but he knew she'd still hear about the conversation, just as she'd hear about anything else that happened in the castle. She always knew everything, eventually. And she was much harder to fool than Alrik.

If Finnvid slipped, even just a little . . . if he let his fingers linger on Theos's arm with no reason, if he looked too often or too long in the wrong direction, if he did *anything* to suggest an attachment, she would know about it. He couldn't take the chance.

"You should see the tailors," Alrik said just before Finnvid reached the office exit. He turned, and Alrik smiled fondly at him. "Your shirts don't fit anymore."

Finnvid moved his shoulders. He'd noticed the tightness when he'd dressed and had dismissed it as part of adjusting to tailored Elkat shirts after wearing loose tunics for so long. But now he looked down to see the shoulder seam threatening to burst, and realized that the fabric was tight around his biceps as well. Everywhere, really; a shirt that had once been loose was now filled past capacity. "Torian training," he said, forcing himself not to think about Theos and his demands on the training grounds. "I'll remedy the situation."

"We need to look like royals and play the part our people expect," Alrik said.

That wasn't something Finnvid could afford to argue with right then, so he obediently went to the tailors, and spent the afternoon wearing one of Alrik's shirts, itself a little on the small side. He ate dinner that night with his mother and Alrik and Alrik's pregnant wife, making appropriate comments about the coming heir and trying to think of a way to sneak off. But his mother was watching him as intently as a hunting falcon. Finnvid was the rabbit, currently under cover; as soon as he moved he'd be spotted and doomed. Only in this case it wasn't Finnvid the rabbit who'd be in trouble, it was Theos the wolf.

So Finnvid stayed still, and then went to bed like a good boy, and the next morning he managed to subtly ask his brother for news of the Sacrati prisoner and was told that he was recovering well and had been moved out of the storeroom.

"Oh, really?" Finnvid tried to sound unconcerned. "Where have you stashed him now?"

"They found somewhere easier to guard him. Now that he's stronger, they wanted him more securely chained."

"Alrik, he's a man, not a god. He can't break chains."

"He got those chains wrapped around the neck of one of the guards last night. There were two other guards in the room with him, and the doctor as well, and they were barely able to save the guard." Alrik looked at Finnvid closely as he added, "He's an animal, Finn. A savage."

Finnvid felt ill, but managed to say, "He's *chained up*, after being ambushed in a place he'd been told was safe and losing all his friends. And you *said* the guards had been abusing him after his injuries—was this guard one of those?" He moderated his tone. "I guess it makes sense to chain him more securely for everyone's safety. But has anyone talked to him yet? Explained the mistake? Shown him the letter? He *should* be enraged, Alrik. He's just being angry at the wrong people right now. We could change that."

"I'm still thinking it over."

"And mother is still pressuring you to . . . what? To kill him, so it's tidy? That's shortsighted, Alrik."

"She thinks it's too late to take your path. She thinks we've committed to the warlord, and there's no going back. So if we're on his side, we need to follow his instructions and kill them all."

"It's too late for that." Finnvid wasn't sure if this was wise or not, but he needed to try. "Andros—the kind Sacrati I mentioned yesterday—he didn't come into the valley with us. I told you, remember? If he sees the Torian regulars going back without the Sacrati, he'll know something's up, and he'll return to Windthorn before they do and make sure the Sacrati side is represented."

Alrik stared at him. "Damn it, Finnvid." He ran his hands through his hair, and for the first time Finnvid realized that being the king wasn't easy for his brother. Alrik always *acted* like it was, but that was just part of his policy of showing the people what he thought they needed to see. "The Torian regulars headed out the morning after they arrived. They're already long gone."

"Then Andros is long gone too. Or maybe he crept in among the regulars—he had friends among them, I know. Maybe he heard the story. But if they're racing back to Windthorn to report? A sole Sacrati will move faster than a band of regulars. He'll arrive first, so we need to keep this Sacrati alive, and we need to make him as comfortable as we can."

Alrik still looked undecided, and their mother came in then so Finnvid gave up the argument for the moment. He'd have better luck speaking to Alrik privately than getting into a duel with his mother.

That day was spent trying to act as if nothing had changed, and the day after that as well. Finnvid tried to catch the rhythms of castle life so he could know when they were disrupted, and did a little more skulking around, trying to figure out where Theos was being held. The valley had no real dungeon; the few prisoners they ever took were kept in chains, usually out in the open. He'd not seen anything of the sort lately, though, and he noticed enough guards heading for the cellars that he decided Theos was likely down there. Not a good sign, if the man was still being held in such unpleasant conditions, especially considering his injuries. But at least he was still alive.

How long could he last for? Finnvid needed to come up with a plan, something more than his continued campaign with his brother. But any overt steps he took would almost certainly alert his mother and result in Theos's death, not his escape.

It was a horrible situation. And it all got that much worse on the fourth night.

Finnvid was a hero, and he'd returned home after a long and dangerous mission. He needed to be celebrated. The queen mother had put together a feast, and there would be dancing afterward. His new clothes were ready, and he'd looked so handsome when he tried them on. The queen mother was delighted.

Finnvid let the planning continue, and tried not to be sick.

CHAPTER 24

Finnvid's skin crawled as he stood in line with his family and they greeted friends and relatives in the Great Hall. No traces of blood left, not there or in the entry, and yet Finnvid was sure he could still smell it. Would he ever again be in the room and not be reminded of the carnage and his own guilt? But he made himself smile, and he ate and drank and after dinner, he danced with some of the eligible daughters paraded by him.

It felt like different worlds were brushing far too near to each other. He wondered whether the sounds of their music and laughter reached Theos in the basement. Did Theos know the fate of the other Sacrati? What was he thinking? Did he feel abandoned and alone?

Finnvid had no answers, and as the questions kept piling up in his mind, he found it more and more difficult to keep his attention on the small talk and dance steps. How was he supposed to care about any of this with so many more important things going on? How was Alrik able to smile and chat when he was responsible for an entire valley, and when he'd given the order to have men killed just days before?

It was getting hard to breathe. The air felt too warm, too moist, as if it had been inside of everyone's lungs already, breathed in and out of this entire incestuous mass of sycophants, all of them playing games when they should be fighting for people's lives. The faces before him seemed unfamiliar, and he fought to control himself.

He heard someone say his name and spun one direction, then another, not knowing who had spoken, or why. And then a firm hand clapped onto his forearm and he looked down to see a familiar, totally human face. Short and plump and redheaded, with bright blue eyes that danced at the slightest provocation. "Gaiera," he whispered.

"I'm feeling faint, my lord. Will you walk me outside?"

"It's winter . . ."

"Just into the entry hall, then—" She stopped when he jerked his arm away, and turned to peer at him more closely. Gaiera had always been friendly, and now she seemed truly concerned. It made him want to cry. "The library, perhaps?" She reached out her hand again, and he managed to crook his elbow and make a somewhat respectable show of escorting her out of the Great Hall.

They walked down the side corridor in silence, and when they paused in front of the library doors, a servant stepped from a nearby alcove and pulled the doors open for them. As if they didn't have hands of their own.

Finnvid didn't object. The lamps in the room were turned down low, yet Gaiera waved the servant away and didn't bother to adjust the lamps herself. Instead, she slipped her fingers from his forearm to his hand and tugged him gently toward the leather chairs by the fire. "You've had a rough time lately," she said as she guided him into a seat. "You looked like you needed a break. I hope you don't mind my interference."

"You rescued me," he confessed, letting his eyes close as he leaned back into the upholstery. "How long do you think we have until they come looking for us?"

"I think we have as long as we want," she said, and as the meaning of the words became clear he opened his eyes to stare at her. She nodded. "They want us to marry. If you're absolutely against the idea, I should go back soon so my reputation won't be spoiled. But if you're willing to consider it— Well, no. If you're willing to *commit* to it, they won't disturb us."

"How do you know this?"

"Our mothers have been at work."

"I only got home a few days ago!"

"They've been contemplating it for a while, as I understand. But something happened since your return, I think, to make your mother keen to move things along." Gaiera's eyes were too bright, making him feel like she saw too much. "We've always been friends, Finnvid. If you don't want to tell me what's going on, I won't make a fuss, but I *will* go back to the Great Hall. I won't marry a man who won't share things with me."

He closed his eyes again, fighting for control as questions began to rise and take over his mind. They *had* always been friendly. Yet never friends, really. That wouldn't have been proper. He might have been friends with a girl who was completely unmarriable, but Gaiera was no such thing. Her father was a loyal supporter of Finnvid's family and a member of the King's Council, and her mother was a member of the royal family from two valleys over. Gaiera was so suitable she'd been considered as a candidate to become *Alrik's* wife and produce heirs to the throne.

"My mother is worried about me," he allowed. It wasn't safe to tell her much more. He opened his eyes. "Why did you and Alrik not marry?"

Her grin made it clear that she wasn't grieving the lost connection. And he could imagine seeing that grin more often, maybe every day. For the rest of his life? Yes, if she smiled like that, maybe he could stand it.

"I believe they decided it would be better to have someone more pliable in the role," she said.

"Are you unpliable?"

"Horribly so, yes."

"Well, now I'm intrigued." Could he do this? It would certainly calm his mother down if he became engaged. "Was there a specific incident that earned you the label, or was it an ongoing situation?"

"Ongoing." Another smile, this one more thoughtful. Then she leaned forward as if she had made up her mind to speak. "But after that . . . after they decided to look elsewhere for a bride . . . there *was* a specific incident. Hushed up, of course, but I believe it may be why our mothers are eager to see me married. And I wonder if it may be similar to the reason they'd like to see *you* married."

Had she been captured and enslaved by Torians, only to find herself falling in love with one of them and having passionate near-sex in a forest during a blizzard? He was tempted to ask the question out loud. "How do you mean?" he said instead, and he was proud of his control.

"I . . . formed an unsuitable attachment," she said carefully.

He supposed that *was* similar to his mother's reasons for wanting him married. Good to discover that he hadn't put her mind totally at ease yet. "With a commoner?" he asked politely.

"No. Well, yes, she—" Gaiera broke off, then raised her chin and stared him down. "She *was* a commoner, yes, but I don't believe that was their chief objection. And when I protested at their sending her away, and announced my intention to seek similar companionship in the future . . . I believe they decided it was best I was married as soon as possible."

He shouldn't be surprised, not after months in Windthorn, knowing how their women carried on. But here, in Elkat? Unheard-of, but he was clear proof that unheard-of attractions were possible, even in the best of families. It was also possible that this was a trap. If he confessed to his own weakness, would she report back to his mother?

He stood somewhat abruptly. "I think we should return to the Great Hall," he said. "I don't think it's been too long yet."

The emotions chased across her face. Anger, fear, disappointment, pride . . . and hurt. No one was a good enough liar to put on such a performance. He stretched a hand down to her, and waited while she stared at him cautiously before lifting her own hand and placing it lightly on his.

"We *have* always been friendly," he said. "And during my time in Windthorn I came to realize that there are more ways to feel and express love than we contemplate here in Elkat. But . . . if I am to marry, I would like to marry someone who wants me, and loves me. Not someone who thinks I will be a convenient curtain behind which she may carry on as she likes."

"You, a prince of Elkat, believe you will be allowed to marry for *love*?" She sounded amazed, but not scornful.

"I expect not. But I believe there are still vows to be made before one is married, and I believe myself capable of refusing to make them." He shrugged. "If I find myself unable to refrain, I will certainly seek you out."

She stood gracefully without putting any extra weight on his hand, and nodded. "I wish you luck, Prince Finnvid."

"And I you." He led her back to the Great Hall and saw his mother frown at their quick reentry. He turned to Gaiera then, facing away from the crowd, and said, "While I may not be interested in marriage at this time, it might be useful for both of us if we *appeared* to be contemplating it?"

"Are you asking permission to court me?"

"To a certain point, yes. If that would be agreeable to you."

She smiled up at him. "It would be lovely," she said with a charming curtsy. "And very convenient. I wonder how long we can put them off for that way?"

"As long as possible." He saw movement in a group of older women and whirled so his back was toward them. "They're coming over," he said, and almost cackled when he saw the expression on her face; it matched his own dread so completely, and it felt good to have an ally. "Do you think it would be too scandalous if we ducked out again?"

"I think it would be the perfect degree of scandalous," she said, already moving toward the nearest doorway.

He followed her, both of them holding hands and laughing like naughty children. The weight of everything would return, of course, but for that one moment, he felt light. They practically skipped along the hallway toward the kitchen: kindred spirits bonded by general disapproval.

And that was when the Sacrati appeared. Not Theos, but Andros. Andros, wearing a rough Elkati cloak, the hood up over his head with snow still on it. And there was someone with him. Someone smaller. They both spun, perhaps because they heard the small noise of surprise that rose from Finnvid's throat, and they both stared. Andros and Gunnald. The fugitive Sacrati and the loyal Elkat soldier, together. And stealing toward the door to the cellars.

All three of them stared, frozen in place. Gaiera was the only one who moved, staring first at Finnvid, then at the others, then back at Finnvid.

He forced himself to act, nodding to the men and then turning to Gaiera, trying to seem normal despite the queasy apprehension roiling his stomach. "Maybe we should go back to the library."

She didn't argue. But as they started walking she hissed, "What's going on?"

Finnvid froze again, then looked at Gunnald rather than Andros. "They're protecting Elkati honor," he said, ostensibly to her yet loud enough to be sure Gunnald would hear.

The old soldier nodded, just once, and then prodded Andros into motion. They disappeared down the stairs and Finnvid spun away, hoping desperately that they had a plan for disabling the guards rather than killing them. Theos needed to be rescued, and Finnvid would accept responsibility for whatever the outcome was; still, he didn't want any more blood on his hands.

He briefly contemplated going down the stairs and ordering the men to surrender Theos, but it was already too late. Andros was Sacrati, and that meant he was quick and thorough. By the time Finnvid caught up, any damage would have been done.

"So we didn't see any of that?" Gaiera said. She sounded willing to follow Finnvid's lead.

That was the end of it. At least, it *should* have been the end. Gaiera would cover for Finnvid while Theos and Andros escaped. The Sacrati would return to Windthorn, and Finnvid would go back to his old life in Elkat, without the dreadful tension of worrying about Theos all the time. He'd have to fret about a Torian invasion, he supposed, but that wouldn't happen for a while, if ever. He could step away from it all and let Alrik make the decisions. Maybe he *would* marry Gaiera.

He frowned down into her kind, confused face, and he shook his head. "I'm sorry, but I need to do something. Can you—would you mind—could you stay in the library? For as long as possible, before going back and telling them you were alone?"

"Alone? Where are you going to be?"

"I have business."

She frowned, but then said, "You'll tell me about it someday?"

"If I can," he promised, and he kissed her quickly on the forehead.

Her eyes were bright and interested as she nodded. "Go. I'll hold off the families."

He ran. Up the stairs to his brother's study, then down the hall to his own set of rooms. Then back to the kitchen, where he hovered indecisively at the top of the stairs. Would they still be down there, or gone already?

Finnvid pushed open the door to the courtyard and the footprints in the snow told the tale, although with the way the wind was blowing the trail wouldn't be visible for long. So they didn't have much of a lead on him. He jogged out into the snowy night, through the walled service yard, and yanked the wooden gate open. A sleigh was right in front of him, two dark horses hitched and ready, blankets piled in the back as if waiting for passengers . . . but no Sacrati in sight. How had he missed them?

He turned, saw a shadow change near the wall, and realized he hadn't missed them at all. The shadow came closer, big and bulky, the movement rougher than he'd expected, and then he saw the man's face. It was covered with dark bruises, cuts and scabs, and one of his eyes was swollen shut. "Theos," Finnvid breathed.

Then Theos acted, far too quickly for someone so battered. An uncovered fist, headed straight for Finnvid's face. His head rocked back, an explosion of pain and pressure across his jaw. And then darkness closed in from the sides, and Finnvid felt himself falling to the cold white snow.

PART ⊹ III

CHAPTER 25

Theos wanted Andros to stop talking. And he would be happier if the sleigh could stop moving, too, because there was something about the shifting slide of it that was making him queasy. But apparently Theos had used up all his wishes just getting out of the dungeon, and had no luck left to make his new dreams come true.

"Are you listening?" Andros demanded. "We might need him to get past the sentries? Fine, but why the hell did you have to hit him?"

That was enough to make Theos speak despite the nausea. "He's the *enemy*."

"You're an idiot. I've told you twenty times that he let me and Gunnald come find you. And then he could have raised the alarm, but instead he came running after us. He must have had important news. And we could have heard it if you hadn't knocked him out!"

"He set up the ambush." He'd caused the death of Theos's friends, his brothers. How to explain the sense of betrayal, the confusion, the absolute tragedy of seeing strong warriors butchered for no reason? He couldn't. "You weren't there, so you don't know." Theos wasn't afraid of violence, and he'd been in his first full-fledged battle at fifteen; but he'd never felt so trapped and helpless before, never been taken so completely unaware. He'd never trusted someone only to have that person betray him so horribly. And there'd been no excuse for it because Theos absolutely should have known better than to trust Finnvid, of all people.

Andros didn't respond immediately, partly because he was busy driving the sleigh; Torians used horses, but it was mostly the women in charge of them. Andros clearly wasn't comfortable with his task. Once he'd gotten the team straightened out and moving as he apparently wanted, he turned back to Theos and said, "I wasn't there. I don't know. But *he let me and Gunnald come find you*. And he *didn't raise the alarm*. So whatever happened *then*, it seems like he's helping us *now*."

Theos didn't bother responding to that. As if there was anything that the Elkati could do that would make up for what he'd *done*.

He glanced down at the lump next to him in the back of the sleigh. They might still need the tied and gagged princeling as a hostage, but it was tempting to just push the body out into the snow. Maybe the coward would freeze to death, maybe he'd live long enough for Theos to return and take revenge against him and the rest of his murdering, lying clan. Either way, at least Theos wouldn't have to sit beside him any longer. Wouldn't have to think about him.

"We should reach the sentries before dawn," Andros said over his shoulder. "We're supposed to just drive past them; Gunnald said they aren't primed for threats from inside the valley, and no one will have raised the alarm yet. Still, keep your head down in case of arrows."

Theos shuddered at the thought of more arrows, but when, after what seemed like a lifetime of gut-rocking sleigh travel, they passed the sentries, nothing flew after them except a few surprised shouts.

They didn't get much farther before the trail became too narrow and steep for the sleigh. "We could keep the horses," Andros said doubtfully as he struggled to unhitch them. "You could ride one."

Theos shook his head. "Turn them loose; I'd rather walk."

"Are you fit for it?" Andros's voice was deliberately casual.

Theos forced himself to be honest. Andros had seen his injuries when he was naked in the dungeon, so there was no hiding the external, but Andros had to know the rest. "They fed me, but not a lot. And I lost blood. I'll be weak."

Andros nodded. "Well, you weak is better than most men strong. Let's play it by ear."

Theos turned and yanked the Elkati out of the sleigh as the freed horses wandered away. If he was still unconscious after so much time, Theos had punched him too hard and done permanent harm. It wasn't a thought that should have bothered him.

Luckily, the Elkati twisted as he fell, getting his feet under him and showing that he was not only awake but quite lively. Theos jerked the bonds on the prisoner's hands, pulling him forward. "If you run, we'll catch you. If you slow down, we'll drive you ahead of us on the tip of our swords. Understood?"

"You want to take him with us?" Andros said in amazement. "I thought you said you just wanted to use him to get past the sentries."

"The sentries gave us no trouble, so I guess he worked. Maybe he'll be useful again." The Elkati's pack was still strapped to his back, so Theos worked his arms into the straps of the pack Andros had scavenged for him, then prodded the Elkati forward and fell in behind him, trying to ignore the protests of his abused body. His muscles would warm up soon enough, and then he'd know for sure how much trouble he was in.

"How will he be useful?" Andros persisted.

"You said you wanted to talk to him. Can't do that if we leave him."

"This is stupid," Andros said. Still, he jogged ahead and took his place at the front of the line, breaking a path for the others. The snow wasn't quite deep enough for the snow flats, but Andros had two pairs of them strapped to his pack, ready for later. Two pairs, not three. Well, let the Elkati fight the drifts. A tired prisoner was a good prisoner.

Once they started up the hill, Theos needed all his energy and concentration just to keep moving. Sacrati training involved a fair bit of endurance work, and Theos knew the tricks. His injured body might give out before it should, but his mind was strong.

He walked until Andros stepped to the side of the path and handed him a pair of the snow flats, and only then did he realize that his leg was damp with something that wasn't sweat or snow. One of his injuries must have worked itself open, and he was bleeding. He should tell Andros. It was the responsible thing to do; his body was a tool, and it needed to be repaired and then maintained if it was to stay useful. But he couldn't bring himself to do it. He was tired of being injured; maybe if he ignored the problem, it would go away.

So they walked on. Dawn came late, the sun blocked by the towering mountains. Shortly after the glare hit the snow, Andros stopped walking and looked behind them. Theos let himself turn, as well. They were on top of a hill and could see almost all the way back down to the mouth of the valley. There was no sign of pursuit.

"Guess nobody wants to get him back," Theos grunted. A part of him was sorry; he would have liked the chance to fight rather than run.

But Andros was frowning at the prisoner now. Without asking Theos's permission or even opinion, he spun the Elkati and untied the gag from his mouth. It was just a strip of sinew; Finnvid should have been able to breathe around it, yet he still gasped and sputtered as if he hadn't been getting enough air. Theos refused to feel guilty about that.

"Why aren't they behind us?" Andros demanded. "Why did *you* come out after us?"

The prisoner wasn't breathing properly yet, but he managed to slip his pack off his shoulder and drag the top of it open. Theos readied himself for the appearance of a weapon; instead the Elkati pulled out a rolled parchment. By the time he stood up, he probably could have spoken if he'd wanted to. He handed the parchment to Andros with a wordless glare in Theos's direction.

Theos glared right back, and after a moment the prisoner dropped his eyes. They stood there, locked in their poses of dominance and submission, until Andros swore softly. "Read this. It matches what Gunnald said, but there's more details." He handed the parchment over and Theos accepted it. He could read, well enough to get by, but it wasn't easy for him, especially with his vision fading in and out as it was. Still, if Andros thought it was important . . .

Theos read. Then he jumped back to the start and read again. The words were impersonal, but to Theos, they meant more than what they said. Ekakios, Heirax, Crios, Balius, Tiro. All the Sacrati, the men Theos had lived and trained with his whole life. If they'd died in battle, he would have grieved them and moved on. The ambush, though? There had been no honor in it, no chance for them to die as the warriors they were. They'd been murdered, and it had come at the behest of a fellow Torian. "Zenain," Theos said. His voice seemed strange, but he continued. "He sent this letter on ahead." He stared at the prisoner, then at Andros. "It came from . . . It was one of *us*. Zenain caused this."

Andros nodded slowly. "It seems so."

Theos tried to make sense of it. A Torian should . . . A Torian would . . . "Zenain," he whispered. The word was a curse.

"Gunnald said he didn't know, and neither did any of the other Elkati. When I snuck into the valley and found him, he told me what had happened. He said Finnvid didn't know."

"I didn't," Finnvid said. He sounded genuine, desperate to be believed and forgiven. But he was such a good liar. He'd fooled Theos so many times before.

Theos couldn't think, not right then. He staggered a little as he turned and looked back down the mountain. "Why aren't they following us?"

"I'm not sure." Finnvid stepped forward cautiously, keeping his distance but peering in the same direction Theos was. "I asked Gaiera to hide my absence, but I didn't think she'd be able to do it for too long. And someone should have noticed you missing, surely."

"Gunnald thought no one would notice until they changed guards in the morning," Andros said. "So if they didn't discover you missing, and your friend didn't report it, they may have only just found out. We've got a good head start."

"Good," Theos said. It was as if the words were coming from very far away, maybe way back in the valley. Maybe from that entry hall at the Elkat castle, where his Sacrati comrades had been butchered. He squinted at Andros, and the expression on his friend's face told him he wasn't the only one who knew their next step. "You'll do it," he said. "You'll take care of it." Andros nodded. That was enough, so Theos tried to focus on Finnvid's face and say, "Go home. Be safe."

But Finnvid didn't seem to be listening to him, or just wasn't obeying. Typical. Theos tried to push the boy, to show him which way he was supposed to be going. Somehow he lost his balance and swayed, and then stumbled. He felt a quick stab of pain from his thigh, reached for it, and managed to miss his own body with his hand. Was he dissolving?

"Catch him," he heard Andros say, and he tried to turn, tried to grab at the Elkati before he got away: Why was Andros telling him to do that? Had Finnvid betrayed them again so *soon*?

Then the world spun a little and Theos was staring at something impossibly bright and dazzlingly blue. He could hear voices, maybe, and that was nice. He wasn't alone. And he wasn't cold. He felt his eyes drifting shut and didn't fight to keep them open.

"I *may* be able to control them if they catch up to us," Finnvid said. "Maybe. I can't guarantee it." If the men were sent by his brother, they'd probably be manageable; if his mother was involved, with her paranoia about Finnvid's state of mind, the soldiers might have been told to ignore his orders. They wouldn't hurt *him*, but they'd kill the Sacrati, or else be killed trying. Finnvid didn't like to think about either outcome.

Andros nodded and looked doubtfully at the man sprawled at their feet. Finnvid had done the best he could with his healing, but Theos's trousers were dark with blood, and there couldn't have been much extra in his body to start with. It probably hadn't helped that Finnvid had been shaking, almost crying, the entire time. To be with Theos again, to feel the beginnings of forgiveness, and then to see him collapse? It was too much, and Finnvid had been hardly any use until Andros had grabbed him by the hair and held his head still while scrubbing his face with a rough hand and icy snow. Finnvid had managed to regain at least some control after that treatment. He was glad Andros was still in charge.

The Sacrati said, "We'll rest here, where we have a view of the trail. We can decide what to do about pursuers when we actually see them coming."

"Did you kill the guards?" Finnvid had been fretting about it since they'd left the castle, and he needed to know for sure.

Andros shook his head. "Gunnald wouldn't let me. He stayed out of sight so there'd be no need, and I just tied them up." A quick look before he added, "You Elkati really should work on your training."

Finnvid snorted, and sank down in the snow beside Theos. They were nestled against a cliff that sheltered them from the wind, and he'd grabbed his warmest clothes before he left the castle, so he wasn't cold, although his hands were still thawing after being bared to help Theos, and from being washed in the snow. Finnvid stared at the reddened ground and said, "If we're followed, they'll think we fought a battle here."

Andros looked around, apparently quite comfortable with the gore. "Maybe," he agreed. Then he turned back to Finnvid. "I've got questions. And we don't want to move him until we have to, so . . . it's time to answer them."

Andros's expression was Sacrati-fierce, and Finnvid braced himself.

Sure enough, the first question was hissed through angry teeth. "What happened?" Andros clearly had to work to bring himself back under control before adding, "Who knew what, and when? What's the situation now? Why couldn't you help Theos in the castle?" He paused as if thinking, then caught and held Finnvid's gaze. "Don't try to tell me you didn't *want* to help him. We're not going to play that game."

"I wanted to help," Finnvid whispered. But how to explain the fine balance he'd been trying to maintain, especially to someone like Andros, someone strong enough to just power through any obstacles? Then he remembered how Andros had been caught in the middle of the mess back in Windthorn, forbidden to share what he knew with Theos even as he watched his friend struggle to figure things out. Andros of all people knew that things could be complicated. He must know that sometimes the best path to a destination wasn't a straight one.

So Finnvid stood up and told his story, such as it was, Andros interjecting with an occasional question, and when it was done, Andros nodded his understanding of the facts. But there was still no hint of whether Finnvid's explanations had been acceptable when the Sacrati asked, "So what are you planning to do now?"

Finnvid swallowed. "I'm not sure. My first plan was just to get to you and deliver the letter. To prove my people weren't your enemy. Or at least, not your *worst* enemy." Well, his first plan had been to see Theos. There had been no logic behind his pursuit, no motivation other than a selfish, desperate hunger to see the man still alive. But Andros didn't need to hear all that.

"And was there a second plan?" Andros asked.

"There's been about fifty, all racing through my head, none making any real sense."

"So you'll stick to the first one. You've delivered the letter. Now you'll turn around and go home." It wasn't quite a question, not quite an order.

And Finnvid wasn't sure how to respond. "I can." There would be consequences for his actions. He supposed he could say he'd been kidnapped while trying to prevent the escape, but he wasn't sure anyone would accept that story. There were too many guards at the castle, and he'd had lots of opportunities to call them to his aid. Still, he was the king's brother, and the queen mother believed him to be mentally unstable. He hadn't actually aided in the escape itself, and the letter wasn't common knowledge, so the family wouldn't have to explain how it had disappeared. If he went back, he would be watched even more closely, treated like an unstable invalid, but he wouldn't be punished too harshly. He *could* return.

"You might need me. For Theos. I'm not sure I can keep them from coming after you, even if I go home. I don't really have anything new to tell them, and they weren't persuaded to free Theos before. If you have to move him by yourself, you'll have to carry or drag him, and both ways seem likely to reopen the wound. If I stay, we could try to rig a stretcher. Also, you may need my healing skills, such as they are. And when you get to Windthorn, I might be useful, too. I could present the letter and explain its authenticity firsthand. I could formally apologize for Elkat's role in the killings."

"Oh, a formal apology? After the slaughter of a band of Sacrati? You think an *apology* will make us forget?"

"No! I don't expect you to *forget*." Finnvid could have stayed at home in his safe, comfortable bed, but instead he'd been punched in the face, bound, and forced to drag himself through the snow for hours in the dark. He'd had enough. "Don't forget anything. You need to *remember*! Remember who started all this. Remember who sent the suggestion that the Elkati do what they did. Remember that Elkat was a peaceful valley for generations before your Torian violence swept over us and caught us up in its current. I'm ashamed of what happened to the Sacrati, but my brother did it because he was told to by the leader of the Torian military. *That's* what I can say."

There was movement near Finnvid's feet. "Didn't sound much like an apology." Theos's voice was low, but clearer than it had been before he passed out.

Finnvid schooled himself to speak more calmly before he replied, "Sorry, I didn't mean to wake you. And you're right, I need to work on my wording."

Theos snorted, then coughed weakly. Finnvid crouched next to him and offered his water flask. "Drink. And if you can eat something, that would be good. I didn't see any signs of infection or other problems, so I think we're mostly just dealing with blood loss."

"Which you should have told us about," Andros scolded.

Theos busied himself with lifting his head to the flask. Finnvid felt a wave of affection for both of them. Theos, strong and brash, hiding from Andros's disapproval. And Andros, kind and sweet, unafraid to poke at his grumpy friend when needed. If Finnvid was going to travel into the winter mountains again, he couldn't have chosen better company. Well, unless he could have chosen a fit and healthy Theos instead of the injured version they were currently dealing with.

"I think I should come with you," Finnvid said.

"Do your people use dogs?" Andros asked. He saw Finnvid's blank expression and added, "To track with. Dogs?"

"To track *people*?" Finnvid shook his head. He'd read of such things, but never seen an animal trained that way. "Our hunting dogs chase the scent they find, not the one we give them."

Andros nodded, and squinted at the sky, then down toward the valley entry. "We should rig a stretcher," he said. Apparently he'd agreed with Finnvid's decision to stay and then moved on. "And we should carry him. If we get very, very, lucky, we'll get a good dump of snow from those clouds blowing in."

"We *want* snow?"

"We do." Andros didn't elaborate. "Do you have anything to write with? And on? Use a chunk of bark and some blood if you need to. Leave a letter for those following us. We'll cut that tree down, there, and lay it across the path, then tie the note to it to be sure they see it. Try to slow them down, or better yet, send them home. Make it clear that you're not a prisoner, and don't need to be rescued. Tell them you have a plan."

"A plan?"

"Make it sound better than what you've actually got, if possible." Andros smiled wryly. "While you're doing that, I'll set up a stretcher. You should take Theos's snow flats."

"He can't carry me," Theos muttered. "Give me a moment, and I'll be able to walk."

"Let him try," Andros replied. "We need you strong. If we carry you now, you'll be ready to *run* later, if we need to." He glanced apologetically in Finnvid's direction before adding, "Ready to fight."

Theos stopped arguing, the prospect of a good battle all that was required to ensure his compliance. Finnvid resolved to remember that trick for future use, and tried not to think about *who* Theos would be fighting if he got his way anytime soon.

There was a ragged sheet of parchment with a stub of colored wax for writing in the medical kit, so Finnvid set about composing his message, glad he wasn't writing in blood. By the time he was finished, Andros had the tree laid down over the path and had the stretcher assembled. Finnvid hadn't written very many words, but he'd tried to choose the right ones, tried to compose the magic message that would make all of this go away. He knew he hadn't come up with anything *that* good, but he hoped he'd at least made the situation clear.

He strapped on the snow flats and helped shift Theos onto the stretcher with as little stress on his wound as possible. "Did that hurt?" Finnvid demanded fiercely. "Do we need to stop and re-dress it? Better you tell me now than later, when you've already wasted more blood."

"It didn't hurt." Theos seemed meek, and Finnvid wasn't sure if he liked it. "I think it's fine."

"It had better be." Finnvid crouched to wrap his hands around the stretcher poles and braced himself to carry half of Theos's considerable weight.

"Look," Andros said quietly. Finnvid straightened, then turned to follow Andros's gaze.

There were soldiers streaming into the base of the trail. From a distance, they looked like a dark river, filling the space and splashing up the hill.

"That's too many," Finnvid whispered. It made no sense. He stared as more and more men appeared. "That's hundreds of men. It's most of our army!"

"They can't mean to attack Windthorn," Andros said. He sounded more thoughtful than alarmed. "That would be suicide." He looked over at Finnvid. "They must be planning to catch up to us. They'd know better than anyone else how badly Theos was hurt, so they'd know we won't be making good time. But this many men . . . Do you think it's because of you? They think you were kidnapped and are trying to get you back?"

Finnvid wished it were that simple. If it were, he could just turn around and stop the men, and Theos and Andros could continue their journey in peace. "No. I don't think so. They must have suspected where I was all through the early winter and they didn't send so much as an envoy to check on me or arrange my release." Finnvid hadn't been surprised by that, given the weather conditions, but the behavior then was in clear contrast to the situation now. "I think they discovered that the letter is missing, and they're coming after *it*. They've decided to back the warlord, and they don't want you to return to Windthorn with evidence you could only have gotten from them. It would look as if they'd turned the information over to his enemies."

Andros watched the distant men a moment longer, then nodded decisively. "So. They're going to follow us, regardless. So take your note down."

Finnvid stared at him. "Why?"

"Because it can't do any good—it won't stop them. And without the note, if they catch up to us, you can claim you were kidnapped. I mean, you *were* kidnapped, right?"

Finnvid wanted to argue. He wasn't sure why, but it seemed important that he make some sort of declaration, to the Elkati *and* the Torians. He wanted them to know that he'd chosen a side. Right or wrong, he'd made a choice.

Andros didn't look interested in his internal musings. "Let's go. Get the note, and grab an end of the stretcher. Let's see what we can do." He peered at the horizon, the clouds that he'd said might bring snow. Finnvid still wasn't sure how that would help anything.

Maybe there wasn't any help to be had. So Finnvid retrieved the note, and they hefted their burden and started walking.

CHAPTER 26

Finnvid struggled, even with the snow flats. Theos was heavy, and Finnvid hadn't slept the night before, and—and it was impossible to forget what he was doing. He was running away from his valley, his home. His family.

When he'd left the night before, it had felt temporary. He was taking a trip, that was all. Eventually he'd go home and grovel a little and be forgiven. But he wasn't sure he could do that, not anymore. With the number of men following him into the mountains, people would know he'd helped Theos escape. It couldn't all be hushed up, not with hundreds of witnesses.

It was treason, he supposed. Strange to think of it that way, when his motives were so pure. He wanted Elkat to survive, and he didn't think an alliance with the warlord was a good way to ensure that outcome. It seemed right that he was taking action.

But it was action against the wishes of the king. And who was Finnvid, to question his brother's decision? A dilettante, a child, interfering in matters far beyond his ken. An idiot.

He trudged on through the snow, and looked down at the man dozing on the stretcher. Even in his sleep, Theos tended to frown, and the determined grumpiness should have made Finnvid impatient and frustrated with him. It *shouldn't* have made Finnvid want to reach down and smooth the tension from the man's face. It shouldn't have made him daydream about waking up next to him and kissing him into one of his sweet smiles.

Finnvid had left home for Theos. He'd like to deny it, even to himself, but there was no use. He thought he was doing the right thing, trying to ensure that the Sacrati took their revenge at home rather than in Elkat, but that wasn't what had made him race through the castle, throwing winter survival gear into his pack before stopping by his brother's office and snatching the letter as an afterthought. A justification.

He'd abandoned his family and betrayed his king for the man lying on the stretcher in front of him. The man *frowning in his sleep*, as if even his dreams couldn't live up to his impossible standards.

The tension was boiling within him, frothing and fighting toward the surface. If the emotions escaped, Finnvid wasn't sure what he'd do. Drop his end of the stretcher, probably, and launch himself on Theos's falling body. But would he attack the man with punches, or kisses? Anger, or love?

Andros stopped moving, and Finnvid stumbled as he tried to recover his balance. Theos's eyes opened with a blurry complaint, then drifted closed again. "Set him down," Andros ordered, and Finnvid did as he was told. He hadn't realized how long they'd been walking until he tried to move his arms and found that his shoulders had cramped into position. He shrugged cautiously and bent his head back, letting the cold snow fall on his effort-warmed face.

It was snowing. That should mean something, he remembered. He squinted at Andros, who was watching the sky intently. Then the Sacrati turned to Finnvid and said, "You need to decide. Commit. It's not too late for you to go home, but if you try to leave after this . . . I'll have to stop you."

Friendly, easy-going Andros was gone. The man in front of him was assessing him like a potential enemy, and it chilled Finnvid more completely than the wind ever had.

"I can't go back," Finnvid said. "I don't think I can. They'll consider me a traitor."

"You can tell them you were kidnapped. Tell them you saw one of us taking the letter and chased after us, and we grabbed you. Torians are cruel, and you were afraid."

It might work. He could make it work. Finnvid felt his panic starting to subside. He *wasn't* trapped. This *wasn't* all beyond his control. And that was enough. "I'll stay. I'm committed."

Andros waited for a moment, then nodded and smiled. "Good. Grab your end and be ready for some tricky ground—we're leaving the trail."

"We are?"

But Andros was already crouched by his end of the stretcher, so Finnvid forced himself to bend and grasp his own handles. His body complained as they stood, but he made himself ignore it.

As promised, Andros turned almost at a right angle and started into the pine forest. He seemed to be picking out a path of sorts, but everything was rougher and harder going, and several times they had to backtrack when they hit an impenetrable spot.

Finnvid didn't ask questions; he just focused on the task at hand. He'd told Andros he was committed, and now was the time to prove it.

Finally, Andros stopped and grunted, "Put him down."

Finnvid was only too happy to comply, and they both stood for a moment, stretching their muscles and catching their breath. Then Andros nodded toward a huge pine with snow drifted up around its trunk. "You should be able to den up in the snow under those branches," he said. "You start digging while I go back and make sure our trail is well covered."

"Wait," Finnvid said. "You said 'you.' Not 'we.'" He paused, hoping to be contradicted, then said, "Where are *you* going to go?"

"I'll probably den up with you, for tonight. And then I'll move parallel to the trail until I figure out where your soldiers are. I want to avoid them, but I can't afford to sit around and wait for them to get tired and go home."

"But *you're* going home? Without Theos?"

Andros dropped his head and peered down at his friend. Finnvid followed the gaze and saw Theos looking up at both of them.

"He needs to get the letter back to Windthorn," Theos said. He still sounded weak, but there was no doubt in his voice. "He needs to make sure the people know—the Sacrati know—that the warlord has attacked us."

"It may be too late by the time I arrive," Andros said, and Finnvid knew he was searching for excuses to stay with Theos.

But Theos frowned at him. "It may not be. It *shouldn't* be, not if you can catch up to Zenain and his band. I don't think the warlord will attack at home until he knows things went according to plan in Elkat."

"What if I hadn't agreed to come?" Finnvid asked. He looked from one Sacrati to the other. "You wouldn't have been able to go on ahead, right?" Andros wouldn't have left Theos behind, not injured as he was. It was unthinkable. But if he hadn't, he would have left his Sacrati friends in Windthorn vulnerable to a surprise attack. Xeno was back there, and so many more. Finnvid shook his head. "You would have just *left* him? You should have told me that before I decided to stay! What if I'd gone back?"

"I'm Sacrati," Theos said quietly.

"That doesn't make you invincible!"

"It makes him duty-bound," Andros said. "He's sworn to fight and die for his brothers. He's sworn to protect the Torian Empire, and Windthorn. You've made no such vow. You have no such duty. For you, there had to be a choice. A real one, not one made out of guilt."

"You gambled with Theos's life!"

"We gamble with our lives every day," Andros said. Then he clapped his hands together, signaling an end to the conversation. "You," he said, pointing at Theos, "instruct our young recruit on digging a nice three-man den. And you," he added, waving in Finnvid's direction, "stop standing around! Get moving! You're wasting daylight, and the wind's picking up. When I get back, I want a nice home and a hot meal waiting for me. And you should have my blankets spread out and airing. And maybe a nice centerpiece of some sort . . ."

"I'll see what I can do," Finnvid said, and that was it. He just got to work, piling and digging and tunneling according to Theos's instructions, and shoulders that had been sore from being in one position for too long became screamingly painful from overuse. But when he was done, he was able to help Theos to his feet, hold him upright while he peed into the snow, and then drag him inside their new den. It was a den Finnvid had made by himself, and it was strong, and once he got a lamp lit it would be cozy.

"I made this," he said out loud, and immediately felt foolish.

But Theos just nodded from his place on the snow floor, and inspected the dim space. "Good job."

Finnvid turned to the packs to hide his blush.

"You . . ." Theos stopped, and Finnvid squinted at him. The Sacrati looked as if he was fighting with himself. Finally, he shook his head and said, "You really didn't know. About the ambush. You didn't lead us into that?"

Finnvid didn't know what to say. After all the lies, why would Theos believe his truth? "I swear," he said intently. "And think about it! The attack only made sense to someone who believed everything in the warlord's letter! My family made a horrible decision, but they did it because they didn't know the truth. They thought I'd been abused, and were seeking revenge. But I knew no revenge was justified. They thought the warlord was the absolute master of Windthorn, and had to be obeyed, but I know there are three leaders, two of whom would strongly object to Sacrati being attacked." He stared at Theos, willing him to hear the words as he said, "I would never hurt you because I never would. Because I respect you and . . . because I don't want you hurt. But even if that wasn't true, the attack was just *stupid*, to anyone who has any idea what's going on in Windthorn! It was stupid, and I knew better. I swear."

When Finnvid was done, Theos was silent for a moment, then nodded. "I believe you," he said quietly.

Finnvid returned his attention to the packs, but his hands were shaking too much to be much use. After so much horror, finally something good. Theos believed him. He gripped the canvas tightly, willing himself to be calm, and then rummaged in the pack with more purpose.

"I found Andros's lamp," he said eventually. The lamp was a little metal dish with a piece of wire holding up a strip of cloth for a wick. Not fancy, but it would do. "But I can't find fat cakes."

Theos made a face. "We're probably out. This wasn't meant to be such a long trip, and we didn't think we'd be sharing with the Elkati horde."

That was another complication. Andros would need the fat for quick energy and warmth on the trail. Finnvid reluctantly reached for his own pack. "I don't— I took food from the kitchens. But we didn't have fat cakes. Elkati don't eat them." After a deep breath, he extracted one of the cloth-wrapped bundles he'd packed. The cloth fell away from the sides, and Theos carefully stretched out and dug a finger into the creamy yellow ball, squashed on two sides but still about the size of a man's head. He brought the sample to his nose, sniffed, then licked it.

"Butter." He nodded slowly, then grinned. "Almost as good, and *much* tastier."

"Will it work in the lamp?"

"Probably. I don't know. Give it a try."

"I will. And then I'll melt some down and fry something in it, and you can eat it."

Theos smiled, slow and lazy, and Finnvid had to turn away again to hide his expression. The smile shouldn't matter so much, but it did. He and Theos were together, and they were getting along. Even if it all went wrong right then, if Elkati soldiers burst into the den and killed them where they sat, Finnvid would still have made the right decision when he left the castle and chased the Sacrati. He'd gotten what he wanted, what he needed, and everything after this was just extra.

Theos's stomach wasn't as enthusiastic about food as he wanted it to be. He forced down some butter-dipped jerky, chewed each mouthful into disgusting mush before making himself swallow it, and then fought to make sure it stayed down. He thought he was doing a good job of hiding the problem, but then he saw Finnvid chopping jerky and dried vegetables into a small pot of water warming over the little lamp, and groaned. "Broth? That's not real food, you know."

"If it's all you can eat, it's better than nothing. I've got some bread as well. You can soak it in the broth and eat it like that, hopefully."

"You said I had to eat a lot to regain my strength."

"Your body isn't so sure. Take it slow. If you sip and nibble all day long, that's just as good as eating two or three big meals, and it's easier for your stomach to accept."

Theos groaned again, but didn't really argue. He was surprised by how much he enjoyed being taken care of. When Finnvid spread blankets out on the canvas-covered floor, Theos tugged Finnvid's closer to his own. He wasn't in shape for anything really fun, and Finnvid likely wouldn't be interested regardless, but just being near, maybe touching a little . . . that would be nice.

And important for warmth, of course.

It was hard to sense the passage of time inside the den, and Theos didn't care enough to try. With Finnvid there next to him, Theos found himself feeling happy and snug in a way he hadn't for far too long. He didn't fuss much when Finnvid insisted on inspecting his wounds, and his groin's response to the Elkati's touch made it clear that he might be injured, but wasn't dead. Finnvid ignored that reaction, cleaned the wounds, dabbed them with some sweet-smelling ointment, and re-covered them with fresh dressings.

A sound at the entrance tunnel caught their attention, but when a scarf-covered face appeared, the eyes were familiar, and Theos and Finnvid relaxed before they'd really had time to get tense. "It's blowing hard out there," Andros said as he crawled in. He brought a wave of cold air with him, and the snow packed into the creases of his clothing was a clear indication that the storm raged on. He looked exhausted, and Theos felt guilty for lying down while Andros was doing all the work. Then he remembered he'd spent several days in a dark cell while Andros had been dancing around outside, free as a bird, and the guilt faded.

Still, he was happy to see Finnvid ease in beside Andros and pull one of his mitts off, wrapping the man's cold fingers around a mug that had been sitting by the lamp. "It's just hot water and honey," Finnvid said. "But it'll help warm you up."

Andros sipped cautiously, then took a deeper swallow. "Thank you," he said.

Finnvid helped Andros pull off his bulky outer clothes and get comfortable, then gave him some food and filled up his cup of warm honey-water and generally fussed just enough for Theos to start wondering why *he* wasn't getting any attention. Then he noticed Andros's smug little smirk and made a face. He wasn't jealous. He didn't *get* jealous. It was just . . . "That honey-water sounded good," he hinted. "I think maybe my stomach would like some of that."

"There's only your broth mug to put it in," Finnvid said sternly. "Finish your broth and you can have honey-water for dessert."

Theos couldn't help himself. "*Andros* didn't have to drink any broth."

"*Andros* will soon be eating a full meal, and not looking like he's going to puke it up on my blankets. *Andros* just came in from the cold and has been walking all day." Finnvid smiled at Andros and then added, "*Andros* didn't punch me in the face for no reason."

Well, that was a pretty hard string of points to argue with, so Theos drank the worthless broth and then held his mug out greedily. When Finnvid took the cup, his self-satisfied grin made Theos want to pull him down and kiss him until he stopped being so pleased with himself and started being pleased with Theos. Unfortunately, he had no strength for such nonsense. Not yet, at least.

They rested cozily after that, eating and talking. But when Andros came back in from a trip outdoors and said, "The moon's rising," Theos pushed himself more upright. While he'd been imprisoned, he'd made a litany of the names of his brothers, chanting them in his mind, swearing revenge for their deaths. They *would* be avenged, but this was something else.

He and Andros sat facing each other, cross-legged, with the lamp between them. Then Theos looked over at Finnvid, and back to Andros. "He knew them too," he said, and Andros nodded.

"We need to say good-bye," Andros told Finnvid.

It was a simple ceremony, one developed for men who routinely lost comrades in battle. There was no need for any officiant, or any remains. Instead, Theos and Andros took turns saying the names of the dead, and after each name, they sat silently for a few moments, remembering. That was all.

These men had lived and laughed, fought and fucked with Andros and Theos since they were children. And now they were gone, and those left behind could only remember them and wish their souls a smooth journey to the next world. It didn't seem like enough. It never seemed like enough.

They talked for a while after they were done, mostly sharing memories. When it seemed like they were wearing down and ready to sleep, Theos crawled outside on his own to pee, although he knew Finnvid was close behind him, keeping a watchful eye.

They stayed on their knees in the trench Finnvid had dug, and even so the wind was fierce and icy. When they crawled back inside, Finnvid was quiet for a while, then said, "I wonder if they found shelter. The soldiers following us. There were so many of them . . . and they wouldn't know about denning up. They could all be freezing to death."

Theos was already close beside him and edged in closer before saying, "They've probably got the Elkati we traveled with. Maybe even Gunnald. They'll take care of the others, make sure they make it through the night. And if they get cold and scared? That's good, really. Maybe they'll send themselves home when the storm breaks."

Finnvid relaxed a little, his warm shoulder tight against Theos's. "I hope they do," he said.

Then they lay down and slept. Theos dreamed, just as he had every night since the ambush, bloody visions full of betrayed, dying friends, but this time when he woke up trembling there was a warm body next to him, a soft voice whispering reassuring words, and a gentle, tentative kiss on his forehead to soothe him back to sleep. Later, he woke again with Finnvid pulled in close to him, Finnvid's back against Theos's chest, Finnvid's ass against . . .

Theos made himself ease away, at least with that part of his body. Finnvid had made his feelings on the issue clear, and while Theos might *hope* those feelings were changing, while their encounter in the woods might *suggest* those feelings were changing, there wasn't sufficient evidence to allow Theos to lean in the way he wanted to. Besides, even if Finnvid *had* changed his mind, Theos was in no condition to do anything the way it deserved to be done.

So he eased away a little more, trying to ignore his morning hardness, and that was when Finnvid stirred and shifted backward, his ass seeking the warmth it had so recently lost.

By the sword, Theos wasn't strong enough for this. But he found some hidden reserve of willpower and made himself move away again. He was at the edge of his blankets now, his own ass cooling against the icy wall of the den, and still, Finnvid shifted toward him.

Shifted, and then rolled over, and the Elkati's eyes were open and aware. He'd been doing it on purpose.

"Are you trying to get away from me?" Finnvid whispered.

Theos shook his head, then reconsidered, and nodded. "I was," he admitted. "But not anymore."

"Good," Finnvid said, and he leaned forward and brought their lips together.

Stale breath, dirty bodies . . . none of it mattered. Their tongues met like old friends, sliding over each other in warm greetings. Theos wrapped an arm around Finnvid and dragged him in tighter—and gasped as the effort stretched something along his leg. Finnvid froze immediately, then jerked away.

"I'm sorry!" he whispered. "I don't know what I was thinking." His fingers were quick and strong as they pulled at Theos's trousers.

"This wasn't quite the sort of undressing I was hoping for," Theos grumbled, but Finnvid ignored him, easing back the bandage from the wound in his thigh and then hissing in dismay.

"It's worse than last night," he said. "It was a little red then, but now it's well on its way to looking infected."

"It doesn't hurt," Theos said, wishing Finnvid would stop getting distracted.

"It's starting to get swollen," Finnvid said firmly. "And there's heat to it. That's not good." He turned away and rummaged through his pack. "I've already used the best ointment I've got. There's medicine I can give you to drink, but it might upset your stomach." He frowned. "It's probably more important to fight the infection than to worry about getting your strength back. I'll give you the medicine, and if all you can eat is broth, that's too bad."

"Have you considered that it might be the broth *causing* the infection?" Theos tried. He didn't know much about medicine, but he knew how he felt about broth.

Finnvid didn't even answer, just kept burrowing through his bag, so Theos lay back down in the dim light and tried to convince his cock that the excitement was over. Unless maybe he could ask Finnvid to check out the swelling down there and see if he had any treatment for it . . .

Theos smirked, and Andros sat up from his own blankets. The shelter wasn't that large, but Andros had still managed to lie down in a way that made it clear he was somewhere else, not part of whatever Finnvid and Theos were up to. One of those little tricks that made communal living a lot easier. Now, though, Andros was clearly back to being part of the group. "Is there anything I can do?" he asked Finnvid.

"Not much any of us can do, really. I'll clean the wound—it's warm enough in here to put ointment on it and leave it uncovered. I'll make him drink some medicine that should help." He frowned in Theos's direction as he added, "And I'll make him drink *broth*, unless he can eat solid food without immediately seeming ill."

Andros nodded with a worried look at Theos. "I need to get going as soon as there's a break in the weather. I'll show you how to set the snares before I leave, so hopefully you'll have some fresh meat to make your meals more interesting—and you can boil the bones for Theos's broth." A quick grin, and then his face fell back into a more serious expression. "If he gets strong, he can get you both to Windthorn, but don't let him bully you into going faster than what's safe for him *and* for you. Just because he can move doesn't mean he's at full strength." He hesitated a moment before saying, "If he *doesn't* get strong..." He winced at Theos apologetically but continued, "If things go bad, and he doesn't make it, go back to the Elkat valley. Blame us. Tell them the kidnapping story. I won't say otherwise, assuming anyone ever asks me."

Assuming he was alive to ask. Theos looked at Finnvid's stricken face and remembered that the Elkati had lived a sheltered life until very recently, and probably wasn't used to life-and-death situations. He needed some time to adjust, so Theos said, "I could sure go for some breakfast. At this point, even broth sounds good. Any of that lying around?"

"I'll make some," Finnvid said absently. Then he whirled toward Andros, his expression fierce. "And Theos will get better, and we will walk to Windthorn *together*, and we will see you there and deal with the warlord and— Well, I don't know exactly what will happen after that. But it'll be something *good*." He shook his head as if disgusted with both of them. "By the sword, the gloom and doom you two come up with! Everything is going to be fine!" He shoved his pack aside, stomping toward the exit tunnel in a manner that would have been slightly more intimidating if he hadn't been bent almost double to avoid contact with the low roof. "I'm going outside to pee," he said firmly. "When I get back in here, you two will be talking about *happy* things."

He dropped to a crawl and headed out through the tunnel, and Andros looked over at Theos with a laconic shrug. "He's a little testy in the morning."

"He's touchy all day long. Must be an Elkati thing."

Andros nodded sagely, then pulled a long strip of jerky out of one the packs and dipped it in the melted lamp butter. "Delicious," he said.

Theos's stomach flipped, and he wasn't sure if it was in anticipation or disgust. "Toss me a piece," he urged. "Quick, before the Prince of Broth returns."

Andros did as he was told and watched with interest as Theos chomped a chunk off the end of the stick of jerky and started chewing. Theos could tell as soon as he began that it wasn't what his stomach wanted. But he chewed anyway, doggedly grinding away, and swallowed with determination. He could practically feel the meat sliding down his gullet, arriving in his stomach—and he and Andros both heard the angry churning as it landed.

Andros leaned over and yanked the rest of the jerky out of his hand. "Don't let him see you with that. If you puke it up, I had nothing to do with this."

Two fierce Sacrati hiding from an Elkati civilian. Probably not a story Theos would want to tell in the dining hall. "I owe him," Theos said softly.

"If you come out of this alive, you will. If you don't, though . . . I'd just call it even."

"That's fair," Theos agreed, and he leaned back to wait for Finnvid's return.

CHAPTER 27

A ndros left in the early afternoon, laden with butter and jerky and bread. Finnvid hadn't been invited into the conversation that resulted in Andros deciding to try the shorter, harsher route through the mountains, hoping to beat the other Torians back to Windthorn. Finnvid was glad he'd been left out. He hated the thought of Andros being in danger, especially by himself, but who was he to tell the others what chances they should take to protect their people? How could he contribute anything but noise to that conversation?

So he'd stayed quiet as they'd talked, washing the bandages he'd just lifted from Theos's wounds, and then crawling outside to let them dry in the sun and freezing wind. He should boil them, but Theos and Andros had decided it was too dangerous to build a fire sufficient for such a task. "You'd need to use wood, and the smell of wood smoke travels. It could be enough to send them searching for us," Theos had said, and Andros had nodded in agreement.

"I'd think the smell of melted butter might tip them off as well," Finnvid retorted, but he knew that the small flame inside the den wasn't producing much odor.

So he hung the cloths and hoped the sun would bleach them clean, and he stood by Theos as they watched Andros set off into the wilderness alone. Then Finnvid took Theos's hand and tugged gently. "Back inside," he said firmly. "You have a fever, and pushing yourself too hard won't help anything."

"Pushing myself to *stand up*?"

"For now, that's too much." Finnvid shooed Theos into the den and scrutinized him as he sank onto his blankets, clearly exhausted. "You need to drink more—"

"If I drink any more broth, I'll drown."

"I was going to say more honey-water. And I'll give you another dose of the medicine. And then you should sleep."

"You'll keep me company?"

Finnvid blushed as if *he* were the one with a fever. "If you want."

"I do."

So Theos drank the honey-water and took his medicine, and then he lay back and lifted the covers, making a cave for Finnvid to crawl into. It was warm and safe, snuggled in against Theos's chest, with the Sacrati's heavy arm draped over Finnvid's torso. He tried not to wonder how many men Theos had held like this. How many women, even. For Theos, Finnvid was just one of many. For Finnvid, Theos was the only one.

"Are you asleep?" Finnvid whispered.

"No."

Finnvid thought about rolling over, but really, it was better to keep his face safely hidden. "What was it like? Growing up in Windthorn? Were you happy?"

"Happy?" Finnvid felt Theos's shrug. "I suppose. I was . . . busy, I'd say. Always running somewhere, always up to some mischief or another. There were lots of kids in the house, and more out in the city, of course. Always someone to play with, or fight with." He was silent for a while, then said, "Sacrati get their own rooms. You saw that. Nothing big or fancy, but . . . our own. It's supposed to be an honor. But for the first . . . well, I was going to say for the first while, but the truth is, I haven't really gotten over it, I don't think. It's still lonely, in there with no one else."

"You have bed partners," Finnvid said, because there was no point in pretending otherwise.

And Theos clearly saw no reason to try to deny it. "Aye. But . . . not usually. Not in *bed*, usually. I'm supposed to *want* to sleep alone. It's a privilege."

"So you do it, even though you don't want to." Finnvid shook his head gently. "No wonder you were so happy to get me as a bedwarmer."

Theos snorted, a warm gust of air against the back of Finnvid's neck. Then Finnvid felt warm lips pressed to the same spot. An agreement, or an apology? Or just another one of Theos's beautiful, casual gestures of affection? Finnvid decided it didn't matter.

They dozed, and then woke and Theos took his medicine and drank some broth with only minor complaints, and then dozed some more. Just before dusk, Finnvid went out to check the snare Andros had shown him how to set, but it was empty. He returned to the den, almost running, suddenly sure that in his brief absence something horrible would have happened. His brother's men would have arrived, or Theos might have choked on some broth or split a wound open and bled out onto the snow, or his fever might have spiked and his delirium sent him wandering into the forest.

But when he crawled into the den, Theos was there, safe and sound, only a little flushed from the fever. Finnvid didn't slow down, didn't stand up, just kept crawling, right across the blankets to Theos's side, and he reached out with both hands to grab Theos's face and pull his warmth against Finnvid's cold, their stubbled cheeks meeting first, then their lips.

Finnvid was rougher than he should have been. He *needed* more than he should. He hungered, craved, seized, and possessed. He pushed Theos's unresisting body back until he was lying down, Finnvid with one knee on either side of Theos's thighs. It didn't mean anything to Theos, so why shouldn't Finnvid take what he wanted?

He groaned into Theos's open mouth, gasped for air, and joined their mouths again. It was wondrous, this kissing. Finnvid imagined he could go on forever, licking and biting and teasing and tasting, and he knew that Theos wouldn't object. He wouldn't pull away, and wouldn't insist on more. Some of Finnvid's confidence came because he knew Theos's state, his physical weakness. But mostly it came from knowing *Theos*. When Finnvid had wanted to avoid this type of contact, Theos had gone along with that. He wouldn't be less respectful now.

So Finnvid took his time, and enjoyed every moment, every taste and touch and sound. When he finally took a break, he had a crick in his neck and he was pretty sure his entire lower leg was asleep, but he smiled down at Theos anyway, and Theos smiled back.

"Not feeling so 'unnatural' anymore?" Theos murmured.

"I may have changed my mind on that, a little."

"Just a little."

Finnvid shifted his weight, then ran a hand gently over Theos's blanket-covered chest. "I should check your wounds. Make sure I didn't pull anything open."

"You didn't."

"Maybe I wasn't trying hard enough, then."

Theos grinned. "You're turning into a true Torian, aren't you?"

Finnvid frowned and eased himself to the side, but he kept one hand on Theos's chest. "If I were a true Torian . . . If I'd been born in Windthorn . . ." He tried to figure it out. "*You* had a busy childhood. Always running around, playing, and fighting. I didn't. I could have, but I didn't want that. I spent most of my time reading, or staring at trees or bugs or watching people work." He'd thought about it before, but now it seemed more important to share his ideas, or at least his questions. "How would I have fit in, if I'd been born in Windthorn?"

"It's not like you *couldn't* have been a soldier," Theos said firmly. "You're fit enough. You've put on some good muscle in the last few months. You could have found a place."

"But I didn't *want* that. It wasn't just that I was denied the opportunity to be part of the mighty Torian military system; I wasn't *suited* to that sort of thing."

"Well, luckily you *weren't* born in Windthorn. I don't understand why you'd be worrying about this." Theos frowned. "I also don't understand why you were staring at trees and bugs all the time. Were they doing something interesting?"

Finnvid squirmed until he was sitting up, a better position from which to emphatically say, "Yes, they *were* doing interesting things! Things you'll never know about, things *no* Torian will know about, because boys in the Empire aren't allowed to sit quietly and watch things and learn about them!"

Theos stayed on his back, body relaxed. "If there's something important going on with the bugs, the women will notice, and they'll tell us about it."

Finnvid was silent for a while. He half turned and made sure there was melted snow in the little pot over the lamp, then checked the butter in the lamp reservoir, then nodded and looked back at Theos. "Women have much more freedom in Windthorn. They're useful, for a variety of things, and they get to *choose* what they want to be. If I were a woman, I'd want to be Torian. If I had a sister or a daughter, I'd want her raised in the Empire." It was a huge concession, and Finnvid was relieved when Theos didn't say anything smug. He just reached over and squeezed Finnvid's knee.

But Finnvid wasn't finished. "If I had a son, though? If I could go back in time and choose for myself, or for any *man*? I'd want him born in Elkat, or some other valley where *men* have a choice! There's more to the world than war, Theos!" He saw the Sacrati frown, but it was too late to stop now. So he said, "Is there even a plan? When the Empire has spread to all corners of the world, as I know you're sure it will, what then? If half of the people born are only good as killing machines, won't they just turn around and start killing each other? Isn't that what's starting to happen already? Where does it end, Theos? What kind of system is that?"

Finnvid risked a glance in Theos's direction then and wished he hadn't. The Torian was glaring at the ceiling as if he were about to attack it. But the *ceiling* hadn't just insulted Theos's way of life.

"I'm not saying being able to fight isn't important," Finnvid added quickly. "And obviously you can do other things—with your survival skills, and your physical—well, perfection, I guess. I'm not saying it's worthless. It's very impressive, really. But if someone *isn't* as physically blessed as you, or if he just has different interests, he can still contribute, can't he? He can still be something worthwhile?"

"Maybe he could be an archer, and ambush *real* soldiers when they think they have a truce." The tone was cool and casual, but the words cut.

Finnvid's nod felt jerky. "Aye. Or maybe something better. Maybe he could do something that *doesn't* involve taking lives."

Theos rolled to his knees, and if his wounds hurt, he showed no sign of it on his face. "I'm going outside," he said, as if it wasn't obvious.

"What for?"

"Air. A piss. Stretch my legs. Check the weather."

Finnvid didn't have a response, and Theos clearly wasn't waiting for one. So Finnvid stayed behind and started chopping jerky into tiny bits to put in the broth, and when he was done with that he straightened the blankets and checked that his medicines were in order and then added a little more butter to the lamp. And still, Theos didn't return.

He was wearing his undershirt and thin leggings. That was all. He might have passed out, or been attacked, or . . . he might have . . . run away? Yes, he might have decided he'd rather freeze to death in the wilderness than go back inside the den while Finnvid was in there preaching about how nasty Torians were.

Finnvid sighed and headed for the tunnel. He stuck his head out into the cold, and Theos was right there, crouched down with his hands tucked in his armpits, leaning against the wall of the trench. "Come in," Finnvid said. He tried to make it sound like a suggestion.

And it worked. Theos leaned forward, almost falling onto his hands and knees, and he shuffled toward the tunnel as Finnvid backed up into the main part of the den.

"You need to drink some broth," Finnvid said, trying to duplicate the tone of voice that had worked outside. When Theos wordlessly reached for the cup, Finnvid felt like a genius. But he decided not to press his luck, and just sat quietly as Theos drank the broth. Then Theos reached over and pulled a blanket from his bed to wrap around his own shoulders.

"I have sons," Theos finally said. "Most of them are like me. They'll be good soldiers. Good Torians. But a few of them . . . I don't know. They might not. Maybe they'd have been better off somewhere else, somewhere they could be . . . something else."

Finnvid was afraid to say anything that might break their fragile truce. But he was even more afraid to say nothing and leave *Theos* fragile. "Maybe they can be something else without leaving Windthorn," he suggested. "Maybe change . . . maybe it doesn't have to be bad. The warlord has done horrible things, and he's gone about it all wrong. And it sounds like *some* of the things he wants wouldn't be good for most Torians. Still, maybe there are a *few* changes that could be made."

Theos didn't answer, but when Finnvid eased over to him and wrapped his arms around the Sacrati's shoulders, Theos leaned back into him and relaxed.

That night, they slept twined around each other, and the next morning Finnvid checked Theos's dressings and spread more honey on the deeper wound on his thigh. The swelling was going down, and the redness was receding, but Theos's body was still tight under Finnvid's hand and his breath quavered when Finnvid touched him.

Actually, Theos's breathing was extremely irregular. Was something wrong?

Oh. Finnvid had been so intent on his task that he'd forgotten the area he was working in. Once he stopped staring at the wound, it was hard to ignore Theos's cock, still covered by the blanket but hard and erect under the fabric.

"Sorry," Theos said. "Ignore it."

No, Finnvid didn't think he wanted to do that. Instead, he shifted closer and eased his hand under the blanket. Just on Theos's thigh, at first, and then up to his stomach. He left it there, eased it down a finger's breadth, and then retreated hurriedly. He tried again, but lost his nerve and brought his hand back to Theos's stomach.

Theos groaned. "Are you punishing me? What did I do?"

Finnvid's laugh was more like a giggle. "Sorry. I just—you know."

"Not really." Theos took a deep breath, then released it. "But, okay. I can take it."

Finnvid kept his hand where it was, his smallest finger tickling and teasing the top of Theos's hair, and squirmed down so he was lying on his side, pressed up tight beside Theos. He could feel his own cock hardening against Theos's leg, and knew Theos could feel it too. "Really, it's okay? If I just . . . If we . . . Can I just . . ."

"You can do what you want," Theos said. He leaned over and kissed Finnvid's forehead. "You're a cruel man, but I'm strong."

Finnvid slid his hand lower, gathered his courage, and wrapped his fingers around Theos's shaft, and was amazed by how right it felt. How *natural*. He slid his hand up and down, shifting the loose skin over the hard flesh, and Theos sucked air in through his teeth. He moaned a little, his eyes closing, then whispered, "I take it back. You're very kind."

Finnvid was causing that reaction. He was lying in a shelter he'd built, with a Sacrati he was nursing back to health, and he was the one making this strong warrior gasp and groan and tighten his fingers in his blankets. "I wasn't exactly appreciated when I was growing up in Elkat," he whispered. "I was *allowed* to look at trees and bugs, but I wasn't encouraged. I was supposed to be a man. Supposed to marry a woman. Men aren't completely free in Elkat, either."

Theos opened one eye. "*That's* what you're thinking about right now?"

"I was thinking that I want to taste you, but then I thought of what that would make me, according to people at home."

Theos rolled onto his side, easing Finnvid onto his back, and propped his head on one elbow while his hand moved to Finnvid's waistband. "Don't think about them," Theos suggested. He leaned down and kissed Finnvid, deep and powerful and sweet. "Think about me."

And that was what Finnvid did. When Theos teased his fingers beneath Finnvid's waistband and looked a question at him, Finnvid nodded, then pulled away to squirm out of his loose trousers. They'd often been naked together. He'd seen Theos hard more times than he could count, and while less frequently, Theos had seen Finnvid in the same state. This was nothing new.

But as he turned back to Theos and surrendered into a kiss, he knew everything was new. Everything was changing. And he *wanted* it that way.

He let himself get lost in the sensations. Theos's soft lips, his strong tongue, the rough skin of his hand as he wrapped it around Finnvid's aching cock. The smell of their arousal, the warmth of their bodies, the sounds of their breathing and their murmured words. When Finnvid gathered enough courage to reach for Theos again, they set a matching rhythm, slow and gentle until the end. Then their bodies arched and thrust in shared ecstasy, and afterward they relaxed together, still touching and kissing. Theos rolled over onto his back, his strong arms bringing Finnvid along until he was sprawled on top of the larger man's warm body.

"Did I mention that I'm feeling better today?" Theos asked between kisses. "Still not perfect, maybe, but definitely better."

"No," Finnvid disagreed. "I think you're very sick. Very weak. You need to stay here longer. Maybe forever. With me."

Theos's smile was a little sad. "You'll get tired of eating so much butter."

"I'm already tired of butter. But I'm not tired of *you*."

"Not yet, maybe. But give it time." Theos didn't seem upset by the idea, and Finnvid was reminded again that this encounter was only special for *him*. For Theos, it was just an enjoyable way to spend his time while stuck in a snow den. Certainly a better distraction than actually *talking* to an ornery Elkati.

Yet, no sooner had Finnvid thought that than Theos said, "It's just you in your family? Your mother only had two children?" He frowned, then said, "Your *father* only had two children? And he was the *king*?"

"I suppose he may have had others," Finnvid admitted. "He and my mother weren't a love match, they were just good partners. There may have been children elsewhere."

"May have been? You don't know?"

"Well, no. It's not the sort of thing he'd have bragged about. They're . . ." Finnvid searched for the Torian word. "What do you call . . . well . . . I guess *all* of your children are born out of marriage. They're *all* illegitimate, technically. So maybe you don't have a special word for them?"

"For children whose parents aren't mated for life? You have a word for that?"

"It's an insult." Finnvid frowned. He shifted a little, so less of his weight was on Theos's body. "Ridiculous, really, but . . . it's an insult. I might have half brothers or sisters out there, and they're considered less than . . . not just less than *me*, but less than most people, just because their parents weren't married."

Theos was quiet for a while. Then he laced his fingers through Finnvid's and said, "The world is strange."

That was a bit more philosophical than Finnvid had been expecting, but it set his brain in motion. He leaned up so he could see Theos's face clearly and said, "Okay, say there's a perfect world. Say . . . say we found a whole new valley, one that's normally cut off by glaciers. But there's a really warm few years and the glaciers melt so we can move in. It's beautiful, with forests and fields and lots of water and game. And we get to choose people to go live there, and we can set it up however we want. And it's going to refreeze after we get there, so we don't have to worry about being attacked or defending ourselves. What would it be like?"

Theos was quiet for long enough that Finnvid began to feel stupid. The Sacrati was a man of action. He didn't play stupid make-believe games, didn't spend his time watching trees or bugs or dreaming of perfect worlds.

But when Theos finally spoke, Finnvid realized that the man hadn't been scoffing; he'd been thinking. "It's cut off *for sure*? No chance of the glacier melting again?"

"No chance," Finnvid said quickly. "There's a rockslide, as well."

"I probably shouldn't go, then." Theos didn't sound sad, exactly. Just resigned. "You don't need soldiers, and that's all I can do."

"No. It's all you've learned to do so far, but it's not all you *can* do! You can learn something else. You can . . . raise goats."

"Goats?"

"Somebody has to."

"The women will."

"And the men will just sit around and do nothing? No, the women don't like the sound of *that*. They say you need to learn a trade."

"I think they should mind their manners. If they want my valuable services . . ." and Theos grabbed himself to demonstrate just what service he was talking about, "they need to spoil me. They should *bring me* goats. I think . . . two goats for a really good night. Five goats guarantees a baby."

"*This* is your perfect world?" Finnvid was torn between being amused and appalled.

"No." Theos paused. "In my perfect world, they'd bring me chickens, and cattle. Oh, and *pigs*. I don't like goat much. And I guess if it's really perfect, they wouldn't bring me the animals, they'd bring me food, already cooked."

"What would you do with your time? When you're not fucking or eating?"

"I'd sleep."

"What else?"

"I don't know. I hear bugs are very interesting. Maybe I'd start watching them."

"Would you want company? A fellow bug-watcher?"

"You?"

"Maybe."

"I was thinking you'd be the bug-watching master. My teacher. I wouldn't know where to start, all by myself. I might do it wrong. I might squish one. Or see a really interesting tree and get distracted from the bugs. Aye, I'd definitely need some guidance."

"Well, I could help you some of the time. But I'll be very busy with running the valley, you know."

"Why will *you* be running it?"

"Because you can't be torn away from your bugs."

"Why *either* of us? Why would *we* be in charge?"

"It's our valley. We found it."

"But the other people live there, right? Shouldn't they get to choose who's in charge?"

"No, it's *our* valley. What if we give power to people and they mess everything up? We're stuck there, remember."

"So we'll have to work hard to make sure they *don't* mess it up."

"We'd have an easier time of that if we kept all the power for ourselves."

"But then *we'd* be the ones messing it up."

Finnvid sighed. He had a feeling he wasn't going to win this argument, and wasn't sure he even wanted to. "So, they'd choose their leaders. Maybe that *would* give me more time for bug watching."

"And fucking."

Finnvid fought to control his blush, and was reasonably successful until he felt Theos's hand brush along the top of his ass, so high up that it could have been considered his lower back. Just one tiny suggestion, barely even a hint, and Finnvid's face flamed. He pushed away, suddenly aware of how little he was wearing.

He'd been lounging there, almost naked, body entwined with another man's, their spilled seed drying on each other's bodies, as if it were . . .

He stopped himself. It *was* natural. Or maybe it *wasn't* natural, but maybe "natural" wasn't such an important thing to be.

Unfortunately, Theos had noticed his reaction. He sat up himself, hissing a little as something hurt, and shifted a hand's breadth away. Theos's expression was still gentle, his body relaxed. He wasn't angry, he was just giving them some space.

Finnvid shook his head. "You must be getting tired of this. Of me, and my doubts."

Theos shrugged. "You're much less annoying now than you used to be, and I managed to put up with you then."

"You threatened to torture and kill me then."

Another shrug. "Of course I did. You were very annoying."

Finnvid knew he shouldn't be pleased. Shouldn't feel as if he were glowing with pride, just because he'd managed to become less annoying to an arrogant Sacrati. But there really didn't seem to be much connection between what he knew and what he felt, not lately. So he let himself smile, and then, when he realized that Theos was still looking away from him, he nudged the man's foot with his own.

Theos turned to him, saw the smile, and frowned in response. "What are you grinning about?"

"I'm not annoying anymore."

"You're *less* annoying."

"*Much* less annoying."

"Well, you started from being *very, very* annoying. There was room for you to improve a lot and still be a total pain in the ass."

"Am I a total pain in the ass?" Finnvid asked it casually, but braced himself for the answer.

Theos squinted at him. "Are you going to make me keep drinking broth?"

"You seem much stronger now. Probably you could eat solid food, as long as you take it easy."

"And are you going to keep touching me? Letting me touch you?"

And there was something about the way Theos said it, something about the lightness in his tone that Finnvid recognized. They were both teasing, but braced to hear answers they wouldn't like.

Luckily, Finnvid could give Theos an answer he *would* like. "I want to keep touching you. And I want you to keep touching me." But he should try to be honest. "Just . . . maybe not—not *too* much."

"Too much touching? How much is too much?"

"Not . . . you know."

"I don't think I do."

He was going to make Finnvid say it. Maybe Theos really didn't understand, or maybe he was just taking a little revenge. Finnvid stared at his foot, still right next to Theos's. "Not . . . what you do with other people. What I've seen you do."

"Eating together? Talking? Oh, *drinking*! You don't want any alcohol. That's fine. We haven't got any here, anyhow."

"Theos."

"Finnvid."

"You still say it wrong. It's Finnvid, not Feenveed."

"Maybe *you've* been saying it wrong."

"I've been saying my own name wrong?"

"Seems like."

Finnvid sighed. He could let the conversation drift, if he wanted to; he knew Theos understood what he was getting at. Still, it seemed like something he should be able to talk about. It seemed childish and ridiculous to shy away from the words. "I don't want you to—to fuck me," he said finally. The words came out too quickly, but at least he'd said them.

"Do *you* want to fuck *me*?"

Finnvid stopped looking at his foot. He stared at Theos and felt his jaw drop open. "I hadn't even thought of that as an option. I don't . . . Do you do that?" In their months together, Finnvid had lost count of how many men he'd seen Theos with, but never like *that*.

"Not usually. I *have*, though. I'm not saying I *will*; I'm just curious about whether you want to. Is it the whole thing you don't like, or just that role?"

"I don't know." Finnvid tried to think about it. His mind was racing too fast, too randomly, to produce any useful ideas. Apparently he'd been wrong, thinking he was ready for this conversation. "I should go check the snares."

He turned and started crawling toward the exit, but before he got far he felt a strong hand wrap around his ankle. They froze like that for a moment, Finnvid not trying to get free, Theos not trying to drag him back, and finally Finnvid looked over his shoulder.

"It's okay," Theos said with an easy smile. "Sex is supposed to be fun. If you don't want to do something, don't do it. It's that simple."

"But *you* want to do it. And you can't because I won't."

"Well . . . yes. But you're not— Finnvid, you're not actually my bedwarmer. You're not my slave. You stayed here to help me get better, not to get fucked. I know that."

"And soon you'll be back in Windthorn, with hundreds of men just waiting for you to fuck them."

Theos frowned, clearly confused by the bitterness in Finnvid's voice. "Well, probably not hundreds. Still—aye, there are other people I can do things with if you don't want to do them. Not right here, right now, but that's not your problem." He took his hand off Finnvid's ankle while keeping his gaze on his face. "The stuff we already did . . . you didn't like that? You didn't want to do it?"

"I liked it," Finnvid said in a small voice. "I wanted to do it." He forced a smile onto his face. "I'm fine. Everything's fine. I just need to go check the snares. I'll be back soon."

"You need to put more clothes on," Theos prompted.

Of course he was right, and Finnvid pulled on heavier pants and a hooded coat and mittens. He managed to do it all without even a glance in Theos's direction.

When he finally got outside, the cold air felt like a slap. A slap that he needed. He'd gotten stupid, forgotten who he was and who *Theos* was. He'd let himself get too attached, and he was going to suffer for it. He stared up at the cold blue sky and wondered how things had gotten so confusing.

CHAPTER 28

Theos had no idea whether all Elkati were insane, or just Finnvid. He looked down at the gash on his thigh, the one that was giving him the most trouble, and poked at the edges. They weren't as red as they'd been, and he didn't think he had a fever anymore, either. The thought of food no longer made him feel ill.

His injuries were healing. He still didn't have the strength to walk all day, or to carry a heavy pack, but it wouldn't be long before he could get moving. And as soon as he could, he would; he needed to get back to Windthorn and see what could be done to make things right.

Theos sighed and flexed the muscles in his leg, watching the honey-covered scabs stretch but not tear. Another couple of days in the den. He could justify no more.

He lay back and dozed a little, and when he heard Finnvid crawling into the den, he kept his eyes closed.

"I caught a squirrel," Finnvid said quietly. He clearly knew Theos wasn't asleep. "Can you help me clean it?"

"I'm weak and feeble. You should do it yourself."

"I'm weak and feeble, too. I've never really learned how to do this. When we hunted, we had people to take care of what we caught."

"I thought you hunted with birds."

"We did."

"So the birds caught the animals, other people cleaned them . . . When you say 'hunting,' do you really mean 'going for a walk'?"

Finnvid snorted. "I suppose Sacrati hunt wolves with just their teeth."

"Teeth? Teeth would be cheating. We just use our bare hands."

"So be a mighty Sacrati and come help me with the squirrel. If you don't help, you can't eat any."

"I don't actually like squirrel all that much."

"Do you like it better than broth?"

Theos opened his eyes and sat up. "We should do it outside. Let me get dressed."

So they cleaned the squirrel, and Theos showed Finnvid how to chop it up and cover the little scraps of meat with vegetable meal and then fry it all in butter.

"It would have been better if we'd hung it up for a couple days," Theos said as he chewed one of the meat chunks.

"Less tough?"

"Aye."

"That would have been nice. But, still, it was good to have something fresh."

Everything was nice and relaxed. If Finnvid hadn't reacted as he had earlier, and if he wasn't still being quite so careful to avoid eye contact, Theos would have thought that the logical end to their afternoon would involve nakedness and skin-to-skin contact. But as it was, he kept his clothes on and waited. Finnvid was tidying and organizing their meager belongings, and when he was done with that, he looked yearningly toward the exit.

"Maybe I'll check the snares again," he said.

"You should leave them alone," Theos said. "If you want to go for a walk, go the opposite direction, so you won't disturb any animals that might be investigating the traps. And make sure you don't get too close to the main path—we don't want anyone to see your trail. And don't get lost." Really, it made no sense for Finnvid to go outside at all. "I'm going to sleep. I'm pretty tired."

At that, Finnvid turned and finally looked right at him. "Do you feel fevered? You just woke up . . . If you're tired again so quickly—"

"I'm not *actually* tired," Theos said. Awkward to have to explain all this for the poor Elkati, but apparently he was as clueless about social cues as he was about hunting. "I'm saying I'll stay over here and keep my eyes closed and leave you alone, if you want. You don't have to go outside to get away from me."

"I'm not trying to get away from you," Finnvid protested. He saw Theos's face and grimaced. "Well, I suppose I am. But not . . . I don't know. I'm not— I don't—"

"Maybe you should have spent a little less time watching trees and a bit more time learning how to *speak*."

"I can speak. If I knew what I was feeling, I could probably express it. But I just have no idea what I feel."

"Neither do I. Know what *you* feel, I mean. I know how *I* feel."

"Okay . . . how do *you* feel?"

"I'm still a bit hungry. Not starving, but if there was more squirrel, I'd eat it. I'm generally warm, and nothing hurts too much right now. The fever's gone." And because it was Finnvid, Theos pushed himself a little more. "I'm impatient to get back to Windthorn and figure things out. But I also kind of like it right here. I feel like this is a safe cave we're living in . . . a little *world*. Just us, with nobody causing any problems. If I wasn't worried about the people back in Windthorn, I wouldn't be unhappy about being here. You built a good den, Finnvid."

It was still hard to be sure what Finnvid's expression meant, but then he nodded. "Thank you. I—I'm not unhappy about being here either. And I'm a bit scared of what we're going to find in Windthorn, so . . . I'd really much rather stay here."

"You don't have to come to Windthorn. You *shouldn't* come to Windthorn, really. You could still tell your family we kidnapped you. You could go home, and maybe it'd be rough for a while, but they'd get over it, wouldn't they?"

"You don't have to take care of me," Finnvid said, raising his chin.

"Well, as we travel, I expect I'll need some help. But when we get to Windthorn—I don't expect to be your responsibility anymore. You don't need to pay for my food and give me somewhere to sleep."

"I don't mind doing that. I told you I don't like to sleep alone. That's not why I think you should go back to Elkat."

"You think I'm useless in Windthorn. I'll have no role to play, and won't be able to contribute. I understand that, and I know you're right. But don't *you* understand? I have no role to play in Elkat, either! I'm useless there too. They were trying to find a purpose for me when they sent me on this mission, and look what a mess it's turned into. First I was captured, then I made friends with the wrong side, and then

I betrayed my people and gave vital information to the enemy. Even if they believe I was kidnapped, I'll still be the one who was stupid enough to let it happen."

He stopped and shook his head, then whispered, "And that's not even *starting* on the other problems." He met Theos's gaze with wide eyes. "How can I go back and pretend to be something I'm not? Pretend to... How can I marry a woman, after what we've done here?"

It was Theos's turn to stare. "I don't understand. You... touching me, just the little things that we've done? They make you— You can't marry a woman now? You're unclean, or something? I don't understand Elkati rules. Not at all."

Finnvid's snort was only a bit shaky. "It's not that. Not exactly. But . . . I'm not like you, Theos. I'm not just interested in finding a warm body to rub against and get inside. All my life, I've known I was supposed to want women, and I never, ever have. There's a woman who helped me get away, and she seems very nice, and I would like to know her better and be a better friend to her, but Theos, I don't want to touch her. I don't want to lie with her, like I want to lie with you. I can't *imagine* wanting to be with any woman, not like I want to be with you."

Theos tried to sort it out. "But before you were with me, you thought *I* was disgusting, too. Maybe you just need to stop *assuming* you won't like things, and try them."

"I never thought you were disgusting."

"Disgusting," Theos said. "Unnatural, immoral, sinful."

"That was— It was never *you*. It was the—the acts themselves. And even then, I never really meant it. I *wanted* to mean it! I knew I *should* mean it. But I never really did." Finnvid took a deep breath and was clearly forcing himself to continue. He looked Theos straight in the eyes, his expression pleading for understanding as he said, "From the first moment I saw you I thought you were beautiful. Dangerous and threatening, but beautiful. And later on, I thought you were arrogant and violent and stupid and horrible and cruel, but I still thought your body was beautiful. And then when I got to know you better, I stopped thinking the bad things—mostly—and when I saw what you can do with your body, the ways you can find pleasure and give it to others . . ." Finnvid shook his head. "I've never lain with a woman. But I've never wanted one, either. Not even a little bit. And with you? Even before I liked you, I wanted you. I didn't understand it, maybe, but I wanted you." He frowned. "How can I go back, and forget all that?" The question seemed to be as much for Finnvid as for Theos.

Neither of them answered it until finally Theos said, "There are some men like that in Windthorn. They don't want to fuck women at all. And there's a few that don't want to fuck men, not ever. Some women the same way. It's peculiar, but it's not really a problem. It's like if somebody wouldn't eat meat. It's their decision and they're not hurting anyone. The less they eat, the more there is for everyone else." He grinned, thinking of the extra women he could be with because there were fewer rivals. Not that he was afraid of competition, but if he got older, he might appreciate a bit of an advantage.

Wait. He was getting off topic. "So . . . aye. You should come to Windthorn. We'll find a way for you to be useful if you want to stay." He shrugged. "That's assuming we make it there alive, and then aren't killed as soon as we step into the valley."

"Of course," Finnvid said. He leaned forward now, looking more relaxed if still not completely happy. "And . . . the—the way we touch. Now. The way we did this morning. Can we keep doing that, even if I don't want to do—if I want to do a *bit* more, but not—"

"Finnvid." Theos tried to keep his voice level, and not growl *or* laugh. "You said it once. You can say it again. Say, 'I want to use my hand and maybe my mouth, but I don't want to fuck.'"

Finnvid blushed, then he pulled himself up straight and prim. "Well, I don't *need* to say it, since you've clearly demonstrated that you understand my wishes."

"Yes, sir. I understand."

"And do you agree to abide by them?" Finnvid was still acting haughty, but Theos could see the tentativeness trying to creep in.

So he smiled, and leaned, and reached out, and grabbed hold of Finnvid's ankle again, tugging on him. "For now," he said, and then he crawled forward and pushed Finnvid down so he was lying on his back, Theos hovering above him. "And if I decide I *don't* like your rules anymore, then I'll just stop playing. You understand?" Surely Finnvid did, after all their time together, after all the restraint Theos had already shown. But if it was as obvious to Finnvid as it was to Theos, they wouldn't be having this conversation. So he added, "I won't change the rules, not if you don't want me to. I'll just stop. And if I do, that's not your problem."

Finnvid still didn't seem completely happy, but he smiled, and laced his hands behind Theos's neck and pulled their mouths together. And after that, Theos stopped really worrying about whatever the problem had been; he had more important things to pay attention to.

Finnvid stretched, and Theos's sleepy mumbled complaint made him smile. They'd spent the last two days horizontal almost all of the time, tangled around each other, intimate and comfortable. Theos hadn't stopped "playing," and Finnvid hadn't needed to face the truth: it might just be a game for Theos, but for Finnvid it was much, much more.

They'd decided that this would be their last night in the den. Theos wasn't sure he could manage a full day of walking yet, but even a half day would be something, and would help him start to get strong again. The day before he'd done some scouting and come back looking confident. He'd seen no tracks on the main trail, suggesting that the Elkati troops had given up and gone home.

"They might still be around," he'd mused as Finnvid helped him out of his snow-covered clothes. "They might have raced along the trail, hoping to catch up to us before we crossed into Windthorn territory. They know I was hurt, so they'd be hoping I couldn't move fast. By now they'll have hit the border and maybe have turned around and be coming back." He'd glanced at Finnvid. "They're your people . . . does that sound right?"

Finnvid had nodded thoughtfully. "Probably. And them knowing you're wounded might not matter too much. They know you're Sacrati, and the way people talk about that? They make it sound as though you can fly. If the mountains were in your way, you'd just lift the mountains up and shove them to the side."

Theos had been quiet for a moment, then said, "They might think differently, now that they've killed some of us."

He'd worn the same expression he had every time he spoke of the attack, and as always, Finnvid had been torn between compassion, his own sorrow, and his sense of guilt. He hadn't known the attack was going to happen, but he *should have*. He'd invited the Torians to the castle, and that had been a mistake that had cost brave men their lives.

Now, lying next to Theos, feeling the warmth of his body, Finnvid let himself admit to another emotion. Relief. He'd made a horrible mistake, and men had died, but *Theos* was still alive. A selfish reaction, yet honest all the same. If Theos had died, Finnvid never would have come alive himself.

"Maybe we could just move farther into the forest," he suggested, not sure if Theos would listen to him or not. "You're still not at full strength; if we get into trouble and have to run or fight, you won't be as strong as you could be."

"We'd better stay out of trouble, then." Theos pulled Finnvid closer to him, then rolled and shifted until Finnvid was flat on his back, Theos on his side and snuggled in close, one leg thrown over Finnvid's so their cocks lined up. It seemed to be one of Theos's favorite postures, and Finnvid had no complaints about it either. "I need to go home," he said softly, his lips tickling Finnvid's jawline as he spoke. "We'll be careful, but I can't stay here. I can't keep lying around, enjoying myself with you, when my valley may be at war with itself."

Finnvid gave a nod, and ended it with his head tilted back, leaving more space for Theos's explorations. Finnvid had shaved when he'd been in Elkat, but now his stubble was long enough to be softening, long enough for Theos to get a grip on it with his teeth when he wanted to. Sharp tugs followed by the warmth of Theos's tongue, little nips immediately kissed better . . . Finnvid wanted to stay balanced like this, wanted to surrender all independence and give his body to Theos in perpetuity. If he could, he'd volunteer to be Theos's bedwarmer again, to be cared for and owned and protected. But that wasn't their future.

Theos was kissing his way down Finnvid's body, now, pushing bedclothes out of the way, leaving a trail of warmed skin to be cooled by exposure. Finnvid had lost track of how many orgasms he'd been given in the last few days, but his body apparently wasn't exhausted yet, responding to Theos's ministrations as enthusiastically as ever. He let himself lie back and surrendered to the sensations, Theos's warm lips wrapping around him, his soft tongue flickering and teasing, his strong hands massaging and coaxing. Finnvid felt like his entire body was liquefying. Well, everything but his cock. Really, it was like all the strength and solidity of his entire being was channeled into one part of his body, the part sliding in and out of Theos's hot mouth.

He found enough energy to prop himself up on his elbows so he could watch. It wasn't the sensations that were important, not really. *Anyone* could perform these acts. Maybe not as well, but well enough. The parts Finnvid needed to remember, the images he wanted to have filed away to comfort him in his lonely future, were about *Theos*. The rough man being gentle, the enemy being a friend. The beautiful, powerful creature abandoning its fierceness and giving pleasure instead of pain.

This was what Finnvid would remember. They'd go back to Windthorn and do what they had to do, and Theos would have hundreds of other men to choose from, not to mention the trips to the city. Finnvid would be forgotten. But he would not forget.

CHAPTER 29

They left their den behind the next morning, kicking at the snow walls and doing what they could to disguise their interference with nature. There were still signs, of course, because several days of human habitation were hard to erase. But it was less obvious than it had been.

Theos kissed Finnvid at the edge of the clearing, and even though they were leaving together, it felt like good-bye.

They moved slowly and carefully, always quiet, and Finnvid could feel his shoulders tightening from the tension. It had been one thing to travel the difficult mountain trail when the only enemy was nature; but now, with the possibility of men out there who would kill Theos and might kill Finnvid, everything was even more daunting.

They'd decided to stay on the main trail in order to make better time. Theos had asked questions about the land, about alternate paths, and Finnvid had been ashamed to realize that, though he'd been a member of the family that claimed sovereignty over this territory his whole life, he knew less about the terrain than Theos had picked up in his one trip through.

Theos believed there were several places where the main path was the only way to travel, unless they were to use ropes and mountain climbing tools, which they didn't have, to ascend the peaks. Finnvid had been forced to accept Theos's decision when he said, "There's no point mucking about in the woods, breaking our own trail, when we'll have to come out on the main trail in some places anyway. If the Elkati are still out there . . ." He'd shaken his head in frustration. "We'll have to watch for signs, and hope for wind to blow our tracks away. We shouldn't wear the snow flats; we've only got one pair anyway, and if they see those tracks, they'll know for sure they're ours. Our best hope is that they found Andros's path up through the mountains and followed it; if they're all up there, we can skip right past them and take the valley route."

"And if they didn't? If they're on the same trail we're taking, marching back toward us?"

Theos had made a face. "That would be bad. But I watched your men on the way here. They weren't good in the mountains, not good in snow. Right?"

It had felt strangely disloyal to agree with Theos's assessment, but it would have been even more disloyal to deny a truth that might be important. "We stay in the valley during winter. We consider it foolhardy to go into the mountains."

"That's good. So whoever is out there will be unhappy. Trudging along like you and the other Elkati did on the way here, with your eyes on the feet of the person in front of you. And if the person in front of the parade is just as disheartened, he won't be looking for anything too intently either. But *we'll* be paying attention, and we'll know they're coming before they know we're there. We'll slip into the woods and let them march right by, and if we're lucky, they won't notice our tracks."

"And if we're unlucky?"

Theos had smiled sadly and pulled a looped strip of leather out of his pack. "If we're unlucky, you stretch this around your wrists and then yank it tight with your teeth." He'd demonstrated, with the loop catching one hand only, and Finnvid had seen how the knot was cleverly constructed to tighten with a jerk, and then not loosen. "I attack, you stay behind. When they're done with me they find you, and you show them your bound hands and tell them your tale of kidnapping and violence."

When they're done with me. Those words echoed in Finnvid's head as he trudged along the snowy trail. After Theos had said that, Finnvid had resolved to stay just as alert as Theos, to be the guardian who would keep them out of trouble. He'd keep the Elkati away from Theos, and then they would *never* be done with him. But as he'd walked, the cold and the effort had drained the energy from him, and by the time they stopped for a midday break, he knew he was just as numb to his surroundings as the other Elkati on the mountain.

"We can get off the trail here, where the rock is windswept so they won't see our tracks, and make a little den," Theos said. He'd been walking in front all morning, breaking the path. "They could walk right by us and never notice. We can rest for a couple hours, then see how we feel. If we're strong, we'll walk some more, then make a better den for the night."

Finnvid nodded. He wasn't going to argue with any plan that involved the word "rest." He followed Theos off the trail and into the trees, and together they burrowed out a two-person sleep tunnel and crawled inside, their packs at their feet to shut out most of the wind.

"I think I'll miss this," Finnvid whispered. "When I get back to sleeping in a regular bed. I'll have too much space, and not be cozy enough."

"You think you're going to be sleeping in a bed when we get to Windthorn? I was planning for you to be on my floor again."

"I'll fight you for the bed."

"You will? I'd better get in shape."

They smiled at each other, and kissed, and then drifted off into a peaceful doze. Finnvid woke when he felt Theos's finger on his lips. The touch wasn't sensual, for a change, and Finnvid opened his eyes cautiously and looked at Theos, waiting for an explanation. Theos just looked back at him, and put the finger to his own lips.

That was when the booted foot broke through the ceiling of their den and dangled for a moment between their shocked faces. A grunted Elkati oath followed, and in that instant, Finnvid saw the expression on Theos's face turn from surprise to fierce determination.

"The cord," he mouthed to Finnvid. He already had a knife in one hand, and Finnvid knew his sword would be drawn as soon as there was room. And as soon as the sword was drawn, there would be blood.

"No," Finnvid mouthed back.

Theos stared at him in disbelief, then frowned and nodded vigorously. "The cord!" he mouthed again.

No. Finnvid knew he was right. He didn't want Theos to fight Elkati soldiers, didn't want to see injuries or death on either side. But if Theos *was* fighting, no matter who his enemy was, Finnvid would be part of it. Even if he wasn't much use, he would not sit idly by and watch Theos killed. So he shook his head, and Theos glared a little more, and then something dripped down the sides of the rough hole left by the Elkati boot. Something yellow, and warm enough that it was melting the snow around the top of the hole.

Finnvid and Theos both drew away in disgust, watching the urine fall to the snow between them. Then they lay there, still as ice, as the man above them crunched off.

Finnvid exhaled, then scrabbled lightly at the snow by their shoulders, covering the yellow stain. As if *that* was all he needed to be worrying about. But it was the only thing he could *do* anything about, and Theos didn't tell him to stop.

When he was done, they kept still for a while, and Finnvid could hear more sounds. Nothing too loud, just the squeak of boots against cold snow, the snap of an occasional tree branch and, more comfortingly, a few casual words here and there. The men outside had no idea how close they were to their quarry, or they never would have been so relaxed.

Theos was listening too, his eyes squinted as if that improved his hearing. When the noises stopped, Finnvid opened his mouth to speak, but Theos shook his head firmly. So they stayed there, silent, for so long Finnvid felt as if his chest might explode with all the unspoken words, until finally Theos shrugged.

"I guess they're gone," he whispered. "But still be quiet."

Finnvid resisted the urge to roll his eyes. As if he'd been about to start yelling. "What were they doing?" he whispered. "Why weren't they on the track?"

"They must have figured we'd stayed behind," Theos said. "Maybe they found Andros's tracks and saw that it was only one man traveling." His eyes focused somewhere over Finnvid's shoulder as he added, "Maybe they caught him. Made him talk. He could have told them we'd denned up off the trail, but it would be hard for him to give them a precise location."

Finnvid shook his head. He wouldn't let himself believe that Andros had been captured and tortured. "Probably just his tracks. Or else it's like you said: they know you were hurt, so they're guessing maybe we denned up somewhere."

Theos nodded tentatively, and Finnvid felt a wave of affection for the man. Theos cared about his friend, and he was worried about him, and it made him seem a little vulnerable. Finnvid cared about Theos, and wanted to comfort him. It was all so pure.

Then Finnvid glanced down and saw the long knife still gripped in Theos's hand, and the complications of the world crashed in on him again. "I won't sit back while you fight," he whispered. He squirmed until he found the leather cord and pushed it over toward Theos. "I'll fight with you, or run with you. I won't be a coward."

Theos opened his mouth to argue, but Finnvid was already there, kissing him quickly, then pulling away as if the decision had been made. "Is it safe to leave, do you think? I don't really want to stay in that man's latrine for longer than I have to."

"We should go," Theos agreed. "And we'll have to move fast. If they're searching off the path, they'll probably find our old den, so they'll know they're right, and they'll have a good idea of how long ago we left it. They'll probably turn around and chase after us."

Finnvid nodded. "Let's go, then."

So they eased out of their den and headed for the path, Theos swearing as they went and he saw all the tracks through the woods. "Idiots," he said. "They have no one on the trail at all? If they did, they'd have seen our tracks, and seen where they ended."

"Maybe they thought we were Elkati. The Elkati military isn't set up for this sort of mission. Our communication isn't too efficient, and we don't have . . . routines. I don't know the word. We don't have processes to follow, ways to expect people to behave. It's probably pretty chaotic out there."

"Good," Theos grunted, and then they saved their breath for traveling rather than wasting it on conversation.

They moved fast, and again Finnvid lost his battle to stay alert and on guard, drifting into a meditative state, focusing only on putting one foot in front of the other. He knew that Theos would be paying attention to the larger world, so Finnvid paid attention to Theos's feet, tromping through the snow ahead of him.

They took short breaks to drink the melted snow from the containers they kept strapped against their chests and to eat quick bites of jerky and even of straight butter. As darkness fell, they stepped just off the trail and burrowed into a snowbank together.

The night was long, and Theos said it was too dangerous to travel in the dark; too much chance of falling off a cliff or running into a camp full of Elkati. Finnvid felt ashamed for his gratitude to the night, but he knew that if he'd asked his legs to carry him any farther, they would have refused. So he loosened his outer clothes and snuggled in against Theos, and they slept, alone again in their tiny world.

The Elkati were camped right where Theos had expected them to be. He'd noticed the spot on the journey toward Elkat and had seen how there was absolutely no way to pass without going through the narrow gap between two cliffs. But it had all been academic then, just one more bit of information to stash in case it was useful someday.

Now it was a serious problem. "We could get off the trail, den up, and hope for a storm," he told Finnvid. "In the middle of a blizzard we could walk right through; no one would be able to see us well enough to know we don't belong. If we were farther up in the mountains, that would make sense; the weather up there is bad as often as it's good. But we're pretty low, here. We could wait a long time and not get much of a storm."

"What's our other choice?" Finnvid asked.

"We don't really have another choice," Theos admitted. He'd been thinking about it for a while, worrying about it, but he'd hoped the Elkati incompetence would continue and they *wouldn't* have seen the importance of the pass, wouldn't have established a camp there. Now that he'd seen not only the Elkati but the *number* of Elkati, his optimism was gone.

"We need to get through," Finnvid said. "There are too many of them to fight?"

"There's about a hundred men."

"That's too many." Finnvid grinned quickly. "Right? Even for a Sacrati?"

"It's too many."

"There's no way around it. We can't fight through it. I like your blizzard idea, but the weather won't cooperate." Finnvid stared through the trees in the direction of the camp. "This is a problem."

"It is."

"We can't just wait it out? Maybe they'll go home."

"The men downhill from us have probably found our den, and they're likely working their way back toward us. They'll be sweeping the forest more thoroughly now, and they'll know what they're looking for. If they're doing a good job, it'll slow them down, but you and I haven't been pushing as hard as we could if I were healthy. They'll catch up to us soon."

Finnvid stepped a little closer and drew a shaky breath. "We've come a long way, you and me."

Theos heard the sadness in his voice. The resignation. "It's not too late for you to go back. Or go forward. Stumble into camp with your wrists tied, say you managed to get away from me . . ."

"Stumble into camp," Finnvid said. He frowned. "I probably could. Not as *me*, just as an Elkati soldier. Everyone will be wearing whatever winter gear they could find; there's no uniforms to worry about. With scarves and beards, it's hard to recognize anyone at a distance. Or even up close."

"That's why they'll have passwords, and a process for identifying . . ." Theos looked more closely at Finnvid. "No passwords? No system for keeping track of who's in camp and who's out?"

"I don't think so," Finnvid said. His voice was cautious, but his excitement was clearly growing. "I've never heard of such a thing. Never seen it done. When we traveled this summer, we did nothing of the sort, and as I said, we don't usually leave the valley in the winter, so we'd have no special procedures in place."

"It would be risky," Theos said thoughtfully.

"No more than sitting here, waiting for the soldiers from downhill to catch up to us."

"You could still go back," Theos tried.

Finnvid snorted and clapped a mitt-covered hand to the side of Theos's face. "You need to hear me when I say this, Theos." He locked his gaze on Theos and slowly, clearly, said, "I'm not going back. I can't live like that. I won't."

"Maybe you could—"

"No. I can't. I won't."

"Just because they want you to marry a woman."

Finnvid sighed. Then he shook his head. "No. Not because of that. Truly, it's because they mispronounce my name. They say it 'Finnvid,' but really it should be pronounced 'Feenveed,' and I just can't stand the idea of living the rest of my life with such ignorant people."

"That must be very aggravating for you."

"It is."

Theos took both of Finnvid's mitted hands in his own and said, "I'd rather you were safe. But, if you're sure . . ."

"I am."

"Then I think we should go at dusk." And they stood together, there under the pine trees, and worked out the rest of their plan.

A few hours later, as the sun dropped behind the mountain peaks, they ran up the hill toward the Elkati camp. They were both genuinely out of breath, but they exaggerated the stagger in their steps and the slump in their bodies.

There were sentries on duty—the Elkati had managed that much—huddled behind a tree, trying to escape the wind, and only one stepped forward to intercept the new arrivals. Theos briefly reconsidered the plan; he could probably kill these three without much noise or fuss, and then there would be no one to sound an alarm. No. There would be time enough for killing if the plan went wrong; no need to rush into it.

So he doubled over as if fighting for breath while Finnvid spoke in Elkati. He would be saying that they had an urgent message for the camp commander. When the sentry would demand to know what it was, Finnvid would gasp out that an army of Torians had snuck around, coming down the mountain route, and were on their way to the valley.

Theos could see the sentry's jerk of panic in response to the Elkati words and wondered if they should have chosen something more mundane, and snuck in on a wave of apathy rather than panic, but it was too late to change, and this approach seemed to be working. The man was no longer thinking clearly, and that was good news. Finnvid barked a few orders at the sentries and then strode into camp, Theos stumbling along behind him, doing his best to look harmless and disoriented.

Finnvid seemed to know where he was going, approaching a large tent—a tent, in the middle of the mountains in the wintertime—and then jerking to a halt as if his attention had been called elsewhere. Hopefully this charade would work if the sentries were still watching them. Finnvid turned and strode just as purposefully off on a tangent, and then, once they were out of view of the sentries, he stopped and waited for Theos to catch up. "Good?" he whispered, and Theos nodded. He didn't see any reason for them to wait around.

So they continued, heading for the far side of the camp, and it was then that Theos saw a familiar face, and then another. The Elkati soldiers who'd traveled with them from Windthorn, the soldiers who'd been Torian captives for months . . . some of them were in the camp, and they were staring at Theos and Finnvid. They'd recognized them.

Theos found his sword. There were too many Elkati, far too many, but he'd go down fighting.

Then he saw one of the former captives raise his hand. A quick, subtle gesture, but unmistakeable. He was telling Theos to stop. Stop moving? No. Stop his attack, before it had even started. The men didn't move. They didn't sound an alarm. And then, as if of one mind, they turned away.

Theos hurried after Finnvid, and they reached the path out of the camp. There were sentries there as well, just as cold and miserable looking as the others, and again only one of them stepped forward. More Elkati words from Finnvid, this time drawled in the bored voice of a soldier sent on a task he considered beneath his dignity, and then they were past.

Still not out of bow's reach, though; Theos could almost feel the arrowheads burying themselves in his shoulders, yet nothing flew at them, and no alarm was raised.

Theos wanted to speak, wanted to yell a celebration, but he didn't dare. So he just kept walking after Finnvid, trudging through the barely packed snow.

When he couldn't stand it any longer, Theos jogged a few steps and caught up to Finnvid. "It worked," he said.

"So far," Finnvid said. "But there are tracks here . . . Elkati have been traveling this path. Keep your guard up and your voice down. Stop speaking your brutish Torian."

Theos was startled into silence and fell silently back into line as they moved on. Finnvid was right; there was no need to draw attention to themselves. But Finnvid didn't understand that it didn't matter if they drew the attention of an Elkati or two. It probably wouldn't matter if they drew the attention of five, as long as none of them were archers. Theos could handle a few Elkati. By the sword, his Sacrati instincts *wanted* to handle them. He'd been nervous walking through camp but unable to do anything about it, and his body was still thrumming with unused energy. It would feel so good to use it, to fight and strain and face death and find victory over his foe.

He scowled at Finnvid, scurrying forward, running away, and was irritated, but only for a moment. Because then he realized the soldiers they'd just escaped from were Finnvid's people. Anyone they fought now would be one of Finnvid's people. Maybe someone he'd grown up with, someone he knew.

The Elkati soldiers who'd looked away and let them pass? Did Theos want those soldiers to regret their actions and spend the rest of their lives knowing that their decision had allowed Theos to go on and kill some of their comrades?

He swore under his breath, too quietly for Finnvid to hear. War was much easier when he didn't know any of the enemy.

They walked on until the moon set, then denned up for a few hours of sleep while waiting for the sun. As they lay on their sides, facing each other, their bodies tight together to share warmth and comfort, Theos wished there was more light. He wanted to study Finnvid's face, wanted to understand how he was feeling. He'd left his people behind, helped someone who might be their enemy, someone who'd only hours earlier wanted to kill some of them just to wear off some energy . . .

"Close your eyes," Finnvid said softly.

"It's dark in here. You don't know if they're open or closed."

"I know. I can feel you staring at me."

"No you can't."

"Are you staring at me?"

"Maybe."

"I wonder how I knew that?"

"Well, now I wonder too! How am I supposed to go to sleep with that on my mind? I need to keep my eyes open so I can watch you and figure it out."

"You can't see me. It's dark in here."

"If Elkati have superior night vision, that's something I should know. It could have strategic importance."

"It won't. Because we're away from the Elkati now. We're only a day or two from the border, and no matter how much they might want to catch us, they won't be stupid enough to cross the border into Torian lands, not after killing Sacrati."

"And you're not worried about that? Not sad? To be leaving your people behind..."

"I'm sad," Finnvid said softly. "And a bit worried."

"I don't like that." Theos was surprised by how true that statement was. He didn't like—he *hated*—the thought of Finnvid being unhappy. He wanted to protect him from it, somehow, but he didn't think there was a way. Well, not for most of it. He couldn't do anything about the sadness, but maybe he could help with the worry. "I'll take care of you. In Windthorn. You can stay with me, and I can pay for your food, just like before. We'll find you something to do. Something worthwhile, something you like." What else? What else would someone like Finnvid be worrying about? "I'll try to... I'm not sure. I'll talk to people. I'll help them understand that the Elkati— I won't lie. I won't say the Elkati aren't murdering cowards. But I'll make sure people understand that the trouble started in Windthorn. I'll make sure that if they're looking for revenge, they look close to home; that's where the *real* betrayal happened."

"We could get back to Windthorn and find the warlord completely in charge. He may have already killed the Sacrati there, and taken over the city."

"Then I'll find somewhere else safe for you until I can get things sorted out."

Finnvid snorted. "If I wanted to stand with you when you were fighting *my* people, do you think I wouldn't want to be with you while you fought your own?"

"I'd like it better if you were somewhere safe."

"And I'd like it better if you came with me to that safe place, and left all this mess behind. But you're not going to do that. I know it. So . . . I'll stay with you, and we'll be unsafe together."

Finnvid's loyalty was touching, but it was Theos's own reaction to it that was truly overwhelming. Theos had experienced comradeship all his life, with the Torians in general and then the Sacrati in particular. He knew what it was like to care about the group more than he cared about himself. But this? For him to care just as much about one single person as he did for all of the Sacrati combined? And for that person to care about him in return?

Theos tugged at the leather bracer on his right wrist. Two buckles undone, and then he ran his fingers over the bracelets. Where was it? That one, with the rounded, smooth surface. He stretched it so the gap between the ends widened, and then he slipped it off his wrist and reached out to find Finnvid's hand. He wrapped the cool metal around warm flesh and squeezed the ends shut tight.

"For me?" Finnvid whispered.

Theos just nodded. He wasn't sure he could trust his voice, and he wouldn't be able to find the right words anyway.

"I wish I could see it."

"I'm still not sure that you can't, with your night vision. But if you can't see it now, you can see it tomorrow." Tomorrow, and the day after, and many days after that.

They slept, then, both of them exhausted, and woke early the next morning to begin walking again. Several times through the day, Theos caught Finnvid looking at the bracelet, or running the fingers of his other hand over the smooth metal, and each time he saw that, he felt . . . he didn't know what to call it. Proud, somehow, and tender, and strangely hopeful. It was hard to understand, and certainly would have been hard to explain, but he didn't think he really *had* to explain it. Because the only person who needed to know how he felt was Finnvid, and every time he touched the bracelet, he turned and smiled at Theos, and Theos smiled back at him. And that was enough.

CHAPTER✝30

They encountered no more Elkati. When they reached the Windthorn border, Finnvid paused before following Theos across. He was leaving his home, and he didn't see how he could ever return. Not only because they wouldn't want him, he reminded himself, but because he didn't want *them*. Not on their terms. So he rubbed his bracelet for luck, kept his gaze on Theos, who had turned around and was waiting patiently, and moved forward.

"It feels like forever," he said quietly.

Theos took his hand. "Nothing's forever. Especially right now."

Finnvid tugged his hand free. "Is that supposed to make me feel better?"

"Better? I don't know. It's just . . . true. It's supposed to make you feel truer."

They had a fire when they camped that night, for the first time since their trip had started, and Finnvid found himself almost mesmerized by the dancing flames and the warmth. He leaned back into Theos and let himself be enveloped by it all. Another moment he wanted to claim and keep and never leave. But as Theos said, nothing was forever.

They walked on and on, until one night when they made camp Theos said they shouldn't have a fire. "We're close to the valley, now. I don't want to call attention to us until I know what's going on."

"And how will you discover what's going on?"

"Tomorrow morning I'll walk down to the sentries' post and see if they try to kill me. If they do, it's a bad sign. If they don't, it's just . . . undecided."

"I'm coming with you."

"You shouldn't."

"Will it make them more likely to attack? If I'm there? Would it be bad for you?"

"I don't think so," Theos said.

"Then I'll be there."

Theos looked like he was thinking about arguing, but then shrugged. "Hopefully it will all be fine."

They denned up and slept, and as they got packed the next morning, Finnvid kept an eye on Theos, making sure he didn't slip off on his own to be a hero. Theos noticed, of course. "You'd be too sad without me," he said with an understanding grin. "Wouldn't be able to go on living. It would be cruel of me to leave you alone. I know."

His joke was too close to the truth, and Finnvid was quiet as they walked the rest of the way down to the valley.

As they approached the sentry post, Theos turned to him, and now there was no humor in his tone. "If this goes bad, step back. I'll be moving fast."

Finnvid nodded mutely. He knew he wouldn't be much good, not if this became a fight.

But before they made it to the final bend in the path, Theos stopped walking, so abruptly that Finnvid almost slammed into his back. "Andros," Theos said, and there was a note of affection and admiration in his tone that made Finnvid squirm with jealousy even as he struggled to understand what was going on.

"He left us a message," Theos said, and he reached up into the boughs of a nearby pine tree and grabbed a small brown bundle. It was the size of a pine cone, if that, but Theos was holding it as if it were something sacred. His smile was radiant as he said, "He made it back."

Finnvid tried to feel good about that. He *liked* Andros, he reminded himself. He liked him very much. Of course he was glad Andros had made it safely back to Windthorn. It was just hard to see the relief on Theos's face and realize how worried the Sacrati must have been for the whole trip. Hard to know that Theos hadn't bothered to share any of that with Finnvid.

"There's a note?" he asked. He could worry about his pettiness later, or, even better, forget about it entirely. "What does it say?"

Theos unrolled the small bundle and pulled out a slip of paper. He squinted down at it and groaned. "Stupid code. I hate codes."

"Code? Really? You write in code?"

"Sometimes. When we have to." He looked toward the valley, then back up the trail. "I need to sit down and figure this out. We need to use numbers, and I'm even worse at numbers than I am at letters."

"Can I help?"

Theos squinted at him, then nodded. "Probably. It won't take long to explain it. Just hard to actually do the work."

So Theos explained, and Finnvid was more than a little amazed by the complex blend of calculations they had to go through, but eventually they had the message deciphered.

Midnight watch. Temple. Second gate.

"A lot of work for not much of a message," Finnvid said. "Does that all mean something to you?"

"It means we're camping out a bit longer. I suppose the men on the midnight watch are on our side in whatever's going on. And I guess he wants to meet us at the temple. The second gate is a way into the city; it's usually barred, so I assume he's done something about that."

"So there *is* something going on."

Theos nodded. He looked discouraged, but then he brightened. "Still, Andros is here! That's good news."

"It is," Finnvid agreed, and by now he was sure he meant it.

The impatience that had been building in Theos as he walked home from Elkat was almost too much to stand, now that he was so close yet forced to sit and wait. He thought about trying to find another way into the valley, but the only other possible approach was a four-day trek through the mountains in the summertime. In the winter the route would likely be impassable.

He considered approaching the sentries even knowing they might be hostile. He'd rather fight than wait, and if they were on the warlord's side they were his enemies. But maybe they weren't really on any side yet and were just following orders. And maybe it would be better if Theos and Finnvid arrived unnoticed. After all, they didn't really know what was happening.

So he waited. Finnvid tried to distract him in ways that would ordinarily have demanded all of his attention, and Theos tried to cooperate, but it wasn't long before Finnvid sat up and said, "You don't have to, you know. You're not *my* bedwarmer."

"I want to. In general. Just . . . not so much right now."

"Because of Andros?"

"What? Andros?" Theos pushed away from Finnvid and then frowned at him, trying to make sense of the words. "What does he have to do with it?"

"Nothing," Finnvid said quickly. Miserably.

"Andros is fine," Theos reassured him. "He left us that message. I'm not worried about him anymore. Well, I'm much less worried than I was when I thought he was alone in the mountains, or maybe captured by Elkati."

"I know." Finnvid smiled, too bright to be real. "I don't know what I was saying. Just babbling, I suppose. After guessing him, I probably would have said something about the phase of the moon, or there being too much snow. Or possibly not enough."

The lie was obvious, but Theos didn't know what to do about it. "I'm just restless," he said. And then they stopped talking.

The temperature dropped as the sun set, so they denned up and snoozed, and when he could wait no more Theos shook Finnvid awake, and they crept down the hill and around the bend. Two dark shapes would be easy to see against the white snow, so they kept to the forest and didn't get too close. They watched as the midnight shift took over the post and the others retreated to the simple cabin to sleep. Theos made himself wait a little longer, giving the soldiers in the cabin time to settle.

Finally, he and Finnvid set out. Theos stopped walking before the sentries could call a challenge, hoping to keep them from making noise that would alert those in the cabin, and then walked forward slowly, hands raised to show they were empty. Beside him, Finnvid was doing the same thing.

"Theos?" The voice was hushed but familiar. "By the sword, Theos, it's good to have you back."

"Achus." Theos stepped closer. "You remember Finnvid? He enjoyed it so much here that he's returned."

"Andros said you two were together." Achus muttered a few words to the other men in the sentry tower, then slid down the ladder and moved toward them. He clapped Theos on the shoulder and nodded at Finnvid. Theos began to tug the bag of soil from around his neck, but Achus reached out and caught his arm. "Better not. They might count the bags and realize you're back."

"Who are 'they'?"

Achus sighed. "Things have gone all wrong, Theos. You need to get into the city before sunup. I'll walk with you and explain as we go."

So they started down the path, and for the first time in his life Theos wasn't relieved to be coming home. Instead, as Achus spoke, he felt himself growing more and more tense.

"The warlord's taken over," Achus said. "He had Tamon executed—claimed the captain had committed treason, been conspiring with the enemy. But he wouldn't give details about any of it. Said the trial had to be private because there were important secrets that might be spilled otherwise."

"Tamon's dead?" Another Sacrati, another comrade, gone. If there'd been a battle, Theos would have been prepared for the loss, but this? His sorrow rose until he pushed it down and replaced it with anger. "We don't have secret trials!"

"We do now," Achus said with disgust.

"What are we doing about it?" The biggest part of Theos's plan had been to get back to the city, talk to Tamon, and find out what to do. Now that was gone, and there was nothing left in its place. "What's Andros up to?"

Achus sighed. "He came back and took shelter in the city, trying to understand what was going on. The warlord found out he was around and invited him down to the barracks to discuss the captain's trial. He made it sound like he'd release the captain to Andros's care."

"But the captain is dead."

"He is now. He wasn't then. Not until Andros showed up to get him. Then the warlord arrested Andros and gave the execution order for the captain." Achus was silent for a moment before saying, "We didn't know about the execution. The Sacrati. We knew the captain had been arrested, but we still thought . . . I don't know. We thought it was a bluff. Thought the reeve could negotiate his freedom. If we'd known, we would have done something, of course. But we didn't know. Not until the warlord dumped his body on our barracks' doorstep and told us we no longer had the right to our own commander." Achus shook his head as if he was overwhelmed by it all.

Theos fought back his anger at the Sacrati inaction. They hadn't had the whole story; the captain had chosen to keep secrets, and that was why he hadn't had defenders when he needed them. If Theos had been in Windthorn, without knowing about the warlord's betrayal in Elkat, he probably would have waited, too.

"And now he has Andros? I understand why you wouldn't have known to do something about the captain, but why haven't you rescued Andros?"

"Some of us want to. *I* want to. He told us what happened with the Elkati, but then the warlord took him before we could figure out our next step. And he's being guarded by regular soldiers. Lots of them. If we want to free him, we'll have to fight them. It'll be Torian against Torian. And if Sacrati attack regular soldiers, the warlord will be able to make it look like he was right all along. People will think that the Sacrati *are* traitors, and we *are* trying to start a civil war. The soldiers will fight back because they think they have to, and we'll fight back to defend ourselves. And where does that end?"

Theos swore softly. He was a simple man and didn't like these complications. They made him feel like he was drowning under all the words, all the possibilities. But then he realized he was walking beside someone who was a much better swimmer.

"Ideas?" he asked casually, as if he were just giving Finnvid a chance to be part of the conversation.

"The letter," Finnvid said quickly. "Unless Andros lost it. If it's still around, it's clear evidence. A bit tricky to know what to do with it, though. Normally you'd give it to whoever's in charge. In this case, that might not work so well."

"It could still work," Theos said.

"You want to show the warlord evidence of his own betrayal? What do you think he'll do with that information?"

"Not the warlord. This isn't Elkat; it's Windthorn. The warlord might be giving orders, but he's not really in charge."

"He still isn't? With the captain dead?"

"No. The people are. The women . . . hopefully we can keep the women out of this. But the men need to know what's going on. One warlord is nothing compared to a couple thousand soldiers."

Finnvid nodded slowly. "So we need to speak to the men. And we need to be safe long enough to make sure they listen. How can we arrange that?"

Theos frowned at Achus. "The Sacrati and the regular troops aren't truly at war, at least not yet. You're still on sentry duty, not stuck in jail. Could I just talk to people? Go to the dining halls, the training yards—"

"And get arrested yourself," Achus said. "You'd have to sneak around, and I really don't know which of the soldiers we can trust. Most of them just want this all to go away, I think, but I know the warlord has spies."

"I can do it. If I'm careful—"

"How long would it take?" Achus asked skeptically. "The warlord has made his move, and he's got Andros. How long will it be before he has *his* trial and earns his execution?"

Achus was right. There wasn't enough time for Theos to talk to the men individually. "We need them all together. Somewhere we won't be attacked and arrested before we're finished speaking." He could only think of one place that would work. "The city. The main square. It's neutral ground. Well, hopefully it's *our* ground. But at least neutral."

"Will the reeve agree to that?" Achus asked. "She doesn't generally seek your counsel, as I recall. And her priority will be the safety of the women, not the politics of the men."

"She understands the situation. She knows that it will be terrible for the women, long-term, if the warlord gets his way." He grinned with a confidence he didn't truly feel. "And I think I can persuade quite a few of the *other* women to help us out."

"You don't have time to seduce them all," Finnvid scolded. "You'll need to appeal to their brains, not their . . ."

"Hearts?"

"That wasn't the body part I was thinking of, no." Finnvid shook his head. "I think you're right, though. The city would be perfect. We just need to find a way to make it happen."

CHAPTER 31

"**Y**ou want me to invite them all in to the city," Photina said. Finnvid and Theos had made their way through the side gate to the city, gone to the temple, requested an immediate meeting with the reeve, been sent to her office in the middle of the night, and now she was scoffing at them. Finnvid had expected a warmer welcome, but understood her reaction when she said, "You want to bring that violence inside our walls, where our children will be exposed to it."

"They're *their* children too," Theos tried. "You know they won't hurt the kids. *Their* kids. They won't hurt the women, either."

"You know that for a fact, do you? Tell me, would you have predicted that the warlord and his allies would order the murder of an entire squad of Sacrati? Or arrest and execute the Sacrati captain without giving him even the hint of a fair trial?" The reeve strode around the office impatiently. "Things have changed, Theos. The warlord was biding his time, setting things up before you left. But now, he's made his move. He's breaking every rule he can find, and he has people helping him."

"How many people?" Finnvid asked. He should probably be keeping his mouth shut, but he'd committed to all this, so he needed to be involved. "Do you have numbers? And how many of them are true believers, rather than just following orders?"

"I don't know." The reeve sighed and sank down into the chair behind her desk. "Andros was looking into all that until they stopped him. But my impression is that there are a lot of men looking for leadership, and with the captain gone, the warlord is the only one providing it. They'll believe what he says because it's easier than thinking for themselves."

"Did Andros mention a letter?" Theos asked. "Did he show it to you, or mention it to the warlord?"

"He did. I saw it."

"Where is it now?"

"He took it with him when he went to arrange Tamon's release. The warlord said he'd trade the letter for the captain. But he lied."

"So the warlord has the letter now. Or he's destroyed it."

Finnvid tried to be positive. "But the reeve's seen the letter, and you've seen it. You can speak to what's in it. And so can I. I can explain how the Elkati were tricked."

"We can say what we want, but will they believe us?" Theos sounded like he was giving up already. And if Theos wasn't determined, there was no way they'd persuade the reeve.

Finnvid hadn't mentioned it before, hadn't wanted to give Theos one more reason to consider Elkat a threat, not without hard proof. But he couldn't refrain any longer. "There may be another layer to the warlord's plan," he said reluctantly. "It's just a theory, but based on the letter, and conversations with my brother?" He took a deep breath. "It's possible the warlord may *want* a civil war, one that weakens *both* sides."

Theos's eyes were narrow. "What would he gain from that?"

"It would kill many Torians, including Sacrati. In the warlord's letter, he also suggested we exchange troops for 'training.' If enough Torians were dead, and if enough of the remaining soldiers were over in Elkat, your valley might be vulnerable to attack, even from a force that wouldn't normally have a chance." He waited for the others to catch up.

It was Theos who whispered, "The Elkati? You think he's planning to allow *the Elkati* to conquer Windthorn?"

"Under his banner, I assume. He'd have to arrange things so it wouldn't look like a sign of Torian weakness. *That* would certainly merit intervention from the central valleys. But a warlord using whatever troops were handy in an emergency?" He watched as the other two exchanged doubtful looks. "I don't know. It's just a theory. But you said no Windthorn soldier would ever attack the city. Elkati soldiers would not hesitate if they thought they had a chance."

"And after killing a band of Sacrati," the reeve mused in hushed tones, "they might just have the confidence to try."

Theos looked toward the reeve, then shook his head as he turned back to Finnvid. "The women would fight," he said. "Whatever Windthorn soldiers were left, plus the women—I don't know that Elkat could win."

"But you don't know that they *couldn't*," Finnvid said. "And that's remarkable enough."

"He couldn't be so ruthless," the reeve said, but there was doubt in her voice. "Or . . . if he *is* that evil . . . what *else* might he have planned? And what does that mean for the women? If he's willing to go that far, would it be better to appease him, at least temporarily? If he's trying to find ways to attack the city, we're in even more danger than I thought we were. We need to be safe and careful until we have a plan we *know* will work."

Finnvid stared at her in frustration, but Theos seemed more resigned. "Maybe she's right. The warlord is unpredictable, so it's too risky to have the meeting in the city. This isn't their problem."

"How can you say that?" Finnvid demanded. "You have *forty-six* children living in this city. The fate of their father is none of their concern, or their mothers' concern? And will the warlord be kind to them all if he takes over?"

"Forty-seven," the reeve murmured. "Alloria had a boy while you were away. She's calling him Toro."

"Toro," Theos said quietly, almost sadly. "He's healthy? And she's well?"

"It was a long birth, but she's strong. They're both fine."

Finnvid couldn't let them get off track. "And in nine years, Toro will leave his mother and go to live in the barracks. How will the warlord treat him? What will the rules be, and how will anyone who dares to stand up to tyranny be punished? If the warlord is mad enough to think about starting a civil war for his own selfish gains, he clearly doesn't value the life of Torian soldiers." Finnvid ignored Theos and stared at the reeve. "And you have other grandsons. If you won't stand up for your son, won't you at least help them? The children of the women you're trying to protect?"

"My grandsons?" Her voice was sad. "I can help the girls, but the boys? They'll go to live in the barracks, and Theos or someone just like him will teach them that their only role in life is to kill and die in battle. Is that really so much worse than whatever the warlord is planning?"

"Theos knows more than that," Finnvid protested. He supposed he was the one being dragged away from the topic now, but he wouldn't stand there and let the reeve be so critical of her son. "Otherwise, *he* wouldn't care about the warlord. He'd just train and rest and wait to be called to battle. He's willing to risk his life to protect the Torian way, the way that's good for the women and children, if not the men. The danger isn't just in battle, but in making a stand like this. He knows what happened to the captain, and what they might be doing to Andros, and still he stands up for what he believes in. If your grandsons learn that sort of strength in the barracks, I think you should be pleased, and proud of them!"

"He's willing to make a stand because the warlord has made himself the enemy of the Sacrati. You may think this is about ideals, but it isn't. Not for Theos. It's just about winning. Destroying the enemy."

"Because Theos can't use his own judgment? He can't decide for himself who's an enemy, and who's a friend?" Finnvid frowned at her. "How sad for you, to not see him more clearly. I've known him for a much shorter time, and yet I've seen him show mercy and compassion and respect. I've seen him change his mind about who the enemy was when faced with new information, and I've seen him walk away from fights I know he wanted to run toward."

She raised her eyebrows dismissively, but there was *something* in her expression as she gazed at her son. "So, I haven't seen you clearly?"

Theos had been staring at Finnvid, but finally he looked at his mother and shrugged. "This isn't important." He stopped, and turned back to Finnvid. "I don't mean . . . What you said . . . thank you. It's important *to me*." Then he told his mother, "It's not what we should be talking about. You don't think much of me . . . I know that, but it's not important right now." He was silent for a moment, then said, "You need to pick a side. You should know that if you choose the Sacrati's side, and the warlord wins, he'll punish you, and possibly the rest of the women. And if you choose the warlord's side, and the Sacrati win? The Sacrati will continue to treat you and the women of Windthorn with respect. So if you want to be smart, I suppose you'll choose to help the warlord." He shook his head. "But I'm hoping you'd rather be *right*. And you know which side is the right side. You know."

"I can't afford to back you if I don't think you can succeed," she said. "If I think there's a chance, then I'll do what I'm able. But . . . what's your plan? You'll gather the men together, tell them the warlord *hinted* that the Sacrati should be attacked—because I saw that letter, and all it really did was *hint*—and . . . then what? They need a leader, Theos. The captain is dead, and the warlord is strong. If you're going to win, you've got to give them an option. They need someone *else* to follow."

"We'll have elections," Theos said. He frowned. "That's what we do. Why would it be different this time?"

"Elections eventually, yes. But not right away. The men can't vote until they're confident they know the whole story, and that will take time. In the meantime, someone has to step up and take charge. Are you willing to do that?"

"Me? There are many Sacrati more qualified. I'm not even an iyatis anymore."

"There may be Sacrati more qualified. There certainly are some who are iyatis. But none of them are *here*, Theos." She shook her head, quickly forestalling his objection. "I don't mean you should take the job because you're convenient. I mean *none of them care enough to take a chance*. None of them came here and tried to find a solution."

Theos looked at Finnvid and the confusion on his face made Finnvid want to find a blanket and a den and snuggle Theos and keep him safe forever. But it was too late for that.

"Five breaths ago she was telling me how worthless I am," Theos said, as if his mother couldn't hear him. "Now she wants me to take charge of the entire military. Are you following this?"

"Not really," Finnvid admitted. He turned to the reeve. "Have you changed your mind about him?"

"Changed my mind? I said Theos would shape his sons to see the world the way he does. I still believe that, and I still don't like the way he sees it." She frowned. "I admit, I may not see *him* any more clearly than I think he sees the world. I need to think about what you said. But, as he said, this isn't about that. We're not looking for a philosopher, or even a long-term leader. We just need someone the men trust, and someone they'll follow. Someone brave or stupid enough to stand up against a would-be tyrant who's shown himself willing to kill those who stand against him."

A quiet, mocking smile, then she added, "We need the sort of man who could bring someone to Windthorn as a prisoner, send him away as an enemy, and somehow return with him as a loyal ally. We need someone who could convince someone to follow him into danger and take his side, no matter what." She glanced down at Finnvid's wrist, at the bracelet, and said, "I gave him that when he left home and went to the barracks. And now I see it on your wrist, and I see you touching it when you want comfort." She raised an eyebrow. "Tell me, Finnvid of the Elkati—can you think of anyone better able to do what needs to be done? Anyone more likely to turn hostility into . . . something better?"

Finnvid felt his face flush, but didn't let it bother him. He hadn't known his affection was so obvious, but there were more important things to worry about than his pride. "I can't, no. I think he's someone worth following. I just want to make sure you won't agree now, and then lose faith halfway through whatever comes and abandon him. He needs to know who he can count on."

She looked at him for longer than seemed necessary, then over at her son. "You've surprised me, Theos," she said softly.

He shrugged. "We need to speak to the men. The city's the safest place to do it. Will you invite them in?"

She nodded, slowly. "Yes. Tomorrow. We can send messengers to the training yards, midmorning, and have the men come here directly. Will that give you enough time to get ready?"

"Ready?" he asked blankly.

She snorted. "You need to give some thought to what you'll say, and how you'll say it. And more practically . . . you look like a bear, and smell like what a bear leaves behind. The men may not want you to look pampered, but they'll at least want to believe that following you won't mean a life of depravation and filth." She turned up her nose. "Go to the temple baths. They'll be deserted at this time of night. And

I'll have someone bring you clothes from the garment makers. What else do you need?"

"I need to talk to Xeno. As soon as possible. Could you send a messenger for him?"

"And new boots," Finnvid interjected. The Xeno conversation was probably important, but so were Finnvid's feet. "Ours are wet and worn. And maybe some ointment for our skin? And food." He realized he was making a lot of demands, yet the reeve just nodded as if she was pleased there was someone able to look after the practicalities. So Finnvid thought a little harder. What else would Theos need? He was about to give an important speech, and he wasn't much for words. "Will there be writing tools at the temple? Something we can use to put down key points?"

"There should be," the reeve said calmly, "but I'm not sure where. I'll put a package together and send it over with the other things."

"Thank you," Theos said, and he started for the door.

Finnvid was half-turned to follow him when the reeve said, "Wait."

So Theos eased back around, but not all the way. Enough so he was looking at Finnvid, not at his mother. And he waited.

"You're a good Torian, Theos." She stepped a little closer. "A good Sacrati. If I— No. *When* I am critical of you, it's not *you* I'm talking about. Does that make sense? I wanted more for my son. More choices, more freedom. I fought for it, and I lost, and it was—it was very difficult for me. So to see you excel in the narrow path they offered to you, to see you become the epitome of what they wanted you to be . . ." She stopped talking for a while, then shook her head. Finnvid saw nothing on Theos's face to suggest that her words were making any impression on him, or that there was any point in continuing. Still, she went on, "I'm proud of you. You're strong and brave." She smiled at Finnvid, then added, "And smart. And apparently you can be merciful and compassionate and respectful. You're a good man, Theos. I'm sorry if I've made you feel that I don't see that."

He nodded, then said, "Can you ask the messengers to send Xeno to the temple baths? We can talk to him there."

"I will," she agreed quietly.

Finnvid followed Theos out of the office and then out of the building, back into the cool night air. It was well below freezing, but after their time in the mountains, neither of them even bothered to refasten their cloaks for the short walk to the temple. "Mothers are difficult," Finnvid said tentatively as they strode through the darkened streets.

Theos frowned at him. "*Preventing civil wars* is difficult," he corrected. "Mothers are just . . . mothers."

Well, then. That was taken care of. So Finnvid tried to shift his mind in a more productive direction. "Do you know what you're going to say to the men? And what will you ask them to *do*? Assuming they believe our story and want to follow you . . . what's next?"

"No idea," Theos said almost cheerfully.

"Oh. Do you think you should figure something out?"

"Probably." Then Theos stopped walking, and Finnvid felt strong fingers wrap around his, and suddenly he was being tugged, shoved, manhandled in Theos's unique manner that somehow made Finnvid feel as if his body was at fault for not having been in the desired position to begin with.

Finnvid ended up with his back against the wall of the building they were passing, Theos's thigh pushed between his as if it belonged there. And then Theos's lips, hungry and demanding, were on Finnvid's. Their kiss was deep and hard; Finnvid drove his head forward, making his own demands, and Theos met them without question. Their hands groped through layers of fabric and found the familiar points of entrance: Theos sliding his hand up the sleeve of Finnvid's tunic to grasp his forearm, Finnvid reaching down the neck of Theos's shirt to find the bare skin at the top of his back. And all of it was just a little more desperate than usual, as if they were both aware it might be their last time together.

Or maybe Theos was just getting rid of some frustration after the meeting. Finnvid didn't really care what was motivating Theos right then; he was too busy responding to the onslaught. Theos rutted against him; Finnvid pushed back, maybe with less coordination but with just as much enthusiasm. It was primal and real, and Finnvid's whole body sang with energy and need. And as they drove each other toward their climax, their clothes no real challenge in the face of their desire, they worked together, fought together, and won together, both of them arching and groaning and then slumping over the other, the wall at Finnvid's back the only solid thing in their suddenly molten world.

Theos was the first to straighten, but he didn't pull away. His kisses were gentle now, even tender, and when he leaned back, his smile was affectionate and teasing. "Where has my prudish little bedwarmer gone?" He asked, and gave Finnvid another kiss. "The boy who turned his head every time I took off my shirt?"

"I was trying to keep from getting hard," Finnvid admitted sheepishly, and Theos rewarded his honestly with a kiss. "I worried that once I started staring, I wouldn't be able to stop."

"You never need to."

"I might," Finnvid said, and he shoved Theos back and turned to start walking, ignoring the damp fabric against his skin. Theos caught up to him in a few strides, and Finnvid said, "If things don't go well . . . if you have this meeting and the men *don't* follow you, the warlord will have you killed." Finnvid glanced over to see Theos beginning to speak, but shook his head. "Don't say you're not afraid to die. This isn't about you, it's about *me*. I don't want you to die! Even if I can get away, somehow, which I doubt will happen, it won't matter. I'll still be . . ." He shook his head, surprised but not embarrassed by the tears gathering in his eyes. "I might as well be dead," he whispered.

Suddenly, he was shoved against another wall. This time, though, Theos held him in place with a forearm across his throat. And then leaned in. Finnvid couldn't breathe. He tried to gasp, dug his fingers into Theos's arm, then just stared, eyes wide, paralyzed with confusion and fear. It felt like forever, but really Finnvid had probably only missed a few breaths by the time Theos pulled his arm away and growled, "*That's* dying, Finnvid. It's not romantic, and it's *not* peaceful. I've seen men drown in their own blood, I've seen them trying to shove their own guts back inside themselves while they leak shit through the holes. If things don't go well tomorrow, that might happen to *me*, but it *will not* happen to you! Do you understand? If I'm captured or killed, you'll *run* to the warlord and thank him for rescuing you. You'll kiss his feet and do what he says and you will *live*, Finnvid. Do you understand me?"

"I'll live long enough to cut his throat in his sleep," Finnvid snarled with what little breath he had. "Or to break you out of his jail. But I won't run away. No. I can't do that."

"You *can*."

Finnvid pulled his head back and narrowed his eyes. "So why don't you do the same? You don't need to stay here. We've proved we can survive in the mountains in the winter. Come with me, and we'll just *go*, and find somewhere new to live. We can leave all of this behind."

Theos frowned. "You know I can't. This is— It's my family. My children, my friends. I can't walk away and leave them."

"*I did*," Finnvid said. "I left everyone who cared about me, everything I'd ever known." He took a deep breath and found the courage to continue. "I did it for *you*, Theos. I ran away from my world, and the space in my heart where it all used to be? I filled it with *you*. And I'm not sorry. I made my choice, and I don't regret it. But if you think I left all that behind, and then if something happens to you, I'll just leave *you* behind and go find something else? You're wrong. And stupid. I love you, Theos. You don't need to love me back; it doesn't change how I feel."

"Of course I love you," Theos said. He sounded confused.

Finnvid was tempted to let it go, then. He could carry on with those words in his heart, and if he and Theos didn't survive the next day he could die with them still ringing in his ears. But he couldn't fool himself. "Like you love Andros. And the mothers of your children. And the Sacrati. And probably even your mother and sisters. Like that."

Theos frowned. "I don't know. Like Andros, yes. He's—he's my close friend. He means more to me than the other Sacrati. More than all the other people you said. So, like that. But . . . but different."

"Different," Finnvid said, and his courage deserted him. Or maybe his wisdom reasserted itself. *Different* was good enough. Being like Andros was good enough. Finnvid shouldn't, *couldn't*, expect more. So he took Theos's hand and tugged him forward. "Baths at the temple. Let's get clean."

Theos didn't budge. It was frustrating to see that he barely even had to brace himself in order to withstand Finnvid's movement, but that was an aggravation for another time.

"What?" Finnvid asked. "You don't want a bath?"

"I want you," Theos said. He still sounded confused, or even angry, but he seemed to be trying to talk through it. "You know that, right? You're . . . special. I want you like I don't want the others. I want to— to protect you? Sometimes. And sometimes I want to strangle you, but less of that, lately. I like talking to you, and sometimes I even like listening to you. You make me think about things I don't really want to think about, but I know that I should. I'm . . ." He frowned, clearly consulting something fairly deep inside himself. "I'm better. Because of you. You're good for me."

"Like medicine."

"Like broth," Theos said, and he grinned, wide and true and beautiful. "But better. Like a big meal, and it *starts* with broth, and I get impatient because that's a waste of everyone's time, but then the good stuff comes. And it's *really* good, and it makes me strong, and even though I don't know all the flavors yet, I like it. I *like* that I don't know all the flavors."

Finnvid nodded. It was more, much more, than he'd expected. Theos didn't have a word that meant what Finnvid wanted; he didn't even seem to have the concept. But he had something of his own, and he'd gone out of his way to share it. He'd struggled to express an unfamiliar emotion because he somehow knew Finnvid needed to hear about it. So Finnvid smiled, and leaned back, and kissed Theos, then tugged on his hand again. "Good. Thank you. Now, a bath. You stink."

Theos moved this time, and they walked through the streets together, both of them quiet. Finnvid repeated Theos's words over in his mind, committing them to memory. And he repeated them in his heart, and committed them to Theos.

CHAPTER 32

Xeno looked as if he hadn't slept in days, but he was eager and alert as Theos explained their plan, such as it was. "The Sacrati don't need to hear what I say, do they?" Theos asked from his seat inside the temple's soaker tub. "The warlord killed the captain without a trial, so the Sacrati are ready to fight. Right?"

"We are," Xeno said, and Theos could see that it was true. He had some questions about why they hadn't already taken action; he supposed they'd been trying to find a way to avoid a civil war, just as he was.

"So you won't come to the city tomorrow, but don't be obvious about it. Then . . . Do you know where they're holding Andros?"

"We have some ideas."

"Figure it out. But don't break in, don't attack. Let's give them the chance to solve this peacefully, if we can."

Xeno nodded grimly. "*Last* chance," he said.

"Aye. I'll do what I can with the soldiers. Hopefully they'll listen, and we'll arrest the warlord and his inner circle—if you have names for that list, let me know—and we'll let Andros go. But if things don't go well in the city, it'll be time to fight. Bust in, get Andros free, and then . . . you know what happens then."

"We fight other Torians," Xeno said. He sounded like he was still having trouble believing it.

"Or don't. Maybe you just head for the mountains and try to find another way. But you'll be leaving your children behind, and the women who bore you those children. Your mothers and sisters." Theos shrugged. "I'll probably be dead by the time you realize things have gone wrong, but if I'm not? I'll be fighting."

Xeno nodded grimly. "Aye," he said. Then he turned to Finnvid, who'd been sitting quietly in the bath, soaking, while Theos and Xeno talked. "And you?" Xeno asked. "Is there a plan to get you back to your people if this goes wrong?"

"I'm with my people," Finnvid said. "As much as I have any. I'll be beside Theos, fighting as well as I can."

Xeno nodded. "That's all any of us can do, I suppose. We'll pick our side, and we'll fight as well as we can."

Theos slipped along the submerged bench and ducked his head under the stream of clean water coming into their tub. Xeno was ready to fight. The rest of the Sacrati were ready. *Finnvid* was ready. Ready to fight and die, for revenge? Or to defend some stupid ideal and maintain a way of life that Theos was already starting to question himself?

Theos had to stop the warlord without starting a war. He wasn't suited for giving speeches; better to persuade someone with a fist and a sword than with words. But once blood started to flow, even a trickle, he feared it would turn into a river. The whole valley was tense and ready, and if he gave them an excuse . . . if things got started, they'd take a long time to finish.

The water was too hot on his face, but he stayed under as long as he could, and when he finally emerged, he saw Xeno rising from the stool he'd pulled over to the side of their tub.

"We'll be ready," he said to Theos. "Whatever happens. Your brothers are with you."

Theos stood, and they gripped each other's forearms. The two of them had never been especially close, drawn together more by their shared affection for Andros than anything else, but in that moment Theos's gut tightened at the thought of never seeing Xeno again, a churning anxiety about getting him killed, along with all the other Sacrati. All Theos's other brothers.

Xeno left, and Theos sank back onto the bench. He needed to scrub himself, needed to shave and find clean clothes, needed to figure out what possible words he could use to persuade disciplined, well-trained soldiers that they needed to defy their commander. It was too much; it was impossible. He was a warrior, not a politician.

He was going to fail, and so many men, *Torian* men, would die because he wasn't who they needed him to be.

Then Finnvid moved, shifting over so he was straddling Theos and staring right at him. "Stop worrying," Finnvid commanded.

Theos just groaned. As if it was possible for him to forget about it all, to just turn his brain off—

"I want us to fuck," Finnvid said, and suddenly Theos's mind was empty.

"What?" he managed. The words had seemed clear, but this wasn't something Theos wanted to have misunderstood.

"I said the word," Finnvid said with the beginnings of a sly grin. "Do I need to say it again? Theos, I want to fuck. I want to use my hand and my mouth, and then I want us to fuck."

Theos's brain had stuttered back into motion. "Because you think we're going to die tomorrow, and you don't want to die a virgin. But that's stupid. Because we might not die. We might, but . . . maybe not. And even if we do . . . fucking isn't all that important, you know."

"It is. You fuck people all the time. You like it. And they like it. I've seen all this, Theos, so it's stupid to pretend it didn't happen."

"I like lots of things. Everyone likes lots of things. Fucking is . . . It's good, sure. But it's not like we're making babies. It's not *more* than everything else we've done."

"But we've done everything else. We haven't done this."

"There's lots of things we haven't done."

Finnvid squinted at him. "Like what? And why haven't we done them?"

"Well . . . mostly because I don't like them much. And since you don't even know what they are, it seems easiest to pretend they don't exist."

Finnvid snorted. "But I know fucking exists, and I know you like it, and I want to do it. I want to feel you inside me."

"Because you think we're going to die tomorrow."

"No. Because we're still alive now, and I want to keep *being* alive, and trying new things, for as long as I can."

Finnvid's eyes were open wide and even in the dim light of the baths they were impossibly blue. He looked pure and young and strong and honest, and Theos felt a surge of something impossible and inevitable in his chest. "I can't fuck you, not tonight. We don't have time to do it properly, and I'm not going to do it wrong. Not with you."

"Theos, I've seen you fuck people. It does *not* take that long!"

"Are you suggesting I lack stamina?"

"Your partners don't seem to complain, and neither will I."

"No. Not your first time. I want to fuck you, but I want to take my time, and make sure you're ready. I want you to be begging for me before I give you what you want."

"Well, I seriously doubt I'm ever going to beg you."

Theos wanted to wipe that smug expression right off Finnvid's face. Well, he wanted to fuck it off, really. But he just shook his head. "You're pretty close to begging already and we haven't even gotten started."

Finnvid stared at him for a moment, then pushed away in disgust, bobbing toward the other side of the tub. "You're honestly not going to fuck me?"

Theos reached out and wrapped a hand around Finnvid's ankle. "Not tonight. Maybe tomorrow night; looking forward to it will give me a reason to keep fighting."

"You're supposed to be insatiable," Finnvid grumbled. "What do you want to do instead? Cuddle?"

"We can still fuck," Theos said slowly. It had been a while, but getting fucked would certainly be easier for him than for an absolute virgin. And their cocks were both proportionate to their body sizes, so regardless of experience it would be easier for Theos to take Finnvid than the reverse.

"You mean . . ." Finnvid looked Theos up and down as if assessing his body's capabilities. "I've never seen you do that."

Theos tugged Finnvid the rest of the way back so they were face-to-face again, then kissed him and pulled him in tight. Then he said, "Just for you." He saw the flare in Finnvid's eyes and knew he'd found the magic words. And they worked just as well for Theos. "Just us," he murmured, and this time it was Finnvid who started the kiss.

Eventually they shifted around, Finnvid sitting on the bench, Theos stretching for the pot of oil and then hovering over Finnvid. He usually liked the power imbalance in fucking. He liked making it competitive, and when he'd been younger he'd loved fighting his partner for dominance, straining and wrestling to see who'd fuck the other. As he'd gotten older and stronger, his partners had stopped fighting, just accepting that he'd play the role he wanted. Was he taking a step back now?

He watched Finnvid's face, saw the strain and amazement in his eyes as Theos lowered himself. No, this wasn't a step back. It wasn't about dominance; it was something else entirely. Theos tried to relax and accept the intrusion. The burning stretch, the protests of a body not used to this treatment; he didn't really care what signals his body sent to him. His mind was in control, and his mind wanted this to happen. So it did. He sank down all the way, and let himself enjoy Finnvid's expression.

Theos was used to giving Finnvid pleasure, but he was usually taking it himself at the same time. Now, with so little preparation and care? And with Finnvid's breath already coming unevenly as Theos moved above him? Theos would have no physical pleasure from this, and somehow that made it sweeter. This was for Finnvid. This wasn't about dominance *or* pleasure; Theos could take both if he wanted, and he knew it, so it was somehow more important that he was giving instead.

Finnvid was gasping, his hands gripping Theos's ass as if he were the one lifting Theos's body. Theos thought about slowing his movements down, dragging things out, but he honestly wasn't sure he could; Finnvid was already too close to the edge. So Theos moved a little faster, tightened his ass, and as Finnvid began to shudder and groan, Theos savored every movement and every sound.

When they finally relaxed and uncoupled, Finnvid frowned. "You didn't . . . did you?"

"Now you can say 'fuck,' so you're going to lose the ability to say *other* words?"

"I don't need to say the words when you know what I mean. And you didn't."

"I didn't. I don't want to."

"You don't *want* to?"

"I'm saving up. For tomorrow night."

"Be a bit sad if you end up getting killed before then."

"I guess I'd better be careful. And you'd better help me find the right words to keep people from *wanting* to kill me." Theos grabbed the soap from the side of the tub and started scrubbing. "First, let's get clean, and shave. Then we'll get dressed, then maybe sleep a little. And when we wake up, you'll tell me what I need to say."

"I'm not sure why you think I'll know how to convince a crowd of Torians of anything."

"You're very persuasive. You've convinced me of all sorts of things."

"Like what?"

Theos had already shared more of himself that night than he had in the rest of his life combined. He'd given all he could. So he shrugged and said, "You persuaded me to drink a lot of broth. That's quite impressive."

"I'm definitely qualified to become your speechwriter, then."

"You're the best of the available candidates." Theos passed the soap over and said, "Get clean. We have a war to stop."

And for once, almost magically, Finnvid did as he was told.

Theos didn't seem nervous. Finnvid was so tense he was practically vibrating, but Theos stood on the stage in the city's central square, watching the men stream in, and appeared perfectly calm. From ten paces away, on the ground at the side of the stage, Finnvid had no idea whether Theos's composure was an act or genuine, which somehow made him even *more* nervous. He'd given up his world, was risking his life, and he couldn't even tell how the man he loved was feeling?

Then Theos glanced in his direction and made a face while taking a deep breath and then exhaling. He *was* nervous. And he was letting Finnvid know something he was hiding from everyone else, because Finnvid *was* special to him. Which made all the risks worthwhile.

He smiled back, trying to seem more confident than he was, and Theos shook his head. "You used to be a much better liar," Theos called to him.

"You used to give me better reasons to deceive you."

Theos grinned, then his attention was caught by a disturbance at the entry of the square. Finnvid followed Theos's gaze and his chest tightened around his heart. It was the warlord, a squad of men following him, and they were heading right for the stage.

The yard was about half-full, more men pushing in after the warlord, moving faster now in anticipation. Finnvid wanted to run. Not away, but toward Theos, so he could protect him. Still, he'd been given his role, and he would play it. He would maintain his discipline and make Theos proud.

So he stood still, and when the warlord reached him and fixed him with a hard stare, Finnvid met the man's gaze. "What are you doing here?" the warlord growled, and for the first time Finnvid saw the hint of uncertainty in the man's face. He really didn't know what Finnvid was doing, and maybe didn't know what Theos was planning, either.

"I'm waiting to find out," Finnvid said. It was honest enough.

"Do you represent your brother? Has he canceled our alliance?"

Finnvid ached to lie, to bluff the warlord into backing down, but he didn't think he could sustain the illusion, and Theos wanted everything out in the open. So he said, "I represent only myself. I cannot speak for my brother."

The warlord nodded sharply, then leaned in. "If you get out of here, *now*, I'll forget about this. But if you stay? You'll be held to your decision."

"As will you," Finnvid replied. The bravado tasted sweet as it passed over his tongue, but it turned to sour fear as the warlord smirked at him and then waved his men toward Theos.

"Arrest this man!" the warlord bellowed.

The warlord's men started forward, and Finnvid shrank back. He'd argued about this, but Theos had won. Finnvid would stay out of the way, and Theos would have no Sacrati bodyguards, no one to make it look as if the Sacrati were in revolt. It needed to be clear that Theos was acting alone. So Finnvid stood and watched as the men climbed to the stage and approached Theos. Twelve of them, battle-scarred and strong. And they all froze the moment Theos drew his sword.

"What are the charges?" Theos asked. His voice was almost as loud as the warlord's, but it was lighter, somehow. Less angry, less aggressive. Almost conversational, if conversations were carried on at such elevated volumes.

"Treason." The warlord stalked up onto the stage himself, but stayed behind his men. "You have conspired with the enemy against the interests of the people of Windthorn and the Torian Empire."

"And if I allow you to arrest me for this, will there be a fair and public trial? Will I be allowed to speak in my own defense?"

"That is the Torian way," the warlord replied as if it were a real answer.

"So you give me your word of honor that you would not *murder* me without a trial, the way you murdered the Sacrati captain?" Theos stopped speaking, then shook his head. "But what use is *your* word of honor?"

"*Arrest him,*" the warlord hissed toward his men, and a few of them stepped gingerly forward.

Theos stepped forward as well, and the men froze again. Twelve men. Finnvid knew the reputation of the Sacrati, but he also knew these were well-trained Torians. Twelve-to-one odds were too much, even for Theos. And the men must know this too. Still, they didn't attack.

Theos watched them for a moment, then nodded, and half turned. He still had his eye on them, but he was facing his audience as well. "The warlord has murdered the Sacrati captain," he said, loudly enough to be heard throughout the square. "You all know this. There was no trial because the warlord had no evidence. Is this the man who should be leading us?"

"We are under attack from within," the warlord bellowed. "In times of war, soldiers follow the orders of their commander! We don't have *time* for trials, and we can't expose state secrets in the name of *evidence!*"

Theos didn't even look at the warlord. He told the crowd, "You know he's lying. You know he's a murderer. And not just the captain. Twelve Sacrati left Windthorn to escort the Elkati home; only two returned. You know this. He's come up with lies to explain what happened, but you know they aren't true. You've spoken to the others who were there, your fellow Torian soldiers, and they've either told you the truth or they've dropped their eyes in shame. They stood by while their fellow Torians were *butchered*, and they did it because they were *following orders*."

The warlord strode forward then, shoving one of his soldiers toward Theos, then turning and yanking the arm of another. "Arrest him, or kill him—I don't care!"

It was too late, surely. Theos had spoken, and the men had heard him, and Finnvid had seen the words hit home. They *did* know. But now that the warlord's men were moving again, reluctantly circling around Theos, preparing to attack, the men in the audience didn't do anything. They stared, waiting.

Not bloodthirsty and waiting for a show, Finnvid didn't think. There was no excitement on their faces, just doubt. The reeve had been right; they wanted to be led, and they hadn't been given an order.

Finnvid was tempted to shout out his own command, but he knew he couldn't. He wasn't even a Torian; they wouldn't obey him, and his attempt would make Theos look weak. Still, he wouldn't stand by and watch Theos die, so he climbed up on the stage, his sword feeling awkward and too heavy in his trembling hands.

The fighting started when he was at the top of the short flight of stairs. He couldn't say how he knew, exactly: his view was blocked by the men in front of him. There was just a sort of collective gasp that told him one or more of the men had rushed in to attack. There was a buttress on the side and back of the stage, and Finnvid jumped onto it, thinking he could run along the top of it and attack from above, but when he looked over at Theos, he froze, and just stared.

Two attackers were already down. Theos was fighting the rest of them, his back against the buttress on the far side of the stage, and he was—he was fearsome, and beautiful. There wasn't room for all the men to attack at once, so only three of them were doing battle, slashing and hacking and being met each time with Theos's quick blade or with a simple absence where his body had been a perfect target a moment before. He was Sacrati, the perfect warrior. He darted forward, fast and light, and one of the men tumbled to the ground, clutching his suddenly red gut.

There was a pause, not even time for a full breath, but it was all Theos needed. "Enough!" he bellowed, and he raised his sword and pointed it toward the nearest men. "Enough. Drop your weapons, *now*!"

They stopped. Finnvid was close enough to hear Theos when he lowered his voice and said, "Is *this* how you want to die?"

They remained still for just another moment, and then one of them looked at the man next to him. "This is better than hanging, and that's what we'll get if he wins. Kill him."

As the men surged forward again, Finnvid surged too. A scream ripped from his throat, a strange, wild sound that seemed likely to curdle his own blood, if no one else's.

Some of the men attacking Theos spun to face Finnvid, and Theos took advantage of the distraction, his sword sharp and deadly. And then, finally, the men in the square were moving. They charged, an avalanche of warriors, rolling and tumbling up and over the stage, wrapping around the attackers, sweeping them away from Theos, away from Finnvid, and burying them under a drift of bodies. It was as if Finnvid's clumsy attack had assured them that this wasn't a private fight.

It all happened so quickly that Finnvid almost forgot his one real job. But as he tried to orient himself, tried to find Theos in the crowd to be sure he was still alive, he saw a familiar face fighting through the chaos. "Stop him! The warlord! Stop him!"

Finnvid leaped after the man, pushing through the men who were too intent on reaching the fighters to pay attention to someone trying to get away. "The warlord," Finnvid yelled into the face of a startled Torian. "Grab him!"

The Torian turned, recognized the warlord, and reached for him. And the warlord whirled, dagger out and slashing, catching the Torian across the biceps and then rebalancing, spinning again, facing Finnvid—and Finnvid put all his weight into a blow. Theos had spent months teaching him how to fight, and it might not have been enough, but it was something. Finnvid could throw a good punch. His fist landed square on the warlord's nose, squishing it in, driving the man's whole body back into the Torian behind him. "Grab him," Finnvid shouted again. "Watch for the dagger."

Things went more smoothly this time. The warlord was still reeling from Finnvid's punch as two Torians flipped him to the ground and pinned him. One of them pulled the dagger out of the man's hand and looked up at Finnvid questioningly. Finnvid wasn't sure what he was supposed to say.

But then Theos was there. "Don't kill him. Tie him—we need to question him and have a trial. That's the right way to do things."

The crouching man nodded.

Finnvid stared at Theos. "They're following your lead."

Apparently inspired by the realization, Theos jumped up onto the balustrade, waving his arms and yelling to catch the attention of the men swarming all over the stage. "No killing!" He frowned down at the bodies his own sword had produced, then shrugged. "As little killing as possible! We want them alive to answer questions, and we need to have trials."

"That takes too long," an anonymous voice objected.

Theos grinned in the approximate direction of the speaker. "We still have a couple months of winter—you have something better to do with your time? Training and fucking fill some of the hours, but we can fit in a few trials too, can't we?" Then his face darkened. "Besides—they're part of it. Sacrati have been murdered. If these men are part of the warlord's plot, they don't deserve clean deaths in battle."

It took a while for the chaos to fade. Theos stayed by Finnvid's side through it all. They didn't exchange words, but Theos was *there*. He sent men to ensure that Andros was freed, then some to find Zenain wherever he was, others to secure the warlord's office and personal space in case there was evidence that needed to be preserved, and another group to start cleaning up the bodies and cleaning the blood off the stage. The rest of the men stood around, waiting for more action, until Theos started waving them out of the square.

"The women have put up with enough of our nonsense," he yelled. "If we ever want to be invited back again, we need to leave when the party's over. And I think we all want to be invited back, don't we?"

As the crowd flowed away, Finnvid noticed a small cluster of boys, wearing the leather tunics of young recruits, trying not to be washed away with the men. He noticed the one in front, a bit smaller than the others, but with a way of standing, a fierce, stubborn expression on his face . . . Finnvid nudged Theos, and pointed his chin in the boy's direction.

Theos stiffened, then relaxed. "I suppose he's old enough," he muttered, and he linked his fingers with Finnvid's, then walked them both across the ground toward the boys. One of his sleeves was dark with slowly drying blood and there was more gore splashed all over him; most of the boys shrank back at his approach, but not the little one in front.

"Damios," Theos said, and the boy nodded seriously. "I'm sorry I wasn't there to welcome you to the barracks."

"You were on a mission," the boy said with clear pride. It seemed that having a father on a mission was even better than having a father greet him in his new home.

"I was. And it was important. But I wish I could have been two places at once."

The boy shrugged, then let his eyes wander to the blood on Theos's sleeve. "Are you hurt?"

Theos shook his head. "That's not mine."

"That's what I thought." And finally, Damios's face broke into a grin, wild and real and so much like his father's that Finnvid's chest tightened. "They didn't even *touch* you! That was good fighting! I'm going to fight like that someday, right?"

Theos glanced at Finnvid, then returned his attention to the boy. "Maybe. If you want to, I can help you learn. But if you want to do something else . . . maybe you could do that, instead."

The boy frowned. "What else *is* there?"

Another look at Finnvid, and this time Theos held his gaze. "There's trees and bugs, as I understand it, and probably a few other things too. I don't really know; I'm just learning about it all myself. But it's pretty interesting. I think, well, I can't say what Windthorn is going to do. We'll have to have elections as soon as we can and see what the new people in charge want. For me, though? I think I'm going to try to learn about some new things."

"And stop fighting?" one of the other boys asked, disbelieving.

"No," Theos said quickly. "We're Torian. We never stop fighting. But maybe, sometimes, we can do other things too."

The boys seemed mostly satisfied with that answer, and Theos squeezed his son's shoulder with his less bloody hand and then sent the group back to the barracks.

Theos turned slowly to Finnvid. "I'm always going to fight," he said. Clearly he'd meant his earlier words as much for Finnvid as for the boys. There was a concession in them, but not a surrender.

"I know," Finnvid said. It wasn't as if he could change anything. And maybe he didn't want to. Would Theos still be Theos without a blade in his hand? He stepped forward and reached out for Theos's bloody arm. When Theos tried to wipe it off on his tunic, Finnvid caught him, and slid his clean white fingers between Theos's red-and-brown ones. "I *know*," he repeated.

It took a while for Theos to drop his head into a nod. "You know," he finally agreed.

And they stood there, together, as the bodies were carted away and the reeve came out to scold them about the violence and badger them about the next steps, and the wind was cold and Finnvid had no home and no belongings and no real idea about his future. But he gripped Theos's hand tight, and he was content.

"You need to decide!" Andros stood up and braced his hands on the table as he leaned over toward Theos. "Now. No more delays."

"Fine. I won't run." Theos smiled. "There, that was easy. Let's go find Finnvid and get dinner."

"No, you rust-stained simpleton, you need to decide the other way! You need to declare yourself a candidate! You're the one who said we should have an interim leader until a new warlord and captain can be chosen, and people like the idea. They like *your* idea, so you should be the one to follow up."

"That's terrible logic. And I'm not good at that sort of thing; I'm not a politician."

"That's why we need you. This shouldn't be about politics, or sneaking around." Xeno sounded confident, and the other men at the table, a mix of Sacrati and trusted Torian regulars, nodded in agreement. "We need a leader. And you can lead."

"I wouldn't know what direction to lead us *in*. I have no idea what the answers are to any of this."

"That's the best part," Andros said. "You haven't got your own agenda, so you won't be trying to push us in any specific direction. You'll just help us set up the rules for discussion, and then you'll make damn sure the rules are followed."

Put that way, the job did seem like something Theos could manage. But he knew there was more to it than Andros was admitting. "Spring's not far off. We'll have to sort out a plan for dealing with the Elkati and the other valleys."

"Aye, we will. And we should do it after lots of talk, and the talk should follow the rules that you set up for it."

Theos sighed. It had been six days since the Sacrati had pulled Andros out of his cell and pushed the warlord into it, and Andros seemed to have spent every moment of his freedom investigating and planning and working. Zenain had been tracked down and imprisoned, the Torian soldiers who'd been under his command had been questioned, and still there was so much more to do.

"Don't you just want to—to eat and drink and have a soak and a fuck?" Theos knew he sounded like a petulant recruit, but he didn't care. "Do we have to be so *busy* all the time?"

"There are things to be done," Andros said.

"And we don't all have a fresh new bedwarmer waiting around, watching us like we're great heroes," one of the soldiers added.

"He's not a bedwarmer," Theos corrected. "Well, he warms my bed. But that's not his *job*."

"But he does *need* a job," Andros said with a smug smile. "And it's too late to make much of a soldier out of him. He'd likely be a good advisor, though, of the sort that might be needed by the man leading the Sacrati *and* regular army. Seems like he could really make a place for himself with that, if only there was a leader elected who would give him a chance..."

"You could do it," Theos said hopefully.

"No, I couldn't. Nobody cares about me. I didn't yell insults at the warlord and fight off his thugs."

"I don't think I yelled insults."

"You said his word was worthless," a Torian regular contributed. "That's insulting."

"Well, I didn't *yell* it."

"I heard you, and I was at the back of the crowd."

Xeno snorted. "That's funny. I didn't think *anyone* was at the back of the crowd that day. The stories I've heard, everyone was so close to the front they got sprayed with blood and could see exactly what the warlord looked like the second before he turned to run."

"And everyone was the first onto the stage too," Andros said with a grin. "Amazing how it happened."

"It was a group effort," Theos said.

"See?" Andros nodded in satisfaction. "Look at you, being diplomatic. You're ready for this. Absolutely."

"I'll think about it," Theos said, pushing away from the table.

Andros grinned at him. "You mean you'll ask Finnvid what to do. And I've already talked to him, and he thinks it's an excellent idea. So . . . congratulations, Theos! I'll see you at the temple first thing tomorrow morning to second your declaration. Don't be late."

"Sometimes I question why it was so important to get you out of the prison," Theos said. "My life would be easier with you locked up."

"It's not about being easy," Andros replied.

Theos left without answering, and headed out of the building and across the yard, then inside his barracks and up the stairs. He supposed Andros was right. Sometimes he needed to do things that weren't easy. But sometimes? He smiled as he opened the door to his small room and saw Finnvid lying shirtless on his stomach on the bed, reading one of the books he'd borrowed from the library in the city. Sometimes, the easy thing was the only thing to do.

"Shove over," Theos ordered, pulling his own tunic over his head and dropping it on the floor.

"Make me," Finnvid retorted.

"Do you really think I can't?"

"You can." Finnvid rolled over and sat up. "But I want to talk to you. If you lie down, we won't talk."

"We might talk a *little*."

"I want to talk about something other than fucking."

"Oh." Theos sighed and thought about pulling his tunic back on. But that felt like an admission of defeat, so he just sank onto the end of the bed and said, "What do you want to talk about?"

"You're going to be interim leader, right? You're going to do that?"

"Andros wants me to. Some others. Maybe I'll run."

"If you declare your candidacy, you'll be elected. I've been talking to people, and I don't think anyone else will even run if you declare."

It would have been easier if he'd been able to believe there was still an element of uncertainty to it all, a chance for fate to step in and find someone better for the job. But Finnvid was good at uncovering information; he probably wasn't wrong about this. "So, maybe I'll do it. Is that all you wanted to talk about?"

"I want to talk about Elkat," Finnvid said. "I want them to have a chance."

"A chance? To do what?"

"To survive, I suppose. I know they made a mistake. A horrible, bloody mistake. But . . ." He frowned, clearly trying to use the exact right words. "The soldiers were just following orders. The archers—they didn't know what was going on. And other soldiers helped us. Gunnald risked a lot for your escape. And the men in the pass, they turned away when they could have turned us in. Right?"

"So you think we have no quarrel with the soldiers of Elkat."

"That's right."

"So who *do* we have a quarrel with?" Theos knew the answer he'd give to the question, but he wanted to see how Finnvid would handle it.

And judging by Finnvid's expression, he had the same answer Theos did. "My family," he said slowly. "My brother. My mother. They thought they were doing the right thing. The smart thing, to protect their people. But . . . they gave the orders. I know."

"It won't be my decision," Theos said. "For something like this? We'll have to talk to the Sacrati, and let them decide how much they can forgive."

Finnvid nodded. "And in general? I mean, if you're planning to attack Elkat anyway, this doesn't really matter. Right? My family will be—" He breathed in through his nose and exhaled through his mouth, clearly trying to calm himself. "They'll be killed or sold into slavery anyway. Right? That's what Torians do to the leaders of the valleys they conquer."

"I talked to the reeve about it," Theos admitted. Probably he should have brought Finnvid along for that conversation, but he hadn't really known how it was going to go, not before he'd started. "She says she and the other reeves—the other ones that border Elkat—they're looking for something different. She thinks we could do well to set up a new kind of relationship with them. More trade, less conquering."

"Really?" Finnvid looked optimistic, and Theos wanted to protect that fragile emotion if he could.

But he didn't want to lie. "That's what the reeves want. The soldiers will want something different. And everyone back in the central valleys? Who *knows* what they'll want? It's all way over my head, Finnvid. I'm not good at this business."

"You're good at being honest and brave," Finnvid said staunchly. "That's the most important thing for now."

Theos shrugged. He hoped Finnvid was right. "We can talk to the Sacrati about your family. Apologies don't mean much, so they'll have to find a way to really show their regret. If they can do that? And if the reeves decide to use their power? Maybe we can do something different. Maybe we can make it work."

"We could trade cultures as well as goods," Finnvid said excitedly. "I know at least one woman in Elkat who'd probably be very excited about the chance to come here and see how things are done, and maybe some of your people—maybe some of *your* sons, the ones you said might not want to be soldiers—maybe they could visit Elkat, and find ways to be useful there."

"Don't make too many plans." Theos shook his head. "It's all just ideas, right now. There's a lot of work to be done, and arguments to be made. This won't be easy."

"But you're on my side? You'll speak in favor of—not forgiveness, maybe, but some sort of understanding? You'll help me?"

"I'm on your side," Theos said. "And the Sacrati side. I'll try to find a way for them to be the *same* side." He reached over and found Finnvid's hands. "And *you'll* help *me*, as I try to do that?"

"I will," Finnvid promised. "We'll do it together."

"I was hoping there might be something else we could do together, as well," Theos said. He'd already taken his tunic off, after all.

Finnvid waggled his eyebrows, then slid down the bed so he was lying on his back. He ran his hand down over the bare skin of his torso and dipped it inside the front of his trousers. "I have no idea what you mean."

Theos grinned and tugged at the drawstring of his own trousers. "I'd be happy to show you."

Finnvid didn't answer with words, but he wriggled out of his already loosened pants, kicking them to the foot of the bed and lying back in his lean, pale splendour. They'd switched roles for sex the night after the warlord's arrest, and Theos had taken his time, just like he'd wanted to, and made Finnvid squirm and beg and *need* Theos inside him. There'd been no going back after that. Finnvid liked to be massaged and coaxed and persuaded, and Theos was happy to play the role of seducer, even if he was tempting the same partner night after night.

He stood quickly, dropped the rest of his clothes with practiced efficiency, and fell to his knees by the side of the bed, leaning to kiss Finnvid on his lips, and then all over. He had his mouth wrapped around Finnvid's hard cock when he heard, "I saw you talking to Aikater today after training."

That didn't seem at all relevant to their current pursuits, but Theos freed his mouth long enough to say, "*Aye*kater, not *Ee*kater. You're saying his name wrong."

Finnvid tightened his fingers in Theos's hair and pulled his head farther away. "Is that what you think I wanted to hear?" He sounded . . . not quite angry. But not happy, either.

Theos thought about it. If Finnvid was genuinely sad, Theos would move the world to make things better. But he was pretty sure Finnvid was just being sulky. "I know how important proper pronunciation is to you," Theos said, and tried to lower his head back where it belonged.

Finnvid didn't release his grip. "He wanted you to fuck him," he growled.

Theos sighed and stopped trying to reach Finnvid's cock. "Aye. He did."

"Did you?" And there it was, the hint of vulnerability that could break Theos's heart.

But he tried to resist the impulse to make apologies and promises. What would the future be like if Finnvid could manipulate Theos so easily? So he said, "No," but then he added, "not this time."

"You have before?" Finnvid asked. The vulnerability was gone, replaced by something almost ferocious.

"Many times. Once, when we were cadets, we spent a festival night together. Two women from the city, and both of us. It was—"

Finnvid tightened his grip on Theos's hair. "Is *that* what you think I wanted to hear?"

"If I was in your position, the only thing I'd want to hear would be slurping and maybe a little moaning. So I don't feel like I can really guess what you want."

Finnvid was quiet for long enough that Theos started to doubt his approach to this conversation. Finally, the tight fingers in Theos's hair relaxed. Instead of going back to his original task, he skimmed up Finnvid's body and looked him in the eye.

"I didn't fuck him. I have no plans to fuck him." But he needed to say a little more than that. "I've been invited to the city, next week. Thea's already got a daughter with me, and she'd like to try for another child. It's been approved by the temple—it would be rude for me to refuse."

"I don't care about the women," Finnvid said. "You want to be a father. You only spend one night with them. I can accept that. But . . . other men . . . I know that's the Torian way. I know it doesn't mean anything to you. It's just for fun; I understand. I've *seen* it, far too many times. I know you like it. I just—"

"Finnvid," Theos said in exasperation. "It's *sex*. Of course I like it. You like it too, now that you're past all your silliness." He brushed the fine blond hair back from Finnvid's forehead and softened his tone. "I've had sex with lots of people. But I don't—I don't *talk* to them, not like I talk to you. I certainly don't *listen* to them. I don't think about their ideas, and wonder if I could find ways to combine their ideas with mine. I don't . . ." Theos stopped. What were the words that would make this better? He'd say them, as long as he could *mean* them. "What *do* you want to hear?"

Finnvid's smile was too sad for Theos to look at for long. "I'm not actually sure," he said, and he ran his hands over the bracelet around his wrist.

Theos reached for his own wrist, and tugged off the first band that came under his fingers. He glanced down at it and nodded.

"This came from my father before he died. I was still young, but he was a great warrior, and I wanted to be just like him." He stretched down and wrapped the metal band onto Finnvid's arm, bending the almost-closed circle tighter to make it secure on Finnvid's thinner body. He looked at it there for a moment, then reached back to his own arm. Another random selection, and he untwisted the clasp of the braided strands. "From Anaya, when she bore my first child. Damios . . . you've met him. It's her hair, blended with mine." He found a spot for it on Finnvid's other wrist, then reached for another.

"Stop," Finnvid said, catching Theos's hands. "Your wrists will be naked! What sort of Torian will you be then?" He was laughing, but his eyes were wet.

Theos leaned closer to him. "What sort of Torian do you want me to be?"

"I want you to be mine. That's all. *My* Torian."

"I am."

"But you're not *just* mine."

Theos sighed. "You want an Elkati relationship? Even though I don't think they make sense in Elkat, where everyone *expects* couples to behave like that? You think we'd do well to behave that way *here*?" He frowned. "You want me to change to be exactly who you want me to be?"

Finnvid didn't answer.

Theos nodded slowly. "Give me a bracelet back."

"What?" Finnvid looked startled, almost afraid, and each of his hands closed protectively around the opposite wrist.

"Pick one. Tell me why it's important to you, and give it to me."

Finnvid hesitated, but he finally undid the hair bracelet and tentatively refastened it on Theos's wrist. "You got this from a woman named Anaya when she gave birth to Damios. I liked having it because it made me feel like part of your family. I know that family isn't the same here as it is in Elkat, but it's still *something*, and I liked having the connection to it."

Theos gave himself a moment to absorb the words, then reached down and undid a new bracelet from his wrist. It was made of metal beads, tarnished by sweat and weather and wear. "Andros gave this to me when I became Sacrati. Three months later I found its match and gave it to him when he joined the brotherhood." He fastened it around Finnvid's wrist. "Andros is my friend. My good friend. But the way I feel about you is . . . It's different. It's . . ." He tried, but he didn't have the words. "It's more, I think. I want to fight beside Andros, but I want to fight in front of you, to keep you safe."

Finnvid was relaxing now, and Theos eased up onto the narrow mattress, stretching out alongside Finnvid's body. Neither of them was hard anymore, but it wouldn't take long to remedy that situation. Sex was easy; it was everything else that seemed to take a lot of work.

Finnvid rolled onto his side and snuggled back, and for a moment it seemed like he was planning to just go to sleep. Theos thought about sitting up and pulling the blankets over them, but then Finnvid squirmed a little more, working his ass into Theos's groin.

Theos kissed the side of Finnvid's neck and savored the way Finnvid leaned his head to provide more room for Theos's attentions. "I'll buy you a bracelet of your own," he whispered. "One for . . . for *us*."

"I'll buy you one too," Finnvid murmured. "They could match." Then he slumped a little. "But . . . that's an Elkati tradition. I shouldn't trick you into wearing it when you don't really know what it means."

"What tradition? Elkati exchange bracelets?" Theos had seen no evidence of that, but it was almost as intriguing as the story about the hunting falcons.

"Not bracelets. Rings."

"Rings? For your fingers? But rings are so small! And how many could you fit onto your hands without making it hard to grip things?" Theos tugged Finnvid's hand up for inspection. Surely he would have noticed . . . "You don't wear rings."

"No. Not like Torians do. We don't gift them as often. But when a couple marries, they exchange matching rings."

Back to that. Theos sighed, and Finnvid twisted around so they could see each others' faces. "I can just buy you a different bracelet. Right? It would be okay if I just gave you one, not a matching one."

"You should hang onto your money. I'll buy bracelets." Theos took a deep breath and a moment to be sure he really meant it, then said, "Matching ones, if that's what you want."

Finnvid rolled right over and kissed Theos while doing some very interesting things with his lower body. Then he ruined it all by saying,

"I want *you* to want it. If you're just doing it to make me happy, you shouldn't." Another strong, deep kiss, and he added, "You already do more than enough to make me happy. I'm happy. I love you, and I like living with you, and I'm already breaking so many Elkati rules with just that . . . it probably *does* make sense for me to let go of a few more."

This seemed a bit too good to be true. They kissed more, familiar and warm and safe, and when Theos cautiously slid his hand down past their hard cocks and reached behind, Finnvid lifted his legs and wrapped them around Theos's hips.

"I feel like I may be stepping into a trap," Theos murmured, but he stretched for the pot of oil by the side of the bed anyway.

"I love you," Finnvid replied. "And I love it when you're inside me. No traps."

"That's just what someone laying a trap *would* say." Theos made little circles with his oiled finger, nipping the tip just inside and then pulling it out for more circles. More teasing, for both of them.

"Fuck me," Finnvid ordered, and Theos just raised his eyebrows and kept doing what he was doing.

Finnvid groaned in frustration. "I could go find someone else right now," he threatened. "Someone more obedient, who'd fuck me when I told him to."

"You could find *lots* of men who'd be more than willing," Theos promised. "I'd rather you didn't do it right now, but if you wanted to, you could." That was a distracting thought. What would it be like if Finnvid was making those breathy sounds for someone else, if his beautiful cock was wrapped in someone else's fist?

"Or if I was with another man, maybe I'd do the fucking," Finnvid said thoughtfully. "I don't really want to fuck *you*, but someone else? Maybe I'd like that."

"You might," Theos mused. How would *he* feel about that? Better than having someone else touching Finnvid's ass, at least. But both options made his stomach tighten in an unpleasant way.

Finnvid ran his fingers absentmindedly over Theos's shoulders. "Maybe I'd like being with him *better* than I like being with you," he mused.

Theos frowned, then saw Finnvid suppressing a smug smile. Theos let his face break into a wide grin. "Impossible," he declared. "Such a man doesn't exist. You could never do better than me."

Finnvid managed to hold off for a moment, but then he wrapped his arms around Theos's neck and kissed him. "I never could," he agreed. "And you could never do better than me."

"Never," Theos promised. And he meant it.

He slid another finger inside Finnvid, who arched his back and rocked against him. "No more talking," he gasped. "Just fucking. *Please*. Theos..."

No, Theos couldn't imagine Finnvid begging like that, not if the plea included any other man's name. "I love you," he whispered.

"So fuck me!"

"What happened to my blushing Elkati virgin?" Theos shifted so his cock slid *almost* into place, but he just teased around the opening. Finnvid shuddered and writhed, and Theos wanted to watch him forever. This was Finnvid, and Finnvid was *his*. *His*. Every groan that came from Finnvid's lips was a song for Theos's pleasure, every shiver of his body a dance Theos could share. He kissed Finnvid's neck, his cheek, his ear, whatever his mouth could reach without taking their bodies apart. "I love you," Theos whispered again.

"Prove it," Finnvid groaned, canting his hips in an attempt to draw Theos in.

Theos ran his free hand down Finnvid's belly, ghosted it just above his straining cock, and then returned it to his ribs. "I could slay a dragon for you. Or rescue you from rock trolls. Fight a star god."

"Or you could skip right to the victory fucking."

Theos let his cock slip just inside, just enough to make Finnvid's breath catch and his hips roll, and then he pulled out again and went back to teasing. He was so hard he ached right up to his belly; the brief touch of pressure around the head of his cock had been enough to make his balls throb, yet he stayed strong.

"Slave," Finnvid barked. "I *order* you to fuck me."

"I don't think I'm—" Theos started, but Finnvid made his move then, twisting with his hips, driving with his shoulders... he didn't have enough weight to actually flip Theos, but there was courage in the attempt, and he should be rewarded for that. Also, Theos loved him. And, of course, Theos was about ready for some victory fucking too.

So he let himself be rolled over, squirmed away from the edge of the narrow bed, and watched with warm eyes as Finnvid straddled him, looked down as if to be sure there was no objection, and then slid down, slowly, steadily, stretching himself around Theos's cock.

Theos gasped and arched his back as his hands found Finnvid's hips and held on. The heat, the slick, tight slide—it was all perfect. All familiar. What Theos still hadn't gotten used to, what he wasn't sure he ever *would* be used to, was Finnvid. Theos forced his eyes to stay open so he could appreciate the view. The beautiful pale body, smooth and unscarred; the fine-boned face, tense with concentration and growing pleasure; and then, when Finnvid opened his eyes and his gaze found Theos's? The warmth, the challenge, and most importantly, the love.

"I love you," Theos said. His self-control was leaving him, but he wanted to say these words before he lost himself entirely. "You're the only one I want. No one else should touch you, or even look at you. You're mine. Always mine."

"Yours," Finnvid moaned. He reached down then, and his fingers found Theos's hair and pulled. Theos moved as directed, let himself be rearranged until he was sitting up, still buried deep, with Finnvid's cock hard and wet between their bellies. "And you're mine," Finnvid whispered, and his kiss was hard and strong.

They didn't last much longer. Finnvid gasped and writhed and then came with a shout, and Theos let himself go too. A few more deep thrusts into a body that spasmed around him, and he found his own climax, emptying himself into Finnvid's warmth.

They collapsed together and lay there, still joined, while they caught their breath.

When Theos finally shifted away, Finnvid turned so they were both lying on their sides, facing each other. A gentle kiss, and then Theos whispered, "I'll buy us bracelets. Matching ones. Or rings if that's important. Whatever you want."

Finnvid's smile was almost shy. "You don't have to."

"I want to."

"Bracelets, then. They'll mean that we don't fuck anyone else? No other men, at least?" Theos nodded. It didn't feel like much of a sacrifice. And Finnvid said, "Good. We can wear them until the next festival."

"What?" Theos drew his head back so he could see Finnvid's expression more clearly. "Only until the festival?"

Finnvid nodded. "And then we'll decide if we want to keep wearing them. We could take them off, or we could keep them but decide they mean something different."

"Why would we do that?" Theos asked suspiciously. "I thought Elkati mated *forever*?"

"We're not Elkati." Finnvid kissed Theos, then said, "I'll probably want to keep wearing your bracelet after the spring festival. I'll probably want it to mean the same thing. But . . ." His smile was pure mischief and joy and affection. Pure Finnvid. "You'll have to earn that. You'll have to ask nicely."

Theos snorted. "We'll see about that."

"Yes. We will." Finnvid snuggled down a little, his head resting on Theos's biceps. "We'll see a lot of things. Together."

"Together," Theos agreed, and they drifted off to sleep, wrapped in each others' arms.

Dear Reader,

Thank you for reading Kate Sherwood's *Sacrati*!

We know your time is precious and you have many, many entertainment options, so it means a lot that you've chosen to spend your time reading. We really hope you enjoyed it.

We'd be honored if you'd consider posting a review—good or bad—on sites like **Amazon, Barnes & Noble, Kobo, Goodreads, Twitter, Facebook, Tumblr,** and your blog or website. We'd also be honored if you told your friends and family about this book. Word of mouth is a book's lifeblood!

For more information on upcoming releases, author interviews, blog tours, contests, giveaways, and more, please sign up for our weekly, spam-free newsletter and visit us around the web:

Newsletter: tinyurl.com/RiptideSignup
Twitter: twitter.com/RiptideBooks
Facebook: facebook.com/RiptidePublishing
Goodreads: tinyurl.com/RiptideOnGoodreads
Tumblr: riptidepublishing.tumblr.com

Thank you so much for Reading the Rainbow!

RiptidePublishing.com

ALSO BY
KATE
SHERWOOD

Novels
Dark Horse (Dark Horse Book One)
Out of the Darkness (Dark Horse Book Two)
Of Dark and Bright (Dark Horse Book Three)
Lost Treasure
Shying Away
Beneath the Surface
Poor Little Rich Boy
The Pawn (Against the Odds Book One)
The Knight (Against the Odds Book Two)
The Fall (Book One)
Riding Tall (Book Two)
Mark of Cain
Chasing the Dragon
In Too Deep

Novellas
Home Ice
More than Chemistry
The Shift
Room to Grow

ABOUT THE AUTHOR

Kate lives and works in rural Ontario, Canada, and can't stand airports or hotels. Fortunately, her imagination lets her travel all over this world and into other ones as well.

She writes about men who are struggling against themselves. Men who want love but can't manage to make it work until someone just as damaged comes along and gives them a hand. They may be lost souls, but at least they're in good company!

Kate can be found on Facebook (kate.sherwood.79), Twitter (@kate_sherwood), and at her website/blog (katesherwoodbooks. com). he loves talking about her writing, once she gets over being bashful—feel free to contact her at any of the sites above or by email at kate@katesherwoodbooks.com.

Enjoy more stories like *Sacrati* at RiptidePublishing.com!

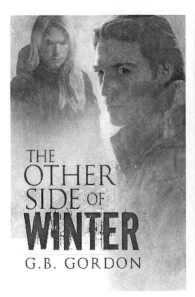
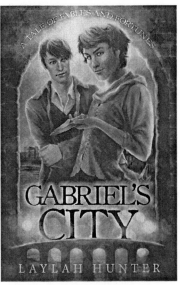

CPSIA information can be obtained at www.ICGtesting.com
Printed in the USA
LVOW07s2317310315

432820LV00004B/275/P